JUST ONE LIE

RUTH HARROW

INKUBATOR
BOOKS

Published by Inkubator Books
www.inkubatorbooks.com

ISBN (eBook): 978-1-915275-60-8
ISBN (Paperback): 978-1-915275-61-5
ISBN (Hardback): 978-1-915275-62-2

PROLOGUE

I t's unthinkable how the perfect moment can turn into a nightmare so quickly. In the blink of an eye, a precious moment in the sun went from wondrous to terrifying. There I was with my little boy in the water. The hot Portuguese sun illuminated his sandy-coloured hair as my hands supported him effortlessly beneath the gentle waves.

It was the perfect day. People were dotted here and there on the beach, colourful and vibrant under the sun. One of them, my spouse, who had reluctantly agreed to let me take our little boy for his first swimming lesson.

The trip had been good for us. Our first holiday together as a family. Things between us hadn't been easy since the birth of our son. Nothing had. But this trip was supposed to mark the start of a new beginning for us. And it was. We were all starting to relax. The troubles of the past were beginning to melt away.

Then it happened. It had started with a tug. Maybe it had already started before I felt the first pull of the water. Had I not been so caught up in our son, I would have noticed sooner.

But I'd been so concerned with making sure his water wings were doing their job, been so determined to keep the salty water from his mouth and nose. I'd been so eager to make sure that he wasn't getting sunburned beneath his broad beach hat that perhaps I hadn't spotted the first sign something was wrong.

All of a sudden, the beach seemed further away than I remembered. We were further out than I had realised. Prioritising the infant in my arms, I tried to get us closer to the sand.

But nothing happened. I fought harder, but to no avail. The current was too strong. It wasn't pulling me under – yet. But how long did I have?

I called out. One arm pulled my son's tiny body to my chest. The other waved frantically in the air, splashing around in the hope of getting some attention.

I called again, only it came out as more of a scream.

Guilt stabbed at me somewhere under the water at the panic in my voice. I did this. It was my fault. I'd put my son in danger. He was paying the price for my stupidity. He was oddly quiet. I'd expected him to cry or start screaming himself once I'd started, but he didn't make a sound. Perhaps he didn't even realise something was wrong. In a way, it was for the best.

It was then that I was aware of just how far the water had swept us. I pushed harder than I thought possible against the water. Some part of me knew that it wouldn't help, but I had to try. It wasn't just my life on the line.

I screamed again. Until all the air was gone from my lungs and I was left gasping for more. I coughed and spluttered as salty water stung my throat, and I put all my energy into keeping my little boy as close to the surface as I could. He had become so heavy balanced on my shoulder, but I didn't dare shift my position. I was terrified he would slip beneath the waves. They were stronger and more aggressive further from the shore.

My legs felt weak. The salt burned my eyes and mouth. I was panting hard from the exertion of fighting against the current. I knew I couldn't afford for us to be pulled further into the sea.

The figures on the beach moved together into a colourful swarm near the water's edge. I knew my partner was one of them. One or two appeared to buzz in one direction or another at high speed across the pale sand.

But I knew they wouldn't make it in time.

1

A sinking feeling settles in my stomach as I stare down at the pile of boxes around my feet; I tear at the plastic document pack on one of them and find the delivery note.

The feeling that somewhere an error has been made rises now; I'll be annoyed with myself if it is my own.

As I scan the list of items included in the packages, I swear under my breath. The backdrop frame I thought I'd ordered as part of the professional lighting kit isn't here. I had been certain there was one included when I ordered it online. I definitely remember seeing it in the pictures. But perhaps it had been depicted purely for demonstration purposes?

How careless of me. I'm usually on top of things like that. I know that recent events are what caused me to overlook such a detail.

I glance around me at the bare shop floor I now find myself in; I had hoped to transform this retail unit into the go-to place for maternity and family portraits. There isn't anything else like it in our little town, even though I know there is definite demand. The idea came to me when I had started to show in my recent pregnancy. Maternity portraits seem to be popular amongst the mothers at the local school, but they had to travel elsewhere to get them.

When my idea was fresh, I had passionately envisaged being the proprietor of a charming little hub with stunning backdrops and sets the mothers would adore and the children would be enthralled by. I even have all the elements of the Christmas set I had planned saved neatly in a dedicated online wish list.

Not that my budget can allow it yet though. The rail of elegant gowns I had pictured my clients excitedly rummaging through has now materialised as smaller-sized Chinese imports. A handful of pieces from the local charity shops hang beside them; I'd had to get them cleaned twice to get them smelling fresh enough to use.

It feels as though everything that could have gone wrong has done. Yet, every one of these things is so far from the worst that has happened lately.

My lip trembles when I think about what I have lost in the last two months. My husband, Dan, knows I am at my best when I have a project on my hands, and he is happy to see me moving forward and thinking of the future once again. His work as a chef keeps him busy. I wish he could be here today to help me, but he has the morning shift. We would be lucky if he gets home before eight this evening.

I need something to keep me occupied now more than ever; engaging tasks keep bad thoughts away.

For the most part it has worked. In the past week, I've been so busy getting everything ready that I am asleep within minutes of my head hitting the pillow. That's the way I like it. The night-time dwelling is the worst.

Unfortunately, I often find that I wake in the middle of the night and can't slip back into the oblivion I so anxiously crave. The rest of the household remain united behind a wall of peaceful slumber from which I am locked out.

Outside on my own, my mind wanders, and I'm dragged back to places I would rather not visit.

I take a deep breath and move over to the window. The dusty glass panes are still buffed with white – another thing on my to-do list before I officially open.

Outside in the street, pedestrians drift by, all puffa coats and hats in the growing October chill. Very few even glance at my shop. From the outside, I must still look like another hole in this road off the high street. I'm still waiting for the signwriters. A pair of young mums pass by, and my eyes are immediately drawn to the bundle of pink blankets tucked snugly inside a trendy-coloured pram.

With a wrench, I tear my gaze away and plunge my hand into the nearest box, tearing into the cardboard with my bare hands. I'd better get the lighting set up in my studio. I was due to open last month, but after what happened, I'm nowhere near ready.

Without any support, I feel overwhelmed in front of the big list of tasks ahead: setting up the desk for my computer and editing equipment; setting up various different sets; finding more props and accessories.

The shop landline screeches to life on the floor in the corner, making me jump.

I take a second to compose myself before I crouch down and raise the old corded set that came with the premises. I lift the receiver to my ear. 'Hello?'

There is a pause at the end of the line before a woman speaks. 'Hello? Who am I speaking with?'

I remember that I'm now officially a shop owner. 'Hello. Sorry, this is Alison Burnham Photography. Can I help you? Are you calling about the job?'

The faint rustling I can hear in the background abruptly ends, and I am left in silence.

I conclude it was a wrong number and put the phone down. Perhaps it was an enquiry for the clothes shop that used to occupy this unit? It had been an independent store that catered for the older lady. The woman on the phone was softly spoken, but there was something that struck me as forced about her voice. She could easily have fitted the target demographic. But someone of that age would have surely been well-mannered enough not to hang up when she realised a mistake had been made.

I sigh. I'd hoped the call had been a response to the job ad I put up. I haven't had a single response.

What would be useful now is a friend, but most I had in school have moved on from their small home town. Life in Rishworth isn't exactly lived in the fast lane. Once an industrial mill town in Lancashire, the quiet high streets are now filled with discount stores, a scattering of small independents and other creative start-ups that don't last all that long. I am determined that I will not be one of them, however. I know this latest idea of mine will work.

One thing Rishworth is not short of is new mothers and young families. They are my main target market. I've seen other towns like ours with chic photography studios that provide aspirational images mothers love to splash over Facebook. The packages aren't cheap, but that's the cost of vanity and living through the lens of social media. Their businesses are booming.

Once the lighting is set up, I push myself to get started on the window display. *If I don't do it now, it will never get done,* I tell myself.

The sky darkens as I fetch a box from my car parked a few streets away.

Deep maroon velvet feels warm and soft beneath my

fingers as I unpack it. I drape it carefully over the crates in the window and scatter a bag of artificial autumn leaves over the whole lot.

From the back storeroom, I find the large, framed pieces I had planned for the window. I've chosen three examples of my work. They all feature my eight-year-old son, Adam. There is one of him as a toddler, dwarfed by the cornfields rising high in soft focus around him. I position another shot of him flashing his perfect milk teeth as his pudgy fingers grip the chains of a park swing.

For the centrepiece, I place a large matt print of Adam against a woodland backdrop when he was a couple of years older; in it he clutches his favourite, worn teddy bear.

Another composition had been in mind for centre stage in the window, but I hadn't been able to shoot it. That opportunity had been snatched away from me. After following a handful of trendy portrait photographers on Instagram for months, I'd come up with a clear picture concept. Adam would have been sat inside a set made up with the red velvet, posed with his newborn sister in his arms. I'd chosen a deep scarlet shirt for him that would have matched the floral headband of the baby cradled in his lap.

But now that picture will never exist. Today, I've put the fabric to use in the window display instead. The other clothes and accessories have been stuffed in a cupboard somewhere. I can't bear to bring all of it into the studio, handed out as mere props for happy new mothers.

The lump in my throat that has been threatening to emerge all day now squeezes its way to the surface. My face screws up as I give in to the wail of misery that begs for release. But I know I shouldn't feel sorry for myself.

Karma is real. What happened wasn't just a tragedy that could have occurred in any household.

If anyone ever found out what I'd done, I know they would agree.

I deserve what happened.

2

I pull my car neatly up outside the house. A traditional stone cottage with a well-tended garden greets me. No doubt, I have my son to credit for the immaculate rows of colourful flowers.

My son's partner might think of herself as artistic, but it seems my son is the one who puts all the work in. His partner certainly is the creative type. I'm not entirely sure I would call what she does real work.

I sigh. If only my boy had found himself a different partner. One with a more traditional career like his. I blame myself for not teaching him better. But wasn't it the right thing to do to let him make his own decisions?

I worked hard to provide as a single mother for many years so that my son wouldn't go without. Perhaps I should have made more of an effort to remarry after his father passed away? I lay awake so many nights worrying whether I was doing the right thing leaving my son without a father figure.

Now I see that it was a mistake. I needn't have spent all

those years alone either. I've lost count of the nights I cried myself to sleep, the loneliness gnawing away at my insides.

But the past can't be changed. My heart hammers in my chest as I stand on the neat porch. I haven't seen my boy for so many months. We often went out together on days out, concerts and dinners. But then he met *her*, and she has found a way to occupy his time, one way or another.

Now I'm lucky to see him at all. Being invited over for Sunday lunch is such a rare treat that I'm actually nervous. I wipe my palms on my floral skirt and wonder if the peach blouse I have paired it with was the right choice.

Disappointment bites me when it's she who answers the door. She greets me with the same false smile she saves for these rare occasions. Today, however, she surprises me when she pulls me close to her and plants the briefest of kisses on my cheek.

Suddenly, I have a bad feeling. It doesn't abate when I am shown through to the living room. My son is standing over a couple who must be his girlfriend's parents. He previously mentioned that they emigrated to the other side of the world in recent years. Their tanned skin confirms the memory. He pours champagne into the decorative glasses in their eager hands. Although, I note they look as bemused as I must do.

My boy looks up as I enter the room and grins at me nervously. His eyes are alight in a way that I haven't seen before as he hands me a fizzing glass with a kiss too.

When we are all seated on the matching sofas, he remains standing and pulls his partner close to his side. The pair both beam around at us parents. He doesn't need to utter the words that spill from his mouth next though. I can already guess their news.

As all mothers everywhere know, their life with their little boy is only a temporary blessing. You are owed a few fleeting years as you nurture and sacrifice for them. But at a certain age, they start to slip away, take care of themselves. Then the day comes when they find a woman to marry, and she is custodian of his world from then on.

Then that's it. It's all over.

I force a smile and raise my glass in congratulations, but it seems the newly engaged couple have more to declare. It's a double announcement, they say. Then *she* presses a hand to her perfectly flat abdomen, and the news tumbles from her full, excited lips. Her mother springs up, her eyes wide and straight teeth bared in an impossibly wide grin mirroring her daughter's.

I hear nothing but a ringing in my ears as I watch. My son pulls his hand free from his future father-in-law's enthusiastic grip and moves over to me, pulling me into one of his warm hugs so much like his father's.

'I wish you both the best of happiness,' I say. 'This is such wonderful news.'

Inside, I have only one wish.

That my future daughter-in-law is blessed with a little boy. So that one day, when someone like her steals him away, she will feel the same pain.

Only then will she know what she has done.

3

Despite the fact I woke up in the early hours of the morning and was unable to drift back off, I still found myself hurrying around the house at the last minute trying to get Adam ready for school. He isn't the easiest person to wake up in the morning. Neither I nor Dan is like that, thank goodness.

My husband has already left for work, and it is left to me to pull back Adam's duvet and cheerlead him through a bowl of cereal with one eye on the clock. Adam has made the most of my lapse in authority these past few months. Since what happened to his little sister, I lost the heart to drag my little boy from the peace of his bed and send him out into the world where any number of accidents and tragedies could strike at any time.

Now I am determined to get our lives back on track. Dan is working hard on getting a promotion at the local restaurant, and I know my latest business idea is going to work this time. It will turn into a massive success. It feels like I have been down this path of a new start-up so many times, I could write a book on it. But I have to believe this is the last time I ever have to start again from scratch.

Only five minutes later than I intended, we step out onto the porch. Beside me, Adam complains. 'Mummy, why are we leaving so early?'

'It's not early,' I tell him. 'If your father was taking you, then he would have left already.'

'But he isn't,' he whinges. 'You are. It takes two minutes to drive there.'

I start down our street of semi-detached stone cottages and march determinedly past the car. 'We are walking.'

Adam makes a noise of complaint and doesn't move beyond the bonnet. 'You told Dad we were driving.'

'Yes, I did. But I wasn't able to get to the petrol station before school, and the tank is nearly empty. Let's go, sweetheart. We will be there in no time. It's not like it is far.'

It's a white lie. I didn't fill the car up because my card was declined at the pump. I have to save the last bit of fuel for trips to the studio whilst I am shifting heavy equipment and boxes. Once I have a few clients under my belt, everything will be fine. I'll have to use my other card for groceries for now. We'll keep our belts tight. That's definitely something Dan and I are used to.

I've been so busy getting my little boy ready that I now realise I've neglected my own breakfast. My stomach rumbles as we set off, as though trying to remind me that the only other chance to eat before dinner is the hasty pack of sandwiches I prepared alongside Adam's packed lunch.

Adam starts off dragging his feet, but after a few minutes he picks up and even shares some details about his latest art project at school. I feel honoured, as it is so hard to get him to talk about what he has done. From the sound of it, Adam's painting has been positioned in the centre of the display board in the classroom by the teaching assistant. I feel a sense of pride that he does so well in creative projects. At least we are alike in that sense.

I took art as an A-level in college and got my degree in graphic design. The period I had designed advertising for a company in Manchester had been the highlight of my career. If I hadn't made so many mistakes in my life, we would have been so much better off now. At least I will be able to guide Adam if he wants to pursue a creative career.

We pass the corner shop where I'm often nagged for sweets, and as we do an elderly lady steps out through the automatic doors. I realise it is one of Dan's old neighbours from before we moved into the cottage together.

She beams at me. 'Long time no see.'

I smile back. 'Yes, it has been a while, hasn't it? Are you keeping OK? You look like you've lost weight.'

'Do you know, the postman said the exact same thing this morning ... or was it yesterday. It's hard to keep track when you live alone.' She waves a frail hand vaguely as she tries to remember.

Looking at her thinning frame beneath her coat, I have a feeling that her memory is so lax she forgets meals. I reach into my bag for the sandwiches I had prepared for myself earlier.

'Here,' I say, handing her the package. 'I think you need these more than me,' I say, ignoring the gnawing in my stomach.

'Oh, I couldn't possibly,' she says in protest. Then she looks down at the offering hungrily. 'Well, I can't say no to a bit of corned beef. It's been a while since I had any of that. Go on then.'

'It's important to take care of yourself.' I wish I had more to give her. I make a mental note to say something to Dan later. Maybe we could take it in turns to look in on her from time to time?

She puts the sandwiches in her handbag, and I hope they don't get forgotten too. Then she shifts her attention to Adam. 'You've shot up, haven't you, young man?'

Adam shrugs as she eyes him critically.

'Such a handsome boy,' she goes on. 'Those baby blues are going to break some hearts one day. Just like your mother, I bet.'

I'm glad Dan isn't here. It has always been a bone of contention that Adam bears little resemblance to him. I had hoped that our new baby girl might have inherited her father's sandy hair and high cheekbones. But I know that will never be.

She addresses Adam again. 'How old are you now, then?'

Adam shifts awkwardly in his shoes at all the attention, rough scarlet patches creeping into the skin of his cheeks. It's adorable how shy he gets sometimes. 'Eight.'

She turns back to me, tilting her head sympathetically. 'Aww, they grow up so fast. Make the most of it. Soon it will be all loud music and girls, I promise you.'

I smile. 'Yes, I will.'

A few minutes later, I drop Adam at his school gates. His cheeks haven't cooled much as I kiss him goodbye. Part of me is reluctant to let him go. I want him by my side where I can see him. Protect him.

Always.

But then he shrugs me off as a couple of boys from his class see and laugh out loud over their shoulder. I'd hoped it would be longer before my little boy was embarrassed like this. I'm sad to think Dan's old neighbour may be right.

As I round the corner and turn onto Mill Street, I see my shop loom into view. I feel a flutter of excitement. The signwriters will be here today. Then my vision will start to become real.

I pull out my keys and let myself in. The state of mind I was in last time washes over me once more. For a moment, I consider leaving the windows and doors open to freshen up the air a little, but October is rapidly becoming chillier. My cheeks are still numb after the walk from school.

I move over to the boxes of flat-pack furniture and decide to set up my desk. I'll need to pop home to pick up the old desktop I'll be using for image editing. Maybe I will combine it with a trip past Adam's school later and take him home in the car?

Before I decide, I am distracted by a dark shape in the window. On the other side of the white-buffing, a large figure moves slowly as though trying to peer in through the ivory streaks. They hover. Not simply a mere passer-by.

The shadow passes to the door and knocks. The sound is loud and abrupt in the dull gloom of the quiet shop.

My heart beats nervously, and I don't know why, but I hesitate for a moment before pulling open the door. A woman in a large puffa coat appears in the door frame.

'Hiya,' she says brightly, chapped lips pulled wide into a warm smile. 'You haven't filled that job vacancy yet, have you?'

'No, not yet,' I say, taking in the brassy ends of the woman's grown-out highlights. She is probably my age or even a little younger, but she has deep lines around her mouth.

'Well, would you mind if I interviewed for it? I was going to call first, but I was in town anyway, and it makes sense just to pop over here, doesn't it? Or would you prefer a phone interview? I can email you my CV if you like?'

'No, that's fine,' I say, glancing behind me at the dull shop interior and mess of boxes and objects. 'Come in.'

Flipping a light switch does nothing, and I glance over to the dusty box of light bulbs I found on top of the kitchen cupboard last night.

'Sorry about the state of this place,' I say as I realise there is nowhere for my potential recruit to sit. 'I was supposed to have finished setting it all up by now. It's just been hard on my own.'

'It's no problem,' she says warmly in her thick Lancastrian accent. She finds a perch for herself on a large upturned crate I have planned for my autumnal woodland set. 'I know it is tricky for new start-ups, especially in this town. My dad used to run the old photo shop on the high street. I used to help out in the back when I was little.'

'Oh, that's a coincidence.' I smile as I flick on a lamp near the phone on the floor. 'So you know a fair bit about photography, then?'

'Quite a bit. Working in a shop like that, you see all sorts. Dad always used to let me watch the film getting developed. I remember he got flustered sometimes when people brought in reels with naughty shots on them. He used to make me leave the room!'

She laughs at the memory, and I feel my face being pulled into the first real smile for ages.

'Some people were more professional though,' she continues. 'I know loads about what makes a good shot, especially when it comes to babies and kids. Plus, I've served behind the till in lots of other places since my dad shut the place down.'

'I assume the digital camera put an end to his business, then? I'm sorry. It's sad when that happens.'

'Yes, it's a shame, isn't it? But I've got loads of other retail experience. I'm great with people, especially kids. Any of my references will tell you that. I used to work at Jumperz, you know, the family fun place?'

'Yes, I remember that place. It shut down after that fire.'

'That's right. I was gutted about that. It was an amazing place to work. Kids are great fun. My sister has four. They are a right handful! They love it when Aunty Rebecca looks after them though.'

I realise I haven't introduced myself properly and extend my hand to Rebecca. 'I'm Alison,' I say. 'Alison Burnham. I guess you got that from the ad though.'

She nods as we grasp hands briefly. 'That was a bit of a giveaway.'

'The signwriters should be here this afternoon,' I tell her. 'I still have a lot of work to do before we open the doors though.'

I don't know what I mean when I say *we*, but I plough on anyway. I had thought when I put that ad on the local Facebook group that I would have time to google the appropriate interview procedure. I've never employed anyone before, and I haven't done much research into the hiring process. Rebecca has caught me off guard here today. She still seems keen, however, so I must be doing something right.

I notice her pale blue eyes darting around the shop as we talk, taking everything in quietly. I feel self-conscious of the bobbly old jumper I pulled on this morning in a hurry and the way the stack of empty cardboard boxes and packaging is strewn all over the floor. I don't know if it is more of a reflection of myself or Rebecca that she still seems to want to work here, given the state of the place now. Perhaps her past retail experience has taught her about new start-ups, how they have to blossom from a small acorn. In any case, she comes across as patient, and I am grateful.

She seems to pick up my thoughts. 'You know, I'm available to start immediately if you need a hand getting things together. It's just you on your own, isn't it?'

'Yes. My husband would help me get things up and running, but he has to work.'

'Oh yeah. He works at that buffet place on the other side of town, doesn't he?'

'Yes,' I say hesitantly. 'How did you know?'

She looks sheepish all of a sudden and lifts her palms guiltily. 'I have to admit I looked at your profile a bit when I saw the job ad. I came across your husband's profile too because he is listed as being in a relationship with you. Well, one click leads to another on social media, doesn't it? Before you know it, you are scrolling through people's old photos for no reason at all. Or maybe it's just me because I'm sort of into photography more than most. I just wanted to get a feel of what sort of person you were. I hope you don't mind?'

'Not at all.' I shake my head and don't tell her that I am unnerved. I shouldn't be, really; everything I put online is for public consumption, for just about anyone to peruse at their leisure.

She grins at me, relieved. 'And while we are on the subject, I have to say that I love your wedding dress. It was just gorgeous. The vintage lace sleeves were stunning – like Kate Middleton had. I like it when classic designs are brought back.'

'Yes, that's exactly what I thought when I saw it in the shop at the time.'

'I bet it cost a fortune though.'

I grimace. 'It did. We – my husband and I – we were much better off when we got married though.'

'Oh? You worked for some big company, didn't you?'

'Yes,' I say again slowly.

She slaps herself on the hand. 'Sorry, I'm so nosy,' she says awkwardly. 'I can't help myself sometimes.'

'That's all right.' I smile. 'Yes, I had a well-paid job at a marketing firm.'

'But you left to come back here?'

'I wanted to spend more time with my son. I didn't like leaving him in daycare back then. Dan works long hours, and it just wasn't working out. So I have to be out of here by three on weekdays to pick up my child from school. That's why the hours are advertised as they are. I thought it might suit someone else who works around the school run.'

'Sometimes I pick up my niece and nephews from school, so it would suit me well. I mean, that's if you wanted to give me the job?'

She looks at me expectantly. The pearly blue tone of her irises seems to gleam in this light, and I haven't the heart to say no.

I nod. 'Of course. With your experience, I'd be silly not to.'

She stands up and claps her hands together. 'That's great! Let me help you with all this.' She points to the box of tools resting hopefully near a shelf. 'That needs sorting for a start.'

Rebecca leads the conversation as we work together setting up equipment, telling me all about her childhood working with her father. She tells me more about the shifty people who wanted their unsavoury pictures developed and the time her father had to call the police about a particular set. From the sound of it, her dad had a great passion for photography, which she insists she has inherited.

'I've always wanted to pursue photography as more than just a hobby,' she says. 'But working in retail means I've never had the money for the gear. All the stuff Dad had is old. You are so lucky. I bet all this doesn't come cheap.'

She glances at the studio lights, and her eyes come to rest on my most prized piece of equipment – my camera. Fitted with my favourite 85mm portrait lens, my Canon EOS 90D rests snugly in the expensive padded backpack Dan got me last Christmas.

'No, it doesn't. I've collected it all over the years though. I never dreamed I would be turning an old hobby into my livelihood. It is quite a risk, I suppose.'

It's more than a risk. Recently, I've spent so many nights terrified that it won't work out, that everything will come crumbling down around me. But I can't let that happen. Not again.

I don't tell my new employee that the last of our savings has been ploughed into this place, that this venture has to work. Failing isn't an option.

Not this time.

I simply tell Rebecca that I have to work. That Dan's income isn't enough for us on its own, which isn't a lie.

'I miss my income at the marketing firm,' I say later as we take a corner of a tartan rug each for the autumnal picnic set and lay it out. 'But it's so important that I spend more time with Adam.'

I suddenly remember what Dan's old neighbour said earlier about children growing up so fast. After all, Adam is to be cherished more than ever after what happened recently.

For a moment, I feel that Rebecca can see straight through me. That she can tell I'm lying about the real reason I left my successful design job. But when I glance over at her, she is busy pulling open a bag of artificial flowers.

She drapes the golden fairy lights around the pumpkins and sunflowers she has been busy arranging. Seeing her put so much care into the arrangement calms me somewhere inside. At least I have made one good decision in hiring Rebecca.

She kneels and works on adjusting a pumpkin. I stand on the crate that she sat on earlier and screw the light bulbs into the decorative crystal light fixture left over from the boutique clothing shop.

'I envy you doing all this,' she says suddenly. 'But I'm so

excited to be a part of it from day one. I think you're really brave.'

I look over at her. 'Brave?'

'I just mean that turning a hobby into a business is only a dream for most people. It's great if it works out though.'

She catches the look on my face over her shoulder and says hurriedly, 'I didn't mean that it won't work – I'm sure your business will be a massive hit. I've seen the stuff on your Facebook albums – and these prints in the window.' She gestures behind her. 'They look amazing. You're really talented. This place is exactly what this town needs. I know people who will pay through the nose for Insta-worthy shots they can show off online. My sister is one of them. Don't think she is getting away without coming down here. She might even be your first customer.'

'Well, you don't have to do that,' I say awkwardly, imagining Rebecca pressuring a faceless woman into turning up here with her brood. I'm not in need of charity.

She gives me a reassuring smile. 'What you're setting up here is really clever. I just know people will love it. I'm excited, Ali.'

The use of my nickname, used only by those closest to me, takes me by surprise, but I find I don't mind. I've relaxed in Rebecca's company over the afternoon, and we have been chatting away so much I haven't realised the minutes ticking by. I hadn't known what to expect from employing someone, but I suppose in a small business like mine we are more like friends rather than master and subordinate. It's been so long since I've had a friend. This afternoon with Rebecca has been nice.

We are interrupted by the signwriters later on, and I realise they are late. I had doubts when they quoted a much lower price than others in the area, but they do a good job. They work quickly too.

I stand back to admire their work, and I feel a rush of excitement when I see my name embellished on the white signage in purple ornate lettering.

Rebecca pads out to join me. She lets out a low whistle. 'It's all official now,' she says. 'It looks amazing.'

'Yes, it does, doesn't it?'

I hand the signwriter a cheque, but he reminds me we agreed on cash in hand, which is a conversation I have no recollection of. But I go into the back of the shop for my handbag anyway and find the cash in my purse I'd been saving for emergencies.

I pause and have to count it twice. I was sure there was more than that in here. I always keep a round hundred for the unexpected. Plus I took out extra for this afternoon. I count some out, sure some is missing, and hand it over to the signwriter anyway. He gives me a flat *cheers* as he pockets it and leaves.

I stare back up at the sign and try to remember when I might have spent the money. My eyes come to rest where Rebecca returns to work on the desk for my computer. Earlier, I went to clear the yard of old boxes and shop fixtures as she insisted on working her *flat-pack magic* when she saw that I was struggling. Could it be possible she had slipped into my handbag when I wasn't looking?

Now I feel stupid for leaving her unattended. She had seemed so warm and genuine earlier when she was talking about her past. After everything she told me, I feel like we have known each other for ages, but I remind myself we only just met today. I don't even know her last name.

I always believed that you couldn't fool a liar. It turns out that isn't true.

4

I feel as drained as my Fiesta's fuel tank when I walk in through the door for the final time later in the evening. Since picking up Adam from school, I've done a quick run with some more equipment for tomorrow. I didn't like leaving him on his own, but it was only for half an hour, and everything is finally set up at the shop now.

I thought I would be relieved that the hard part is behind me. But I've been fretting all evening, wondering how to approach the situation with Rebecca. I have no real basis for an accusation. And if I'm honest, part of me would be disappointed if I confronted her and was proven right.

It startles me how quickly I have grown to like her. I even started to consider her as the friend I have missed so much in recent times. Besides, I thought I was a better judge of character than that.

The pipes hum as I enter our cramped galley kitchen. Dan must be home and handling Adam's bath time. My heart pounds as it always does when I'm forced to do something duplicitous. My hand reaches into one of the high cupboards, and I take down the rusting biscuit tin no one ever uses. The perfect hiding place for what Cash Generator handed me for my mother's old pearl necklace. It isn't much by anyone's standards, but it will help us along for now.

At least Mum won't notice. It's been a year since I last saw her. The lid comes off the tin with a pop, and I freeze as I stare inside. I thought I'd cleared the last of the hidden cash in the tin, but I was clearly wrong. There must be over two hundred in here.

Unease bubbles in my stomach as I realise I've made a mistake. But I can't for the life of me understand how I made such a miscalculation. Guilt stabs at me when I imagine my mother's pearls sitting on some grubby shop shelf next to long-dulled gold chains and battered old DVDs. My grandmother had passed them down to her.

Then I think of how I turned Adam down for the milkshake he so wanted on the way home. He reminded me of the reward I had promised for getting top marks in yet another spelling test. He sulked for the rest of the afternoon before I relented and let him watch his favourite cartoons back-to-back as compensation. None of it was necessary, it seems.

It also means Rebecca is innocent after all. It disturbs me how quick I was to accuse her. What else have I done without realising?

'Ali, I didn't hear you come in.'

With a gasp, I spin around. 'Dan, you scared me.'

Beneath his sandy hair, Dan pulls his face into one of his crooked smiles that illuminates his dark brown eyes. He nods to the biscuit tin in my hands. 'You got the munchies?'

'What? Oh, a little. I made stew for dinner. Do you want some? There's a bowl in the fridge.'

'No, thanks. I ate after my shift.' He walks over to the sink and places a used mug on the side. At six feet and broadly built, my husband and his fuller figure seems to make the tiny kitchen in our cottage look even more of a joke than it already is. 'We had loads of garlic bread left over today for some reason. Hardly anyone ordered starters.'

'Saves money, I guess,' I say over my shoulder as I slip the biscuit tin neatly away. 'We aren't the only ones cutting corners.'

My husband potters around with the kettle and doesn't answer. There is a sudden change in his broad shoulders. Arguments about money come up so often. I wish I hadn't said anything, but I was keen to keep the conversation flowing to cover my hidden stash of cash. And nothing is more natural for us at the moment than to argue.

He hasn't mentioned much since we lost our baby. But I know this is simply the eye of the storm.

He makes us both a hot chocolate, and I catch sight of the side of his face; he is chewing the inside of his cheek, which is never a good sign.

'It was freezing in here when I got home,' he says abruptly as he leans against the kitchen worktop. 'Someone had turned the thermostat right down.'

I shrug. 'Yes, that was me. It's still only autumn. It will be a while before we need to use the heating.'

'What about Adam?' Dan knows how to hit me hard, and my stomach twists again. 'He was chilled to the bone when I got back.'

'He has slippers and plenty of thick jumpers if ever he decided to wear them. But he always complains he is too hot. You know how awkward he is.'

'Yes. I know where he gets it from. It certainly isn't me, is it?'

I shake my head and say nothing. Dan hasn't talked to me like this for a while. Not since it happened. I'm too tired to deal with this today. Maybe I will accept the cut, lick my wounds later when he is fast asleep and I'm lying awake staring at the ceiling.

When my husband speaks again, his voice is so much gentler that it startles me. 'If you want to bring some more money into the household, Ali, there are some easy things that we can do.'

'Like what?'

'Well, there is all that stuff upstairs we know you won't be using now.'

My mouth opens in shock. 'You mean the baby's things?'

He nods gently, avoiding my eye. He must know the agony this wrenches inside my chest.

'No,' I say, horrified, thinking of the cot lined with soft blankets and plush toys, all still with their tags on, all waiting in vain. We gave Adam the large room when we brought him home as a baby, as our own bedroom was too cramped for him along with our things. It took me by surprise how much paraphernalia a baby needs. Now there is a brand-new set I know we have no use for. 'It's too soon,' I say. 'I still need those things.'

He looks at me, surprised. 'What for? It's been two months now, Ali.'

'I know that.' Has it been that long already? It seems like just days ago that my little girl was handed to me for the first and last time. Her delicate weight is still felt pressed in my arms. I had made a silent promise to her that I would never let go.

It can't be time to send her carefully chosen possessions back to where they came from and pretend that she never existed.

I take a deep breath. 'I just need more time.'

Dan moves over and envelops me in his strong arms. There was once a time when I felt safe here. Now my own arms ache for something that has been taken from me forever.

My husband's breath is hot against my ear, his voice low. 'I know it's hard, but we need to move on with our lives. You said so yourself. That's why it's good that you are going back to work. You need to stay focused on the future, Ali.'

I swallow down the lump that has formed again in my throat. 'I know. I will sort everything out. Just not yet.'

'We will be lucky if they let us return it at all. They aren't legally obliged this late on. I will take care of it all though. You don't have to worry about it.'

'I just need a little longer,' I whisper. 'Please, Dan.'

He sighs. 'All right. But remember we need to be strong for Adam. It's not good for him to have part of his room still dedicated to the baby.'

Adam. Our surviving child. The one we must cherish. Dan knows that's the only way I will ever let go of all those things laid out neatly upstairs, gathering dust, no doubt. It hasn't been possible to examine any of the items too carefully.

I haven't dared touch anything. Disturbing things might ruin the lie to myself that everything will still be OK.

It can't ever be. Not after what I've done.

5

BEFORE

The motion of checking my phone for messages and missed calls feels like it is wearing me thin. I wouldn't be surprised if my joints start protesting soon. So far, I have managed to avoid the sorts of problems other women my age face.

My new daughter-in-law certainly wouldn't be disappointed to see me less mobile. She must live in fear of a surprise visit, bypassing the appointment system that seems to be in place at my son's house these days. It has been so long since I have been allotted a slot.

Does my daughter-in-law peer out of the decorative little windows and worry that she might see my car pulling up at any given time?

She should. Over the past two weeks, the thought has flitted into my mind so many times. Isn't it illegal now to keep a grandparent from visiting the children of their children? I'm sure I have rights. It is equally tough to imagine that *her* mother hasn't seen the new arrival yet.

One of my wishes came true, at least. My son and his wife welcomed a little boy into the world. Five pounds, six ounces.

Or so I was told unceremoniously via text. Later an email came through with a photograph of my newborn grandson. It disappointed me that I saw little of my son in the sleeping infant. Part of me was hoping to relive some memories of when my boy was small himself.

I've already spent a fortune on the same storybooks I read him so many bedtimes ago. I cast a glance at the pile of pristine hardbacks I've invested in. The decorative blue curling ribbon I had used to embellish the bundle seems to mock me as it sits waiting patiently alongside companions of the most charming little socks.

I wasn't able to contain myself in the shop and indulged my excitement by choosing the most adorable blue bunny. My fingers caress the long fluffy ears idly. My eyes flick to my answering machine again, and I chastise myself for my moment of hope. My son still hasn't returned my last call.

There have been so many excuses. My son tells me it wasn't an easy birth. The labour was long and complicated. Then the midwives detected a heart problem, and the baby had to be taken to the neonatal unit for care. That's understandable; these things happen quite often, after all. But they were discharged after just a few days. It's been well over a week since they got home. Surely they have had time to adjust to home life and be ready to receive just one little visitor?

I can just imagine my daughter-in-law's mother has been welcomed into the cottage already. The picture of her seating herself down carefully with the new baby haunts me. In my mind's eye, I keep seeing a vision of her slipping her own excitedly chosen plush toy next to my grandson. What if my grandchild takes an instinctive liking to her gifts? It renders me quite useless through no fault of my own.

The only contact from my son recently has been a series of hurried texts full of mistakes. It isn't like him. He must be snowed under with childcare. I know how much time and energy a new baby saps.

My daughter-in-law doesn't know how lucky she is to have my boy by her side. My husband had left all the work to me when our son was small. Then later, he was gone forever. In a way, I've lost my boy now too. Only to my daughter-in-law this time and not natural causes.

The best I can hope for is a brief visit or a photograph here and there.

But hope is a dangerous thing. It can lead you to believe you can still clutch onto something when you know deep down it has already gone.

Then you realise you are left with nothing.

6

'Are you sure you can't get the cost of this course refunded?' Dan asks me again over dinner. Adam forks at his cheese and mashed potato pie with a glazed expression. I get the sense he is trying not to listen to what we both anticipate might become a row. The poor thing probably enjoyed the break Dan and I have given him in recent months.

But as my husband says, we must get back to normal. And this is the norm for us. In the last few years, anyway.

I nod as I swallow down another forkful of grainy mashed potato. The melted cheese stubbornly sticks to my teeth. I glance at the clock with a thrill of nerves. The last thing I need is to be late for my first session.

'I told you, I can't. The course is non-refundable. It says so on the website.' I wash down my food with a gulp of water. Now that the weather is turning, the taps seem to be dispensing the chilled liquid we so craved during the heatwave we had in summer. Now it just makes me shiver.

'But have you called them and explained the situation?'

'Yes, of course. I'm committed now, Dan. I booked the

thing and paid ages ago. Anyway, the fact I'm doing this means we will have more money in the long run. My business needs a website, and I need to learn how to get one up and running.'

Dan shakes his head as he pushes a floret of undercooked broccoli around his plate. I'd been distracted while cooking, not paying proper attention. It isn't like me, but my stomach was swimming with nerves. Dan isn't helping. I should be thinking of the evening class I have ahead of me. I need time to prepare myself. It isn't helpful to be forced to tell the same lie to the same questions over and over again.

My husband frowns. 'But you already know how to set a website up. You've done it before, for that jewellery-making business you started a few years ago.'

'That was different,' I insist, aware of how this heavy meal sits uncomfortably alongside my squirming insides. 'It was years ago, and the technology has changed since then. All websites need to be designed for smartphones now. And the one I did wasn't great either. It didn't get much traction in the search engines. This course will teach me everything I need to know about getting spotted online too. We need this. I wouldn't go otherwise, would I?'

'I suppose.'

Once I am in the car and away from the pressure at home, I take a deep breath. I'm so nervous. I hate having to lie to my husband. It isolates me. I'm on an island with no way back to my only partner in life.

Dan and I were so close once. We made a promise to each other, after all. 'Til death does us part. Now our lives seem only connected by one lie after another. It seems to be the only way to get through each day. I didn't mean for it to be this way, but I've no map for the route back to the way we were before.

Indeed, I booked this course back in the summer. I did it

with the anticipation of having paying clients by now. Dan also expected a promotion by now too. It's also true that the website says it is non-refundable. But I haven't pushed for the money back as I told Dan.

He wouldn't understand why, but I need to attend this course. I can't imagine letting this opportunity slip away from me.

So here I am tonight.

Darkness is falling by the time I park up at Lakeside Community Education Centre near Accrington. A short drive away, this place runs a handful of evening courses for adults.

White street lights start to twinkle against the bare trees. Little yellow squares reveal snapshots of the classrooms inside. Figures with their focus on a computer screen or in chairs with their gaze trained on a tutor. Walking along the brightly lit corridors inside the building, I pass a pottery classroom and a room with a circle of chairs that looks like it could be used for group therapy.

In a classroom on the first floor, my new tutor instructs us all to choose a workstation, and I land at one positioned in the circle near the middle of the room. My fingers are cold and clammy as I take hold of the warm mouse to log in.

It's so hot in here. My top starts to cling to me beneath my jumper. The heating must be on full blast. Or maybe I chose a workstation directly underneath a heater? I glance up and see nothing but uniform ceiling tiles. Perhaps I'm just not used to the luxury of heat. I think of Adam at home in the cold cottage, hoping Dan turned the thermostat back up when I wasn't looking.

I get a fright when I realise the tutor pauses directly behind me as she walks around addressing the class. Suddenly this doesn't seem like such a good idea.

Why did I come here?

I glance at the door, but it may as well be in another

building now, as far away as it seems. Simply walking out isn't an option.

My clumsy fingers fumble with the keyboard as I try to remember the password I thought I memorised. I was sent the email a few days ago, so it must be accessible on my phone. I grab my bag from beneath the desk.

Suddenly, I sense a shape moving behind me, and the tutor's arm reaches across for my mouse. There is a split second where our fingers collide as I move mine out of the way. She makes a few rapid clicks and quickly types a password in for me.

As she leans over, I feel her warmth and breathe in her delicate scent. It is subtle; it might even be her deodorant. It feels too intimate, purely something only someone up close to her would detect. A sudden rush of emotion washes over me, and I feel light-headed. I'm glad that I am seated.

She pulls back as my computer loads. 'There you go. Looks like you're in.'

In one sweep, her almond-shaped eyes take me in. 'Don't be nervous.' She smiles warmly. It seems genuine, like she cares. 'We're all beginners here, Alison. We'll take it one step at a time, OK?'

For a moment, I am worried about the fact she knows my name. But then I realise she must have seen it openly on the screen in the username box.

She moves on to the grey-haired man beside me, who hasn't even managed to bring up the login box at all.

She thinks I am one of them, clueless and terrified of the technology they sit in front of. My shoulders relax a little as I realise she has no idea who I am.

Of course she wouldn't. I suspected as much when I booked the course all those months ago. There is no way I would have turned up if there was any chance she would recognise me for who I really am.

I HOPED to drop Adam off slightly earlier at school this morning and have time to talk to his teacher, Mrs Evans, who is also the deputy headteacher. We are approaching the school photograph season, and it would be a massive boost for my new business if I could get the contract. I know it is Mrs Evans who is in charge of choosing which company takes the project on.

There have been many complaints about the national chain that came in to take last year's shots. I have all the necessary equipment. Surely the school would be keen on a reliable local business instead of a faceless organisation driven only by profits? I wanted to put across how passionate I am about quality and care in my work.

But as I trot briskly along with Adam this morning, I realise I've missed the opportunity on this occasion. The bell has already rung as we approach the gates, and only a scattering of parents are left behind chatting to one another.

One of them is Adam's best friend's mother, Helen. I must catch her eye as she speaks animatedly to Mrs Evans at the edge of the playground, as she gives me a vague wave before returning to her conversation. We were close once, especially in secondary school and college. But that was a long time ago.

I kiss Adam goodbye, but he shrugs me off impatiently. He quickly looks around to see if anyone is watching before hurrying into the school building. My heart aches as he disappears.

Despite being a few minutes later than I planned for school, I still have an hour before I arranged to be at the shop with Rebecca. She said she would bring her old prom dress today to donate to the rail of gowns.

'I haven't worn it for sixteen years,' she said. 'I probably won't ever wear it again. I'd be so lucky just to have the occasion, let alone have it fit me.'

I'm on foot this morning, so I wander away from the

school. I feel at a loose end after being so busy with setting up the shop.

Dan is at work this morning, and I have nothing but a visit from my mother-in-law to look forward to after I finish at the shop for the day.

It's just so much easier to keep extended family at bay. The post-partum months weren't exactly the highlight of my life. Far from it. Adam's birth wasn't easy. He was taken from me almost as soon as I held him, and rushed to the baby care unit. I'd only just recovered from the problems I'd had when I was dealt another unexpected blow. That one had knocked me right off my feet.

The streets of Rishworth are so familiar to me that my feet automatically carry me up the busy main road. I know it will lead me through a development of large detached houses, each one unique and full of character.

When I was little, I always padded these roads expecting to live in one of these homes one day. It had looked like a possibility when I started working for the marketing company and was earning a decent wage. But it had all turned sour when Adam was still small.

For a long time, I've avoided doing more than glance at the thatched roofs and period stonework that I pass by now. Today, however, I'm starting to fall back in love with the stunning homes. In my head I decide my favourite and consider how different my choice is compared to when I was young and walking these same haunts.

When my new business takes off and Dan gets his promotion, we can realistically start looking for something bigger again. Adam can have the bedroom he wants, and both he and Dan can have the games room they so often dream about.

Even before I arrive, I realise where I will end up next. This town is so familiar to me I would recognise any part of it, even in isolation. So it is no surprise when the long-established trees and golden wrought-iron gates of the Rishworth cemetery come into view.

The catch clangs loudly in the quiet of the cloudy morning. A quick glance tells me I'm the only one here, almost. There is the distant figure of an elderly lady further up the slope of the hill, laying down a pot plant at a headstone.

Mum had my father cremated, as he always wanted. He often used to joke he wanted it that way to avoid any mistakes. I know my mother misses him terribly; she keeps his ashes close.

Guilt stabs at me whenever I think of her on her own now. I could do without the unexpected reminders of her like the one this morning. I've only ever done what I thought was right.

Even if it wasn't.

One thing I am sure of is that the past can't be changed. The thought is sobering. It hits me now like a train when I see the headstone I knew I would reach. Dan doesn't know about these visits. Somehow I haven't been able to find the words to tell him.

There is only one bunch of flowers left. White and pink roses, many heads still not fully opened. I wonder if whoever laid them meant that to be symbolic. They are shrivelled and dark looking now. How quickly fresh buds wither.

To me, the memories will always be fresh. The grief will always be too real. I will never be able to forget the opportunities lost to me forever.

I'll never forget the child I never had.

8

The shop landline rings almost as soon as I let myself in. I feel flustered. There are surely only a few minutes before Rebecca shows up. She has a habit of being highly punctual. And I am aware that after my visit to the graveyard, my mascara has likely swirled into black clouds around my eyes.

With thoughts of the sink in the tiny toilet, I drop my coat and handbag down behind my desk. The phone stops ringing and then immediately starts again.

It occurs to me that it could be my first customer calling, and I rush back out to where the handset now sits next to the computer on my desk.

'Hello?'

I am met with silence. 'Hello? This is Alison Burnham Photography. Hello? Can you hear me?'

There is a faint rustling. 'I think we have a bad line, sorry. Can I help you with something?'

There is a pause before I am met with silence once again.

A strange feeling creeps up on me as I put the phone down, but I shake it off. I pick up the receiver again and press redial. An automated message informs me that the number that called me was withheld.

A sudden flurry of activity behind me makes me jump, and I gasp.

'Hiya.' Rebecca bustles in brightly in her long, padded coat, a bundle of mauve chiffon in her arms. She catches sight of my face and does an immediate double take.

'Alison, what's wrong?'

'Nothing.' I gesture to the phone in my hand. 'Just a wrong number, that's all.'

'Are you sure? You look upset.'

I suddenly remember how my make-up must have run. The phone call had pushed it out of my head momentarily. 'Sorry, I just ...'

Words fail me, but Rebecca suddenly looks knowing.

She puts her arm around my shoulders and squeezes tightly. 'It's OK. I understand.'

It occurs to me that Rebecca knows all about the recent tragedy my family suffered. I wrote a simple post above all the excited maternity and pregnancy musings on my Facebook wall that would tell everyone what they needed to know. It wasn't easy tapping out the words, but I put something together to explain why I suddenly wasn't posting continuous updates anymore.

Rebecca must have seen it and put two and two together now. 'Why don't you go and wash your face, and I'll put the kettle on for us, eh?'

'Thanks.' I slip into the bathroom and dab at the black smears with a wet tissue.

When I emerge a few minutes later, she is busy at the rail of dresses. They bloom from their wooden hangers in shades ranging from pink and red at one end to gold and purple at the other. Rebecca's donation is perfect for the collection. It is fitted under the bust with a loose flowing skirt dusted with silver sparkles. It will make for some stunning maternity shoots.

'It all looks beautiful,' I say. 'Thank you.'

'No problem. It was just gathering dust in my wardrobe. I feel good that someone could make use of it here.' She eyes me somewhat warily as she sets a cup of hot tea on my desk. 'How are you doing? Are you feeling up to keeping the shop open today?'

'Yes. Of course. I just had some time to kill earlier and ... well, I went to visit the graveyard this morning.'

'Oh. I'm so sorry.' She squeezes my arm sympathetically. 'You should have said. I could have come with you, given you some moral support. I don't like the thought of you being on your own up there.'

I shake my head. 'That's very nice of you, but it was a spur-of-the-moment sort of thing. I just ended up there. I suppose I'm still looking for closure. Dan thinks we should move on with our lives. He wants to send all the baby's things back.'

'But you want to keep them?'

'Not forever. I know it isn't practical. To be honest, we can't afford to keep a whole set of things that we don't need. Deep down, I know he is right. That's why it is so difficult to argue with him over it. It's just that those things are the only tangible connection to the baby I've got. It's like it is proof our baby existed.'

'I'm proud that you stuck up for yourself. You should be able to have as much time as you need. Don't give the things back until you are ready. And if that's never, then that is fine too. You will regret it forever if you do something you know in your heart isn't right.'

For a moment, I think I see a glimmer of something in Rebecca's eyes, but she blinks, and I'm sure I imagined it. I'm only projecting thoughts of my own past onto others.

We spend the morning and most of the afternoon with our heads buried in a screen each. I'm at my PC, starting work on the website that should have been up and running by now. Rebecca uses the laptop I brought in to start work on designing leaflets advertising my services.

I make space for her at my spacious desk, and she pulls up a stool to face the wall behind me whilst I sit guiltily in the large computer chair I ordered months ago.

My offers to swap fall on deaf ears. 'Don't be silly,' she says every time I make the suggestion. 'I'm fine. This is cosy.'

I glance at her now and then. Her face is screwed up in concentration as she works on the promotional flyers. With the amount of effort she puts in, I know I couldn't ask for a more diligent employee. I'm lucky to have her.

Part of me thinks I would do a better job on the flyers, as it used to be my job back in the day. But I can't do everything myself, and the website is my priority, as more people will see it.

A large part of what went wrong in the past was down to me not asking for help when I needed it. I kept everything bottled up, and things just got too much. Now my whole family is paying the price.

The afternoon flies by, and before I know it, it is time to call it a day. I forgot that I have an evening with Julie when I get home, and when I remember, the warm bubble I have experienced for most of the day working with Rebecca dissipates instantly.

I'm half-tempted to text Dan and tell him I'll be working late, but I know that wouldn't go down well. So I say goodbye to Rebecca when it is time to close for the day.

It's Friday night, and I wonder if Rebecca has plans with anyone. She hasn't mentioned a boyfriend or partner in any of our chats.

9

The morning routine is as hectic as usual. Adam is the slow and fussy eater he always is, and it is hard work getting him into his uniform, warm from the dryer, and out the door on time.

Dan has the breakfast shift again at the restaurant and offers to take him to school, but I insist on doing it myself. I am determined to speak to Mrs Evans this morning about getting the school photo contract before she settles on another business. Our school portraits are always done in December, so I'm aware that I'm running out of time.

Luckily, Adam's teacher is on duty in the playground in the morning, and she moves over to the gap in the diamond-patterned fencing to greet him when he arrives.

'Morning, Adam,' she says formally, as she does with all the pupils. From what my son says, his teacher this year is someone not to be tried.

He doesn't need to tell me though. It is immediately obvious from her straight posture and the way she holds her broad shoulders. She is a far cry from the leggings and plim-solls most of the other staff wear here, in her suit jacket and trousers. Perhaps she is already preparing to move into the top job when her boss, Mrs Bradley, retires; surely that must be soon, as she was teaching when I attended myself.

Mrs Evans watches Adam pad into the playground. I feel the usual tug of trepidation as he moves out of my protective radius.

His teacher turns her shrewd gaze back to me when she realises I haven't left yet.

'Adam has settled in nicely this year. I couldn't ask any more of him,' she says.

'Thank you. That's so nice to hear,' I say, aware that I'm wearing my old mud-stained walking shoes, not the smart heels and neat black skirt like a mother who steps past me now. She waves goodbye to her child over her shoulder, no doubt in a hurry to get to her office job.

Mrs Evans's eyes give me the briefest going-over. I could almost miss it. 'What is it you do?' she asks. 'Adam tells me you have your own business.'

'Yes, that's right.' I'm delighted the subject came up naturally. 'Actually, I'm a photographer. I specialise in family and children's portraits.'

'How wonderful.' Her attention is suddenly snatched away by a pair of boys who have taken to shoving each other on the other side of the playground. Unfortunately, they have done so near the teaching assistant from Adam's class.

Mrs Evans shouts over to her, gesturing to the pupils nearby. The assistant snaps around and visibly reprimands the pair, sending them to separate corners of the grey stone yard.

Mrs Evans mutters more to herself than me, 'Not even five minutes into the school day this time ...' She glances at me again. 'It's a good thing they aren't all like that. It's luck of the draw what I get to teach in a year. As I said, I'm so delighted with how your son is getting on.'

when I round the corner and pull out my keys to open up my little shop.

She greets me brightly with her illuminating smile that is hard not to return. 'Hiya, Ali. The weather has taken a turn, hasn't it? I'm freezing out here. Had a good weekend?'

'Not bad,' I lie, thinking of the visit from my mother-in-law. 'You haven't been waiting long, have you?'

'No, I just got here. But the bus went straight past me earlier, and I had to walk all the way over instead. I think he was running late, the grumpy old sod. It was that wind that got me. It might take me a while before I can feel my face again.'

'How horrible,' I say, standing back to let her into the shop, which doesn't feel a great deal warmer than outside. I shut the door behind us. 'You don't have far to walk though, do you?'

'It's quite a trek on foot.'

'Oh.' I think of the CV Rebecca sent over after her interview. I looked up her address after realising I had money missing, and knew she lived on the outskirts of town. 'I thought you lived in one of the houses by the train station? The big Tudor-style ones?'

She shrugs as she hangs up her coat on the stand by the door. 'Well, it's a fair way in this cold. I didn't want to be late either.'

'Don't worry about that. It was mean of that driver not to stop for you.'

'Too right it was. I'd like to report him, but I don't want to give him another minute of my time. I've let it go already. Must be all those endorphins from the exercise. But I'm not one to hold a grudge, anyway. I do need a cuppa though. Coffee?'

'Yes, please. Can you make it–'

'Semi-skimmed milk and no sugar,' she finishes for me with a wink as she disappears into the back room.

I smile. 'That would be great.'

It's a dark morning. The sky outside the only shop window is a dark stormy grey. I flick on the light at the wall, and nothing happens. My fingers click the switch a few more times to no avail.

My desk lamp is the same when I try it.

Rebecca calls from the kitchen, 'Ali, I can't get the kettle to work.'

I try the switch for my computer too and groan. I realise now why it is so cold in here. 'The electricity has gone off.'

The wind catches the door and tugs it from my grip as I step out into the damp yard. It bangs behind me, echoing loudly.

The battered old fuse box is a mess of wires and faded handwritten labels. It is dark in the enclosed yard and hard to see. Not that I know what I am looking for.

The beam of Rebecca's phone flashlight appears over my shoulder. 'Well, that's weird,' she says.

'What?'

'There doesn't look like there is anything wrong at all.'

'Well, something has gone wrong somewhere,' I say, dreading the thought of getting hold of an electrician. How much would that cost?

Rebecca seems to read my thoughts. 'The landlord should take care of it. Look at the state of that electrical box. That is a long-overdue repair. Have you got their number? I'll call them if you like.'

'It's OK. I'll take care of it.'

After almost forty minutes on the phone, I manage to get Andy, the landlord, to arrange someone to come in after lunch and look at the electrics.

We treat ourselves to a pasty and a cream-topped latte at

the bakery around the corner. 'At least it's warm in here,' Rebecca says as we find a seat.

I nod, thinking of how behind I will be at the end of the day, even if the problem gets resolved soon.

The stout electrician turns up much later in the afternoon than arranged in an old blue Transit van.

Rebecca rolls her eyes at me behind his back as he crouches down at the box with a torch. I'm so glad she is here with me today.

'It's short-circuited,' he says after unplugging various wires and running tests with a handheld device. 'Water has got inside the system.'

He gestures, but I don't know what I am looking at.

Rebecca frowns at him. 'Water? How could it? It hasn't rained properly for ages.'

The electrician unclips part of the casing with a loud snap and tips out a small stream of clear liquid to prove his point. 'It must be recent – it hasn't gone black or mouldy. At least that's something. There's a hell of a lot in there though. You're right. It shouldn't be like that.' He shrugs. 'Andy will be pissed at having to pay for this. It should take a fair few hours to fix. I reckon if I start now, though, it will be done by half-six.'

He gets to work, and I pull out my phone to text Dan. I had wanted to pick Adam up from school and take him for that milkshake I'd promised him. Now I'll be spending my afternoon here instead, and Dan will lose his time off. He has worked so hard for so many years taking care of us when I was unable to.

Rebecca sees the message I am typing out over my shoulder. 'I can stay here whilst this gets sorted,' she says.

'I couldn't ask you to do that,' I say. 'I can't pay overtime either.'

She shakes her head. 'Don't worry about it. You set this

place up so you could have more time to spend with your son. It defeats the objective if you miss seeing him altogether.'

I hesitate awkwardly. 'Are you sure?'

'Absolutely. As you said, my house isn't far from here. You've been working so hard, Ali. You deserve it. This wasn't your fault.'

'You have too, and it isn't your fault either.'

'I know.' A faint frown line appears amongst the freckles on her pale forehead.

'What's the matter?' I ask.

'Nothing, it's just that ... well, have you seen the gate?' She gestures behind us over her shoulder.

She shows me pale gouges on the exterior, fresh and new against the rest of the rotten wood. 'It looks like someone has broken in.'

10

The waiting has become too much. They can't seriously expect me to contain myself any longer. It's now officially three weeks since my grandchild was welcomed into the world. And still, I have not been allowed to visit.

It's hard not to take it personally. My daughter-in-law is lucky I don't hold grudges. All I want is to see my grandchild in person, hold him in my arms. Despite what my son says about his in-laws not flying over yet, I'm sure his other grandmother must have had the opportunity already. I'm not asking too much.

I've given up waiting for an invite. So I've planned a brief visit as I pass by on my way home from work. They can't argue with that. Just half an hour won't hurt.

My heart starts to flutter uncomfortably as I pull my car over to the usual spot outside the little cottage. The sense that I shouldn't be here is almost overwhelming, and for a moment, I even consider starting the engine again and leaving.

But I can't. I'm so close now. The last picture my son

emailed yesterday was just too adorable; in it, his baby son was bundled in a fluffy blue bear romper, his perfect little face in peaceful sleep. There surely isn't a more beautiful little angel anywhere.

My boy can't expect me to stay away after sending that image. I'd have to be heartless not to feel the rush of love as soon as the pixels filled my screen.

My uninvited feet trespass up the quaint little path. I am hopeful that the bundle of gifts in my arms affords me entry, an offering before the new little prince.

The afternoon is dusky as sunset approaches, and there is the warm glow of light from the living room. Someone is definitely home.

When I ring the bell, I'm almost holding my breath. It almost feels like an eternity before someone answers. With relief, I realise it is my son's tall figure that I see approaching through the frosted glass.

He can't hide his surprise at seeing me when he opens the door. After a moment, he catches himself and invites me inside the warmth of the house.

The scent of their home has changed. There is no trace of the expensive fragranced designer candles my daughter-in-law has always enjoyed. There is a much more appealing aroma now – that special perfume that is added to most baby products. It is unmistakable.

My son doesn't greet me with his usual hug. Instead, he directs me to the kitchen sink, where he awkwardly asks me to wash my hands.

I set down the bag of gifts on the kitchen worktop carefully and do as I am told.

He apologises and tells me they are taking every precaution. 'We can't be too careful,' he says, muttering something about my line of work. Is that why I haven't been invited? Because I am in contact with so many?

I try to reassure him. 'The hospital wouldn't have discharged the baby if there was any risk,' I remind him.

It isn't like him to be a germaphobe. This can only be *her* influence. I want to tell him that people were far less careful in the past. That children have survived without being coddled for countless generations, thousands of years, even. But I say nothing. I don't feel welcome here, and I feel ashamed now that I couldn't resist the temptation to drop by.

'I was going past anyway,' I tell him, but I don't think he truly hears me.

Up close, I realise how tired my boy looks. The dark circles under his eyes are accompanied by red rims and bloodshot whites. I've never seen him so tired.

Doesn't he know it's the new mother who usually looks like that? Not the father. I'm sure I did, but I barely had time to notice back then. My son must be doing too much. He is overworking himself as usual.

His tone is further hushed as he leads me through to the living room, where a Moses basket rests on the plush carpet beside the sofa.

He informs me that his wife is taking a nap upstairs.

As I suspected, I think to myself. I perch myself gently on the edge of the sofa ever so carefully. Even so, the baby stirs as I settle myself down.

I can feel my son almost holding his breath beside me, willing the infant to stay asleep.

I pray for the opposite.

Tiny fists clench and flail around, and after a few moments of fidgeting, the narrow eyes open. I get my wish.

My son scoops up his son, and there is almost a reluctance when he is handed over to me. He instructs me further back in the seat so that my arms are propped up on the oversized cushions around me. No chance for any accidents.

My son leaves the room hurriedly to warm some milk as

the baby stirs gently in my arms, moving his head from one side to the other, fruitlessly mouthing his fists.

Here it is. This is the moment I've been waiting for ever since it was announced all those months ago. I've been denied this for so many weeks now that the longing has turned into something else.

Any resentment melts away now I'm trusted with such a precious little package. And yet, I'm left with something else. A feeling I can't identify.

All the time spent staring at the pictures didn't prepare me mentally. Or was part of me still expecting to find a more obvious trace of my son in the newborn's delicate features – one that the camera lens missed?

I'm feeling a little deflated. There was so much build-up to this visit that it feels anticlimactic now that I am here.

Why did they have to keep me at arm's length? It has made this all seem so unnatural.

When I leave, I try to get my feelings better organised. I tell myself that it is probably normal to be this way. This marks a new chapter in my life and that of my child's. Neither of us will be the same again. He is a father now, and I, a grandmother. We have new identities to fill and grow accustomed to. That is probably all it is. I had been so intent on visiting, I was emotionally unprepared.

As I pull the car away and leave the cottage behind in the rear-view mirror, I'm still not sure what I'm feeling. I'm disoriented, confused, disappointed. All of them. Or maybe none. I still am not sure.

Maybe they were right to keep me away. I was only let into the palace with some reluctance because I forced my way in. I invited myself and was only allowed to see my grandson after I had washed my hands. I feel dirty, contaminated.

Maybe they were right to keep me away.

11

F inding a venue for the exhibition is tough. All the obvious local locations are fully booked with winter crafts events and Christmas fairs.

Rebecca tries to make helpful suggestions when I explain my frustrations after being on the phone all morning to no avail.

'Have you tried the theatre?' she asks thoughtfully.

'Yes. There isn't any availability until March. Same with the town hall and the community centre,' I say wearily, resting my head on my hand. It's not just the exhibition that seems to be doomed. Despite Rebecca and me printing and distributing hundreds of leaflets, I haven't had a single enquiry. If it weren't for the shoot we have booked with Rebecca's sister today, I would be feeling quite panicked at this stage.

Rebecca suddenly pauses her rummaging through the box of prop flowers and stares at the wall. 'I just remembered,' she says suddenly. 'My dad had an exhibition of his work at the library once. He got quite a bit of exposure from that. The best part was he didn't have to stand around or anything. They put his prints up behind the glass display cases near the doors. He didn't sell any of it though, but it wouldn't hurt to look into it. I don't think it cost him anything either. It could be a good way to get the word about.'

'That's a good idea,' I say, considering how my more creative pieces would look next to the book-return bin and peeling posters explaining the town's textile history. I suppose there is the possibility it could turn out to be the ideal place to sell some local landscape shots. The printers gave me a discount for getting the A1 prints at the same time as the leaflets. I think of the stack of them in the back room. I'm quite committed.

I make enquiries with the library, but by the time I put the phone down, I have got no further than adding my name to a waiting list that stretches into next year.

A few minutes later Rebecca places a mug of coffee on my desk. 'You could always have the exhibition here.'

I laugh, then realise that Rebecca is quite serious.

'Why not?' she says. 'Loads of people advertise events online these days to bring people to them. And you said yourself, that's where your market is. You could put the event up on Facebook and host it here. It would cost hardly anything that way. And everyone will know exactly where to come when they want their family portraits. It would put you on the map.'

I feel a flutter of excitement when I realise she is right. 'That could just work.'

'Of course it could. I'm not just a pretty face, you know.'

By the time we have to leave for the photoshoot, the arrangements for the exhibition are made. It is to be held next Saturday evening, and I'm back to feeling enthusiastic about the business again. I've never experienced so many ups and downs with any of my previous start-ups. I feel a little like I'm on a roller coaster of emotions, not knowing what jolt is to be felt next.

I take extra care as I lock up the shop, mindful to take any removable valuables with me, even my laptop, which I don't need on this outing. I installed an extra bolt for the gate so it can't be opened from the outside, at least not easily. It troubles me that someone forced their way into the yard. Nothing was taken either, which disconcerts me further. What did the intruder want? Mindless sabotage and nothing more? Or was it a coincidence the electrical cupboard was filled with water?

Rebecca promises to invite as many of her friends as possible as we set off together. 'It's going to be amazing,' she says as we load my car with the equipment and get in.

I'm becoming unceasingly nervous as we drive closer to Rishworth Woods. I've never done a shoot with anyone outside of the family before. From what she has said, Rebecca's niece and nephews sound like they may take quite some directing to get a decent shot their mother would be happy with.

On the other hand, I suppose I should be grateful for my first paying customer, even if they didn't find out about me as organically as I had hoped.

My Fiesta's engine protests as it starts the climb up the dirt track leading up the hill. Halfway up, we get out at the car park, and I take a moment to look around. The views from up here are enviable. Virtually the whole of the town is visible, stretching far into the distance.

This is the first time I have set foot here since back in May.

If this place hadn't felt so oppressive in the last few years, I would think it more beautiful. There are other rows of pretty cottages like ours splayed out here and there like long fingers, the original homes of the industrial workers from the local textile mill. The green square of the public park is visible near the middle of it all; from up here, the bright orange hues of various autumnal trees are striking against the drab grey of the buildings in town.

But I don't want to include any of this in today's compositions. I already have a perfect set of images in mind. I want the same background of evergreen trees that were in the photos I took with Adam before summer. It looked amazing.

It's just a shame I can't locate my maternity photos. Not that long ago, I wasn't sure that I even wanted to keep them. Now that they are gone, I want to see them more than anything.

Once Rebecca's sister and her children arrive and the photoshoot is underway, I start to relax. The children certainly turn out to be boisterous, but they take instruction from me, a stranger to them.

'They aren't like this usually,' Rebecca mutters to me as we switch from a seated shot upon a fallen log to a standing position along the same path I captured Adam on. 'I guess they haven't come out of their shells yet. Too bad they can't stay in them more often.'

I laugh. 'I'm sure you don't mean that.' This is exactly how I imagined running the business would be, having a nice time with the clients.

Dusk is falling now, making the string lights we hung in the nearby trees twinkle enchantingly.

Rebecca helps me weave flowers into her sister's and niece's long hair. I notice the three of them all share the same mousy shade. The little girl is adorable. She gives me the widest gappy grin as she dashes off to join her mother and siblings for the next shot. The burgundy dress Rebecca found for her seems to flow eerily in her wake.

I work quickly, making the most of it before darkness falls completely.

Rebecca helps retrieve the props at the end of the shoot in between supporting her sister loading her brood into their car.

As the light fades, I move quickly, winding the string lights into a roll in my hand. It isn't easy, and I leave the bulbs switched on to light my way.

I swiftly step forward to retrieve the power supply I had strapped to a tree earlier. A twig snaps beneath my trainer, and the sound echoes back almost immediately from somewhere in the dark of the woods.

I suddenly sense someone waiting in the gloom of the trees, unseen. Watching.

There is a moment when I imagine us both staring at each other. Only I have the disadvantage. I'm watching blindly from one thick crop of trees to another.

Where are they? What are they waiting for?

I don't dare move or even breathe as I brace myself for an attack.

A rustle from close behind me has my heart pounding wildly in my chest.

I spin around in time to see Rebecca drop an armful of artificial flowers into a nearby box. 'Well, that lot are off to McDonald's for tea. They have had a great time. Are you nearly ready, Ali?' She shivers. 'I'm chilled right through here. I think we've got time for a quick coffee before we call it a day.'

'Yes ... we probably do.'

I glance back to the green gloom of the surrounding trees, but the moment has passed. Now that I'm not alone, it's easy to convince myself that what I experienced could easily have been a dog walker. Perhaps I heard the sound of the hound scouting off into the branches alone.

In the car as we drive away, it occurs to me that I could have imagined the presence entirely. The thought does nothing to comfort me, however.

The thought that my mind is betraying me is unwelcome. I can't let things slip now.

Not again.

12

The shop is busy in the morning. I'm excited to take the first real enquiry and booking by phone. The rest of the morning is spent at my desk, processing the set of photos from the shoot with Rebecca's sister. The shots look great, but I just want to add my unique touch by editing, cropping and applying the finishing touches to each one. It's been so long since I last did this that I have forgotten how time-consuming it can be. By lunchtime, I'm almost finished working on the first of the three photos chosen from the collection.

I can't find my usual colour and style filters in the photo-editing software. I was counting on those to provide the finishing professional touches.

The last time I used any of the effects was when I was pregnant, and I conclude that they must be on the laptop, which I was using at the time. I sigh, remembering that I've left it at home for security purposes after the attempted break-in. I'll have to pop home and pick it up if I want to have any chance of finishing the project in time for the exhibition.

I also can't wait to hear how happy my client is with the final result.

At home, I let myself in and head straight for the laptop bag I stashed in the cupboard under the stairs. I swing it over my shoulder and am almost back at the front door again when I freeze.

There was a noise upstairs.

I listen hard, hardly daring to breathe. The floorboards creak quietly above the living room.

Someone is here. In one of the bedrooms. Adam is at school, so it can't be him.

I pause and glance behind me towards the front door. I could slip outside undetected and call for help. Dan is on shift at the restaurant a short walk away. He will be entering the lunchtime rush right now.

But what would he do that I can't on my own?

I force my hand onto the bannister and creep up the stairs.

The activity has stopped as my shoulders draw level with the top of the stairs. I pause. Have I imagined things again? Perhaps the sound was coming from the next-door neighbours' instead? Sometimes, I feel that we almost live with the elderly couple next door, the way they have their television turned up so loud in the evenings. Sometimes it sounds like they drop something heavy, and it reverberates through our floorboards. Maybe that is what has happened just now? They are usually around the house in the day, after all.

Then, without warning, the door to Adam's bedroom swings open.

There is a gasp.

'Alison?'

I let go of a breath I didn't realise I was holding.

'Dan? You scared me.'

I take in his chequered plimsolls and chef's whites as I ascend the last few stairs. 'What are you doing here?' I ask him.

'Our food delivery didn't show. Most of the stuff is off the menu – the best sellers too. Nigel was practically having a fit when he realised he couldn't get another supplier at short notice. You should have seen him. I've never seen the bloke more stressed.'

'He shouldn't be running the place. You should. I bet you would have worked something out if that had happened when you were in charge.'

He runs his hand over his unshaven face. 'I guess. Anyway, that's any chance of overtime blown this week.'

'That's annoying.' I glance over his shoulder through the open door. The slats of the unused cot are visible from here. 'What were you doing in Adam's room?'

He shrugs. 'Nothing. I was just wondering when we can start moving forward, that's all.'

My arms fold automatically across my chest in an act of defence. It doesn't go unnoticed by my husband.

'Don't get worked up, Ali,' he says with a sigh. 'You know we have to do it at some point. It's not easy for me either, having to live with all this stuff, you know. It's like a constant reminder.'

'Are we supposed to just forget?'

He turns and pads back inside the bedroom. I follow him in.

It's been a while since I've looked at all these things properly. I'm not prepared for this right now.

I look around at the cot lined with plush toys and blankets and at the changing table set with various packs of nappies and pots of cream.

It's all so overwhelming.

When Dan speaks again, his voice is lower, gentler. 'What about what Adam feels? All this is the first thing he sees in the morning and the last thing before he goes to sleep at night. The situation is confusing and upsetting enough for him.'

I think I would prefer it if he shouted; I could have put my guard up then.

I feel my eyes watering as I stare at the plush rabbit in the cot, one of the many soft toys in this section of the room.

I let myself get carried away when shopping for the baby. I indulged myself in a way I hadn't during my first pregnancy. This time, I was determined that the baby would have everything it could want, even if it stretched the budget a little. I chose each thing proudly and with such care.

You know what they say, pride comes before a fall.

Dan speaks to me in that gentle tone again. 'Why don't we just take one thing at a time? Let's start with the cot. It's taking up the most space ...'

My husband might think he is being sensitive, but I just find it patronising. I'm not his equal. Not anymore. I was once, back when I had a successful career. Perhaps I was even more than that. Apart from the money troubles, part of me thinks Dan might even prefer it this way.

The baby was supposed to change everything. Put right the wrong between me and Dan. There has been so much of it, at least since Adam.

Before he was born, we were happy. Everything went wrong between Dan and me after Adam came into our lives. And yet, I would never give him up. Not for anything.

Dan's voice drifts back to my consciousness. '... And I wouldn't need to do overtime at all if we sent these things back. What about that water bill that came through this morning? How are we going to pay for that? I noticed you slide it into the kitchen drawer when you thought I wasn't looking. You can't just bury your head in the sand, Ali.'

'I'm trying my best. You know how much I've put into making the business work. It won't be long now before we start seeing things turn around. I've already had one paying client. I booked another today. It will work this time, Dan.'

'I think you are putting too much into the business, if you ask for my opinion – which you won't.'

I stare at him, bewildered. 'What are you talking about?'

He shakes his head. 'You just ... You know what you're like. You tend to get things in your head ... and you have trouble letting them go.'

'I don't know what you are talking about.'

He sighs and rubs his eyes. The dark circles are more pronounced than ever. 'You know how you are with things. You have ideas – which are great – like taking up photography again. It's a nice hobby. But then you get, I don't know. A little ... obsessive.'

'I needed to find a way to earn money to support us. You said it was a great idea.'

'No, I didn't. I said it could work, but you shouldn't put the pressure on yourself.'

My mouth drops open. I'm sure Dan supported my suggestion of starting the shop. He didn't stop me from getting the premises, entering a fixed-term lease and buying all the equipment. I can't believe he is saying all this to me now. Especially when things are starting to pick up. Why would he even mention it when I'm so committed?

He sighs heavily. I've never seen him so weary. It should be me who is exhausted. He sleeps soundly all night, and I've lost count of the hours spent staring at the ceiling.

'All I'm saying is you just need to learn to let go of things sometimes.' Dan gestures around him. 'Like all these possessions you don't need. I'm worried that what you've set up here is turning into a shrine. This is how it started last time. You can't get like that again. It's not healthy. For Adam's sake, at least. He was too young to remember at the time. You won't get that luxury again.'

13

BEFORE

I t is thought that most of our experience of the world is a reflection of ourselves. Our lives are not simply determined by the actions and whims of those around us. So what does that mean for me?

There must be a flaw in me. For so long, I longed for a grandchild. Now he is here, the experience isn't what I expected. It can only be my fault. I allowed myself to indulge in glowing visions of what life would be like with the little one in it. The bare-faced reality didn't meet up with my expectations, and it left me feeling flat. That is all. If I'm disappointed, I only have myself to blame.

Nevertheless, it has been wonderful watching the little one develop over these past few months. Pushing for the visit paid off. It seemed to unblock the connection between my son and me. Remind him that I still exist. I've been allowed a handful of visits so far. All of them over too soon. It is a wrench to have to hand over the baby again, especially when it is *her* waiting arms that reach out for him.

There is an adorable little shop that sells baby products on the high street. The display of shiny silver christening gifts in the window catches my attention, an array of choices from pocket watches to compasses and personalised christening gowns. The poster behind promotes a monogram embroidery service.

I smile to myself as I imagine the new parents' faces when I present them with something so charming and personalised. Something that will take centre stage at the event. Little Miss Perfect wouldn't be able to push it aside or donate it easily to a local charity shop.

Even if the gift gets stowed away out of sight in a box somewhere and my grandson happens upon it one day, he will appreciate that I cared.

A week's wages down and with a newly packaged box in my hands, I realise that it is my son's choice of wife that has thrown a spanner in the works. If he had met someone else, then we all could have been happy together. My family would have been extended, not segregated.

I was so excited at first, so determined to love my grandchild that I pushed aside thoughts of who the mother is. Nothing is stronger than the bond between mother and baby. Perhaps it was foolish of me to think I could ignore the fact that the child ultimately belongs to my daughter-in-law when all is said and done.

Things would have been different if I had a maternal link to their family unit. I bet my son's mother-in-law is given priority in everything: priority access to visits, the first invite to special occasions, the most thoughtful gifts. Even if they live abroad sometimes, I'm sure the little one is pushing the other grandmother into sticking around.

But as things stand, I'm just the *other* grandmother. I'm the one being squeezed out.

I am the one who has to work the hardest to stay in the loop.

No matter what it costs.

14

By the time I get home, it is already dark. Someone broke into the shop through the front, smashing their way in to get to my computer. I'd foolishly left my camera equipment on-site overnight too. The lot was gone by the time I got to the shop and went inside, my boots crunching over the smashed glass to assess the situation.

Inside the cottage, it is dark. I hear noises from upstairs, but there are no lights on. I make my way up the stairs gingerly, terrified of what I might find.

The sounds come from Adam's bedroom. I call out for him, but he does not respond.

My heart is pounding when I push his bedroom door open.

The room is bare. Everything has gone. Not just the baby's things but Adam's too. It is like neither of them ever existed.

Dan stands with his back to me, stripping the cornflower-blue wallpaper with his bare hands.

I hear the shock in my voice as I ask him what he is doing, but he doesn't turn around. He simply responds in a flat voice, asking me why I didn't turn up to Adam's funeral.

My mouth opens in shock. I hadn't realised that Adam was dead. Then I realise I had forgotten. How could I have failed to remember something like that? My daughter is gone, now my son too.

I've lost them both. I've lost everything.

I collapse to the floor in a flurry of despair. Dan still doesn't look at me as I start to scream.

My eyes snap open. My breathing is quick and shallow. My hot legs are tangled in the sheets of the bed.

Even though it is dark, the familiarity of our bedroom washes over me as I look around wildly.

The back of Dan's head comes into focus by my side. He sleeps in silence, his breathing deep and quiet as usual.

From years of sleepless nights, I've learnt to judge the time from the degree of light on the curtains. The street light outside is still prominent, so the sky can't have lightened at all yet. Day is still far from breaking.

I take a deep breath, trying to steady myself. I bury my face in my hands. But when I shut my eyes behind my fingers, I immediately see the vision of Adam's empty bedroom again.

The images are too sharp and real. When my guard is down, so is the barrier between reality and fear. In the dark, anything feels like it could be possible.

It is becoming more obvious by the moment that it was all a nightmare, but I want to check. The only thing that will assure me now is seeing my little boy sleeping soundly in his bed, surrounded by his toys, books and posters.

I slide carefully out of the bed so as not to disturb Dan and pad along the landing to Adam's room.

My stomach drops to the floor when I see his bedroom door is wide open. He has always insisted on leaving it shut, to keep the monsters out.

When I round the corner, I am flooded with relief to see him tucked up inside his green dinosaur duvet. The floorboard creaks beneath my bare foot as I creep forwards, and his head snaps over in my direction. His eyes are open; the dim light casts a fearful glaze in the whites.

'What are you doing awake?' I ask him, wondering what could have dragged him from his usual deep slumber.

'I had a bad dream.'

'Poor baby. Me too. What about?'

He shakes his head, unwilling to speak of whatever horror upset him in the middle of the night. It makes me sad that he doesn't want to confide in me. Dan always laughs that our little boy is a closed book even at his young age.

'What was your nightmare, Mum?'

'Just silly things.' My hands move automatically to tuck him in, smoothing out the sheets and adjusting his pillow.

He eyes me closely. The deep hue of his irises still glow, even in the gloom. 'Why do grown-ups have nightmares?'

'The same reason children do, I suppose. Things you try not to think about in the day come back to visit you at night. Things that you bottle up. That's why it's good to talk to people. Is there anything bothering you, Adam?'

He shrugs, slipping his chin beneath the duvet.

I sigh, knowing I will get no further. 'Why was the door open? Did you want some water?'

He shakes his head. 'I needed the toilet.'

I sigh, realising that is probably why I'm awake now too; our bedroom is in between Adam's room and the bathroom. With the rickety old floorboards and noisy pipes, it is almost impossible to make a quiet visit. At least my little boy rescued me from my nightmare.

'Go back to sleep,' I say gently, kissing his smooth forehead. 'You've had a busy week at school. You need to rest. And I've got a big day tomorrow.' I stroke his head gently, relishing how warm and real he is.

No one can ever take him from me, I tell myself silently. It was just a nightmare, that's all.

I'VE BEEN nervous all day, but the panic and excitement bubble over. Now, I find myself walking back and forth unnecessarily into the back of the shop, checking the arrangements for what feels like the hundredth time.

The prints I had selected for this evening hang in bold statements on the wall, illuminated by warm picture lights. We leave the photo sets as they are, lights on, as though ready for a client to walk right into. A relaxed way to show people what I do and how the process works.

We don't officially open the exhibition for another half an hour, and the waiting is killing me. I'm starting to second-guess everything. Like whether the cheap bottles of supermarket label fizz are good enough. Have we purchased too many? Or if the quantity of nibbles laid out on disposable plates is too much. What if no one shows up? And if they do, am I dressed appropriately for the occasion in simple black trousers and a plain jersey top?

I regret not setting the opening time earlier in the evening. Then it would have started already. It's well and truly dark now, and I feel strange not being at home with my family, keeping them safe. At least Dan is taking good care of Adam at home.

I move to adjust one of the prints under the pretence of straightening it, but I am just glad to have something to do with my hands.

Rebecca's heels click noisily on the laminate floor as she appears by my side. 'Don't worry, Ali. Everything is going to be fine. This evening is supposed to be fun. You'll see.'

'I hope so.'

She gives me a reassuring smile. Rebecca has put significantly more effort into her appearance than I have for the night. Her faded highlights have been pulled back into a neat high ponytail. Her bright blue eyes are carefully framed with smokey eyeshadow in a way that I could never pull off; they are complemented by the pearly shimmer on her high cheekbones.

I've broken out in a cold sweat by the time people start filtering in. A large group appears shortly after we open the doors, they all seem to know Rebecca, and I suspect she invited them personally. I feel a wave of gratitude towards her. I couldn't ask her to put in any more effort than she already has.

Although they don't appear to want to buy any prints, they are very complimentary of my work. One of the group, a man with a beard, takes his time gazing at the print of Adam as a toddler; it's the one where he is dwarfed by the tall cornstalks that flank him. I stare at the back of the man's head, wondering what is going on inside it.

It felt too exposed placing the pictures of Adam in such prominent positions. But people and children are what my business is all about. I've placed the prints featuring Rebecca's sister and her children in pride of place in the centre of the wall. As I watch people drift inevitably from one picture to the next throughout the evening, I feel their eyes linger the longest on the shots of my little boy.

Or is that my imagination?

Later on, an older couple starts talking to me about the landscape shots, which seem to have been largely forgotten for most of the evening. They purchase a print of the view from the main hill in Rishworth. The lady tells me it is a gift for their son who used to live in the town before he moved away and became a solicitor in Manchester. I feel a pang of jealousy that I'm still stuck in the town I've spent my whole life in. I had opportunities once.

As I smile and say that I hope their gift is well received, I spot a flash of Dan's sandy hair in the doorway. He steers Adam into the shop by the shoulders, past a cluster of people.

'Dan,' I say in surprise, 'what are you doing here?'

He shrugs, smiling and looking around at the prints on the wall. 'We thought we should pop down here and say hello. Adam hasn't even seen this place yet. He wanted to see what his Mummy has been up to.'

I hear the clip-clop of heels, and Rebecca is by my side, introducing herself with a little wave. 'This must be the star of the show,' she says with a beaming smile at Adam.

'Yes, I suppose so,' I say awkwardly, aware the man from earlier is still hanging around, although I'm sure most of the group he came in with are gone. When I look around, I realise he is close by Adam, apparently busy choosing himself a glass of sparkling wine from the table behind.

I move to pull Adam away from any potential danger. I'm always uncomfortable about him being near glass. Why hadn't Rebecca picked up those disposable plastic flutes instead?

'Why don't you go and take a quick look at the pictures of you I've got up here?' I say to him, gesturing to the walls. 'You've never seen these shots so big.'

He shrugs. 'I've seen them on the computer loads of times. One of them is the wallpaper on your phone. Why would you even need it printed out?'

'It's different when you can reach out and touch them. Plus it doesn't need any power. It's saving the planet too.' He says nothing. I see he's spotted the plate of miniature cheese-cakes and eclairs on a nearby table. Adam edges around a woman staring intently at one of the prints on the wall just as an elderly man has a sneezing fit by the plate.

I am forced to steer Adam out of harm's way again. 'Haven't you already eaten?' I ask him.

He tuts loudly. 'Dad didn't give me anything for pudding. I'm starving.'

'You can have some toast when you get home.' I rub his back and realise how clammy my hand is. Having Adam thrown unexpectedly into a flurry of potential hazards is making me nervous. 'Your father will take you now,' I add pointedly as I reach Dan again. He looks at me from where he stands with Rebecca, who seems to be trying to engage him in conversation.

Once I see Dan and Adam drive away safely in the car, the evening seems far from over. Warm bodies continue to bustle and press in around me.

I fold my arms across my chest and smile as more people drift in as the hour gets later. There is nothing to complain about, I remind myself – I couldn't have asked for a better turnout.

The type of person wandering in through the door seems to change, fewer are asking questions, and they avoid catching my eye. Most make a beeline for the free alcohol, and the din of the room seems to become louder and rowdier. I worry for the residents of the flat upstairs, as it is getting late now.

When I look around, I realise I don't recognise anyone who's turned up. It's hard to differentiate who's from somewhere within Rebecca's circle and who the general public is.

At the end of the evening when the doors are shut and the two of us are clearing up, I notice we completely ran out of food and drink. I wonder how many of the attendees were only in it for the freebies.

Still, I sold five landscape prints at full price, which more than covers the costs for the evening. Plus between us,

Rebecca and I gained three new bookings, and a handful of people said they would seriously think about it.

If I weren't so tired, I would be elated. Seeing Adam suddenly sprung in the middle of everything has unsettled me too. I thought he was safe at home. Now the feeling usually exclusive to night-time horrors creeps over me. It must be the lateness of the hour, my body and mind preparing me for the night again. The same old routine.

Hopefully, I will be so tired I might for once sleep right through. I'm just not ready to examine what I saw last night so soon.

I work quickly, aware time is ticking away as I sweep up the last remnants of flaky pastry from the corner of the room. Now I'm near the most recent shot of Adam from the photo-shoot I did with him in May.

I look up, expecting to see his handsome face looking back at me with that muted smile of his.

Instead, I'm staring at the bare wall surrounded by a frame of woodlands. There is a rough section in the forest scene missing where Adam should have been.

15

On Monday, I have what could be described as a great day in the shop. We take on another two bookings and handle our second ever photoshoot – the first in the new studio.

A soon-to-be grandmother has purchased the premium package for her heavily pregnant daughter. She chooses the burgundy dress I wore for my own maternity shots and poses her in the autumn set, amongst the pumpkins and leaves. It seems she has a vision for the shoot and directs everyone, including me, to fulfil it.

I am happy to oblige. Not only am I grateful to have a paying customer, but I'm also thankful to be kept busy, especially after what happened on Saturday night.

Once our morning clients leave, Rebecca sets about making us a coffee. As she stirs in the milk, she stares at the wall where the print had hung. In her mind, I'm sure she can still see the hole and the wall behind.

So can I, every time I close my eyes.

Rebecca seems just as shaken as me. She was horrified, blinking back tears after I pointed out the damaged print.

'I still don't get why someone would do that,' she says
again as she hands me a mug. 'Or how. We were both here.'

'It could have happened when I went to the car with Dan
and Adam. There was only one of us in the room then.'

'I suppose.' She nods, taking a sip of her coffee, then pulls
a face, forgetting it would be far too hot. Her eyes look watery,
and I hope it is only from the drink. I thought Rebecca would
shrug off the incident and make me feel like every possibility
I'd considered was pure paranoia. The fact that my otherwise
carefree employee is also worried only troubles me further.

She sets a plate of biscuits down on the desk between us
and takes one thoughtfully. 'You know, a woman asked me
how the process worked just as you were leaving. Said she
wanted it for her pregnant friend's birthday. I went for it,
trying to make it sound like the perfect gift. It worked though
– she made a booking. But someone could have done something then. Goodness, Ali, I didn't think to *guard* the prints on
the wall! I didn't think anyone would try to mess with them.
Why did someone have to do something so weird?'

'I don't know.' I grip my own mug. The heat burns my
palms in a pleasantly distracting way. I've tried not to think
about who took the scrap of the photo of Adam. I don't want
to consider whose pocket it was slipped into. Or what they
might be doing with it. For some reason, my mind springs
back to the bearded man every time the subject comes up.

I haven't said anything to Rebecca, as I don't want to
throw out random aspersions on someone she may count as a
friend. I just know to be more vigilant in the future. Now that
another potential danger has shown its face, I know what to
look out for.

Nothing will come and snatch my little boy away. I won't
let it.

THE FAMILIAR FLUTTER of nerves starts to tickle at my insides as the evening goes on. Dan seems nervous too. He keeps glancing at the clock now and then when he thinks I'm not looking. The sense of expectation hangs in the air, and I almost feel an argument is about to brew.

But nothing is fired my way. I don't get a single comment or remark as I pull on my coat and pick up my keys.

Relief starts to creep in at the realisation that Dan has accepted that I am going to my evening class regularly. Now that I have started, I have every intention of finishing this course.

Once I have taken my seat at the usual workstation, the tutor starts talking about what we will cover during the session.

She moves around to the front of the class as she speaks and writes on the whiteboard to further demonstrate her point.

Her voice is soothing. Somehow she doesn't come across as patronising even though she must have run this class past hundreds of different faces over the years. I've wondered for so long what it must be like to be one of her students.

I glance around at the class. Do they know about the woman who stands before them?

Her story was in the local paper at the time. It was a small piece. Not front-page material. It was the names that caught my attention. I can imagine that the article most likely escaped the attention of the majority. I only noticed because of the relationship I'd had with her husband.

But she isn't to know that. I can't imagine he would have breathed a word to her either.

When I get back home later, the house is quiet. Dan emerges from upstairs and tells me he has just put Adam to bed.

'You're a little late if you want to say goodnight,' he says, watching me take off my coat in the hall.

'Don't be silly. I got stuck behind a tractor on the way back, but it didn't set me back much. Anyway, it always takes him a while to get to sleep. You know how he is.'

'I've already settled him down, Ali. Let him sleep.'

I slip my shoes onto the rack and look around at my husband. 'What are you talking about? Dan, he's only just gone up. I'll just be two minutes.'

I carefully open the bedroom door and peer into the dark room. Adam turns his head to see me, clearly awake, as I knew he would be. He has always tossed and turned to get to sleep. Ever since he was a toddler.

I step quietly through the door, and as soon as I do, I'm aware that something is wrong.

The room is nothing but various tones of navy, but I can tell that a large shape that should be pressing in on my peripheral vision isn't there.

I flick on Adam's bedside lamp, and we both blink in the brightness for a moment before I turn around.

The baby's cot is missing.

Images from my nightmare come flooding back to me, more real and vivid than ever, except the room isn't empty. The cot has been plucked from the scene, and everything else seems to have shifted, as though the item of furniture has created a vacuum. Now the soft toys, blankets, clothes and products have been moved clumsily around, as though Dan thought I wouldn't notice if they were stacked up in the empty space.

'What happened?' I whisper out loud, more to myself than to the child beside me.

'Dad sold the cot.' There is a soft rustling as Adam settles himself back onto his pillow, rubbing his eyes with his fingers the way I always tell him not to in case they aren't clean. 'A lady came and picked it up when you were out.'

'What lady?'

'I don't know. Just some lady.'

'Well – did she say her name? What did she look like?'

There is a hiss from the door. Dan's stony face appears in the gap. He nods his head towards the staircase. 'Come on,' he says quietly. 'Adam's got school tomorrow. He needs his sleep.'

Out of routine, I kiss Adam goodnight and tuck him in mindlessly. I feel numb as my feet tread the long-flattened carpet down the stairs. Is this why Dan was so quiet before I left for my class this evening?

Dan shuts the door behind us when we reach the living room.

I turn around to face him, arms folded across my chest. My lip trembles threateningly. 'How could you lie to me?'

'Please don't get upset. You know it had to go. We discussed it.'

'You said you were thinking of sending it back. You didn't say someone was coming around for it. Who was she?'

'No one I know. I tried to get the company to take it back, but they said they couldn't do it. We've had it for too long. Someone offered me a good price for it on Facebook.'

'Facebook?' Great. Now everyone will know. And I've been walking around oblivious.

I wipe my tears away with my sleeve. 'How long ago did you set up the pickup? Did you arrange that when I was at work? Or when I was upstairs helping our child in the bath?'

Dan shakes his head. 'I knew you would do this. That's why I didn't tell you. I thought it would be easier if I took care of it while you were out.'

'You shouldn't have gone behind my back.'

'I didn't want to. I just wanted to stop you from getting upset. I thought it was for the best.'

I stare back at Dan. Did he think he was doing me a favour by arranging this sneakily? He honestly seems to think he was being compassionate. He has no idea what I have truly lost.

He will never understand.

16

Dan is eager to take Adam to school this morning even though it will cut it fine for the start of his shift at the restaurant. I know it is because he is trying to make up for having the cot taken away.

But I am equally eager to show him that I have everything under control, that I am willing to move on with our lives. Deep down, I know he is right. I had just wanted more time than he understands.

Part of me wanted to keep everything of the baby's. Bits and pieces slipping away on my watch was never part of the bargain. I'm still hurt and confused by what happened to our little girl. I wanted to keep hold of everything until I had figured it all out. Then again, the rest of me knows exactly why this happened to us.

Adam munches his way drowsily through his cornflakes without so much as a glance at the clock. Despite my best efforts, we both eventually trot off on our way later than I had planned.

Adam's pudgy mitt slips from my grip once we round the

corner, and he turns to face me, walking backwards. 'When can I go to school on my own?'

His balance looks precarious as he walks blindly in reverse. A broken glass bottle lies malevolently at the side of the path. One slip and we will be making an unexpected journey to the hospital.

'When you are much older,' I say, taking him by the shoulder and correcting him. As we near the school, he almost knocks into the wing mirror of a battered green car. It has a scrape down the side that makes me wonder what sort of careless driver it belongs to.

I'm mindful that I need to be at the shop earlier than usual today to take delivery of new props. The delivery window starts soon, and I am anxious about the box being left outside after recent events at the shop.

We are just passing the bungalows with well-tended gardens near the school when I am aware of a metallic rattling behind me.

Out of the corner of my eye, I see the white shape of a Transit van pulling along the road beside us. The pace slows as it approaches. The whir of the electric window is audible in the quiet street as a pale face appears, facing determinedly in our direction.

I move my hand to the rough canvas of Adam's Spiderman backpack, urging him to quicken his pace a little.

'Excuse me, love. You couldn't help us out with some directions, could you? We've got a bit lost.'

I glance over my shoulder but don't stop. 'Sorry. I'm in a hurry.'

The van pulls along the road to match my pace. The unshaven passenger lifts a large map. His skin looks grey, and there are heavy circles beneath his eyes.

I sense the driver watching from the dark of the cabin, but can't see his face properly other than to notice he seems to have a beard. 'The satnav has led us all over the place. Can you show me where Clifton Avenue is?' He gestures to the map again.

I shake my head. As I do so, I notice there is nothing written on the side of the van to say what they do. Neither occupant is wearing any kind of uniform, and the vehicle is old and shabby looking. 'You are on the wrong side of the bridge for that. Once you get to the other side, it should be the first turn on your right.'

I don't get a response, and I pick up the pace, applying more pressure to Adam's shoulder. It isn't until I get to the end of the road that I glance behind me and see the van performing a three-point-turn and heading off in the opposite direction.

'Remember, never talk to strangers,' I remind Adam as I kiss him goodbye at the safety of the school gates.

'But you just did.'

'But I'm a grown-up, and I didn't stop *or* go near the vehicle. If someone was to do that to you, just keep walking and don't turn around.'

'But what if they need help?'

'They will find someone else. Never talk to anyone you don't know.'

I glance around me as Adam steps under the watchful gaze of his teaching assistant but see nothing but other mothers and fathers hugging and waving off their children. They all drive family cars, people carriers and economic estates. There is the smart, sign-written black van belonging to Hazel Greenwood's mother, who owns the trendy home interior shop in town. But no white vans.

The feeling the encounter left me with remains with me all the way to the shop. I find myself looking over my shoulder now and then. I don't know why, but I get the sense that eyes linger on me longer than they should.

When I look around, however, I realise that no one is staring.

As I round the corner with thoughts of getting started on the business website, I am surprised to see Rebecca waiting outside already. She doesn't start until ten.

'You're here early,' I say to her as I arrive. The surprise on her face makes me worry for a moment that I'm the one who has made a mistake and lost track of time.

'We have that shoot that was booked at the exhibition. Do you remember? The lady who needed an earlier slot because of her child's dentist appointment?'

'Yes, I remember. It just slipped my mind on the way over here. That's the one who's due next week with his little brother?'

'Yes, that's right. It feels a bit precarious, doesn't it, her doing this so close to her due date? What if she goes into labour early?'

She glances at me, and her face changes suddenly when she sees mine. 'Sorry, I didn't mean to ...'

'It's fine. I don't think it's likely though.'

'Yeah, I guess. I was just blabbering on, really. You seem a bit distant this morning. Are you OK?'

'I'm fine. Just tired, really.'

I'd like to confide in Rebecca over yesterday's debacle with the cot. I'd like to get some outside thoughts on whether Dan was doing the right thing or not. But I know she would take my side by default. Her opinion wouldn't be objective enough to be helpful.

Our morning client is punctual, arriving at exactly nine thirty as arranged. I feel a little flustered by the time she arrives, as I've been rushing around getting the studio and props set up for her as she had requested. Like our last client, this one has the perfect shot in mind.

Normally, I would be excited about making her vision a

reality, but I'd completely forgotten about this morning's appointment. It was a good thing Rebecca was here to remind me. If it was obvious the booking was a surprise to me, she says nothing. Between us, we get everything prepared just in time before the shop door opens and in comes the client.

A lady with straightened dark red hair walks in. Her toddler walks in neatly holding his mother's hand. I step out of the winter-themed studio set and onto the main shop floor.

'You must be Alison,' she says with a smile displaying a perfect row of whitened teeth. It's more of a statement than a question.

'Yes, that's right. You must be Taylor?' I greet her, feeling grateful that I managed to check her name on the appointment list before she got here. I return her smile with interest as she removes her long black trench coat.

My eyes automatically move down to her bump, which seems a little too flat.

She sees me looking. 'I always carry small,' she says, moving her hand across her belly as an explanation.

I nod. 'Yes, some women do. My mother-in-law was one of them, apparently. She never missed an opportunity to mention it when I was pregnant with my first child.'

Her eyes meet mine, and I can tell she must have been rooting through my social media too. 'That's mothers-in-law for you.'

Her little boy struggles with the zip on his puffa coat, and Rebecca bends down to help him. Despite the fact he can't be older than three, he gives her a clear and sweet, 'Thank you.'

'You're welcome, young man.' Rebecca straightens up and puts her hand on her heart. 'Aww, bless! If only my nephews were that polite.'

I show Taylor to the winter set and talk her through the process. Rebecca keeps the child entertained on the swivel chair behind my desk. She spins him around gently to the most infectious little chuckle.

A few minutes later, his mother smiles as she emerges from the back room, having changed into the dress of her choice – Rebecca's old prom gown. 'I want to thank you for fitting James and me both in at short notice. When I heard what you were doing, I thought it was a great idea. I'm glad I heard about it before I gave birth. It's about time someone did this sort of thing in this town.'

I smile as I show her to the box of floral props. 'That's OK. We love what we do.'

'Also, I wanted to point out that I'm not really stalking you.'

'What do you mean?' I ask.

'Well, because I got my new baby's cot from you.' She strokes her subtle bump again. 'I picked it up last night. Your husband said you had popped out when I arrived. I mentioned that I had a booking with you today. It was his surname that made me ask. I guessed it wasn't a coincidence, and the fact that it was still brand new ...'

'Oh. I see.'

She looks at me for a moment, as if worried that I might crumple as I set up the camera on the tripod. But then she continues, 'When I saw it, I knew it was exactly what my partner and I were looking for. So thank you. It's really beautiful.'

She smooths her palms down her flowing mauve dress and gestures at the glittering silver and white set around her. 'You obviously have great taste in everything.'

'Thank you.' I struggle with my camera, trying to adjust the aperture, wondering why I can't do it. Then I realise the mode dial has been moved to a setting I never use. It must have been knocked at some point.

Since the gate was damaged and the electrical fault, I've

been worried that someone has been trying to break in and steal my things, especially since my nightmare. But I keep the camera and lenses secure overnight. I stash them away out of sight. No one else could have touched my camera. And besides, only I have the keys to the shop.

Taylor is very set on getting the shot she wants. She tries to describe it to me, but I have a hard time understanding what she means. I just hope I have it covered in the hundreds of images I take during her shoot.

It's not just the fact that this is her vision, or I'm unused to being the one directed. I find the fact distracting that the baby growing inside her belly will be sleeping in what was supposed to be my daughter's cot.

I curse myself for not listening to Dan sooner. If the item of furniture had been sent back to the company warehouse within the return window, then I wouldn't have to face the new owner directly. I wouldn't be adjusting her rich-coloured hair to flow over her bare shoulders. And I wouldn't see how her little boy's round features mirror hers. Now, I can picture the face of the baby that will sleep in the tastefully designed ash cot I'd spent weeks browsing online for.

I explain all this to Rebecca once Taylor and James have left, when she notices how watery my eyes become as I wave the pair off. Through the shop window, we see that little James doesn't stop waving all the way down the street.

'Oh, Ali. You should have told me about the cot. I thought you said you were keeping it until you were ready?'

'Well, I was. But Dan thought it was best it went.'

'That's bang out of order,' she retorts quickly.

'You think so?'

'Absolutely. I hope you told him so.'

'I didn't want to start an argument about it. I was tired after a long day.'

'Make sure you set him straight when you get the chance

though. You don't want him pulling that sort of stunt again. Where does it end?'

'I suppose you are right. I just wish I'd listened in the first place and sent it back to the store I bought it from. We would have had more money for it, and I wouldn't have to see the new owners. It's too easy to imagine what the baby who will use it might look like after seeing little James just now.'

'Yeah, he takes after his mother, you can tell. You can sort of imagine what he'll look like when he is older.'

'Exactly. I'll never get to see what my own daughter would look like when she was older. It was hard to judge who she took after when I got such little time with her.'

She puts a sympathetic hand on mine. 'At least you have Adam though. You can sort of picture how your little girl might have looked as she had grown. She would have been gorgeous like her older brother.'

I flip through the new images on my camera sightlessly. 'I guess.'

That night, I find myself unable to get to sleep at all, unable to leave thoughts of the photoshoot behind. Every time I close my eyes, I see Taylor's face. She and James had looked so perfect in their photographs. She did have the perfect little family, with another one on the way. It breaks my heart to think that I'm not in her position.

By 1 am, I realise that sleep is on a distant horizon still. I glance across at Dan. His chest rises and falls steadily.

I reach for my phone and slip downstairs quietly in my dressing gown, using my mental map to avoid the creaky steps. In the living room, I carefully close the door and switch on a lamp, determined not to wake anyone up.

On Facebook, I search for Taylor. Even though my business hasn't the formality of a dentist or therapist, it feels like I am breaking some kind of client confidentiality. I even glance around me at the dimly lit room before I tap on her profile.

I scroll through her pictures. James features heavily, surrounded by gifts and expensive toys. She has a beautiful home. A handsome husband. I don't even need to visit his profile to see he owns a lucrative refrigeration company. Taylor mentions it at least twice in just the handful of posts I see. Appearances mean a lot to her. I smile grimly. She was exactly the client I had in mind when I first got the idea for the business.

Soon she will have more inspirational pictures to splash up on her digital wall once they have finished post-processing.

As I've been scrolling, I've tried to ignore the little red circle in the corner of my screen. I stopped looking at my Facebook messages a while ago.

After what happened, so many people sent messages of support and encouragement. I wasn't interested in their sympathies when all I wanted was to come home with my daughter in my arms as I had expected to. So I stopped reading them.

But now I suppose some of the messages might be enquiries about the shop. It wouldn't be professional to ignore them.

I scroll through and dismiss the ones that tell me how sorry they are, the same hollow words and hug emojis over and over. I try not to look too closely either at the flowery words of one or two, so delicately chosen, not wanting to be dragged down by their meaning. I can't bear to dwell on what I have lost.

I tap out an answer to a booking enquiry and wonder briefly afterwards what the recipient will think of receiving a response at this hour.

The newest message sits at the top of the list. The name is unfamiliar, and the photo is a generic one, a foreign-looking beach somewhere. I tap to open it, expecting to deal with another potential customer.

My dry eyes take in the words on the screen, black and all in uppercase.

I KNOW WHAT KEEPS YOU AWAKE AT NIGHT

17

My head breaks the water, and I struggle for air. I was under for so long that time, I thought I wasn't going to make it to the surface. I stare around me in all directions, coughing and spluttering. I realise Adam isn't up here with me.

I'm flooded with panic. Salt water burns the inside of my mouth and throat. It stings my eyes as I dive down looking for my little boy.

I can't find him. My vision is obscured by a stream of bubbles emerging from the dark water, and I'm forced back to the surface. The current drags me away, disorienting me.

Adam is down there somewhere. I know I'm losing him with every second that passes.

The waves grow and swell. The roaring grows louder in my ears.

I open my eyes.

I'm just in time to catch the brief glow from my phone in the dim room. Sunlight glows on the hydrangea pattern of the curtains.

I breathe deeply, gripping the damp duvet cover. It grounds me. Reminds me I'm at home in my own bed.

I reach for my phone and am shocked when my bleary eyes take in the time. A notification sits below the clock; that must have been what woke me up.

I throw back the covers and get to my feet.

How could Dan let me sleep like this? He must have gone to work already and hoped I would be up in time to get Adam to school. We'll have to take the car, and he can eat toast on the way if we are to make it.

I hurry down the hall to Adam's room but find myself staring at an empty, but neatly made bed.

'Adam?' I call down the stairs.

No reply.

It quickly becomes apparent I'm alone in the house. The feeling from my nightmare has not left me, and I'm worried part of it will come true like it did last time.

Has Dan taken Adam to school? Or has he attempted the walk alone whilst his father goes to work?

Part of me says my husband wouldn't do such a thing, but then another makes me question it. I hadn't seen what he did with the cot coming either.

Bile rises in my throat at the thought of our little boy making the journey by himself. I think of the white van yesterday, of all the busy roads in between here and there and that scraped car near the school, and the message I read in the middle of the night.

It isn't possible that someone knows what I did. But what else could those words have meant?

Danger lurks everywhere, watching and waiting. It's the moment you let your guard down or relax when bad things happen.

I'm shaking as I snatch up my phone again and call Dan.

It takes my nervous fingers a few attempts to tap the right buttons.

The phone rings through and reaches voicemail. I immediately try again. And again.

I pace frantically back and forth in the bedroom, torn between keeping the phone glued to my ear and getting dressed and following the route Adam could have taken.

I'm in tears, trying not to imagine all the horrible things that could be happening to him right now when the ringtone is interrupted. I hear Dan's voice.

'Ali, what's going on? Are you OK?'

'Is Adam with you?'

'No. I just dropped him off at school.'

'Why did you do that?' I retort quickly. 'That isn't what we arranged. I've been thinking all sorts. Why didn't you leave me a message?'

'I didn't think I had to. Wasn't it obvious? You were so tired. It isn't like you to oversleep like that.'

I sink onto the bed and try to stifle the sobs that erupt from me. Dan hears though.

'Look, I'm on my way to work,' he says. 'Do you need me to come back?'

I recover myself, rubbing away my tears with my pyjama sleeve. 'No. It's OK. I'm fine.'

'Are you sure?'

'Yes. I have to get going to the shop soon too.'

There is a pause. 'Don't go putting pressure on yourself, Ali. It's not good for you. You were up late last night photo editing. Maybe you should give yourself the day off. You are your own boss, after all.'

'No. I have too much to do. I have another client booked, and I have loads more processing that needs doing. And I need to work on marketing. I'm fine, honestly. I'll see you later.'

I shower quickly and dress, not wanting to linger too long with the feeling of water on my skin after my nightmare.

I rush around, grabbing my keys and slipping on my coat. I grab my laptop bag stored safely in the cupboard under the stairs, and as I lift it, something small falls out onto the worn carpet.

It's a flash drive. I pick it up and stare at it. Something tugs at my memory. I'd forgotten I had this second, spare drive. I slip it back into the bag and zip up the front pocket.

It was clumsy of me to leave it open in the first place. I always used to tell my mother off for leaving her handbag carelessly unzipped as she went around town.

I feel a twinge of guilt as I settle into the car and think of Mum. We haven't so much as spoken in so long. When I arrive at the shop, I catch the tail end of the phone ringing. It stops just before I reach it. I try to redial, but get the same message telling me the number was withheld.

I'm annoyed with myself for not catching the call. It could have been a company with a larger project in mind. I've contacted a few local schools and playgroups and wondered if they might return some interest. This is about the time when some of the additional staff have some time on their hands for that type of enquiry.

Before I settle down to get started on editing yesterday's shoot, I decide to give my mother a call. The feeling of waking up from a nightmare left me feeling like a lost child again, in need of parental comfort. Besides, I've been meaning to contact her for ages.

She doesn't answer. Knowing her, she should certainly be up and about by now. She has become more and more of an early riser in her senior years. Or so I believe. Since Adam, I seem to have lost touch with my mother. My hands were full with caring for a demanding baby, then a toddler. Dan and I weren't getting along great then either. Then I stopped working for the company in Manchester.

Once I settle down at my desk, I remember the flash drive I found this morning. My mind goes blank when I try to remember what is on it. Perhaps I've stored some useful photo effects on there that could enhance my work further. I didn't find everything I was looking for on the laptop, after all.

I plug it in and realise this is where I was keeping the winter effects I was thinking of just last night. Then I notice a folder titled *May*. I open it and am not prepared for the hundreds of image thumbnails that now fill the screen.

These are my maternity shots. I haven't lost them after all. I rack my brains, and something tugs in my memory. I must have moved these images onto the flash drive to stop myself from seeing them. It's like a digital Pandora's box that I couldn't bear to think about.

I think of the money that I stashed away in the biscuit tin and forgot about. Dread eats at me when I think of Mum's pearls and how I sold them thinking I needed to. All the parking slots were filled by the time I arrived here this morning, and I had to walk down the high street. The necklace was gone from Cash Generator's window when I went past. They are gone forever.

At lunchtime, I think about giving Mum's phone another try, but then get cold feet just before I hear the ringtone.

My stomach rumbles. It's Rebecca's day off, and I miss her doing the lunch run to the bakery around the corner. I push thoughts of friendly chatter and a pastry with a creamy filling out of my head as I work on Taylor's photographs. As I lighten the whites of her eyes, I notice that she had lined them with pastel eyeshadow that matched the dress she selected. Little James too, has cufflinks on his shirt of a coordinating hue. His mother certainly has attention to detail. After last night's snooping, I can picture a few options as to where these shots might go up in their house. I start feeling guilty again. Then a sudden gust of movement in the doorway makes me gasp.

Dan appears clutching two bulging brown bags bearing his restaurant's logo in his thick hands. 'I thought you might be hungry. Are you all right? You look startled.'

'You just made me jump, that's all. It's quiet in here without Rebecca.'

He snorts as he puts down a heavy paper bag in front of me. 'I can imagine it would be.'

'Don't be like that. She's actually very nice. She's done so much for the business too. It's a shame she isn't here full time. I miss her when it's her day off. Are you on a break?'

Dan pulls Rebecca's stool to the desk and starts unpacking the bags. 'Yes. It's been quiet this week.'

'Even at lunchtime?'

He shrugs. 'That new Thai place has opened across the road from us. People seem to love it. Their prices are really low.'

'Are you worried?'

'No. It's just because it's new and different. People don't want spicy food for breakfast. Our place was heaving this morning. We ran clean out of bacon.'

'You need to be in charge of running the place.' I unwrap the chicken burger Dan has brought for me. 'I've said it for ages.'

'I am working on it.' He eyes me critically over his food. 'You look tired. How did you sleep? You seemed pretty out of it this morning when I got up.'

I shrug. 'Not too great. I didn't get much exercise yesterday. That's probably what did it. You know what I'm like.'

He nods. 'I do. I don't want you stressing yourself out running all this.' He glances around at the colourful sets.

'I'm not stressed,' I say firmly. 'Just tired.'

'Why are you so tired? You were practically unconscious this morning.' He fiddles with the lid on his paper coffee cup. 'Is there something else going on?'

'Like what?'

He drops his voice low, as though about to say a rude word. 'Like postpartum depression again.'

'I don't think that's relevant. It's not like I'm exhausting myself running after a baby this time, is it?'

'It's still the same principle whether you are looking after a baby or not. Doesn't giving birth change the chemicals in your brain or something?'

Dan is floundering. 'But it's been months now,' I say. 'I don't know how else to tell you that I'm doing just fine.'

'You didn't seem it this morning. That's not like you, Ali. Anyway, you were down for a long time after Adam was born. Not just the first few months.'

I find it hard to swallow my mouthful of food all of a sudden. I take a large gulp of coffee, even though it is too hot. My eyes water. 'That wasn't Adam's fault. You didn't exactly give me an easy time of things, did you?'

He looks awkward. 'I'm sorry, Ali. You know I didn't mean to. I didn't know what I was doing. But that phase you went through, it went on for a long time then. Then you had that relapse after Adam's first birthday.'

I chew my food quietly. I don't like the way Dan dismissed his part in my breakdown. I thought he had forgotten about all that. He hasn't mentioned it for years.

I'm glad I haven't mentioned the message I received in the middle of the night or the van that was acting suspiciously in my opinion. I'd thought about talking to him about what I thought happened after the woodland shoot. I'm now relieved that I didn't.

He thinks I'm not coping as it is. He doesn't need to know about any of that.

We don't have the kind of relationship where I could casually mention such things. I would love to ease the burden from my shoulders, maybe even laugh it off together. But things aren't like that between us.

Not anymore.

18

This morning, a large white coach is pulled into the bay beside the school. I pull Adam close to me once again, squeezing him tightly and breathing in the special smell of his hair: mint, mixed with his unique scent. I'd know it anywhere.

'Mum, get off!' he says, his small hands pushing into my shoulders. 'You're making me look stupid.'

'Don't be silly,' I say to him. 'No one is even looking.'

'Jack Pearson is. He's laughing, see?' He turns along the loose row of parents saying goodbye to their children. I try to follow his gaze, but find my attention caught by Helen and her boy, Eric, who is eager to clamber up the coach steps.

'You shouldn't worry about what other people think of you so much. I'm going to miss you, that's all.'

'We're only going to the zoo, Mum. I'll see you later – if you ever get off me. Dad – tell her.'

'Come on,' Dan says from beside me. 'Put the poor boy down. It's only for a few hours. It's not like he hasn't been there before. It's good for him to get out and about.'

'I'm just worried about him. This is the furthest school

trip he has ever been on.'

Granted, Blackpool Zoo isn't a million miles away, and yes, we have been there before. But this time is much different. I won't be there to watch over Adam today. I'm putting his safety in the hands of virtual strangers.

I have an eye for dangers looming on the horizon; I always have done. It's a skill imperative to every mother.

The engine turns over impatiently as all the little passengers mount one by one, weighed down with heavy backpacks that look too big for them. Dan's gentle pressure on my shoulder convinces me to let Adam go with them without another word. Adam waves off enthusiastically before he slips out of sight behind the tinted windows of the massive vehicle.

There was an article in the news not too long ago where a coachload of passengers crashed on the motorway. There was an embedded picture to accompany the story, which I will never be able to banish from my mind. That time, the victims had been elderly care home residents. But I know accidents can happen to anyone.

———

THE PHONE RINGS shortly after Rebecca enters the shop. My heart leaps when I answer. It's the headmistress of a local school getting back to me about their photo contract. She says they have been let down by their chosen company at short notice and are looking for quotes from people who are available next week.

Rebecca gets the gist of the call from my end of the conversation. She nods and gestures vigorously at certain sentences, but I find her distracting. She is more ruthless than I am when it comes to selling, but I don't want to come across as pushy.

When I end the call, Rebecca hovers uncertainly in front of my desk with a hesitant thumbs up. 'Did we get the go-ahead?'

'They said they would seriously consider me.'

'Oh.'

I glance over from my computer. 'She likes that we're local. But she needs to get some other quotes first.'

'Maybe I should call them back later? See if I can swing it.'

'I think I'll just see what they say first.'

She pulls a face. 'That will be the last you hear from them if the next person puts the pressure on. Trust me.'

'If I don't hear back before we shut later, then maybe I'll give them a call.' I hope now that I quoted low enough. I'm sure the headmistress understood that I am the most enthusiastic and professional too.

At lunchtime, I pop to the high street to pick up lunch. I've felt guilty every time Rebecca has gone instead. Especially as I see her as more of a friend than an employee.

As I pass the toy shop laden with paper bags of hot food, I take a second to peruse the window display. This place has sold toys since I was little. It surprises me that it has managed to survive the opening of a Smyths nearby in Blackburn retail park. The trendy scooter that Adam pointed out a while ago still sits proudly on display in the window, colourful and bright in the downlights, albeit slightly dusty.

I make a promise to myself that if I get another booking before the end of the week, I will buy it for Adam's upcoming birthday. It would be supporting an independent business too, which I always try to do.

In the afternoon, I get so much done. I am just applying the finishing touches to my latest client's photos when my mobile rings.

'Mrs Burnham?'

'Yes, speaking.'

'This is the first-response team at Rishworth Primary. We need to inform you that Adam has become separated from the rest of the group on his school trip.'

'What?' I gasp, horrified.

Rebecca peers her head in from the back room, where she is steam-cleaning one of the dresses.

I press the phone closer to my ear. 'What do you mean *separated*?'

'His trip partner informed Mrs Evans that he left the picnic area at lunchtime.'

'Lunchtime?' I glance at the clock on my computer. 'That was over an hour ago! Why hasn't anyone done anything? I wouldn't call this the first response!'

'There isn't any reason to panic. Everyone is working hard to find him. Staff at the zoo are conducting a search, as well as a member of our teaching staff.'

'I need to be there,' I say, getting up so fast that I catch my keyboard and lift it with me. It crashes noisily back down onto my desk.

Rebecca is wide-eyed and frozen on the spot. The garment steamer in her hand still spouts clouds of hot vapour. She mouths at me, *what is it?*

I shake my head at her. 'I need to find him before anything happens,' I say into my phone with a quavering voice. 'Someone could have taken him, and you're doing nothing!'

'Mrs Burnham, please calm down. We are doing our best, given the situation. There isn't any cause for alarm. I'm sure we will find him soon.'

'The *situation* wouldn't have occurred at all if you were doing your job properly!' I yell as I pull on my coat and grab my keys. 'I need to get to my son. Something terrible has probably happened to him.'

19

Excitement bubbles in the pit of my stomach as I step over the threshold. I'm finally being allowed to babysit, not just allowed to visit, whilst the watchful parents scrutinise my every move.

I'll be taking care of my grandson today. I will be the one catering to his every need. He will be dependent on me. I've been offering for so long only to hear one excuse or another that I thought it wasn't going to happen.

Surely all new parents jump at the chance for all the help they can get? Unless, of course, they are getting help from the maternal branch. But I try not to think about that.

Today must be an ordinary day. Nothing special or important is going on, so it is free to be tossed to me, the paternal grandmother.

As second-in-line, I get to help out whilst my son goes to work. He looks almost as tired as when I last saw him. Child-care is so demanding in these first few months. At least he gets a break of sorts in his other job.

He arranges the hand-over of his son before he leaves. His wife seems reluctant to let go of the bright baby in her arms.

She folds them defensively across her chest once they are empty as if they ache at the loss.

She watches me closely as I hold her child close to me and coo at him. He is so much bigger than the last time I saw him. The baby talk that I must have used once on my own son comes back to me now as if I never spoke any other way in the absence of a delicate baby in my arms.

His attention wanes quickly, before I can get so much as a smile out of him, and he stares mindlessly at the wall. I suppose it is because he doesn't recognise me. I'm such a small percentage of his life that he doesn't register me as being any more significant than the health visitor or the weather presenter he must see on the television.

I put my cheek close to his impossibly soft one instead and stroke his fine hair. Over his little shoulder, I notice the baby spit-up dried onto his mother's jeans. Despite the weight she has gained, the fabric is stretched and baggy, as though her clothes are overdue a wash. Her hair is pulled into a rough ponytail. Not like the high, sleek ones she used to wear that looked effortlessly glamorous. Just pulled back as though her tresses were in the way of meeting her little one's needs.

She makes small talk with me for a few minutes. Only to reiterate what her husband has said, as though she is unable to think of anything original. She tells me that the baby has been more demanding than they expected. I smile at their naivety. No one ever said looking after a baby was easy. What had they been expecting?

Despite the dark circles under her once perfectly framed eyes and the pasty hue of her cheeks, her words do nothing but make me sad for my boy. He has worked for years to build a reasonably comfortable life for himself and his wife. Will they ever get to enjoy it now that they've made such a commitment?

Things get easier once they get older, I tell her. But I can tell she doesn't believe me.

After a few minutes, my daughter-in-law seems satisfied that her duty is over for a while. She wanders from the room and disappears upstairs. A few moments later, I hear the pipes roaring to life as she runs herself a bath.

My son was worried that she hasn't been able to get enough rest since the birth. Doesn't she know that the baby is the star in the movie of her life now? She is just a supporting role.

No one cared that I was overtired when I was raising my son. I would be so exhausted during the night feeds that dragged on for months that tears would run down my cheeks the whole way through, and even beyond when I'd put the baby down and collapse into my own bed beside my thoughtless husband. It was only when he was older that my boy became the friend that I'd realised I'd been missing the whole time.

Now he belongs to someone else.

I just hope he hasn't made a terrible mistake.

20

T he journey to the school passes by in a strange sort of panicked blur. I'm flooded with gratitude when I see the figure of Adam up ahead waiting beside the coach. His school bag hangs heavily from his fingers as he waits with a member of staff.

Despite the fact I've been driving at speed for over an hour, I've managed to arrive here late for pickup. I initially set off for the zoo before receiving another call from reception to say that they had found my little boy. He had apparently wandered into the zoo gift shop, and by the time they told me this, the class were already setting off back for school.

The result is that the coach has beaten me here. I dodge other straggler parents leaving with their children and race over to my little boy.

I pay little attention to Mrs Turner, the teaching assistant who watches as I pull Adam close and hold him to me tightly.

I let go and look at him. 'Why did you go wandering off like that?' I say to him. 'You knew you had to stick with your partner and the rest of your class. Why did you leave?'

He shrugs, staring at his shoes morosely. 'I don't know.'

From the way he verges on tears, I imagine he has already received a telling-off from one or both of his teachers.

'You scared me,' I say. My anger fades, and I bite back tears myself.

'Yes, Adam here gave us all quite a fright,' Mrs Turner says sternly. She looks every bit as strict as her colleague, with her unyielding bun of mousy hair and the taut lines around her mouth that I can imagine aren't there from too much laughter. 'Mrs Evans is already planning a piece for tomorrow morning's assembly on why we shouldn't wander off unsupervised and the dangers of talking to strangers.'

'Was he with someone?' I say, looking up into her dark eyes in horror.

'No,' she says unsmilingly. 'But we thought it prudent to remind the children. We like to reiterate that sort of message from time to time. It's very important that, as a school, we remind the children to remember how to stay safe.'

It isn't until I'm pulling into our familiar row of cottages that I feel a true sense of relief. I have my baby home again.

He is safe here.

When we get inside, I make Adam a hot chocolate, not bothering to fret about how much sugar is in the sachet of powder. For dinner, I forget all about the leftover roast chicken I had planned and make Adam's favourite instead, macaroni cheese.

He is quiet as he empties his plate, and I realise he has probably had almost as much of a bad time as I have this afternoon. I certainly wouldn't want to get on the wrong side of Mrs Evans, or Mrs Turner for that matter.

I leave him to get on with his dessert and go about sorting out his school bag for tomorrow. I take out his lunch box with his half-eaten ham sandwiches inside. What had possessed him to leave during the lunch break, I still don't know. He wouldn't tell me in the car, and I didn't push him, just grateful that I could bring him home alive and in one piece.

Underneath his Star Wars lunch box is a scrunched-up map of Blackpool Zoo. There is also something else inside the depths of the dark canvas. My fingers sink into soft black fur, and I pull out a plush gorilla.

The tag dangling from its paw bears the Blackpool Zoo logo. There is a little white label with the price tag, and my mouth opens in surprise. We have always avoided the gift shop on days out, wanting to avoid tantrums and disappointment when we have to say no.

I stare at it for a moment before I go back and show it to Adam, who still sits at the dining table, nursing his pie and custard. 'What's this?' I ask him, showing him the toy.

After the briefest of glances, he shrugs, returning his focus to his food. 'I don't know.'

'It must be something. It was very expensive. We didn't give you any spending money.'

He ignores me, intently working on dissecting his food in the way that always annoys Dan.

'Adam?' I step closer to the centre of his field of vision. 'Why do you have this? Did you take it without paying?'

'No,' he says quietly. 'They gave it to me.'

'The shop assistant gave it to you – for free?'

'No. Someone else.'

'Who?'

'I can't tell. They said it would be our little secret.'

I feel my mouth open in shock. 'Who said that? Did he ask you to do anything?' My mind races with all sorts of horrible possibilities. Is this why the school took so long to find Adam – because he was with someone else?

'It was a lady.'

'What lady? Who was it?'

He shrugs again, working on creating a pile of apple filling distinctly separate from the pastry. When he speaks again, it is barely more than a mumble. 'She said not to tell.'

21

'I still can't believe they chose us,' I say as Rebecca and I set up our equipment in Ashton Primary's school hall. This job will be an amazing boost for the business, and not just for cash flow. The nod from an established local institution like this school will look great, especially on the business website I've started working on.

Rebecca grins as together we put up the abstract cyan backdrop. 'You are great at what you do. Other people see it too. Just as long as you keep getting the word out, you're golden.'

Unfortunately, us being here today means letting Adam go to his after-school disco, as neither Dan nor I will be there for pickup time this afternoon. Ashton's school hours are slightly longer, so I just wouldn't make it in time.

Besides, he has been nagging me about it all week. It's just a shame I'm breaking the vow I made to myself to not let Adam out of my sight more often than he needed to be.

Dan complains that I coddle him. That I amplify dangers. But it isn't like I imagined Adam's school letting him out of their sight on that school trip. They allowed some random stranger to get close to him, even interact with him.

I couldn't get any more out of Adam about his period of absence. It makes me shudder to think who could have come so close to my child when he was unsupervised. It is even more baffling the fact Adam says it was a woman.

The school denied all knowledge of the incident too when I called them the next day. The teaching assistant said she hadn't seen anyone near Adam when she had found him. He had been alone. Now I don't know what to believe. Had there been a stranger at all?

When I think of the Facebook message I received, it makes me consider all sorts of possibilities. It is easier to push that out of my mind than consider what it could mean. It is easier to consider the fact that Adam could have lied about the stranger because he thought it would upset me less. He has done things like that before.

Adam can be so hard to read sometimes. The thoughts that spill from his head in the form of play or drawings often surprise me. A lot is going on with him that I don't always understand. I just hope he doesn't drift away from me and become even more distant as he gets older. I want to be a part of his life always, and I hope we have a better relationship than Dan or I do with our own mothers these days.

I set up the lighting umbrella, positioning it to the right angle, and consider what Dan said that night after the trip. He thinks Adam invented the whole interaction. He even accused him of stealing, which reduced our little boy to tears before I intervened and dismissed the notion.

If either of our parenting styles is to be criticised, it is my husband's for being too harsh. He has always been that way. Sometimes, I feel like I have to overcompensate with extra affection to offset Dan's cavalier attitude.

The headmistress enters just as Rebecca and I have finished setting up. She introduces herself.

'It's so nice to be able to put a face to the voice on the phone,' I say, recalling our previous conversation.

'Likewise, are we nearly ready to go? Morning nursery will be ready after registration, so they won't be long now.'

'Yes. We're ready. Thanks again for choosing us. We'll do a great job.'

'Good, good,' Mrs Clarke says brusquely, rocking on the balls of her feet. She comes across as quite a fun head-mistress, with her colourful chunky necklace and toadstool-patterned blouse. 'Yes, the other company tried to reschedule us. The booking has been in place and up on the school calendar for so long, it wasn't practical to rearrange at such short notice. So booking with you made sense – especially since you made us an offer we couldn't refuse.' She smiles and winks at Rebecca, who grins back and busies herself moving our empty equipment bags out of the way.

I glance between them and smile too, hoping I don't look too blank.

'Well, you'll be receiving the first batch soon,' Mrs Clarke says as she moves to exit the hall. Her flat shoes squeak on the polished floor. 'Should be easy enough with all your experience of school photography. The young ones are still sweet and obedient. You'll have a Year Four class later that I will warn you are quite a handful! See you in a little while.'

I glance at Rebecca. 'Is there something you want to tell me? She seems to think I've done school photography before. And what offer is she talking about?'

'It's OK.' Rebecca puts her hands up in defence. 'It turned out she got a much better quote from some other company in Blackburn, but I made a deal and managed to talk her into using us instead.'

'How would you know she got a better quote?'

She has the grace to look a little sheepish. 'Well, I called her back when you left to go and pick up Adam after that school trip.'

'I told you I wasn't going to do that.'

'Yes, that's why I had to do it. We wouldn't be here now if I hadn't. The school would have chosen someone else for the job instead of you. And you will be amazing at this.'

'Well, I just don't want to pressure people into a sale.' I feel as though I have been undermined here, but I can't deny this is a wonderful opportunity. Despite going against my ethos, Rebecca only wanted to help. And she has secured the contract. Perhaps I should trust people more often?

She shakes her head. 'You can't be shy about these things. Not if you want people to take you seriously. You want to make a real success of this, don't you? I've seen what happens when you just let things slide. That's what happened to my dad. He wasn't proactive enough. That's why he had to shut down his shop in the end.'

'I'm not sure I have that killer salesperson instinct though.'

'That's why you have me.' She grins.

I smile. 'I suppose. So what deal did you make her? How much less did you offer?'

'None. You are doing it for the price you quoted, but we are doing staff photos for the school website too as a bonus.'

'Today?' I feel a flush of rising panic. 'I need to pick Adam up after his school disco. Dan is working. He can't do it.'

She nods quickly. 'Yes, I know that. We will be out of here in no time. It shouldn't take long. It's only a small school. It's another twenty shots max – and the teachers are easier to manage than the children. We can do this, no problem.'

Mrs Clarke was right; the nursery class are easy enough to handle. The first part of the school is a breeze with Rebecca in charge of directing the subjects into the seat, leaving me free to operate the camera. She is wonderful with the kids. I imagine she would be a natural mother, and I find myself wondering why she isn't one.

It is lunchtime before I know it, and Rebecca and I are eating our packed lunches out in my parked car.

'Now it really is like being back at school.' She laughs as she pulls out a corned beef sandwich. 'I have to admit I never looked so great in my school photos though. I somehow managed to get my hair messed up by the time it was my turn. Mum used to go mad about it. She still bought them though, every time.'

'Your dad should have tried for the contracts.'

'Yeah, that would have been fun, but he never had a go. It would have been better to adapt than to just let the business fizzle out slowly. He should have made the effort, but he didn't. That's why I think you need to make sure you get these jobs. I didn't mean to butt in, you know. I just thought you needed a little nudge.'

'I know. You were only trying to help,' I say, watching a male teacher cross the car park with a mug of steaming coffee. 'I'm really glad you did. Today has been great so far.'

'I know what you mean. I can't wait to do the rest after. It's nice seeing all the kids in their best. I bet the mums had great fun putting all those little bows and ribbons in their little girls' hair.'

'Yes. That was something I was looking forward to doing after raising a boy all this time.'

Rebecca glances at me tentatively over her Mars bar. 'Sorry, I didn't think.'

'It's OK.' I realise for the first time how little I know about Rebecca's personal life considering all the time we have spent working together. I feel almost like we could have been childhood friends based on what I know of her parents and early memories. But I know very little about the current adult

Rebecca and what she does when she isn't at work. There are large pieces of her life missing from my mental collage of her.

I look over at her. 'I'm just surprised you don't have your own little one yet. You are so good with children. I suppose you just haven't met the right person yet?'

I realise immediately I've said something wrong when Rebecca's face changes. For a moment, I think she might burst into tears or shout at me, but she simply shrugs and looks out the passenger side window.

'I guess not,' she says, reminding me of Adam when he decides to close up. I know from experience with him that I won't get any further, and I don't want to upset Rebecca any more than I already have.

The obligation feels on me to try to change the subject. 'You know, I've started work on the website,' I say, in an overly airy voice that makes even me cringe. 'It should be online in a few weeks or so. Thanks to you, I'll be able to list Ashton Primary as one of my clients.'

Rebecca is quiet, but I still can't see her face. 'That's great.'

She is notably more withdrawn for the rest of the lunch break despite my best efforts. I take the opportunity to put together a draft tweet thanking the school for a wonderful photoshoot. I'll post it later just before we leave.

Rebecca visits the toilets and returns to work with such professionalism that I could almost have imagined that she seemed upset before.

As she predicted, the staff are very obliging for their portraits, and we are packing up with time to spare. She helps me load the car with the equipment before grabbing her handbag off the back seat and looping the long strap over her head. 'I'll be off, then. See you tomorrow.'

'What?' Her words take me by surprise. We drove here together from the shop, as we always do for on-location shoots. 'Don't you want a lift back to the shop?'

'That's OK.' She smiles. 'They've got a Co-op at this end of town. I've been craving one of their ready-meal curries for ages. I can pick one up on the way. It's just what I need in this weather.'

'Are you sure? We can stop on the way back if you like? I still have some time.' I feel bad leaving her in a place that is different to where I picked her up, especially in this October chill.

'Don't worry about it. I'll see you tomorrow.'

I watch as her long green puffa coat disappears out of sight around the corner. I thought she had recovered from my comment at lunchtime. Is she still upset? I wonder if I should pop round to her house later and check she is OK. I have her address from her CV. She doesn't live far out of town. I could use the pretence of popping back to the shop for something.

The car park is emptying now, and I decide I need to get back to Rishworth Primary to pick up Adam. The disco will be finishing soon.

I open up my Twitter profile and post the message of thanks I had drafted earlier. On my Facebook account, I see I have some new messages. I know I shouldn't get bogged down with them now, but I decide to take a quick peep so I can mentally prepare answers for later.

I have two general enquiries and another from an account that suddenly douses my insides with dread – the one with the strange message I read in the middle of the night. The one that kept sleep away for hours.

I feel as though I shouldn't open it, but temptation gets the better of me.

YOU SHOULD HAVE KEPT A BETTER HOLD OF YOUR BABY

I blink and stare around me through the car windows,

convinced someone is out there, watching. My fingers find the central locking button, and they click securely in unison. It doesn't make me feel any safer though.

I dismiss the message and hastily stash my phone away. But the words burn in front of my vision. They are all I can see as I start the car and make the drive across town to Adam's school.

Why is this happening?

A confused jumble of thoughts flashes through my brain as I hurry down one road after another. Who would send me such messages? I'd managed to convince myself the first one was a mistake. A prank meant for someone else.

But now I can't ignore the fact that someone meant them for me. And they must be talking about Adam.

I have to get to him.

An old man raises his walking stick angrily at me as he steps back onto the pavement. I lift a hand vaguely in a gesture of apology, but he is already becoming tiny in my mirror.

The bass beat of a trendy pop song reaches my ears as I park and rush around to the school hall exit. As I round the corner, I am also aware of the chattering of many parents. The first in the queue starts to leave as the children are released one by one, and I merge in with the front of the group. There is a sudden outbreak of outraged hissing from a pair of mothers behind me, but I ignore it determinedly.

When it is my turn, I peer my head around the hall doors anxiously.

I don't see Adam.

Helen Parker looks at me in surprise. 'Alison,' she says in her overly sweet voice, 'where did you come from? I didn't see you there.'

I ignore her, stepping over the threshold onto the polished floor. 'Where's Adam?'

She gestures at me to step back and points at the strip of white tape stuck clumsily across the doorway. 'Sorry, parents aren't allowed over the line. You know the rules.'

'You're a parent,' I say, stepping around various clusters of children. 'Adam?' I call, realising I sound frantic now.

'Well, I'm running this school event.' She draws herself up importantly. 'I must ask you to step outside now, please. I will send your child out when it is your turn.'

There is a rippling in the row of children to my right, and Adam emerges. I let go of a breath I didn't realise I was holding.

'You're OK?!' I reach out for his hand, so relieved I could cry.

There is tittering now from the group Adam emerged from, but I don't care.

Adam, however, pulls his hand away and shrugs me off. 'Mum, you're embarrassing me.'

Helen moves closely behind us as we exit, her arms out on either side, unnecessarily ushering us out. As she does so, I unwittingly catch her eye over my shoulder. She watches us go, with something unidentifiable in her expression that makes my stomach clench.

22

I've been promoted. I must have proven myself in the trials I've been put through. Now my son and Little Miss Perfect have seen fit to let me babysit unsupervised.

They are out together for the first time since they welcomed their child into the world. A dinner date. My husband didn't ever think to take me out after my son was born. It's not as if he never went out on dates though, just not with me. He would come home late with unfamiliar scents worked into the fabric of his clothes. All the time he thought I didn't know.

Before she left, I caught a glimpse of my daughter-in-law in her finest; from a casual glance, you could think she looked like her usual self again. That is, aside from the baby weight she still hasn't managed to shift; the waist belt on her black cocktail dress strained to meet at the back. And no amount of concealer could cover the dark circles beneath her eyes, which seem almost permanent these days.

Left to our own devices, my grandson and I have a

wonderful time. I can see why his parents struggle though. He is a rather difficult baby. Without fail, he fights his feeds, and he kicks and fights during changing and dressing. And whatever you do, don't try to handle bath time alone; he thrashes about so much I fear I might drop him beneath the surface of the water.

Perhaps it is the lack of the rewarding connection that my daughter-in-law finds disappointing. A smile from the infant is fleeting. For me, it might not even be a bad thing that we don't get many – it makes me feel honoured when I do get one. With no one else here, I know it is just for me, and it makes everything else worthwhile.

By bedtime, I've exhausted the supply of storybooks, and I'm having a hard time keeping the attention of my charge. I take him in my arms and step over the various discarded toys scattered over the carpet. The vacuuming hasn't been done for a while. Crumbs from hurried pieces of toast sit blatantly atop the thick pile.

I point out various household items as we go. Rug. Front door. Stairs. Wardrobe. Bed. Mummy's clothes. Mummy's jewellery.

Where once everything had its place in pretty, tidy little boxes and drawers, there is now mess and haste. Very little thought has been given to the scattering of possessions that lie dusty above the surfaces. Fingermarks are surrounding the necklaces and bracelets on the bedside cabinet, as though each piece has been briefly considered for the rare date. Dusty expensive jewellery over a now too-small designer dress. Glamorous adornments for something of once-splendour. As though she is trying to paper over the cracks, the way she did with the make-up beneath her tired eyes and pale complexion. The strain is still obvious though.

As it is with this room. I close the door carefully when we go back downstairs, leaving it just as it was.

My findings all add up to the same thing though. It's as I suspected.

Things are slipping between my son and Little Miss Perfect.

23

'Happy birthday, baby,' I say again, kissing Adam's full cheek. I've lost track of how many times I've said the words today.

He immediately pulls a face as he sits on the carpet in the lounge. 'I'm not a baby, Mum. Stop embarrassing me all the time.'

My mother-in-law, Julie, laughs at this. She arrived earlier. The first part of the day was made up of awkward small talk as I got our small cottage party-ready. It isn't much, but I've put up banners and taped balloons here and there.

Cheap and cheerful, Julie had said as she had hovered behind me with a glass of lemonade.

'We'll have less of that,' Dan says to Adam now from the sofa. He is sandwiched between his mother and Helen Parker. 'You're not a teenager yet, you know. Your mother has gone to a lot of effort here today. You should be more grateful.'

'Thanks, Mum.' Adam mumbles the words so quietly they are barely audible as his fingers work hungrily on the paper of the first present in a decent pile.

We all sit perched around him on the edges of the sofa and the chair in our cramped living room. We allowed Adam to choose one friend from school to invite to his party, and he selected Eric Parker. He kneels on the floor beside Adam, peering just as eagerly into the wrapping paper.

Helen decided to stick around rather than come back to collect her son later, as I'd hoped she would. She has wasted no time in engaging Dan in conversation at every opportunity. It's times like these that make it hard to forget that they used to go out with each other in college. The three of us had been inseparable at the time until Dan and Helen fell out, and he and I became close instead.

She has made too much of an effort for a children's party in my opinion. Above a low-cut top, her face bears a thick layer of foundation, topped with sparkling eyeshadow and thick lashes.

Rebecca arrives almost at the end of the present-unwrapping. When I open the door, the sight of her is obscured behind a huge bunch of pink and white roses.

'Wow,' I say in surprise. 'Thanks. They're gorgeous. But you didn't have to bring flowers, you know.' I find myself distracted by them; they are the same shade and bloom I've seen when I visit the graveyard.

She shakes her head quickly as she steps inside. 'Oh, I didn't. They were just lying on the doorstep. There's a note in there somewhere, I think.'

In the kitchen, I pluck the small card that has been stuck to the cellophane and turn it over. I feel like my heart has done the same thing all of a sudden when I read the words.

For you, in your time of mourning

Rebecca reads the note over my shoulder. 'That's weird. It must be a mistake.'

'Yes.' I peer through the kitchen window at the deserted street outside. 'Did you see anyone on your way over here?'

'No.' She eyes me strangely. 'Do you think the delivery person got the wrong address?'

Something in her voice tells us both she doesn't think that at all, but I manage to nod as I hastily slide the card back into the flowers and find a much-needed bit of worktop space for them. Part of me doubts anyone will show up looking for them, however. Maybe later, I will look into whether there was a genuine recipient. Not only would it allay my own fears, but I would hate to think that someone is missing these because of my own paranoia.

I'm still unnerved, but offer Rebecca a drink before we go into the lounge.

We settle down in the living room, and I want to catch Dan's eye and maybe get him alone so I can tell him what just happened. But every time I look, Helen is holding him in conversation or pulling expressions at him with the reveal of each gift.

Rebecca hands Adam her present. I notice she has taken care in wrapping it in blue shiny paper and topped it with a premium silver bow.

Adam unwraps it carefully. His movements are different now. He doesn't know Rebecca well enough to not be shy around her.

'Thank you,' he says politely to Rebecca as he pulls out a new set of walkie-talkies.

'You're very welcome,' she says, beaming at him. She has opted for a colourful character jumper today, which seems to make her eyes sparkle even in the absence of make-up. 'I hope you enjoy using them.'

'Cool,' Eric says over his shoulder. 'The range is awesome. Now we can talk to each other from our houses.'

I catch Helen's eye, and we both return our attention to

the boys on the floor again. I make a mental note to make sure her little boy doesn't leave with one of the handsets.

There is only one gift left now. Adam has saved the largest until last, and I am delighted to see his face light up when he sees the new scooter he has wanted for so long.

Dan sets it up for him.

Adam looks up at me eagerly. 'Can I go and try it out?'

'You can later. We're going to have some tea first.'

I leave Adam nagging his father as I go and prepare the food. I hear Julie ask Dan a question about work as I step out of the lounge.

Rebecca joins me in the narrow kitchen as I'm chopping up some carrot sticks. 'Bless, he looks like he is having a nice time,' she says as she empties a large bag of crisps into a bowl.

Helen's raucous laugh sounds loudly from the lounge.

'Yes, I think so. Thanks for the present; he'll love using those things. You didn't have to though, you know.'

She shrugs. 'I can't turn up to a birthday without a gift, now, can I?'

I smile, glad she is here, especially with Julie and Helen in the other room. It feels good to have someone else on my side. For a while, I thought I had upset my friend. But now she seems back to her usual self.

The sit-down tea I had in mind seems to turn into more of a walk-around buffet. Adam and Eric are too excited by all the new toys and games. They go back and forth from the lounge to the kitchen, upstairs and even out into the garden with bits of food. I try to keep a watchful eye on the boys when they are outside, mindful of the flimsy low gate at the end of the small enclosure.

They could slip away without me noticing. It would only take a minute or two to lose track of them in the rows of cottages. And what if there is someone out there, lurking just beyond my sight? A stranger could take advantage of the opportunity in the blink of an eye.

I sigh when I turn from the window and see how many vegetable sticks are left beside the hummus on the table. I've completely lost track of what Adam has eaten and hope he has had enough. I've never known such a fussy eater before.

Dan appears abruptly. He stuffs a sausage roll into his mouth. 'I'm just going to take the boys out for a few minutes.'

'But what about the cake? I'm going to light the candles in a few minutes.'

He shakes his head. 'Adam is desperate to have a go on his new scooter. You must have known he'd be excited when you bought it for him. He wants to have a go on it before it gets dark.'

He crosses the kitchen to the hallway, where he pulls on his shoes by the front door.

I open my mouth to argue further, but Helen appears too.

'Some fresh air will do them good. Kids don't want to be cooped up for too long indoors.' From the hall beside Dan, she glances back at me in my tiny galley kitchen. 'We won't be long.'

Helen reaches out for her shoes – some sparkly red heels. 'Whoops.' She wobbles slightly and reaches out for Dan's arm for balance as she slips them on.

The house is suddenly much quieter now with much of the party moving down the street. I see the lights on Adam's new scooter becoming smaller by the second as he glides away. Eric runs to keep up by his side. Helen laughs animatedly, and I see her move her head close to Dan's as she says something. He laughs too as they round the corner.

I'm highly aware that my husband has left Julie here for me to entertain whilst he takes Adam out. She had declined to go, as she didn't think she would be able to keep up. Panic sinks into me as I imagine Adam scooting off into the distance and Dan not being able to find him. If it weren't for Rebecca being here too, I think I would be feeling more anxious. Although, she is taking a while in the toilet upstairs.

In the lounge, I drift around collecting scraps of discarded wrapping paper and empty toy boxes and stuff them into a bag. Julie swipes through her recent photos on her phone. From what I can see of her screen, it seems she has managed to capture much of our living room in the background.

The thought of her posting them on social media is unwelcome. Her snaps are too personal. They seem to be more intimate pictures of Adam when he is relaxed at home in his natural environment than the staged compositions I had printed and on display at the exhibition. Now I even regret those with everything that has happened since.

Could I ask Julie not to share the images of her grandson? Really, Dan should be the one to say something. Is it possible to say something without him thinking I am being critical of his mother? I know I am in the right.

Everything I have ever posted online has been carefully considered and posted without too much personal information included.

I cringe when I think of someone scrolling through pictures taken inside my home and making judgements, familiarising themselves with the layout of the cottage. Like the way I had done with my client Taylor. In that case, I know my actions were harmless though.

But who is monitoring my accounts online? I feel more self-conscious since I received the strange Facebook messages. I've blocked the sender, but still have no idea who was behind the profile. Or what they could mean by their words.

It could be someone with a mild grudge against me. An old school-friend or colleague who typed in my name out of curiosity, perhaps? I certainly have my share of alienated acquaintances from over the years. It's a shame things ended so badly at my old workplace. I had loved that job. It had given me purpose. I'd been happy back then.

I pick up a staple from near Julie's foot, weak at the thought of Adam ending up with it in his foot later. 'Would you like a cup of tea?' I ask her.

'No, thank you, Alison. I think I've had enough to eat and drink for one day. I think something hasn't agreed with me, actually.' She puts a hand to the waistband of her floral skirt and crinkles her long nose, so much like her son's. 'It's a shame Dan didn't cook. I was looking forward to one of his delicious spreads.'

I smile back politely. 'He does enough cooking at work. I thought it was nice for him to have a day off. I'm putting the kettle on anyway, if you change your mind.'

In the kitchen, I take out some mugs. Rebecca loves a pick-me-up coffee in the afternoon, and I'm sure the others will be frozen when they get back. I peer out the kitchen window, but the view is becoming limited now as the light fades. One of the street lamps flickers on outside.

I do hope nothing has happened. What if Adam falls off his new toy? He could break a bone, his neck even if the fall is at the wrong angle. It will have been my fault. I chose the thing in the first place.

I'd slid his bike helmet on and clipped the straps together securely before he left. But what if he takes it off and lets Eric have a go? Helen would surely insist on safety for her own child. Would Dan make sure Adam is wearing it before he gets back on? Or is his attention elsewhere?

From the hall, I notice some crisps have been dropped on the stairs carpet. I jog up to go and pick up the pieces before they get trodden in, but I see it is too late. As I swoop to brush up the mess, I see that the light is on in Adam's bedroom. I don't want the boys coming back up here when they get back. It is getting late now, and I need to get the cake done and bring an end to the party so I have time to clean up before I'm exhausted. Plus, I don't feel like playing hostess for the entire evening.

I reach the top step and move to switch it off, but gasp when I see a figure inside facing the collection of baby things opposite Adam's bed.

I put a hand on my chest. 'Rebecca.' I laugh in relief. 'You scared me. What are you doing in here?'

'I didn't mean to be nosy.' Her ponytail swishes as she turns to look at me. 'I just noticed there were some bits of food on the carpet and wanted to tidy up. I know it's tough running around after kids and trying to keep your house clean at the same time.'

'Yes, it is impossible sometimes.'

It's then that I realise she has something in her hands – the plush bunny I'd chosen for my baby girl. She follows my gaze and looks down at it too. 'Sorry, you must think I'm having a right old snoop. It just looked so soft.'

She places it carefully back in the gap among the other soft toys. Her movements seem subdued somehow, reminding me of the Rebecca who seemed upset the day of the school photos, not the one who has grinned from ear to ear throughout the party.

It's only now that I realise what a mess the room is. In the absence of the cot, everything is in disorganised piles and stacks. I haven't had the chance to come in here and sort everything out. Or rather, I haven't wanted to.

But I know my friend won't judge me. Will she? Was her comment about keeping the place tidy a suggestion that I should make an effort to have a clear-out? I can't imagine when I will feel strong enough to do it. The time when I can go through all of these things one by one and let them go feels like an eternity away.

'I do mean to sort all this stuff out at some point. It's just that I've been so busy with looking after Adam and getting the business off the ground and everything ...'

There is an eruption of activity that breaks into the quiet of the house downstairs, announcing the return of the children.

Rebecca insists on taking charge of lighting the candles in the kitchen so I'm free to be with my little boy. It's a great idea. From my seat beside him, I can see his eyes are unusually wild with excitement. His round cheeks are still flushed bright red from the cold outside.

We all start a chorus of 'Happy Birthday', aside from Helen, who decides to pull out her phone and start filming. I want to tell her not to, but Dan catches my eye and shakes his head. I make a note to approach her before she leaves.

Rebecca treads carefully into the room with a fully lit cake. Despite the fact there are only nine candles, the waving flames give off enough glow to illuminate her face. I can't tell if it is the limited light or not, but her eyes look glassier than usual.

I clear a space on the dining table, and she sets down the blue dinosaur-themed cake in front of Adam.

'Make a wish,' I say to him.

He blows out the candles in one go, plunging the room back into darkness. Dan starts a round of applause, and as he does so, it suddenly becomes obvious that there is another flickering light coming from the kitchen. The small shadow dances erratically on the dark wall.

I stand up and rush through to the kitchen, but I freeze when I see what is happening.

Flames are attacking the blind at the small window.

Dan swears behind me. He pushes past my frozen form in

the doorway and races for the fire extinguisher. I can do nothing but watch as he stifles the flames in a few quick bursts.

Somewhere upstairs, the smoke alarm screams to life with its piercing and unrelenting shriek.

24

On Monday morning we set up our latest shoot. Today, our client requested a family portrait in the garden of her home. It felt good to officially park outside one of the large detached houses I've always dreamed of living in and walk up the driveway with a genuine reason to be here.

This garden is vast and could likely fit our entire row of cottages along the length. An elaborate wooden summer-house sits amongst the bases of some evergreen trees and bushes in varying shades of deep green. It's a grey autumnal day, and Rebecca and I take a few minutes to set up string lights around the branches of the lower trees to add some background sparkle.

Rebecca is still fretting over what happened at Adam's party. 'I'm so sorry, Alison.' She groans as we set up. 'I still can't believe what happened. I'm mortified.'

'I've told you, don't worry about it. It was an accident. It could have happened to anyone.'

'But it had to happen to muggins here, didn't it? I was sure

I'd shaken the flame out of that match. I thought all I had to worry about was not dropping the cake.'

'It's fine, honestly,' I say, reaching out to put my hand on the arm of her puffed coat. 'Adam had a great birthday. He didn't really notice the fire. He was in the other room eating cake. And he loves the walkie-talkies you got him. He keeps getting me to have the other one so he can talk to me from his bedroom.'

Her face relaxes slightly, but she still looks awkward. It's unusual to see her embarrassed. The lines that are usually pulled into one of her wide smiles are tensed in a downward position. 'But everyone left in such a hurry afterwards, didn't they?'

'The party was coming to an end anyway. It was getting late. I didn't feel like entertaining Helen Parker or my mother-in-law for much longer. You helped me out.'

'Yeah, that Helen woman did seem like a bit of a bitch. Why did she stick around for the party anyway?'

'I don't know. We used to be close friends in school and then later in college. She dated Dan for a while back then. But we haven't really had much to do with her since. That's why I was surprised she hung about. You'd think she would enjoy an afternoon off whilst Eric was at the party.'

Rebecca looks thoughtful for a minute. 'Do you think she wants him back?'

I laugh. 'Of course not. Why do you say that?'

She shrugs. 'It's the way she was dressed, I suppose. She was pretty glammed-up for a kid's party. Then she started telling a joke when you left the room to do the food, and she had her hand on Dan's knee. It was a bit awkward.'

I feel a stab of annoyance. 'That would have been too blatant if she meant anything by it. I mean, his mother was there too. Helen just ... I don't know. I never really thought of it before, but maybe she likes to pretend to herself that she could get back with him. I don't think she is serious though.'

I suddenly feel silly for not thinking about it sooner. When I saw the way Helen went out of her way to get herself beside Dan, I just saw it as a minor nuisance and nothing more. Laughable, even. Perhaps I have underestimated her. Does she have plans on taking my husband?

Rebecca shrugs. 'I guess you won't have to see much of her now anyway. Only at the school gates.'

'Actually, Dan got talked into letting Adam go over to Eric's house after school tomorrow. It must have been whilst I was clearing up the mess in the kitchen. I'm not looking forward to picking him up afterwards.' I glance across at Rebecca. 'Do you think she invited Adam for another reason – just to see Dan again?'

She shakes her head. 'Oh, I was just jabbering on. I don't always think about what comes out of my mouth sometimes. You know me. I'm sure this woman doesn't mean anything by it. I just thought it was funny that she got all dolled up to eat jelly and ice cream, that's all.'

Rebecca works on a knot in the string lights, and I can't tell if she is just trying to appease me now, or if she meant what she said. As if I wasn't feeling anxious enough about letting Adam out of my sight again. I want to call the whole thing off, but Dan reminded me that it's just an hour and a half, and it's only inside Helen's home.

He said I can't let irrational fears get in the way of Adam's childhood. But he doesn't know about the Facebook messages. I just don't know how to tell him. The whole thing sounds bizarre, and I don't want him to think I am taking ordinary things and making them seem malevolent. We both know the consequences of such thoughts, and I don't want to go there again. I'm mindful now of my behaviour after Adam was born, and I don't want it to happen again.

I get my camera set up, and the family group that has been huddled inside the French doors keeping warm all spill out onto the immaculate lawn.

It's tough trying to direct them all, as pairs of them have individual jokes and conversations they have little interest in breaking up. It was much easier posing the children at the school, as they were better behaved.

I'm sure our client, Liz, had told us it was going to be a group of ten. There is almost double that here today. From what they say to each other, it sounds like some have been invited at short notice.

I gesture with some difficulty, directing people where I think they should go. The weight of the camera strains my wrist, and I have to repeat what I say several times. Even Rebecca struggles.

'It's like herding sheep,' she mutters under her breath as she nears me.

I try to smile back but worry that it comes across as more of a grimace. The bustling of bodies too close to me makes me anxious. There are so many people here they seem to bob about almost as though submerged in water.

Even in the autumnal chill, sweat starts to cling to my back beneath my thick coat. Memories start stirring in the back of my mind, vivid and real as if they were recent. If I turn my head, I'm worried I might see a powerful wave sweeping towards me.

Rebecca makes herself heard over the chatter, and she manages to get everyone's attention. She gestures, and the group ripples along so the glowing lamps of the summer-house are central in the background. I stumble as I step back out of the way of the mass, aware of how heavy their collective weight would be if I was to become trapped beneath it. It would take too long to get me out. I would suffocate the same way as if I'd have drowned.

Rebecca gives me a thumbs up, oblivious to the way my hands have started trembling. I take a deep breath as I move into position and turn around to take the first shot.

By the time we get into the car afterwards, I feel quite unsteady on my feet.

Rebecca stares at me as I reach for the ignition. 'Alison, are you OK?'

'Yes, fine.'

'Are you sure? You look so pale.'

'Fine, honestly. Just cold. It was freezing out there, wasn't it?' I keep my tone light and breezy. I just hope Rebecca doesn't notice how my hands still tremble as they reach for the parking brake.

25

The next day, I have another on-location shoot, up in the woodlands again. But this time, I experience the most difficult clients I have come across so far. Unfortunately, it happens on Rebecca's day off. She seems to have a gift for being able to talk anyone around.

The expectant couple opts for the cheapest package I offer, but they manage to draw out the afternoon session well over the time I had allotted. It's a good thing that Adam has an extension after school by being over at his friend's house; I would have been worrying about getting to the gates on time now if he hadn't.

I'm feeling quite irritable by the time I pack the equipment away in my car. The string lights are a hassle to put away on my own and get snagged on various branches, almost as though they have a mind of their own and are doing it deliberately.

I hope that once I've driven down the hill and across town that I've calmed down. Helen has a way of getting my back up, and right now, I'm not in the mood for any conflict.

I wonder whether our tense relationship is really because there is some truth in what Rebecca said. Could it be possible that Helen still harbours feelings for my husband after all this time?

Eric's father is long gone. He didn't even stick around long enough to see his son born. Over the years, Helen has occasionally turned up at the school gates with a new face by her side. But none of them stayed long.

I suppose she probably is lonely. If she had been a better friend to me, then maybe we could have brightened up each other's lives. But that isn't the case. I shall have to watch her more closely from now on though, especially near Dan.

I sigh as the traffic grinds to a halt yet again before I even reach town. I'm disappointed that Helen witnessed the incident at Adam's party.

If there was one way to guarantee that everyone will find out about what happened at the weekend, it's through Helen. She was always the same. I once told her the identity of a boy I had a crush on in college. By the next day, the whole class knew, including the person himself.

She had just thrown her head back and laughed when I confronted her about it. It hadn't occurred to her that she had embarrassed me. From my experience of her outside the school gates, she doesn't seem to have changed much. She is always gossiping about someone. After the party, I know the topic of the week will be me.

Brake lights illuminate my windscreen yet again in the growing darkness, hurting my eyes. My head starts to throb. My fingertips strike an impatient rhythm on the steering wheel, and I glance at the time. At this rate, I won't make it for the time Helen arranged. Will she call Dan to pick up our son instead?

My insides squirm at the thought of Helen left unattended with my husband. Would she invite him in for a coffee to stave off the chill?

'Come on,' I mutter, craning my neck in order to see the road ahead. There are tailbacks in every direction, and impatient horns blare from somewhere ahead of me.

I start thinking back to the last few hours and how difficult the couple was. They insisted on reviewing the pictures before the session ended. I cringed at the way the woman had taken my camera from me, her short fingers jabbing at the buttons. Not like any of my other clients who have been polite and grateful for my service. I start wondering if they know Helen somehow ...

Could she have orchestrated this whole afternoon? What if I have been naive? I've been too busy with the business to pay much attention to Dan. I thought when things were up and running, we would have more time, but between the business, Adam and my course, we have hardly seen each other. Would he look to someone else for some attention? He had accused me of cheating on him a few years ago. His mind obviously springs to adultery faster than mine.

My heart suddenly beats faster when I see a woman who strongly resembles my class tutor, Charlotte, walking past my stationary car. She has made it almost into the distance and around a corner before I can decide whether or not it really is her. What would she be doing in this part of town at this time of day? I thought she had classes throughout on this day of the week. I wonder if she has been to visit someone, that's if it was even her at all.

The traffic hardly moves in the next half an hour. If I had been on foot, I would have made it over there by now. I glance at the time. I don't want to give Helen an opportunity to call on Dan.

With a heavy heart, I phone Rebecca. It's her day off, and

she could be anywhere. But she is the closest thing to a friend I have had for years.

My only friend.

And if she happens to be near or at home, she won't be too far from Helen's house anyway.

To my relief, she answers quickly and is more than happy to pick Adam up.

'I wouldn't ask,' I say. 'But I'm stuck in traffic, and I just can't get there.'

'It's no problem. I'm close. I can be there in five minutes. No worries. See you soon.'

The traffic doesn't seem to move as slowly now that I know Adam will be safely picked up. It bothers me a little though that Rebecca arranged to take Adam into town rather than her own home. I feel as though I've overstepped the mark by making such a request on her day off. But I asked her as a friend, not my employee. I hope she understood that.

Maybe I'm overthinking it. She didn't say where she was when I called.

'Thank you so much,' I say when I finally catch up with Rebecca and Adam over an hour later. They sit together on a bench outside a bakery. Adam bites into a large gingerbread man when I get there.

'I'm so sorry I had to call you, but I didn't know who else to call. Dan is at work, and there wasn't anyone else.'

Rebecca smiles at me and shakes her head. 'That's OK. We had great fun, didn't we, Adam? We went shopping. He found a great thing to blow his birthday money on.'

She winks at Adam, and he grins back.

It's then that I notice the large bag wedged between Adam's ankles. The top of a large Fortnite figure pokes out of the bag. I recognise it as one of the toys Adam asked for recently, but I deemed it too violent. I don't want him being influenced by things like that. He isn't one of those boys.

My heart sinks when I realise how much it would have cost too. I don't imagine there is much left of the money his grandmother gave him.

On the way home, I insist on dropping Rebecca off outside her house despite her protests.

'You didn't have to, you know,' she says as she gets out of the car. 'You're cheating me out of the exercise.'

'Don't be silly. I'm the one who called you away, and I don't want you walking home in the dark. You've done me a massive favour this afternoon.'

Adam and I wave her off as we pull away. It's completely dark by the time we let ourselves into the cottage. Adam pushes the hasty dinner I'd prepared around his plate and scrapes the peeling orange coating from his fish fingers with his fork. The food is less well done than I would have liked.

'There won't be any pudding if you don't eat all of that,' I say to him from the kitchen doorway.

'Good. I don't want any.'

I think of the gingerbread. 'I suppose you've already had that in town.'

'Eric's mum made cookies too. They were really nice. She let me have two.'

'Did she now? No wonder you aren't hungry for real food.' I feel a stab of guilt when I eye what's on his plate. It's not entirely my fault though. If he weren't so fussy, I could cook healthier meals.

I empty his school bag, noting that there is still half a sandwich left – again. He seems to have eaten the blueberry muffin that accompanied it, however.

There is a scrap of paper folded neatly inside the depths of Adam's school bag. Automatically, I feel my stomach tense. Is it time for another round of fundraising from the school already? I had to delve into my purse twice this month already to donate to the good causes the school is supporting.

I unfold the paper, only to find it is not a letter from the
school demanding money, but a hasty handwritten note.

*YOU WERE WRONG TO LET HIM OUT OF YOUR
SIGHT*

26

Things are changing between my son and his wife. I knew they would once the baby came along. They've lost the energy and the camaraderie they once had. Now they are more like room-mates or colleagues, shuffling around one another in a daze. These days, they only really seem to talk to arrange their schedules and the care of their son. Although they have me for that now.

My daughter-in-law has arranged to go back to her old job around my own working week. She may do it under the pretence of needing the income, but I can see through her. She only returns to work as it is far less taxing than her real job as a mother. But she has chosen to quit that and hand much of the daily duties over to me.

I don't mind though, as it means I get to see more of my lovely grandson.

Little Miss Perfect takes one last look in the hallway mirror before she leaves. She has put on what she obviously thinks is her sharpest outfit – a fitted long-sleeved top and expensive-looking trousers in a matching dark grey. She tops it off with some of the jewellery I know she had considered for her date. I wonder if she has dusted it off first before she disappears through the door.

It unsettles me that she simply waved off her baby with a smile before she left. I wouldn't have resisted an opportunity to cuddle him and kiss his soft cheeks. It couldn't be more obvious how delighted she was to skip off and leave behind her real duties. If only I'd had the chance to ditch my responsibility when I was young with a baby on my hip.

No one helped me.

My grandson returns to his soft building blocks, swiping at them with his pudgy mitts. He seems blissfully unaware that his mother has abandoned him for the day.

I pick him up and hold him close, relishing his weight. He seems significantly heavy now, far removed from the underweight baby he was in his first few weeks. I indulge him with my sing-song voice that he seems to like.

What do we want to do today?

Shall we go for walkies around the house again? Yes?

The little baby in my arms stares around with interest at the colourful prints on walls. I can tell immediately that his mother is responsible for them. Like everything else, they are covered in a layer of dust.

There aren't any pictures of my grandson even all these months later. Nothing much has changed in the house since the birth other than the fact it hasn't been taken care of. His parents seem to be struggling to keep on top of things. Now it's starting to show.

I open a kitchen cupboard and pick up a shiny saucepan. I turn it so that it shines in the light from the window, but it doesn't hold the baby's attention long.

I open another cupboard, but he doesn't seem interested in the many tins and packets of salty junk food, even the colourful ones. Is this what my son's diet has been reduced to? It's very far removed from the wholesome dishes I used to serve him growing up. I wonder if I should start batch cooking so I can drop off some fresh meals now and then.

I'd have thought the couple would have found their routine by now. Having a baby should have been a natural progression of their relationship. To me, this is further proof that they weren't right for each other. The baby has only added extra notes to the dissonance.

I count the steps in my baby voice as we climb the staircase. In the bathroom, there is only one bar of soap. It is worn thin, dry and cracked. Bottles and tubes of products are scattered here and there. More mess.

There is an airing cupboard along the upstairs landing. My grandson seems unfamiliar with it as he stares at the towels in various shades of blue and pink. At the bottom is a roughly folded duvet and pillow. This clearly isn't for guests, as it is simple and plain and stuffed hurriedly inside this cupboard out of the way. I also spot a toothpaste mark on the pillow.

I suddenly have a vision of my son taking this out every night and setting up a measly bed in the other bedroom, or even on the living room sofa. Is this what his life has come to?

I was right, but the thought brings me no pleasure.

Now the cracks are starting to show.

27

I've made a vow to myself: Adam is not to be allowed to go anywhere other than school from now on. Helen cornered me at drop-off this morning and tried to talk me into letting him go to the after-school movie evening that was announced last week.

She clucked her tongue sadly when I said no. 'Eric will be so disappointed if Adam won't be there. He was looking forward to it. I'm not sure I will let my boy go now. I hate to see him let down though.'

I smile through gritted teeth. 'I haven't decided either way yet. If not, I'm sure Eric will find someone else to sit next to.'

Privately, I have no intention of letting Adam out of my sight longer than he has to be, especially near Helen. It wasn't just the note that was put in his school bag. Adam had an upset stomach after being at her house that day. There is no way I would allow him back there. Helen did something to his snack on purpose. That must have been why she scribbled that note telling me I was wrong to let him out of my sight. I'm outraged that she dares to talk to me today as though she has done nothing wrong.

I've concluded she must be the one sending the Facebook messages too. Helen knew I was starting the photography business. I knew I was right when I thought she invented that cousin of hers to snatch the school contract from me too.

The snaps came home from school yesterday. I researched the company that did them online. I can't see any connection between the proprietor and Helen. There is nothing on his social media account to suggest they even know each other. She must have picked a photography outlet at random. She invented the whole thing just to spite me.

I just wonder what else she did when Adam was under her care. I'm still at a loss as to what he consumed. Food poisoning was a danger I had potentially overlooked.

I need to wake up. A case of infection transmitted through food can quickly turn nasty in children, even fatal. I've read so many cases that I can't believe I let Adam wander such a dangerous road. I've failed him yet again.

But I will make sure that Helen never gets the opportunity to do anything else. I've blocked and reported the problematic Facebook account she created. She can't reach me like that again, nor will Adam be spending any after-school time with Eric.

We don't have any clients booked today, and I'm all caught up on photo-processing for now. I'm hoping I'll get some bookings in for Christmas shoots soon, but things seem to have slowed a little on the enquiry front. The flurry of activity I enjoyed seemed to stem from the exhibition.

My next project is to get the website I've been working on finished. That should boost the business. I've just been strug-gling for time. Perhaps I will get some of it done today while I'm at home?

I'm not opening the shop today. There is little reason for us to be there, so I've given Rebecca the day off out of fear that she is being overworked. Even though she was polite about it, I still worry that I interrupted her day off when she picked up Adam from Helen's house.

This morning, I feel I should take a fresh look at the baby's things. Finding Rebecca in the room on Adam's birthday made me feel self-conscious.

I hadn't ever considered other people handling these delicate possessions. I'd only ever imagined them in use for my own baby. These things will one day be distributed to other households and happy expectant mothers. But not me. I suppose I should face up to the fact and sort things out. Then at least Adam can have his room back.

I realise as soon as I step inside the bedroom that I have left the bin bags I took out on the worktop downstairs. Maybe I will just look through everything first. That way I can catalogue what is here and prepare myself mentally for the task ahead before throwing anything out.

As soon as I start picking up teddies and onesies, I find myself slipping back into the mindset I'd been in when I happily went shopping for these things.

This baby was supposed to be a fresh start for me and Dan. I thought it might reset us, fix our marriage. We fell apart after we had Adam. We never really drifted back again. Not properly.

I wanted to do everything right the second time around, learn from the mistakes we both made.

With this baby, I wanted to be the perfect mother. And Dan would be the perfect supportive father. We wouldn't row in between night feeds and countless nappy changes. He wouldn't accuse me of cheating on him this time. I wouldn't find myself so desperate to put an end to his fears that I would arrange a DNA test.

Our little girl was going to make everything right again, but now she will never have the chance.

It is only when I hear the sounds of movement downstairs that I realise my cheeks are wet from my warm tears.

I put down one of my favourite items, the Babygro with the slogan *Daddy's Little Princess* and step carefully over to the door.

I hear a cough and realise it is Dan. What is he doing here when he should be at work?

I take a few moments to clean myself up in the bathroom, wiping away my ruined mascara. It's impossible to hide how red my eyes are though as I tread down the stairs.

Dan seems startled as he looks around at me in the kitchen, where he boils the kettle. 'Ali, you scared me. I thought you would be at the shop.'

'No, we don't have any shoots booked, so I gave Rebecca the day off. I was just going to have a sort-out and then do some work at home. You're back early.'

'I only went in to take a delivery. I told you, the freezer has broken down at the restaurant.'

'I don't remember you saying that.'

'I had a feeling you weren't listening. So what were you sorting out?'

It's then that Dan looks at me properly, and a look of realisation spreads across his thick features. 'Oh.'

It feels almost obligatory when he wraps his arms around me now, but I appreciate the gesture.

When he releases me, he spots the roll of bin liners on the worktop and reaches out for them. 'Do you want me to help?'

I nod. 'Yes.'

Upstairs, I notice Dan eyeing the changing table. I suppose that will be the next thing to go. Then there will be hardly anything left. The already tiny footprint the baby left on our lives will shrink further. I take a deep breath. This has to be done at some point.

Now that Dan is here though, I have second thoughts. I

wanted to go through everything in my own time. I didn't want things unceremoniously thrown into a bag for a charity shop. I wanted to go through each item at my own pace and make peace with it before letting it go for the last time.

Dan starts with the nappies and toiletries, filling up the first bin bag. I know he is annoyed we didn't take them back to the shop when we had the chance.

But this is the first time I have even entertained the idea of letting anything go. And even now I'm regretting coming in here with intent.

Next, my husband turns his attention to the clothes. As he looks down at them all, I can tell he's calculating the cost of everything in his mind. Most are supermarket multipacks, but together the price is not easily overlooked.

I suddenly feel a wave of panic when I consider the tiny clothes disappearing from my possession. I gesture to the bin bag in Dan's hand. 'That will probably do for today. I've got lots of work to do, and I'm running out of time before Adam gets back from school.'

'Ali, you can't bury your head in the sand. We're making good progress here. It isn't good for you to keep all these things.'

'We can just do a bit at a time.'

Dan sighs and pinches the bridge of his nose. 'We have been through this already. This is for the best.'

He picks up the Babygro I'd been clutching earlier and stares at it. I'm satisfied to see a flicker of something in his eyes in a rare display of emotion. Sometimes I feel as if he is numb and uncaring. I'm pleased to be proven wrong now.

I keep my voice soft and gentle. 'We'll keep some things, won't we? I thought maybe we could keep a memento or two. I mean, not out on display or anything. But just so we can look at it now and then if we want to remember. I thought that set of sleepsuits might be nice? There is another one like that somewhere. It's bright pink and has *Mummy's Little Angel* written on it.'

I look around me and lift soft toys. I check underneath the seat of the plaid baby bouncer in case it has slipped down. But I can't find the other Babygro anywhere.

Dan searches vaguely too, even though I can tell he does not know what he is looking for. 'Maybe it was something you saw in the shops, but didn't buy in the end?'

'No, it was definitely here. It was a coordinating set to go with the *Daddy* one. It had the same lettering. It was in the same shades of grey and pink.'

'Ali, it isn't here. We would have seen it.'

I insist on lifting everything and seeing with my own eyes. Beside me, I can tell Dan grows impatient. But I am determined to check under the blankets on the changing table and every other place I can think of. After a few fruitless minutes, I can see Dan is right. It isn't here.

That set was the one thing out of everything that was the most precious. I wouldn't have let it go.

I feel a chill when I realise what has happened. 'Someone has taken it.'

Dan stares at me. 'I don't think so.'

'Then where would it have gone?'

'Maybe you put it somewhere else in the house? You've been a bit absent-minded lately.'

'No, I didn't. I wouldn't have misplaced that. Someone has been in here. They have taken it.'

Dan laughs hesitantly. 'Don't say something so silly. Who would do that?'

'I don't know ...' I think back to the birthday party. Helen was in the house. As was Julie. And Rebecca – I know she definitely came into the room. But I didn't see her take anything. Then again, there was so much chaos and confusion when the fire started ...

'It was Helen. Maybe she started the fire as a diversion.'

Dan shakes his head. 'What? You're not making any sense. The fire was Rebecca's fault, but it was an accident. It looked like she wanted to sink through the floor afterwards. She didn't do it deliberately. And Helen certainly didn't either.'

I stare at the disbelieving look on his face. 'Why are you so quick to defend her?'

'I'm not. You just aren't thinking straight if you say things like this.'

'Maybe she didn't do it deliberately, then, but she could have taken it when she realised we were distracted. But it was she who took it. She was the one who gave Adam food poisoning and stuffed a note in his school bag when he was at her house.'

'What note?'

I hesitate before I tell him about the slip of paper I found after Adam came home. So far, I've kept the note and the messages a secret from Dan, not wanting him to think I'm unsettled by an anonymous prankster.

But now it all seems so clear. Helen has been behind all of this. I can't believe I let myself be so bothered by it. But now she has gone too far in stealing something from this room.

My husband is quiet for a moment as he mulls it all over. 'Where is the note now?'

'I threw it away. Why?'

'I just wanted to take a look at it, that's all. I think I would know if it was Helen's handwriting.'

'Of course you would. I try to forget how close you two were. But who else would have done such a thing?'

Dan stares at me and shakes his head. He seems unable to think of anything to say so moves towards me and pulls me into another of his appeasing hugs. He rubs my back in what he must think is a consoling way, but it just comes across as patronising. He doesn't believe me. Does he really think I've invented this? Perhaps he doesn't believe there is a note at all.

'You can't talk like this,' he says quietly. It should be soothing, but it sounds something like a threat, as though my behaviour might cause our outwards appearance of domestic bliss to shatter. 'Let's not go down that road again. Please. Everything is all right. You've just misplaced one little thing, that's all.'

'Yes, you're right.' I somehow manage a weak smile. 'Maybe I've jumped to conclusions. I just wasn't expecting it not to be here. It will probably turn up.'

But I know the garment won't magically appear when I have searched everywhere. And everything is definitely not all right.

Someone has come into my home and stolen something from my baby.

28

M y lack of sleep once again causes my eventual slumber to spill over into the morning. Even with the resulting rush, I find myself dropping Adam off at school late.

I park my car near the dark green one with the scrape along it and am forced to take Adam in through the reception entrance to get him signed into the dreaded late book. The teaching assistant from his class, Mrs Turner, comes out to collect him. She thanks me with a contorted smile as I leave. She must still be thinking of when I lost my cool during the zoo trip debacle.

Even after I have exited the school gates, I feel the heat of her eyes on me. I catch the gaze of a few other people on my way into town, and I wonder what they are thinking. I tell myself it is paranoia from the messages I've been sent and once again tell myself that they are a simple prank from my old friend. If I didn't believe that, then I know I would return to lying awake wondering who sent them and what they mean.

After all, they can't mean what I initially thought they did.

It's not possible. No one knows what I did. They can't, or I would have heard about it sooner.

Wouldn't I?

Helen must be behind it all. She could have left the flowers on the doorstep when she arrived at the house for Adam's birthday. That explains why Rebecca didn't see a delivery van around.

I pull up to park the car on a residential street on the outskirts of town. All the spots closer to the shop are taken, and this shabby street of badly maintained terraces isn't ideal. I might have to give more thought to where I would leave a nicer car, but it's not something I worry about though.

As I pull out my keys, a noise nearby startles me. A crackling sound that puts up the hairs on the back of my neck.

It's coming from my handbag. I reach over to the passenger seat and rummage around.

My fingers close around the walkie-talkie Adam insisted I carry with me. It's been switched on and forgotten in my handbag. We haven't had the chance to use them. When we're not at home, I'm either ferrying my son back and forth from the school, where he is by my side anyway or safely inside the gates. The school has a strict policy against taking toys into class, so I hope Adam hasn't defied it without me realising.

For a second, I imagine it is my little boy trying to get through to me from his handset. Then I vaguely recall I saw it on his bedside cabinet this morning as I pulled his duvet back and opened the curtains. So it can't be him.

The range is good enough on these things to reach the school and beyond from here, even the house. My mind offers an image of a faceless someone walking around my home unattended, touching my children's things. I'm glad now that I didn't let Helen's son take the other handset. The last thing I need is for her to get ideas too.

Through the windscreen, I see some workmen in high-visibility jackets moving back and forth on some scaffolding. Scraps of plastic wave around them in the wind. Any one of them could be carrying a walkie-talkie like this one. That's probably the sort of thing that would get picked up by mistake if we were on the same channel. In fact, anyone on the default frequency could get through to me. Or Adam. What a dangerous gift for Rebecca to give. She must not have realised the potential ramifications. I switch my unit off and throw it back into my handbag, making a mental note to confiscate the other one when I get the chance. I do hope Adam is all right at school.

Being forced to park further away than normal sets me behind by over half an hour. I'm out of breath and sweating as I round the corner onto Mill Street. I'm mindful that I don't want to keep Rebecca waiting in the rain that attacks the dingy brickwork of the town. But as I squint from beneath my hood, I notice she isn't here. Am I so late that she has given up and left? Feeling guilty, I raise my keys to unlock the door.

But there is no resistance. It is already open.

As I step over the threshold, I spot Rebecca in the back room. The kettle boils behind her.

'Hello, stranger,' she says brightly. The smile fades from her face quickly as she takes in my soaking wet and confused appearance. 'Are you OK? I hope you don't mind me letting myself in. It was chucking it down out there, and the door wasn't locked.'

'Wasn't it?'

'No. I thought it was odd. And you were late too. Then I thought maybe you came in early and then got called away somewhere. I couldn't see your car anywhere. I tried calling you a few times but got no answer. I assumed you were driving. So I came in and got started rearranging the

Christmas set the way we talked about. Are you sure you're OK? Has something happened?'

'No, I'm fine. Just soaked through. I wonder why the door wasn't locked. Have you checked that nothing is missing?'

I move through the shop and look at everything of any potential value, mentally checking them off in my head. Nothing seems out of place.

'Maybe I forgot to lock up when I was here last?'

'Perhaps. You seem a little distant sometimes.' Rebecca pauses in my peripheral vision.

I look over, and I see her staring tentatively at me the same way Dan did when we went to sort through the baby's things.

I shrug, trying to make it look like I'm not bothered by the thought of the potential violation. I try to make it look like the thought doesn't make me tremble. I've spent so much time here now that I feel like this place is an extension of my own home. My voice wavers slightly when I speak again. 'I just thought I should check that no one broke in.'

Rebecca nods. 'It's a good idea, but I think we might have noticed if that had happened. No one is getting in here with me around though, so don't worry.'

I try to smile back, but find my face contorts with the sobs I have been holding back for weeks.

I put my face in my hands and hear Rebecca's boots clop over the laminate before she envelops me in a hug.

'I could tell you were upset about something,' she says softly near my ear. 'You know you can talk to me, don't you?'

It somehow feels wrong to be crying on the shoulder of someone who is supposed to be my employee, but I can't seem to help it. My tears flow, and Rebecca listens with a caring ear as I tell her my woes. She sits me down in my chair and pulls her stool around to my side of the desk.

She looks shocked as I mention the note I found in

Adam's school bag. 'This Helen woman sounds like a total nightmare. It's bad luck Adam chose her son as his best friend.'

'I know. I'm so stupid for letting Adam go over to his house that day. He could have been killed by whatever it was she gave him.'

Rebecca goes quiet for a moment, and I realise she's looking at me uncertainly now.

'What is it?' I ask.

'It's just ... Are you sure she gave him bad food on purpose? It could have been an accident. Or it might have been something he had before then. It can sometimes take days for tummy bugs to take effect.'

'The note must have been her though. Where else could it have come from?'

She looks out the window thoughtfully. 'Maybe Helen had someone else over, maybe a boyfriend or something. I don't really know anything about her. Is that likely?'

'No.' I think of the woman who looked like Charlotte coming from that direction that afternoon. Immediately I shake the thought away. I wasn't even sure it was her, and why would she have anything to do with Helen or do harm to Adam? Dan would describe that as an unhealthy thought if I told him. Not that I would dare. He knows nothing of what I know about Charlotte or how I knew her husband.

Rebecca sighs. 'I suppose a kid from Adam's school wouldn't write something like that.'

'No, certainly not.'

'And you pack Adam's bag every morning, right?'

'Yes. It definitely wasn't there in the morning. I would have noticed. It must have got there in the afternoon. And it happened to be when he was at Helen's house. That can't be a coincidence.'

She frowns. 'What do you think the message meant?'

I shake my head. 'All the messages have been about Adam.'

'Apart from the one on the flowers,' Rebecca points out.

'That could have been a genuine mistake,' I lie. I never did manage to track down anyone who had missed them. 'Helen must know how much I worry about Adam. It must be obvious when I say goodbye to him at the school gates. All this started after I lost my baby girl. My worst fear is that something will happen to Adam too. Helen was right with her first message, fretting about his safety does keep me awake in the middle of the night.'

She puts a supportive hand on my arm. 'But how would she know that? Did you mention something to her?'

'No, of course not.' I stare into the cup of hot tea Rebecca made for me. The thought has been bothering me too. How did Helen know that I'm kept awake at night?

'I told Adam that I'd had a nightmare one night. Maybe he mentioned it at school, and it got back to Helen through Eric?'

'Maybe.' Rebecca looks sceptical again.

Now I'm glad I didn't mention the other fear I have been mulling for weeks – the possibility that someone is watching the house. They could have seen the lights go on downstairs and seen me.

Up until recently, I haven't closed the living room curtains at night. Now I realise someone could have been outside our home without us noticing.

Now I know someone has been watching.

29

My worries at night-time are worse than ever, and I seem to spend the days exhausted, in a sort of trance. I haven't been this tired since Adam's newborn months. The mornings are the usual rush, but at least I haven't turned up too late at the school gates in the mornings.

One bonus is that I mostly avoid having to make small talk with Helen. She has less of an opportunity to corner me when I hastily kiss Adam goodbye and watch him across the playground before turning and leaving for work.

I manage to get the business website up and running one quiet afternoon in the shop. There isn't time to admire it, however; the project took longer than I anticipated, and I have to leave for pickup time. Ideally, I would have looked at it from an outside perspective and checked everything works as it should, but there isn't time.

I get caught in the school rush traffic on the drive across town, and as I pull into my usual quiet side street, I realise that the children have already started being released.

As I dash up towards the school gates, I see a sight that turns my insides cold.

Adam's bright red Spiderman backpack and coat bob up in the distance.

He disappears intermittently amongst the flurry of other parents and children moving back and forth between traffic. His arm looks angled, as though he is holding the hand of an adult. The figure is obscured by a group of gossiping mothers in trendy coats and leggings.

I race up the street.

I almost collide with a pair of young boys chasing one another before I reach the pair in my sight.

'Adam!' I shout, reaching out for him.

The figure turns abruptly, and I realise it's my husband.

'Dan – what are you doing here?' Relief floods me, and I feel foolish tears in my eyes.

'I came to pick up our son from school.' He looks alarmed as I wipe my eyes subtly with the back of my hand so Adam doesn't notice Mummy crying. 'Ali, what's the matter?'

I shake my head. 'I'm supposed to be doing the school run this week. We agreed.'

'I know, but we had that email from Mrs Evans earlier, and I thought we should come and pick Adam up together this afternoon. But you weren't there, so I thought you'd got held up. I sent you a text to say I'm bringing him home. Didn't you read it?'

'No.' I pull out my phone and see a stream of notifications I've missed. I was so completely caught up in trying to get the website launched today that I didn't check my phone as often as I would normally. It isn't like me.

'What was in the teacher's email?' I ask, looking from Dan to Adam, who looks slightly red around the eyes again.

'We'll talk about it on the way home.'

I lead the pair over to where I parked, but as I turn and

open the door for Adam, I notice that he has tears running down his face.

I pull him into a hug and hold him close to me. It's awkward with his padded coat and large backpack. 'What's the matter?' I coo softly. 'Has someone been picking on you at school? Was it Eric?'

Adam shakes his head but remains silent. I glance over my shoulder to Dan. 'Is that what the email from Mrs Evans was about?'

'No,' Dan says flatly as he opens the driver door. He waits until a mother with a reception-aged girl walks past the car before he speaks again. 'She caught Adam with another child's toy in his bag. She thinks he was trying to steal it.'

'What? That's ridiculous. That can't be what happened. Can it, sweetie?'

I look down at Adam, but he doesn't answer. He just sobs harder into my shoulder.

I pull him closer to me and stroke his shiny dark hair. Something uncomfortable stirs in me. I thought Mrs Evans liked Adam. She had come across as a fair teacher, albeit strict. I'm very disappointed to hear that she is jumping to outlandish conclusions at the drop of a hat.

'We don't know what really happened,' I say to Dan after securing our little boy in the car and shutting the door. 'We haven't heard Adam's side of the story. I know our son. He isn't a thief.'

Dan sighs impatiently. 'You haven't heard the teacher's side yet either. She says Adam admitted that he was wrong.'

'Well, she probably bullied a confession out of him.' As I settle into the passenger side, I twist and glance over my shoulder at Adam's blotchy and distraught face in the back seat.

I reach back, even though my muscles scream in protest at being so twisted. Adam's hand fits snugly into mine as I give it a reassuring squeeze. 'What can we do to cheer you up? I'll make you one of those special hot chocolates with the swirly cream when we get back. How many marshmallows do you want?'

Adam opens his mouth to speak, but Dan cuts across him, suddenly angry as he brings the car to life. 'For what he has done, he should be punished, not rewarded.'

'What are you talking about? It's all a big misunderstanding. He's been subjected to enough punishment and bullying already, don't you think?'

Dan stares at me incredulously for a moment but says nothing.

I lower my voice as the car comes to a halt before a red light. 'You've seen the teacher, haven't you?' I ask him. 'She is probably terrifying to a child. It's outrageous that she is in charge of a class of children at all, when you think about it.'

It unsettles me to imagine the psychological harm Mrs Evans might be inflicting upon the helpless youngsters under her so-called care, especially our son. Teachers like her should be rounded up.

'I don't think so,' Dan says. 'From what she said, everything sounds fair enough.'

My mouth drops open. 'Why are you taking the side of a virtual stranger over that of your own child?'

'I'm not.'

I shake my head, tears in my own eyes again now as I look out the window and see our row of stone cottages come into view. Dan has always been this way towards Adam.

We pull onto the driveway, and Dan hands Adam his keys to let himself into the house and instructs him to get changed out of his school things.

'We'll be there in a minute,' Dan says out the window to him before he rolls it back up again and turns to me.

'Ali, I know you're always going to take Adam's side, but

you must see what is happening here. Why would the teacher make something up?'

'I don't think she invented it entirely. She probably just got the wrong end of the stick and blamed our son for whatever nonsense went on. It's just a big mistake. Maybe I'll talk to her about it tomorrow when I drop Adam off.'

'I can take him to school for the rest of the week if you want. I think it might be better. You've spent enough time rushing around. I think you are overdoing it. You don't want to get run-down.'

'I'm not.'

'You were late this afternoon.'

I shrug. 'Only by a couple of minutes. I got there just as you were leaving. I wasn't that far behind, was I?'

'Mrs Evans said Adam has been arriving to school late recently. I can take him in the mornings. It's no trouble.'

'Maybe we should look into switching schools?' I wonder out loud. It sounds like Mrs Evans is taking too much of an interest in Adam.

Dan shakes his head. 'I think the problem is a little closer to home, don't you think?'

'The only problem,' I snap at him, 'is that you instantly believe something negative about your son without even questioning it first.'

My fingers unclip my seat belt. I slam the car door, and I'm in the house in a few short movements.

I half-expect Dan to storm in after me, but he doesn't. When I peer out the kitchen window, I see he remains behind the wheel of the car, staring out at the long-withered remnants of the flowers that once lined the garden path.

I remember how my husband used to come home from work when Adam was a baby and do something similar. I used to watch him as he pulled the car up and seemingly steeled himself before he entered the house. I used to fear the day he wouldn't drive home at all.

We had rowed constantly during that time. He would accuse me of cheating, and I would call him heartless and uncaring, looking for excuses to run away from his responsibility. Adam hadn't been planned, and it had been thrown in my face so much back then.

I feel like we are moving backwards now, becoming those people again.

Only this time, I don't have thoughts of quietening Dan by shoving proof into his face that I am a faithful wife. It turned out I couldn't back then.

Even though I was certain Dan was Adam's father, I couldn't show him the results of the DNA test I had taken during our bad patch.

I couldn't show him because I would have been proven wrong.

Dan isn't Adam's father.

30

'That's amazing, Alison. Everyone, take a look at Alison's progress. This is exactly what I was looking for. She's even applied what we learned last time about using bold and italics.'

My face reddens as my tutor, Charlotte, steps back and gestures for the others to peer at the simple spreadsheet on my computer screen. The baby-boomer beside me puts her glasses on to take a closer look at my work.

The task for today's lesson was to put together a basic household budget calculator. Charlotte is delighted with my progress. She even projects my display up on the board at the front of the classroom for everyone to see. Her praise lands heavily on my guiltily squirming insides.

My course at the Lakeside centre is going so well. Unusually, I'm at the top of the class. I hope I haven't let myself get carried away tonight. It wouldn't do to make it too obvious I know all of this already. The last thing I want is for Charlotte to think I don't need to be here. I don't want her to realise she is the only reason I turn up.

My only regret this evening is that Rebecca wasn't available to babysit, as she had already arranged to watch her niece and nephews. Dan is on the late shift tonight, and the only person available to look after Adam was my mother-in-law. I know he will be well cared for, spoilt rotten even, but I don't like the thought of coming home after a busy day to find her in my house.

On the other hand, Rebecca would have been a warm welcome. Perhaps she could have stayed a little longer when I got back. We could have had a drink together and got to know each other a little better. Instead, I'll have to make small talk with Julie.

I'll worry about it later though because I have more important things on my mind right now.

Towards the end of the session, there is a small test to probe what we have learned. To not appear over-competent, I throw a couple of mistakes in here and there for good measure and hope it looks plausible.

When the class comes to an end, however, Charlotte calls me back as I pull on my coat and bag.

Panic prickles in my chest. Has she noticed what I did? Could someone who went skipping ahead breezily filling in formulas in cells not know how to name a file properly?

I should have put more effort into the lie. She will surely see straight through my deliberate errors. What have I done?

She leans back on her desk, one step away from sitting on her hands. It isn't until the last person leaves that she smiles at me with that warmth of hers, her dimples working in unison.

I'm still on edge though. What could she possibly want to say that couldn't be said in front of the others?

'You look worried, Alison.' She laughs, and it illuminates her symmetrical features. What she has been through hardly shows on her face at all.

She shakes her head and looks thoughtfully at me for a second. 'Don't worry,' she says simply after a moment. 'I just wanted to tell you that you are doing great. I'm so pleased with your progress, especially today. You just need to learn to relax a little. I think you are a bit nervous during our classes.'

'I guess.' The tension in my shoulders softens. I'd been so sure Charlotte was about to say something else to me but changed her mind. 'Thank you for being so patient. You're a great teacher. Have you been doing it long?'

Something crosses her face, and I realise that I've overstepped the mark. She must feel it's too much of a personal question. We are merely student and teacher.

Or so she thinks.

'I've been working here several years now.' She recovers her perfect smile. 'I find it rewarding helping people become more confident with technology. Our lives are becoming more digitalised all the time. It's sad when I see people struggle, especially the elderly.'

'Yes,' I say, thinking of George, who sits beside me during class. He is so keen to get to grips with computers and the internet just so he can do his own online shopping. 'I suppose it's tricky for the older generation. They never got to grow up with what we take for granted.'

She nods. 'That's what surprises me about you, Alison. You seem to have some computing knowledge. You're amazing in some areas, but less so in others. Didn't you have IT lessons in school?'

'Some. I guess I wasn't very academic though,' I lie, realising a mistruth is just as easy to invent for Charlotte's benefit as it is for Dan's.

'You went down a more creative route?'

'Yes,' I say slowly. 'What makes you say that?'

'I have to be honest – I know someone who went to the exhibition you had recently. They told me about your photography studio. I ended up seeing your Facebook profile. Your work is amazing. Your son is lovely too. He makes an excellent subject.'

'Thank you.' I'm aware of how red my cheeks are. I feel a mess in the presence of the immaculately composed Charlotte. It is some comfort to me, however, that she can be this way after everything that has happened in her past.

She leans over and rummages in her desk drawer. 'You know, I suppose it's less important with social media and everything, but I think a photographer would benefit from having an official website. Have you ever considered an online portfolio? It might be useful in your line of work. I can help you out. I'd love to help you get something up and running.'

More heat rises to my face. What if she looks me up and sees I've already got a website? A decent one too. I suppose I could always say a friend did it for me.

She hands me a card. On it is her name, email address and home phone number. There isn't an address, but I already know where she lives. Sometimes I like to drive past her house, even though it is out of my way. I thank her as I slip the card into my handbag.

I know I'll store her number in my phone when I get home later, but I will never call it. Somehow, though, I find it reassuring to have this new line of contact into her home. Especially now the one via her husband is severed forever.

'Even if it's not website related. If you have any questions or concerns at all, I hope that you will give me a call.' A strand of blonde hair falls across one of her full cheeks, just the perfect shade of pink. This is the face of the wife I had spent so long imagining. Things could have been so different if her husband had lived. Who is to say what might have been if our lives had travelled down a different path?

What I've lived through instead is an archive of missed opportunities and horrible arguments with Dan as we've grown apart. What might have been will surely haunt me forever. Charlotte's husband could have changed everything.

All of our lives might have been so different.

I long for the cold air and privacy of the dark car park outside, but I'm physically shaking as I leave the classroom and feel the need for something sweet from the vending machine. My head starts to throb as I reach the ground floor and make my selection. The white overhead lights reflect painfully off the glass. I squeeze my eyes shut and take a deep breath.

It's then that I notice a set of footsteps slow as a figure hovers close by.

I turn abruptly and find myself looking at the last person I expect to see.

Rebecca.

She looks as though the feeling is mutual. She seems frozen in the corridor as she stares back at me.

'This is a surprise,' I say to her. I don't know why, but the moment feels awkward. 'What are you doing here? I thought you were babysitting your sister's children tonight?'

Her shoulders slump beneath the straps of her backpack. 'Oh ... that was earlier this afternoon. I picked them up from school, that was all.'

'My mistake. I didn't realise you came here. Are you taking a class?'

'No, well, sort of. My sister thinks I should get myself out and about more.' She jerks her thumb vaguely over her shoulder. 'As if I'm going to meet a hot guy in a pottery class. Try telling her that though.'

I sense that she isn't being truthful. The artificial lights inside the building reflect off the glass front doors, and

Rebecca is quick to disappear into the darkness beyond them.

It's then that I realise I'm not the only one who can quickly roll a lie off my tongue when I need to.

31

R ebecca is late for work. She has never been late
      before. Even when I was delayed, I found my
      employee here already. I find it unsettling. I'd
grown used to the routine we'd fallen into. Rebecca has been
one of the only things I could depend on.

And now she isn't here.

I am acutely aware that the minutes are ticking away until
my next photoshoot – a group shot in the festive set. A couple
with their three young children want the image for the front
of their Christmas cards this year. I had been relying on
Rebecca working her magic with the children.

Before I employed her, I imagined having a special
rapport with the kids myself, but now I've seen her doing it, I
know I couldn't do it any better.

With twenty minutes to go, it dawns on me that she isn't
going to turn up. I've been calling her mobile all morning,
but I can only assume it's switched off, as it goes straight
through to voicemail every time.

I make myself an extra sweet coffee with the hope of it
calming me. I drop down into my computer chair and pull up

the CV Rebecca emailed when she first started work. It has her home address on it, as well as her landline number, which I have never had reason to call.

I don't have high hopes, but unless she has pulled out the plug, she can't very well ignore a ringing landline. That is if she is at home at all. She could be anywhere.

I use the shop phone and tap in the number. For a split second, I think I have reached my wayward employee, but then I quickly realise it is an automated message. It tells me the number has not been recognised.

I check the number I dialled is correct and try again, but get the same message. I frown at my computer screen. The number Rebecca gave me has been disconnected. My mind whirs. Was it ever hers at all?

The image of Rebecca at the Lakeside centre floats again before my eyes. The way she had frozen when she saw me has played on my mind since last night. Her usual air of confidence was gone. She even seemed to shrivel under my gaze, as though she had been caught out doing something she shouldn't.

I find myself breaking into something of a cold sweat as my clients arrive. It is a struggle to get the compositions I had planned without help at my side.

The pictures are probably good enough, but they aren't examples of my best work. I had hoped to add these to my online portfolio and make people desire the Christmas set. I had envisaged being overwhelmed with demand. Looking at the results, however, I'm not sure that even I would make a booking.

When I am alone again in the shop afterwards and all is quiet, I call the Lakeside centre with an idea. The receptionist puts me on hold a lot, but I eventually get put through to the appropriate tutor – the one for the pottery class. When Rebecca told me that she had come from this classroom, I had been immediately certain it was a lie. But it's been bothering me since, and I can't think of a reasonable explanation as to why she would make something like that up. After all, she is my friend.

Surely it isn't normal to suspect her of something when she provided such a reasonable explanation? It's another one of those erroneous thoughts I've been fearful of.

I finally get through to the class tutor. She is short and sounds harassed.

'Can I help?' she says in her deep voice. 'I'm told you have a question?'

'Yes, I'm sorry to bother you, but my friend takes your class. She has lost something, and we are trying to retrace her steps. Has anyone handed anything in?'

She sighs impatiently. 'What is it she has lost?'

'Her phone. She can't be reached on her mobile right now, so she asked me to help.'

'No one said anything in my classes. Who was it, please?'

I hesitate. 'Rebecca. Rebecca Taylor.'

'I'm not sure who that is. Which class does she take?'

'The evening pottery class. You are the only tutor, right?'

The only sound from the other end of the call is the shuffling of papers for a few moments. 'That's correct. But there is no one by that name currently enrolled. Perhaps you have made a mistake.'

'No, she was there just last night. I was there with her.'

'Were you in the class too?'

'No. I came from my IT class upstairs. I saw her in the hallway near your classroom door.'

'There are a variety of different classes going on in the evening. Perhaps you got the wrong one. I'm sorry, I have to prepare for my afternoon session now.'

There is a click, and I'm left in silence again.

32

BEFORE

My grandson and I get to spend the entire morning together. I fear this may be one of the last full days we get like this. My son tells me he and his wife have started using the local daycare service and will use it more when she is back at work full time. Indeed this set-up isn't agreeable with my own working hours. But I tell him I can arrange myself around my job.

For now, I focus on my grandchild. He has grown so much but doesn't seem to be any easier to look after. Getting his attention is tougher than ever, even when I pull out all the stops. I level with him on the dusty carpet and animate his brightly coloured toys with all the energy I can manage.

He enjoys it though when I take hold of his hands and we walk around the garden in the late summer air. I am even treated with a rare smile when we see a bright butterfly flap past us. I can't let go of his little mitts even for a second to leave him unsupported. I wonder how often he is given walking practice.

I imagine my daughter-in-law leaves him in front of the television for long periods whilst she amuses herself elsewhere in the house. An electronic babysitter would suit her nicely for when I'm not here. She wouldn't have to make awkward small talk with it for one thing. It saddens me to think of how she is neglecting her child. The thought makes me want to refuse to leave at the end of the day. If only I could take the little boy with me when I go home. I would make sure he is looked after properly.

It starts to rain, and we are forced back indoors before we have exhausted the outdoor resources.

After a tricky lunchtime where most of the food ends up on the floor, I try a few times to put him down for his afternoon nap. I'm unsuccessful, however. He is restless, and I wonder how I can entertain him for another few hours. I decide a round of our usual game would be in order. This afternoon, we are round-the-house explorers again.

The child in my arms manages a smile as I bouncily count the stairs, and the small interaction warms me a little inside.

In the bathroom, I entertain the little boy with counting all the colourful bottles and tubes. I point out that Daddy's toothbrush is bone dry. Was he really that pushed for time as he left for work this morning? I tell him that his father was never that lax under my care when he was a little boy.

'I think Mummy might be able to help out a little more, couldn't she?'

In the master bedroom, it is clear that Mummy still isn't letting Daddy sleep beside her, even after all this time. What does she think she is doing? I wonder if she is having second thoughts about her marriage. Doesn't she know she wouldn't last as a single parent?

I set my grandson down on the thick carpet and let him roam a little. He obviously doesn't come up here much, and he moves off with as much gusto as he can whilst clinging onto the furniture for support. Something catches his attention under the bed, and he drops onto his bottom and reaches out. He reels in his pudgy fist and shakes about his new acquisition – a colourful set of cardboard tags.

I kneel down beside him and see that he has pulled them from a brand-new large suitcase. Unlike the other items stuffed beneath the master bed, the case isn't covered in a layer of dust. It may be partly because there is a sheet thrown carelessly over the top. Only the brand tags would have been visible from my grandson's level.

My son wouldn't notice something hidden beneath the bed he seems to have been banished from either. I know this is something my daughter-in-law has put here.

She took care to hide it.

What is she planning?

33

The rest of the week sees me working by myself in the shop. Each time I let myself in and work in silence, I tell myself that it is just Rebecca's day off. I've come to rely on her for the duties she performs and also for her company. And moral support, like an emotional crutch.

I feel guilty for feeling that way, especially when it was clearly wrong to become so reliant upon her.

Dan uses his lunch break to bring me some sandwiches one day. I admit to not having time for breakfast and take them gratefully. We sit and eat them at my desk, with my husband perched on Rebecca's stool.

He frowns in between mouthfuls of bread. 'You shouldn't let yourself get worked up about these things. Rebecca must have a flaky personality, that's all. It's good you realised it now and not when you needed her to do something important.'

'Well, that's just it. She was there for me when I needed her, and now she has disappeared. It's strange that she isn't here.'

'Don't let it get you down. You can find someone else. Or just cut the opening hours a bit.'

'I can't do that. We have a load of bookings that need to be honoured. Things are starting to get busy. Or they were. I don't have time to respond to all the enquiries I've been getting. Whilst I'm on a shoot, I can't be looking for new clients. Rebecca was good at talking people around who were on the fence.'

'It's a shame she isn't as good at answering the phone to you. Did you get a response from her landline yet?'

'No. The number must be wrong.'

'Or it was never hers to start with.'

I stare at my husband as he picks the raisins out of his iced bun. 'What do you mean by that?' I ask him.

He catches the look on my face and shakes his head. 'I didn't mean anything sinister by it. I mean, some people just make things up for their CV, don't they? I've done it myself. She might have just jotted some bits down to make herself sound better. She might not even have a landline. Or she might live at a dodgy address or something and didn't want to write it down.'

'That wouldn't show from the number though, would it? The area code is still the same, and she doesn't have a bad address. It's actually very nice. She lives in one of those posh houses by the station.'

Dan's eyebrow twitches. 'Does she? And she has a part-time job here to finance it? What did she do before you came along anyway?'

'She has loads of experience. It's all on her CV.'

'Did you call any of her references before you hired her?'

I shift in my seat, remembering how, as a novice employer, I hired Rebecca on the spot without giving it much thought. 'No. But she told me all about her previous jobs. I didn't think I needed to check up on her.'

'If you had, maybe they would have told you she was unreliable.'

I stare at the wall behind Dan's head and think about the expression on Rebecca's face when I'd last seen her. 'I agree there is something else going on. I just don't know what.'

'Ali, it isn't anything elaborate that needs figuring out. This is why employers always ask for references, because of people like this. Forget about her and move on. Just don't bite off more than you can chew is all I'm saying.'

I nod, not wanting to argue. It seems Dan has forgotten about our disagreement over Adam's teacher. Or rather, we have come to an unspoken compromise, and neither of us is willing to break it.

What Dan said about Rebecca inventing things on her CV bothers me throughout the afternoon. Even when I'm uploading my latest client photos to the portfolio on my new business website, I do so with another tab open. I'm simultaneously taking a virtual stroll down Rebecca's home street on Google Maps. Could it be that Rebecca doesn't live in this house at all? The familiar image of a respectable Tudor-style house fills up my screen. in the daylight, I see a classic red postbox is located almost exactly outside the neat wooden fence of the property. This is definitely the place I dropped Rebecca outside of. She even returned my wave before I drove away that day. But then, I didn't hang around to see her venture inside the property, or even set foot on the driveway. Have I been lied to this entire time?

I glance at the time and realise that if I shut a little early, I can stop by the house briefly and still make it in time for Adam's school. I've been extra careful to make drop-offs and pickups with time to spare. I won't slip again. I don't want to give Dan an excuse to worry about me, for one thing.

For another, it stops anyone with undesirable intentions from being able to wander off with my little boy before I can get to him. The sight of him drifting away from school up the street without me still makes me shudder. It has given me new material for my nightmares, not that they need it. I was just lucky that it was only Dan who was leading him away on that occasion.

I take extra care, as I have all week, and make deliberately slow and mindful movements when I lock the door. I can't afford any accidents, especially now I seem to be on my own.

It doesn't take long to drive over to Carriage Drive. Neat gardens and shiny cars stand proudly outside each property. I feel as though I'm intruding as I pull up uninvited outside number twelve.

Beyond the red postbox, there is a newish BMW on the driveway, and I tell myself it could belong to Rebecca's partner. Not that she has ever mentioned one. She could have either a girlfriend or a boyfriend for all I know.

I haven't asked for any form of documentation from Rebecca. Nor has she willingly provided me with anything other than what she has told me verbally. I had considered her a friend, after all. Should friends have to prove themselves to one another? If that is true, then where do we draw the line when considering people we see every day?

I think of Charlotte and how she thinks of me merely as a student in her classes. I know first-hand how people can be easily deceived. Was I naive to think that others would be truthful to me in return?

It feels like I'm trespassing as my flat shoes slap noisily on the neat dark tarmac of the driveway of number twelve.

I ring the doorbell and wait. A dark shape moves beyond the small squares of frosted glass, and there is a moment of hesitation before I hear the click of a lock.

A young woman with broad features pulls open the door and looks me up and down. 'Can I help you?'

'Hi,' I say brightly. 'I'm looking for Rebecca. She hasn't

shown up for work for a few days, and I was worried about her. She does live here, doesn't she?'

The woman shakes her head with a blank expression. Her loose bun flaps from side to side, as does the thick gold chain around her neck. 'No. I don't know who that is.'

My heart sinks.

A slightly older man in a muscle-fit T-shirt appears behind her in the hallway and stares at me. 'What's going on?'

'I'm sorry. I was looking for someone who works for me. Rebecca Taylor. This is the address on her CV. She hasn't shown up all week, and I'm starting to worry.'

He takes hold of the door, shifting his shoulder so that his companion has to move back into the house. She disappears with a tut.

'I don't know. Why don't you call her?' he says. 'Or give her the sack if she hasn't turned up at work? That's what would happen to me if I didn't bother to get out of bed in the morning.'

'I've tried, but ... I'm not getting through.' I don't mention that one of her numbers has been disconnected. 'Have you lived here long?'

Something flashes in his muddy-coloured eyes, and I realise I've overstepped the mark.

'Ages.' He is suddenly aggressive and shrugs abruptly. 'I've never heard of this person. She obviously gave you a fake address. Can't help you, sorry.'

The door slams in my face. Through the frosted glass, I see the distorted image of the man's white T-shirt move down the hall.

As I turn to leave, I'm sure I hear the muffled sound of bickering voices inside. But I'm not sure if I'm imagining it over the wind.

I TAKE my time when I make Adam's dinner that night. I've been putting extra care in to make sure it wasn't me who inadvertently poisoned my little boy.

The situation with Rebecca plays on my mind as I probe a chicken fillet with the new thermometer I bought online. Have I been wrong suspecting Helen of wrongdoing all this time?

Rebecca had been the one to raise my suspicions in the first place. She was the one to suggest an interest in my husband from his ex-girlfriend. The idea wouldn't have entered my head if it hadn't been for what she had said. It's burrowed into my brain and altered my decisions. But perhaps I've been suspicious of the wrong person?

Rebecca had given food to Adam that afternoon too. And now she is gone.

My hands shake as I slice carrots, and I have a near miss with the sharp blade.

Has everything Rebecca told me been a lie? I feel violated. I let her into my business, my home, my life. I cringe when I think of when I found her looking through my baby's things. She had been holding the pink plush rabbit I had taken so much care to choose.

Now it feels tainted. I want it removed from Adam's room. I use the knife to slide the vegetables and potatoes into the pan of water and slip upstairs for a minute to grab the toy bunny.

Adam is in the living room. A snatch of his favourite TV show graces my ears as I jog upstairs.

I switch the light on and scan the dwindling collection of items in the bedroom, but once again I can't see what I'm looking for. I lift things here and there hurriedly, aware of the unattended dinner downstairs.

My shaking hands become more frantic as the possibility of finding the soft toy looks more and more unlikely. Just as I couldn't find the Babygro I so treasured, I know I won't find what I'm foraging for now.

I stand and stare blankly at the products I've disarranged. What if Rebecca started the fire at Adam's birthday on purpose? It would have served to distract me if she wanted to help herself to something up here.

My thoughts are disrupted by a shout from downstairs. 'Mum!'

My breath catches in my throat, worried about what I will find as I race down the stairs to find Adam hovering uncertainly in the hallway.

'The saucepan is overflowing!'

I hurry through to the kitchen, but Dan beats me to it. The entire surface of our stained old cooker is flooded with starchy water.

Dan turns to me, still in his thick winter coat. His cheeks are rosy and flushed with cold from outside. 'Ali, what's going on? Why did you leave that to boil over? Haven't I told you how dangerous that is?'

'Yes, I know that!' I snap back at him, scalding my fingertips as I mop up the mess with a threadbare old tea towel.

The excitement over, Adam disappears back into the living room as Dan rounds on me. 'Where were you?'

I take a deep breath. Whether it was the adrenaline or the rage stemming from finding something else has been stolen from beneath my nose, I can't stop myself from shaking. 'Upstairs,' I say. 'There's something else missing now.'

Dan shakes his head as he pulls off his coat. 'What are you talking about?'

'That little soft toy. The rabbit one. It's gone.' I throw the sodden rag into the washing machine with Adam's uniform.

More laundry for me later. Perhaps it's just as well that I've forgotten to start the wash cycle already.

I turn to Dan as his face forms the confused expression I've grown to hate recently. 'Don't you dare try to deny it was ever here this time either,' I say fiercely. 'You even had it in your hand when we were looking for the missing Babygro – another thing that has been stolen.'

He shakes his head again. The gesture is dismissive. I know what is coming will be something patronising to keep me quiet. The last thing I need right now is to be blindsided by someone else close to me.

'I don't know, Ali,' he says, staring at the fresh brown stains on the electric hob. 'You're obsessing over such trivial things. You keep thinking too much about material possessions.'

'That's because that's all I have left!' I snap. 'And if they don't mean anything, then why do people keep taking them from me!'

'Calm down. No one has taken anything–'

'Yes, they have. Someone has been in our home – in Adam's room – and stolen things! I thought it was Helen before. But now I know it must have been Rebecca.'

'Please, Alison. You're not making any sense.'

'Yes, I am. Just this morning, you were the one who said she had given me a fake address. You were right too. I went to the house today and spoke to the people who live there. It turns out they have never heard of Rebecca. I've been such an idiot! She must have started that fire deliberately and put that note in Adam's backpack. She was alone with him that after-noon. Anything could have happened to him, and it would have been my fault for leaving him with a woman I know nothing about!'

I stop and take deep breaths. My cheeks are flushed with heat, and angry tears run hot from my eyes. Dan looks alarmed. He reaches out for me. 'Come here,' he says quietly.

'No.' Without thinking, I slap his hand away. He can't dismiss me this time. I want him to acknowledge something is going on. 'I didn't imagine any of this. Why won't you agree that none of what has happened is right?'

'Just calm down. There will be a simple explanation for everything. Everyone isn't out to get you. It's–'

'It's not my imagination! Don't you dare say that! I'm not depressed either, so don't say that either.'

'I wasn't going to. Look, I told you, people lie on their CVs. It doesn't mean there is a big conspiracy against you.'

'Why are you so quick to take everyone else's side other than mine or that of your own child?'

He sighs and rubs his eyes with his palms. 'I don't need this,' he says quietly. 'Not after I've been at work all day.'

'I've been working too! And whilst I've been gone, someone has sneaked in here and taken something else from our baby! And you don't even seem to care!'

'You need to stop this, Ali. I don't know how much more of this I can take.'

'I don't know how much more of your attitude I can take! This morning, you admitted that something didn't add up about Rebecca, and now you are defending her! Why not defend me and Adam for a change?!'

'There's nothing to defend against! Stop it, Alison.'

'Get out,' I say to him.

'What?' He suddenly looks up at me, startled. Should this come as a surprise to him? This has been brewing for a long time.

'You know things haven't been right between us for so long.' I swallow down the lump forming in my throat. 'If you aren't going to support me anymore, then I don't want you in this house. Just go.'

34

The time I have feared in the last few years has finally come. Except it wasn't Dan who failed to come inside the house after hesitating outside. It was me who drove him out.

I roll over and find his side of the bed empty and cold, as it has been all night. The room has never felt less comforting with him gone.

I lost my temper, and Dan didn't see it coming. But now that I have had the chance to calm down, I feel a sting that he went without much persuasion. I check my phone again. The motion seems worn out; I've done this too many times overnight.

There are still no messages or calls.

I have no idea where Dan has spent the night. My guess is he is with his mother since she doesn't live too far away. I wonder what Julie thinks of me now. I thought I could sink no lower in her opinion. Obviously, I was wrong. I dread the moment when I have to face her next.

As I go through my usual daily motion and get Adam ready for school, I keep looking over my shoulder. Part of me half-expects Dan to turn up when I'm making breakfast or urging Adam into the car.

Is this really the end of my marriage? There was a time when my husband would never have walked out on me so easily. I suppose this might be the way things are now, having to do everything by myself as a single parent.

Adam asks me several times as we get ready where Daddy is, and I don't know what to tell him. What if something has happened to Dan? It's not like him to leave me hanging like this.

After the school run, I manage to secure my favourite parking spot on an adjacent street and walk to the shop. As I round the corner, my heart jolts when I see a figure hovering outside the door. For a split second, I think the figure in the distance will be Rebecca, come to rescue me in my hour of need with a plausible explanation for everything that has gone on, but it's Dan.

Relief is unwelcome, but I'm still wary. My husband has made no attempt to get in touch overnight with an apology for not sympathising with me.

He smiles nervously as I approach the shopfront. 'I thought I might find you here.' His breath mists between us.

'Well, of course you would. It's how I've been earning money for our family. It's not just a hobby you know.'

He nods towards the door. 'Are you going to let us in, then? It's cold out here.'

Inside, I flip on some lights in the early-morning gloom and settle myself at my desk. Dan once again fills Rebecca's seat, as he did just yesterday. Although, it feels like so much longer than simply twenty-four hours ago.

'Shouldn't you be at work too?'

'Mark is covering for me until I get back. I wanted to come and talk to you ... after what happened yesterday.'

'What more is there to say? You didn't put up much of a fight, did you?'

'You weren't listening to me. You get so blinkered, and I didn't want to argue with you. I thought if I went, you would have time to calm down and think about what I said.'

'I certainly had that all right. I have hardly slept all night. Not that I usually do.'

'I know that. It's not good for you to be this way, Ali. You need to take it easier. You put too much pressure on yourself.'

'You know we need this business. Especially if we ever want to make our lives better. The cottage feels even tinier now that Adam is bigger. And I did have someone here helping me, but now she is gone, and I don't know why.'

The pain and confusion at Rebecca's abrupt departure bubbles over again, and I bury my face in my hands. The fresh memories of the argument with Dan yesterday and his abandonment flash before the darkness, and I feel tears moisten my fingertips.

It's a relief when I feel Dan's warm arms wrap themselves around me. It's just like old times, and he is back by my side again. How could I ever have pushed him away?

'Oh, Ali,' he says softly after a few moments. 'You've let these things get on top of you. And this is what's happened. This Rebecca is just unreliable. You've never hired someone before, but there are plenty of lazy people around who don't show up on time. I've seen loads of them over the years at the restaurant. Rebecca has done you a favour. You've been working too hard. I think a break from all this would do you good. You've done good business since you started. We can afford some time off.'

'But I've got loads of people booked for shoots over the next few weeks. I need to handle it all on my own now too.'

'Can't you just cancel them? I'll call them up and explain if you like?'

I shake my head. Dan just doesn't get how important this is to me. It's not just a business or a hobby. It's both. It's giving me the purpose and meaning that I have lost elsewhere. I used to feel fulfilled as a mother, and once as a wife too. But I've failed on both counts.

Dan sighs. 'You know we can't go on like this. I've been treading on eggshells for weeks now. I've been seeing you work yourself into the ground. You're turning up late at Adam's school.'

I look up at him in surprise. 'I've been on time recently. I've made a special effort.'

'You shouldn't have to. You should be able to get there on time anyway. Maybe you could just reschedule your bookings so that they don't conflict with school times.'

'I already do that.'

'So why not shut the shop earlier? Or open later? You could stand to cut down your hours, at least.'

I shrug. 'Fine. I suppose I could do more of the admin side of things from home.'

Dan smiles. 'I think that would be a great start. I can look into helping you out with the photoshoots and see if I can wing them around my shifts at the restaurant. When is the next one booked?'

The thought of having to instruct Dan from scratch in how I operate on a shoot fills me with dread. Rebecca had been a natural. Or perhaps her experience with her father had been something she was telling the truth about after all. How much of what she had said was a complete fabrication?

'Thanks,' I say to him, wrapping my arms around his waist. 'But I can handle them by myself. I don't have to set up on locations for the next lot. Everyone wants to be booked in for the Christmas set.'

'You need to learn to ask for help if you need it, you know.

Don't keep things bottled up. I know that's what you've always done. But I'm here for you. I just wish you would talk to me.'

Fresh tears form at the corners of my eyes. I press my cheek against the rough cotton of Dan's chef's whites so he doesn't see. When I have recovered myself, I change the subject. 'So what did you tell your mother when you turned up at her doorstep last night?'

He shrugs. 'She was married for over thirty years. She must know people argue sometimes.'

'I can only imagine what she must be thinking of me now.'

He presses his lips against my forehead. 'You worry too much about what she thinks.'

With Dan gone, I finally fire up my computer and check my emails. I have a new booking request, and my fingertips hover guiltily over my keyboard when thinking of the reply.

I think of my fresh promise to Dan about cutting down my working hours. Yes, we could afford for me not to take on more work. But I think of all the things we need. A bigger house, a newer car. Then there are all the things Adam asks for. I know in my heart we could use the extra income. And besides, Dan is worrying over nothing. I can manage the extra work by myself. Although, I could use someone here. Perhaps I could repost the job ad and take on someone else?

I respond and confirm the new booking, feeling confident Dan and I are OK again, and I've got plenty of work to keep me busy. Everything is going well. *I can do this.*

I work through the rest of my emails and Facebook messages one by one. It's mainly junk, but there is an enquiry from the headmaster of a school in Manchester. He explains that he has heard much praise from another headmistress about my service.

Thank you, Mrs Clarke, I think to myself. I hadn't been allowed to post any example shots of the school contract I'd completed to my portfolio. It's so nice of her to spread positive word of mouth like this.

I excitedly type back a reply. I check it over and over before I hit send, hoping I am selling my services well enough to secure the deal. This is where Rebecca would have shone. Although, it seems like it would be hard to mess it up, as Mr Neal's words are highly enthusiastic and full of adulation already.

It's only after I send the reply and have checked for a response several times that I realise I've broken my promise to Dan to do less again.

I decide I can remedy the situation though. I scour through my Facebook timeline and bring up the job ad that had attracted Rebecca. I repost it and share in as many places as I can think of.

I'll find someone else to help me. Dan was right. I've let myself get carried away; coincidences have spawned wild thoughts. The only thing my employee has proven herself to be is unreliable. That's all.

I'm sure I will find her easy to replace.

35

Over the next few days, I find myself trying to think of a way to explain to Dan that I have secured another amazing deal with another school. Mr Neal got back to me very quickly with another enthusiastic response, and we have arranged to meet up in person to discuss the details.

The trouble is, I know Dan will overreact and think the job is too much for me. Since we've made up, I feel like I should make an effort to at least make it seem like I value his opinion. He might even try to talk me out of it, and I'm not willing to let the opportunity to provide school photos for such a high-profile school pass me by.

It's a lucrative deal too. Mr Neal is happy to pay almost double what Mrs Clarke did. Granted, he is in charge of a slightly larger school, and I would need to travel further to get there. But he seems very keen on using me after what Mrs Clarke told him.

In the end, I resolve not to mention anything to Dan. The meeting with Mr Neal, or Richard, as he insists I call him, is all set after an afternoon of short emails back and forth. I feel a buzz of nervous excitement. This will be the biggest project I have undertaken. Last time, I had someone to help me. I hope I can find another assistant before I have to complete the shoot.

The feeling that I could never hope to find someone as good as Rebecca lurks somewhere deep inside. The camaraderie we shared and her instant rapport with any child just could not simply be replaced.

Other than a few casual responses to my job ad, nothing has come from it. The meeting with Richard Neal looms closer, and I wonder if I will have the confidence to commit to the job if I don't have any support. I can hardly take Dan up on his offer either, as I have no intention of telling him about the potential deal at all.

When I arrive at the shop one morning, I notice I missed a call on my phone. It must have been whilst I was driving. Then I see Rebecca's name on the screen.

I haven't heard from her for weeks now. My many attempts to call and text her have all been met with silence or a generic voicemail message.

I stare at my screen uneasily as I let myself in. I move over to the shop window and stare out at the street. At this hour, the town is quiet, and there are only a few elderly pedestrians drifting about here and there. No sign of anyone else.

I wonder what Rebecca wants. I have a stab of regret in the pit of my stomach when I remember the job advert. She must have seen it. That's why she is calling. What if both Dan and I were wrong? What if there was a perfectly reasonable explanation for everything after all?

I take a deep breath and call back. The phone rings this time. The first time in ages that I don't call a switched-off device.

But I don't get an answer. I try again after half an hour or so to no avail. I check my emails and my phone several times throughout the morning, but there is nothing today. All is quiet.

What is she playing at?

The voice inside my head that Dan has so desperately tried to quash now stirs. What if I was right all along? What if she worked her way into my life just to get at me?

I think again of how her warm and bubbly demeanour changed the day we worked on the last school contract. She suddenly clammed up when I asked her about her personal life. What was she hiding?

The landline suddenly screams to life in the quiet of the shop, making me jump. I answer it hastily with thoughts still full of Rebecca.

But it's not her. It's Rachel, my next client booked for a Christmas-themed shoot tomorrow.

'It's lovely to hear from you,' I say. 'Are you still OK for 10 am?'

'Well, I was,' she says slowly. 'But I heard you were cancelling all your bookings, and I just wanted to clarify what's going on?'

'Cancelling bookings? No, everything is still arranged for your shoot. I've added the nutcracker props now too, just like you asked for.'

'Oh.'

'What made you think I was cancelling bookings?'

'It's just that someone told me you were shutting down.'

'What?'

'I know. I thought it was weird too, as I'd not long booked in the first place, and you seemed so keen on doing my shoot. But then I saw the message on your website ...'

'What message?' I adjust the phone under my ear to free

up my hands. In a few taps of the keys, I bring up the site I spent weeks working on.

I expect the screen to fill up with the graceful design and carefully chosen snaps from my portfolio. Instead, my eyes are met with a glaring white page, blank apart from some scruffy jet-black words at the top.

It is with a heavy heart that I write this. Due to unforeseen circumstances, I have decided to close my business down. As of today, I will no longer be taking bookings, and anyone who has already made arrangements for one will be reimbursed with immediate effect. I'm sorry for any inconvenience this has caused.

Thank you all for your support in making my time in this venture so special. You've allowed me a taste of the success I could have had if I could have stuck with this venture. Today, all my dreams have come to an end. But I'm sure you can find someone to replace me.

All the Best,
Alison,
Alison Burnham Photography

I gape at the text with my mouth open. 'What the hell?'

A tinny voice nearby reminds me my phone is still in my hand. 'I'm sorry,' I say breathlessly. 'I've just seen the message. Please ignore that. I – I must have been hacked or something. I didn't write that.'

'Right. That's weird. I guess I'll see you tomorrow, then?'

'Yes, absolutely. Don't worry about anything. I'll have everything set up for when you arrive at ten.'

I thank her and end the call, grateful to have reassured her everything was fine and wishing I felt that confident myself. I put my hands on either side of my face as I reread the message over and over.

My website has been hacked. But it isn't some faceless organisation just doing it for fun. This was personal, targeted at one of the most important things in my life.

This act was aimed directly at me.

36

BEFORE

S ince I discovered what my daughter-in-law has kept hidden beneath her bed, I've half-expected my son to make some sort of grim announcement about the failure of his marriage. I've been dreading the moment his heart is broken in two when his wife declares she is leaving him.

Or perhaps the suitcases were for my son's belongings to be tossed into rather than for her own use.

It seems my daughter-in-law must have decided to keep him hanging on longer. I'm sure she has it all planned out. Perhaps there is another date in mind? Does she want to wait until after their son has turned two? Then it won't be long. Now that her mother has passed away, Little Miss Perfect might have designs on her father's house in Australia? There is probably room for her and her little boy to move in. She would have to be pretty ruthless with her many possessions to fit her life into that case though.

My stomach sinks at the thought of my grandson being whisked off to the other side of the world. On my income, I would rarely be able to afford to visit. If I'm even allowed, that is.

I've seen evidence of how this marriage has unravelled during my visits. She thinks I don't know. But I've seen how my son has been cast from the master bed. Did she think I wouldn't notice the pillow and sheets stuffed carelessly away in the upstairs cupboard?

I've seen the things she had before she gave birth become irrelevant and turn to dust, even as she has tried to cling to them.

Only I know about her thoughts of leaving. I haven't yet told my son about the empty luggage hidden away under the bed he has been banished from.

I know all her secrets.

Unfortunately, it will be my son and grandson who pay the highest price. She will find herself someone else of course. My son and I will have limited access to the little one once things have been made official.

Then it will all be over. I just wish I was wrong.

The only way I can console myself in the meantime is by giving my little grandson the most love I can. He will soon be old enough to start retaining the memories he makes. I'm determined the ones with me in them are amazing.

That's why I'm planning something special for his second birthday. Even if he can't quite remember just yet, at least he will see what I did in the photos. And as with his christening gift, he will know how much I cared.

When I arrive at the house today, something feels different. But something *is* different. It's a Sunday, and they asked me over for lunch, which is unusual. I'm normally nothing more than a free babysitter for when they are at work. Both of them are hovering around, and I feel an announcement in the air.

I feel a shock of dread for my son, but he doesn't seem

perturbed. In fact, he seems happier than he has been for a while.

He has taken charge of the kitchen today and cooked a Sunday lunch.

'This is wonderful,' I say when we are all seated around the dining table and eating. The little one sits in his high chair and fusses about with chunks of potato, ignoring the meat completely, much to his mother's dismay.

It is when we have finished our food that the announcement comes. But it is not the one I had been anticipating. Nevertheless, it's no less of a shock.

'We're going away for a few weeks,' my son tells me. 'Our first holiday together. Just the three of us.'

'But I won't be here for my grandson's birthday,' I say. Bitter disappointment stabs at me as I realise the implications of what has been said. 'It's not every day he turns two. I don't want to miss it.'

'Maybe we can have a second little party when we get back?' he insists. 'You're not the only one not thrilled about this, you know. The other grandparents aren't that pleased, either. They had planned to come over from Australia. But I thought it would be a nice idea if just the three of us went away on our own.'

He walks me to my car afterwards and hands me some of the home-made ginger cake he had made for dessert. The foil package is heavy in my hands as he passes it through the window. He explains to me how adjusting to motherhood hasn't been easy on his wife.

'It's been such a struggle,' he says. 'For both of us. We haven't been blessed with the easiest ride. Some time away would be good for us, for our relationship.'

I reach out my hand and squeeze his, wanting to tell him I know what a state his marriage is in; I don't know how to explain to him I know he doesn't sleep with his wife anymore without him thinking I have snooped.

It's some comfort to me that Little Miss Perfect isn't planning on giving up on him any time soon. She is just being afforded a luxury I never had when I was in charge of a young child. I wasn't whisked away for expensive holidays to Portugal when I was raising my son. I never had the support of such a wonderful man.

I still don't. And I'll have plenty of time to reflect upon that when they are away sunning themselves and having a fantastic time without me.

I'll be alone here on the sidelines, doing nothing but awaiting their return.

37

The incident with my business website has unnerved me. I still don't know who was behind it. No one I know in my personal life would have the know-how to hack a website. And I'm always careful about my passwords. I don't write them down or share them. Not even with Dan.

The way the message was worded was eerily similar to what my husband said he wanted me to do. If I didn't know him better, I would think that this is his way of telling me he wants me to stop trading completely. But he wouldn't do something so cruel.

Luckily the headmaster, Richard Neal, doesn't appear to have noticed anything untoward regarding my online presence. I've fixed my website so that it no longer displays someone else's words, but I don't have a backup of the original.

So now there is simply a basic contact form for enquiries and nothing else. The professional portfolio showcasing my work is lost. When I'm not so busy, I will put another together.

As I'm making Adam's packed lunch in the kitchen one morning, my phone buzzes with another email from Richard. My heart pounds as I read it. He wants to make sure we are still on to meet face to face. I tap back a hurried confirmation.

As I set my phone down, I contemplate how Rebecca wouldn't have agreed with so many emails going back and forth. She would have insisted on calling him instead. In all honesty, she probably would have arranged the deal by now. But this is my business. I'll secure the contract myself in my own way. I don't need her for anything.

I jump out of my skin when Dan's arms come out of nowhere, snaking themselves around my shoulders. The butter knife I'm holding falls onto the worktop with a loud clatter.

'I didn't mean to scare you. Are you all right?'

I smile, willing my heart to resume a steadier rhythm. 'I'm fine. But don't sneak up on me like that.'

'Sorry. I just hope I'm not catching you working too hard.'

I bat at him playfully over my shoulder, then fold some ham into the slices of bread. 'I'm not.'

'Oh. I thought I saw you checking your emails. It's not another booking request, is it?'

I turn and search his eyes for a moment, wondering if he knows otherwise. Then I shake my head. 'No. Just a general enquiry. I won't take it though.'

Dan squeezes my shoulders. 'Good. Remember, I'm taking Adam to school this morning. Are you still OK to pick him up later?'

'Sure.'

'Great. Make sure you don't overdo it today at home either.'

'It's not possible to overexert myself when I'm only doing photo-editing in the house. I promise to have a relaxed day.'

Once I've said goodbye to Adam and Dan, the little

cottage seems unnaturally quiet and still. It's almost as though the very walls have eyes and stare back at me critically, disapproving of the secrets I'm keeping.

The strong feeling of being watched is upon me, and I peer out of a few windows before I can settle down to work.

I manage to have a productive morning, and I'm just starting work on post-editing the next set of images when my mobile rings. At first, I think it will be Dan. Then I consider the fact that Adam could have had an accident at school. Or the pair of them have both been involved in an accident on their way in this morning and it is the hospital calling with terrible news.

It will have been my fault, I think as I rush over to the device demanding attention. *I should have taken Adam to school myself.*

When I answer, my breath is knocked out of me. It is bad news, just as I had thought.

From the hospital too. But it isn't my husband or son who is hurt or injured.

It's my mother.

THE WEATHER IS UNACCOMMODATING, and after a nightmare journey on the bus, my feet are cold and damp through the thin shoes I threw on thoughtlessly.

The grey hospital building looms into view. It suddenly strikes me as I approach the front desk just how little I have seen of my mother over the last few years, how neglectful I have been. She has no idea why, either. Goodness knows what she must think of me. My only comfort is that my brother looks in on her.

I suppose it is something that I am still listed as her next of kin, however. If she had held any resentment towards me, she could easily have wiped me off all her paperwork.

'Hello,' I say as the receptionist puts down the phone and gestures me forward. I burn under her gaze, as though she can tell how I have failed miserably as a daughter.

'I'm here to see Dorothy Wiley. I was told she had a fall. I'm her daughter,' I add, as though it justifies me being here. But she must know. How many estranged relatives has she directed around the building in all her years?

She tells me where to go, and I make the trek up to the second floor of the hospital as though moving along the halls of a courtroom on my way to be judged by unsympathetic jurors.

As I reach the ward and approach the end of my mother's bed, my vision becomes blurred by a glaze of tears. Mum is more frail and elderly than the last time I saw her; her mousy hair has so much more grey in it. Her face is pale and somehow smaller – an image reaffirmed by the large plaster affixed to the side of her forehead.

I force the cramping muscles of my face into a smile. 'Hi, Mum.'

She turns her head when she sees me and smiles. 'Alison, I wasn't expecting you.'

Her voice wavers, and it alarms me to hear how softly spoken she is. She had been such a strong authority figure when my brother and I were small. It breaks my heart to see her reduced to this.

'I got here as soon as I could,' I say. 'They said you'd had a fall.'

A bloom of colour comes to my attention from the bed one along, and I realise I have turned up empty-handed in my rush to be here. I hadn't known what to expect, but I was determined to arrive as soon as I could. I've failed my family on yet another level.

'You didn't have to do that,' she says again in a weak voice. 'Your brother will be here later. Alma from next door called him. I know how busy you are looking after little ones. Especially with a new baby. I wouldn't want to think you've left your tiny precious girl with someone else just to come over here and visit an old crow like me.'

There is a pause where we look at each other, and I'm frightened to see pale blue eyes so much like mine staring back at me blankly.

She is confused. In her mind, I've delivered my baby safely. Has the bump on her head affected her memory, or has it been slipping away gradually, unnoticed? I make a mental note to ask my brother later.

Anger stabs at my insides. This shouldn't have happened. I should have taken better care of my own mother. My brother and I are all she has left, but I wasn't there. Now it may as well be too late.

I smooth down the thin blanket on her bed unnecessarily, mostly to avoid looking up into those unknowing eyes again. I'm tempted to lie. I don't want to utter the words that will break her heart again. But my lips can't betray the daughter that I'll never hold in my arms again.

Now it's my turn to speak in a shaky voice. 'Mum, you only have one grandchild. Remember? I told you that – that little Dorothy – she didn't make it. She passed away.'

I chance a glance up at Mum and see that her expression of confusion is weaker, yet more watery.

'I'm so sorry, Alison,' she says. She touches a hand to her injured temple. 'I – I'm forgetting things these days. What a horrible thing for me to say. Of course she's gone. I'm so sorry …'

'It's OK. You haven't been well. I'll visit more often, I promise. I'll bring Adam too.'

'Adam, yes.' She nods, as though trying to command her

memories. She takes hold of the hand I've been using to smooth the blankets out. 'Life can make you reflect on what you've lost. But you have so much. Adam is a wonderful boy. At least you have him.'

I don't know whether it is the fact that I feel like I'm sitting talking to a stranger, or the fact that I am reflecting on everything that has gone wrong, but I can't hold back my tears anymore.

I bury my face in my free hand, unwilling to look into the eyes of a stranger once again. My shoulders shake, and I hate myself for breaking down like this. This is the last thing Mum needs. I've failed as a daughter. And as a wife.

Worst of all, I've failed as a mother.

I can't explain to Mum what is really wrong. Her words should have brought me comfort, but they have only caused me immeasurable distress.

In the same way, I can't explain to Dan why he isn't the father of the child he has raised for years. I don't want to tell Mum that she isn't Adam's grandmother. It would destroy her to think that she has no grandchildren at all, and I won't do it. Especially now.

I can't bear the fact that Adam doesn't belong to me either. He was never mine.

I'm not really his mother.

38

If I thought that Little Miss Perfect was a paler shade of her past self after becoming a mother, then I'm not sure what she is now. A mere shadow, perhaps. A ghost, haunting an eerily quiet and empty house.

I'm not sure what she has eaten since her return from Portugal. I've prepared sandwiches and soups, but I've found most of it ends up being thrown away after being vaguely picked at. It's absurd to think of how she has now taken on the role of the fussy infant.

The cheekbones I know she missed since her pregnancy have emerged again, but the look doesn't suit her. Her slender face now looks too thin.

She was on the phone with her father for hours the day she got back from Portugal. She repeated what I'd been told, almost word for word. She must still be in shock. I couldn't do anything else but listen again. Certain phrases stab at me as I hear them. I know I will never forget the words.

The current had got the better of them ... It was too fast ... Even an Olympic swimmer couldn't have fought against such force.

It had taken over an hour for the emergency services to

reach them in the water. The currents take tourists all the time, so she had been told. Only the locals really know the dangers. They must see it happen all the time. How can they bear to live so near something that claims so many unsuspecting lives?

There doesn't seem to be any plan for her father to come over for a visit. I got the impression he was busy with his new wife. He didn't waste much time. He was far from the shining example of a husband and father that my son had been.

I appreciate the irony that it's left to me to take care of her now. Now that my son and grandchild are gone, we only have each other. It's a compromise no one ever wanted or imagined.

But now here we are.

Four weeks after the devastating news, I now find I have to work just to get my daughter-in-law out of bed and dressed in the mornings.

I'd always insisted that my son be dressed and ready for the day no matter what. Even during school holidays and at weekends. The structure was good for him.

Every day is just a blur of caring for a fully grown woman who has never truly liked me. I half-expect her to protest at any minute. To kick me out and tell me I have no reason to be there anymore. But she doesn't. I have a feeling she hasn't truly processed the fact that I am here. She is too absorbed in shock and grief.

She has forgotten about work. She would forget about her own mortality if I wasn't here. She needs me. And I need her. For when I throw myself into taking care of her, I can forget. I don't have to think about what has happened when I'm cooking, cleaning and taking care of the house in between my days at work.

Together we work in a strange sort of new equilibrium. We exist to forget.

39

The weather has cleared now. The incessant rain has turned into golden sun. Dark grey clouds still linger, but a rainbow is still able to descend somewhere behind the hill in the cemetery. The whole scene feels symbolic after my visit to my mother and what she said about Adam. As though I should give hope where there is none.

After everything is said and done, he isn't my child. And after burying my baby girl here, I know I have nothing real left. I've spent years clinging to the dream of Adam. But my efforts are wasted. He isn't mine. No more is he Dan's.

I lay a single pink chrysanthemum at my baby girl's headstone. It was taken from the vibrant bouquet I had found for her grandmother and namesake in the hospital gift shop earlier. Someone else has laid a fresh bunch of yellow sunflowers here, and I wonder who it could have been.

My skin prickles uncomfortably, and I glance around, expecting to see some figure watching me. But there is no one. I'm all alone.

I rotate my shoulders in an attempt to shake off the feeling and read the inscription on the headstone once again.

Dorothy Burnham,
Born sleeping, and forever after

Dan must have felt something was off as much as I did when we brought Adam home from the hospital as a baby. The pregnancy hadn't been planned in the first place. I wasn't ready. Neither was Dan. Yet there we were. Nothing had felt right back then.

The birth was tough. The labour had gone on overnight. Too long. I was exhausted. Then the midwives had noticed a problem with my baby's heartbeat, and he was taken from my grip just moments after he was born. He was placed in an incubator away from me. It was over a week before we were allowed to take him home.

When we got back, things didn't just slip into place or fix themselves as it seemed to for other new parents. The first six months were tough. Dan and I were truly separate people for the first time in our marriage. He eventually formed words for his disquiet surrounding Adam and accused me of having cheated on him. I was outraged of course, as I knew I was innocent.

Adam's lack of resemblance to either of us hadn't bothered me as much as it had Dan. But after months of awful arguments and accusations, I was at my wit's end and ready to prove the truth. I decided to arrange a paternity test. He had been taken aback when he was presented with it and seemed to take my sheer willingness to take the test as proof enough of my innocence. He had broken down after we sent it off and apologised. His behaviour was almost sheepish after that. Once again he resembled the person I had married.

I had been ready to shove the results in Dan's face if he ever suggested again that Adam wasn't his.

Only, I couldn't show him the proof when I received the

results. The truth was something I hadn't expected. Thankfully, Dan's guilt seemed to keep him from mentioning the test again. In the harsh light of day, the fact he had spurred me on to arrange the test seemed to be a reality check. He hasn't mentioned it since, even to this day. And I'm grateful. What would have happened if Dan had forced my hand? Our lives would have been uprooted. Would we have lost Adam? Would the revelation have torn the two of us apart completely and signalled the end of our marriage?

I take a moment to check that I am truly alone before I move on to the next headstones. To anyone else, I would appear to have no valid reason to trespass upon this section of grass.

But the place is deserted. There is only me. I've come to like it that way when I make these trips. I can't explain it to anyone I know. They wouldn't understand, so I can never reveal the truth.

I take the remaining flower I extracted from the bunch and lay it to rest carefully upon one side of the double memorial. The blue head reflects dully against the texture of the black marble.

It seems a pitiful offering. But it is the most I can get away with giving to the child I never had.

I'd held the baby in my arms briefly before he was taken. Just like I had with my little Dorothy. Like so many times before, I close my eyes and try to remember him in those brief moments.

I'd been so tired after the long labour. His tiny body had felt so heavy in my arms. I had longed to rest but didn't want to let him go. There was no way I would have done if the midwife hadn't noticed something was wrong. Despite reliving the moment over and over again all these years, I still don't remember her face. She is just a vague figure and pair of arms reaching to snatch away what should have been my little boy.

Suddenly there were stethoscopes and monitors on his tiny body before he was rushed off to the neonatal intensive care unit. My shaking arms had tried to force myself up to follow, but my legs were still paralysed from the epidural.

If only Dan had been there, he could have gone with our baby. But he had been in between visits when I'd finally given birth.

An overnight stay in an overcrowded maternity ward hadn't done my sanity much good. Being surrounded by new mothers cradling their babies only emphasised what I could lose.

Over a week later, Adam had been discharged with a fresh bill of health, and we'd been finally allowed home, but it hadn't been the relief I had expected. I had felt out of sorts. Everything felt up in the air. Adjusting to motherhood was the most unnatural thing in the world, and then I'd slipped into postnatal depression.

Those first few months are a strange haze now. I know I'd been forgetful and snappy with my husband. At times, I'd been aggressive, paranoid even. Adam was thankfully too young to remember, but I know Dan will never forget.

He was so worried I would become like that again after Dorothy's birth. He doesn't understand why I was so distraught during the first year of Adam's life. He didn't know what I'd discovered.

There was no way he would know what an impossible scenario we were in. Our baby was missing. After leaving the overcrowded maternity ward, he could have gone to a variety of places. Was I brave enough to make a call and start in motion events that would change everything?

No. I was a coward. I was terrified that Adam would be taken from us. That my arms would be left empty potentially forever. I lived in constant fear of being left with nothing; that had fuelled my paranoia. Every time the phone had rung, I'd feared it was the call I'd been dreading – someone had realised the mistake. I imagined what would happen if they forced me to hand over the baby I had nurtured and breastfed for over six months.

What if Adam was taken into care? What if the authorities couldn't locate my real baby? The other family clearly hadn't said a word either. In hindsight, it is obvious they had been blissfully unaware of the fact they were raising my and Dan's child instead of their own.

I'm vaguely aware my fingernails are digging painfully into my palms. If only it could distract me properly from the pain I feel every day when I think of what has happened. My whole life has come to a crashing halt ever since. Nothing I've done has worked out right. Not even my new baby girl.

Dorothy was supposed to be our fresh start. And it breaks my heart that I have to leave her behind here in this cold damp place and go home to all I have left: a marriage hanging on by a thread and a child who isn't mine.

A voice somewhere behind me causes my eyes to snap back open, and it takes me a moment to remember where I am.

An elderly lady with a bunch of flowers looks at me with pity. 'It was a terrible thing that happened,' she says. 'I remember reading about it in the newspaper at the time. I hope you don't think me nosy, dear, but I notice the memorial every time I come past here to visit my dear old Arthur.'

She gestures behind her with the flowers. The cellophane crinkles noisily in the still air. 'He's up on the hill.'

'Oh.' I don't know what to say. She has assumed I'm the mother who has been left behind after the double tragedy. She isn't wrong. But she doesn't realise I'm not the wife of the man buried in the same memorial beside us, the man who had held my little boy as they had both drowned in the Portuguese sea.

'I've often wondered about you. Are you getting on OK?' She nods encouragingly and looks at me with expectation.

'Yes,' I say slowly. I feel as if something is being drawn from me. The lady's wrinkled face is kind, like Mum's. She is another person who doesn't understand the connotations of my situation. 'It's not been an easy few years.'

She nods sympathetically. 'I'm sure they haven't. I'm sure you think of them still every day.'

'I do. I keep thinking about how I want to go back and change things. But I know I can't. The past is set in stone.' My voice breaks, and I tear my gaze away from the lady's enquiring eyes, and it comes to rest upon the double headstone. 'Quite literally.'

She ambles over. I notice her shoes and the bottoms of her tights are sodden from the wet grass. My feet are soaking wet and cold too, I now realise.

Her hand is a comforting grip on my forearm. 'It's not easy to understand why these things happen. But you can't torment yourself with what could have been. It will drive you mad.'

'I know,' I say quietly. I don't say that I fear it is too late for that. My lip trembles threateningly. 'I just can't stop thinking about what I could have done differently. How I could have stopped this.'

I've lain awake so many nights trying to put everything right in my head. It is maddening, frustrating beyond belief.

By some fortuitous coincidence, I found the other family who had my baby, even though they hadn't known it. Through a series of mistakes and misfortune, this man and his wife had been the ones to take my and Dan's child home with them.

But even when I discovered the truth, I hadn't worked up

the courage to take the first life-changing step. Then all too quickly it was too late. The baby and his non-biological father were involved in an accident and drowned. My inaction cost me everything, and the opportunity to remedy the situation was gone forever.

The old lady sighs deeply. 'It isn't for us to decide how fate twists us,' she says. 'At the end of it, all you can simply say is that what is done is done. We can only erase what hasn't been written yet.'

'Yes,' I say, recovering myself finally. I attempt a weak smile. 'You are right. I know that no matter what I do, I can never bring them back.'

40

The journey to Adam's school is miserable. It starts raining again, and there is an accident with a motorcyclist up in the road ahead. I peer out the window of the bus as paramedics tend to a leather-clad rider. He lies sprawled and immobile beneath his smashed bike.

Realising I'm not going to make it for pickup time, I tap out a reluctant text to Dan asking him if he can get Adam from school instead. I'd so hoped to be on time. My husband doesn't need to think I'm unreliable. I am managing; it's just that things keep coming up that aren't my fault.

I try to explain this in the text, but when I read it back, it sounds jumbled and might be construed incorrectly by my husband. If only we had the relationship we used to, it wouldn't be an issue. Now I feel like I have to change my behaviour so it seems like I'm coping just fine.

I can see how Dan might think I'm slipping into post-partum depression as I did before, but I'm not. I would have noticed.

I wish I could talk to my husband. I've wanted to tell him the truth so many times over the years. But I've never found the words and have been held back by the fear of what would happen if he ever found out.

His reply buzzes in my hand.

Don't worry. I'll take care of it xx

I lean my head on the cold window. It rattles my skull in a numbing sort of way. If only my thoughts were so easy to drown out. The truth has kept us apart for so long, I wonder if we could ever be close again, even if I told him everything.

But I don't dare. Adam is the only thing I have left now that both of my biological children have passed.

Deep down, I know it's selfish to cling onto Adam when his real mother is out there. Does she lie awake every night like I do and reflect upon what she has lost?

I joined her evening class to get close to her. I wanted to judge her well-being, her mental state.

I'm not sure what I have learned. Charlotte is a closed book, just like Adam. My guilt hasn't been allayed much. I've gleaned that she seems to have moved on with her life, but not much else.

I tell myself that the set-up we have now is for the best. Adam is free from the heartache of the truth. As far as he is concerned, he has a father. He would be distraught to learn that Dan and I are not his real parents.

We are the ones he has spent his whole life with. I'm the one who read him bedtime stories every evening, who cleaned his wounds when he fell over on the pavement; I was the one who waved him off on his first day of school. We were the only company we had during the endless night feeds when he was a baby. Does that not make me his mother?

As far as I'm concerned, Adam is my son. Dan and I are his family, and I'll never let him go. Especially not now he is the closest thing to a child I have left.

My heart aches for him when I slide my key into our cottage door after finally arriving home. The winter evenings are well and truly drawing in now, and the darkness outside is bleak and foreboding. It feels like a warm hug just to be back with my family after the day I've had.

As soon as I tear off my coat, wet shoes and socks, I move through to the living room. Adam is on the sofa, watching television. His bright blue eyes certainly aren't like Dan's dark ones and are so much richer in colour than my own. They are trained on the cartoon characters on the screen, and he doesn't even glance in my direction as I enter the room.

But I don't care. It just makes it easier to pull him into a hug.

'Mum!' he protests, shifting his head so his ears don't miss a second of cartoon dialogue.

'I'm sorry. I just missed you, that's all.'

He shrugs me off, still engrossed in his program. 'Then why didn't you come and pick me up from school?'

My heart aches. 'I was on my way, but there was an accident in the street. I wanted to be there. I bet you had a nice ride back in the car with Daddy though, didn't you?'

'No. Granny brought me home in her car. She said it was lucky she had the day off work. *Her* car has heated seats. It's so cool.' He turns to face me at last, eyes glazed from so much screen time. 'Why can't we have those in our car?'

I release my grip on his shoulders and glance around. 'I didn't realise your grandmother was here. Is she upstairs? Where's your father?'

'He's outside fixing a new car seat for Granny.'

'I didn't see her car outside.'

Adam shrugs. 'She had to park down the road. Some other car was blocking our driveway when we got back.'

'Why does Granny need a new car seat?'

'So she can bring me home from school. Dad said I can stay over at her house sometimes too. To give you a rest.'

I stand up abruptly. 'I don't need a rest. If your father hadn't insisted on taking you to school in the car this morning, then I would have been able to drive and pick you up myself today. There wouldn't have been a problem.'

'But Dad said it would be good if you had some time off.'

'Time off what?' I laugh in outrage. 'You're my little boy. I can look after you just fine.'

Adam shrugs and turns back to the television even though it's only adverts. 'Everyone at school sees their grandparents,' he mutters miserably. 'They get bought loads of stuff. They even have sleepovers.'

I sit down next to him and rub his back placatingly. 'Well, maybe they are harder to look after than you are. Maybe your friends' parents are struggling. But you're my sweet little angel, and I can look after you no problem.' I sigh. 'I'll be right back. And then I'll make you something special for dinner, OK?'

'Granny already ordered takeaway. She said I deserved a special treat after you didn't turn up to pick me up in time.'

'Did she now?'

I slip my still-crinkled toes into some dry walking boots and step outside. I draw my thin cardigan around myself and peer down the dark road from our driveway. I can make out Dan's back bent into a small Nissan. Julie hovers nearby, watching her son as he works on fitting the new car seat.

The conversation they are having as I approach comes to an abrupt end when they spot me.

'Hello, Alison,' Julie says stiffly as always. I wonder if she is harbouring any new resentment towards me after my and Dan's recent falling-out. 'How's your mother doing?' she asks me now. 'I hope her fall wasn't too serious?'

I open my mouth in surprise for a moment. 'No, it wasn't.

Well, she hit her head, but the nurse said she will be fine. She can go home tomorrow.'

Dan straightens up. 'Mum, why don't you go and wait with Adam? The food will arrive soon.'

'I suppose I should. It's freezing out here. You don't want to be caught outside in a thin outfit like that, Alison. Are you coming back inside too?'

I smile. 'In a minute.'

When she is out of earshot, I turn to Dan. 'What is she doing here?'

He shrugs as he adjusts the seat belt in the small car. 'I was busy at the restaurant, and I asked Mum to pick up Adam for me. It's no big deal.'

'Well, he could have gone to the after-school club if you had said something, and I would have got him later. I was on my way there, Dan. I just got caught up.'

'Yes, I heard.'

He sees the question on my face and answers it before I can form the words. 'I heard the message the hospital left on the home phone. I assume you went to go and see your mother, and that is why you were late?'

'I didn't realise they called the landline too.' Had I been so engrossed in my work this morning that I had missed it? What if it had been the school calling to say Adam had been involved in an accident? Or had gone missing again?

He shrugs again. 'Doesn't matter now. If your mum is OK, then it's worked out for the best. We got this seat this afternoon. So now she can help with school runs. She can take Adam off us now and then.' He glances at me with something I haven't seen in a long time. 'It would give us more time together. I think it would be good for us.'

I remember what happened the last time I let Adam into the company of the people I had deemed harmless, and give Dan a vague, 'Maybe.'

He sighs as he slams the car door shut and locks it. 'Alison, it's time for Adam to get to know his grandmother a little better, don't you think?'

'I think he is safest where we can keep an eye on him.'

I still haven't forgotten the little remarks Julie made when she first encountered Adam as a baby. Did she see the obvious? She may have even been what had fuelled Dan's doubts about his paternity in the first place. It must have been obvious to Julie, the woman who had handled Dan as an infant, that Adam shared no physical resemblance. It was then that I decided to keep grandparents at a safer distance.

'He isn't a delicate little baby anymore, Alison,' my husband goes on. 'There is no excuse now. And you got to see your mother today. Why shouldn't I see mine?'

'That wasn't a social visit. She was in hospital, Dan.'

He stares at me soberly with those deep brown eyes of his. They were part of what I'd fallen in love with years ago. But now they look at me, searching and critical.

'This isn't the first time you've slipped off somewhere, is it?'

'What do you mean?'

'I mean you go off somewhere sometimes. Alone. I don't know what you're up to, but sometimes you aren't where I think you are. I like to think you just go and see your mother, as we see her so rarely. I know you're so protective of Adam that you don't even like our own relatives near him, but I thought maybe you visited your mum by yourself sometimes?'

I stare at the spiderweb stretched across the wing mirror of Julie's car. The street light illuminates the moisture droplets on it. I can't tell Dan about my graveyard visits. I don't know the occasions he is speaking of, but I think he is probably talking about the time before we lost Dorothy. How could I tell him I had visited such a place? I used to visit our son's grave when I was pregnant with her.

Now that's where she has come to lie too. It's surely my fault. The combination of bad luck or karma has banded together to do this to our family. Ultimately I'm responsible, however. Would Dan see otherwise?

'Yes,' I lie. 'I've seen Mum a few times without you knowing.'

He nods. 'I thought so. Then you won't mind if we start seeing a bit more of my mother too. Just get used to it, Alison. She will be a bigger part of our lives from now on. It's a good thing though. I promise.'

41

Dan sets a plate of toast down beside my morning coffee. 'Eat this,' he says. 'I don't want you leaving the house again this week without breakfast. You need to take better care of yourself. It sets a good example if nothing else.'

'Thanks.' Chewing is difficult with a dry mouth. I'm due to meet Richard in Manchester today during his lunch break. The nerves are getting the better of me for some reason. It's not like I haven't met with clients before, but this time feels different. My stomach flutters uncomfortably because I'm hiding the fact from Dan after promising not to take on any more work.

It's not because Richard Neal is a particularly attractive, young headmaster. I couldn't resist trawling his online profiles. He can't be much older than I am. We have so much in common too.

Dan sits at the dining table next to Adam and eyes me critically. 'Are you sure you can't just take the day off today?' he asks. 'You look a little pale.'

'I've got a booking at lunchtime. I can't let them down. I'm honestly fine.'

'Are you still OK to pick up Adam later? I can see if Mum is free today.'

My hot drink scalds as I gulp it down too fast. 'No. Don't worry, I'll do it. I should have plenty of time.'

I feel guilty for the lie, but it isn't entirely untrue. I'll be over twenty miles further away than my husband thinks, but I've ensured that I will leave the meeting with enough time to spare.

When Adam is safely at school, I bring up the satnav app on my phone and input the postcode of the coffee shop Richard suggested. The place is at most a forty-minute drive away. I've been scrolling through the journey on my phone during the sleepless hours of the night. I could probably follow the right route without any help, but I leave the voice directions on anyway for some company. I find it helps calm my nerves, a distraction from my wrongdoing.

As I find a slot in the shadowy multistorey car park, I force myself to think of how beneficial this contract would be for my family.

I'm not running my photography business just for my own good. True, it gives me a sense of purpose and provides a distraction from everything else going on in my head. But it's my family who would benefit the most from the income it provides.

That's why I'm so determined to get a lucrative deal like the one on offer today. I'm confident I have a good chance of gaining this contract if Richard is as keen as he is in his emails. Although it surprises me that we haven't managed to come to an agreement yet via our messages, I'm hoping I'll walk away with a firm booking today.

I'm here far too early for our lunchtime meeting, but I decide to make the most of my trip to Manchester and spend an hour or two scouring the shops. A lot has changed since I was here last. Living in Rishworth is as far from big-city lights as it is possible to be.

Only now do I truly realise how much I have missed it here. Even the drive up brought back so many memories. When I used to work in the city, I'd been happy. I was a different person back then. Whole and full of promise for the future. Even when I'd discovered I'd fallen pregnant when Dan and I weren't trying, I still had hope we would build an amazing life for ourselves.

What happened after I'd had the baby changed everything. My life was in pieces. My return to work hadn't been the triumphant one I'd originally planned. I'd envisaged my colleagues in the office gushing over my new baby when I brought him in for a visit. I imagined they would like and share all the precious baby snaps I would upload online.

But all those ideas went out the window in the aftermath of the birth. The first year of Adam's life was the toughest of mine.

When I finally resumed my position in the office, things had gone wrong straight away. One of the girls in the office had asked me where Adam got his gorgeous eyes from. Maybe it was my lack of sleep, or the way I was out of sorts with city life, or the pressure of having to return to the real world after being away from everything I knew for so long, but I just flipped.

In hindsight, it had likely been an innocent remark. But I'd got into a silly argument over it at the time. Things had turned sour after that in the office. The other staff hadn't looked favourably upon me after witnessing my flare-up. They had taken the other woman's side instead. Members of her clique made sure I had plenty of unpleasant encounters etched into my memory before I'd felt compelled to leave.

I'd worked in that building for years and loved every

moment before the end. That job was my identity; I'd once been fulfilled and happy there. I knew I wouldn't find another job like it, as much as I tried. After yet another rejection letter from a vaguely similar position, I started seeking out ways to be my own boss. Running my latest business has made me feel like a success again. I would miss it terribly if I ever had to give that up too.

Christmas markets have sprung up in the city, and I take my time perusing them. I trail along New Cathedral Street and find scented lavender soap that I know Mum will love.

Once or twice, I find my attention being pulled from browsing the various handmade wares splayed out on the stalls in front of me. I glance around at the many faces nearby and am surprised to find they aren't facing in my direction as I had suspected. Men and women browse and examine the products on display just as I do, oblivious to what is around them.

I try to shake off my paranoia as my feet carry me to more market stalls along King Street, but I can't focus on what is on offer there.

Instead, I find myself looking around distractedly. I can't shake the feeling that someone is watching me. Nor can I find anyone who even so much as glances in my direction. I must be innocuous in my long winter coat and woolly hat, just like everyone else. There is no reason anyone here would pick me out of a crowd in a bustling street.

My feeling of unease takes all the fun out of the Christmas shopping I'd been planning on doing whilst I was here.

I still have almost an hour before I have to meet Richard, but my feet carry me in the general direction of the coffee shop he suggested anyway. I'm so close to where I used to work now that it seems almost petty not to stroll by and see the place again. The place is in a hub of so many other companies and office spaces that nobody could argue that I didn't have a valid reason for walking by.

The route along the river takes me right past the building. The water is as black and still as it always was.

If someone found their way below the murky surface, they wouldn't have a chance of getting out again before it was too late. The edges are steep, and there is nothing to get any real purchase on.

I slow my pace and peer through the uniform pattern of the steel fence, wondering how deep the water is. A dark-haired man with a large Just Eat bag eyes me as he walks past on his phone. Do I look like I'm contemplating jumping?

Just then, my old office building comes into view. The many glass-panelled windows reflect the cloudy sky above. I move forward to get a better view of the front entrance, but I resist the temptation to try to see my old workspace. It would probably look odd if I was spotted.

Just as I have the thought, I think I see a flash of movement and a figure behind one of the tall panes of glass I was looking at. I resume my walking pace and turn my face down into my scarf, supposedly against the wind. I shouldn't be here.

This place isn't a part of my life anymore.

42

I'm still too early for the meeting when I get to the coffee shop. I tell myself it's a good thing though, as I manage to secure a table near the window for Richard and myself before the lunchtime rush.

I settle myself down and get my laptop set up and ready with examples from the other school photos I took. I wanted to show off some of my other work too on my online portfolio, but I haven't managed to put one together since my website got hacked.

It bothers me that I can't display my work any better than this, but I tell myself that I've tried my best. *Haven't I?*

What if Richard is expecting something more elaborate? What if I don't look professional enough? He mentioned he is in touch with other photographers. I bet they are bigger companies too.

Now that I'm here in the cold light of day, my *best* doesn't seem good enough. Why haven't I taken the time to put together a better presentation? I could have done it last night instead of lying awake staring at the repetitive pattern of the dark bedroom curtains.

It's too late now though, I tell myself as I look at the time on my screen. It's quarter past twelve. Richard should be here any minute.

I look around expectantly. The shop is getting full now. The smell of food reminds me that I hardly ate anything at breakfast time. But I still can't eat. I'm too nervous.

I decide to pass the time by making a Facebook post mentioning I'm meeting with a client for a big job today. I try to keep my social media active. It makes the business seem busier and inspires other potential clients.

Dan doesn't check my social media. But I'll have to tell my husband about the job at some point if I get it anyway. Posting an update gives me the boost of confidence I so needed.

But it doesn't last long.

The minutes tick away, and my nerves grow. It's half past now, and I start wondering if I misunderstood Richard's message. Perhaps he meant his lunch break *starts* at quarter past? That would explain his absence.

Even so, now that I reflect on it, he would have a hard time getting through the traffic, park and be here in such a short space of time. What time was he planning on arriving?

Then again, he could have been caught up somewhere? Perhaps there has been an incident with a pupil; that would be an unexpected matter that needs addressing.

I check my phone, but there is nothing. It would have been nice if he had contacted me to say he would be running late.

But then, it wouldn't look professional if he called or texted in front of his students. These days, he probably spends much of his time telling the children off for doing such a thing.

A young couple on the other side of the room catch my attention. The woman catches my eye and quickly glances away, smirking at her partner, who takes a look over his shoulder too. He immediately receives a slap on the arm from his companion. She mutters something into her coffee, and I realise it must be obvious I'm due to meet someone who hasn't turned up.

I want to get up and explain to her there must be a valid explanation. There surely must be a ridiculously simple excuse for why I've been sitting here for over forty-five minutes alone, nursing the same lukewarm latte.

Mainly to avoid the looks the flustered waiting staff give me now and then, I engross myself in my laptop. The school's social media accounts might yield some announcements. Perhaps there has been an unexpected fire alarm or some other sort of emergency instead?

As I scroll through the tweets, I notice that the most recent one was posted just a few minutes ago. It's a shot of a handwritten thank-you letter from the manager of a local food bank to the school for their recent kind donations.

I zoom in on the picture and notice the backdrop is an expensive-looking walnut desk. The caption reads:

So proud of our pupils. Well done to everyone who handed something in. My staff also deserve a mention for making the class deliveries out of hours too!

These must be Richard's words. Why is he tweeting from his office when he is supposed to be meeting me? He's obviously forgotten all about our arrangement.

I hope the couple I still feel watching me can't see the colour now flushing to my cheeks. Richard didn't give me a contact number, as everything was arranged via email. I consider calling the main school office, but wonder how long it would take for the receptionists to get hold of the headmaster if he is busy elsewhere. So in the end, I feel I have no choice but to tap out a message on Facebook. When I hit send, I'm left to wonder how long it will be before Richard even receives it.

I tap back to the Facebook profile Richard used to initially contact me on. Now that I look at the account critically, I realise that it looks quite plain. There aren't any friends listed, and there is only one picture – the same one that is on the school website above all the other staff.

I now realise how odd it is that there aren't any posts in the timeline at all. At the time, I was so excited at receiving such a promising enquiry, I didn't look at Richard's profile itself. I learned everything I know about him from the school website. The lack of footprint on Facebook could simply be the headmaster's way of distancing himself personally from parents and pupils with endless questions and messages.

I simply googled Richard Neal and saw his other social media accounts. I visited the school website, imagining how great it would look on my client list to win the contract with such a high-profile institution.

Now that I'm looking at the profile with fresh eyes, I don't see much difference between this account and the one that sent me mysterious messages. Was this whole thing some-one's idea of a joke?

I look around me again at the faces nearby. None of them seem familiar. Many have come and gone in the time I have been sitting here too. I glance through the large glass-panelled windows to the street outside. Has someone been watching me from afar? I hardly so much as glanced outside this whole time. Anyone could have passed without me noticing.

I take another look at the Facebook post I put up earlier. The words are full of pride at the promise of such a wonderful contract. Now I see how stupid I've been and delete the post, hoping no one has seen it.

After another ten minutes without a response, I decide it's time for me to leave. I stand up to abandon my half-drunk coffee, and a waitress swoops on it before I've even pulled on my coat.

Outside, the streets are busier than ever. It must be lunchtime for a lot of people now, and I'm inadvertently in the crush too. Bodies push near me as I make my way down the street. Too close. For years now I've been unable to avoid noticing how gatherings of people bob about like they are bodies suspended in water. The mere thought makes me cold when I've spent so long picturing what happened to my baby in Portugal.

I didn't anticipate the streets being this busy. I didn't consider the droves of mindless Christmas shoppers combined with office staff rushing here and there. I was too caught up ensuring I didn't miss the too-good-to-be-true opportunity that had dropped into my lap.

It's now I realise my heels have blisters from the impractical boots I opted to wear with thoughts of making a good impression.

Crowds are one thing I don't miss about the city. I simply forgot as I looked back with a skewed view of how good life used to be.

My laptop bag feels so much heavier now I'm trudging back disappointed, dodging people coming the opposite direction. It makes me feel bulky as it bangs repeatedly against my thigh every other step. I start to sweat beneath my thick winter coat and scarf.

I shouldn't be here. This whole thing was a waste of time. And money. I consider what spontaneous treat I could have purchased for Adam with the money I spent on petrol and coffee.

I follow the route I believe leads back to the car park.

Much of this section of the city has been revitalised since I worked here. It feels as unfamiliar as a new place.

A flash of pale blonde hair up ahead makes me think of Charlotte. But then the woman is gone before I can scan her face. Visions of her haunt me recently, even though there is no logical reason for her to appear where I am. She remains oblivious to the truth.

A section of pavement takes me past another part of the black river. I feel unsteady on my feet as I stare down the drop to the murky water below.

I put out a hand to steady myself, but the diamond fence feels flimsy beneath my grip, and I once again imagine what it would feel like to plummet into the filthy water far below. The blood rushes in my head, and I wish I were anywhere but here.

People continue to pass me by. They bustle past hurriedly, all with purpose and somewhere to be. The sense that I'm being watched won't let me go.

Then a voice breaks through the sound of chatter and many footsteps.

'Ali?'

43

BEFORE

Isn't it funny how one little slip can nudge time backwards? Roles reverse. They transform in the blink of an eye.

My new set of keys slides easily into the lock, and I'm back again. For so long, I'd wanted to meet with less resistance upon entering this house. I never wanted it to be like this, however. The silence that now resides in this property will never leave me. It had been so bustling and full of fresh new life before. Now all is still.

I pick up the untouched post from the mat and shuffle through it. There is nothing of any importance to us anymore, so I drop it in a drawer out of the way with the rest.

In the kitchen, the dish of casserole I brought over yesterday remains untouched; it sits unrefrigerated and spoiled on the worktop. I scrape it out into the bin and look at the clock.

It's past 10 am. My daughter-in-law should be up by now. This is getting out of hand. I never allowed my son to sleep in this late. I stride into the bedroom and pull open the curtains.

'Rise and shine,' I say out loud. My sing-song voice is

quickly stifled by the oppression of the room. The air is still and stale. It makes my eyes water.

I sigh. When was the last time she bathed?

All of a sudden I've found myself in charge of a grown woman instead of a little boy, as I'm so used to. These past few months, I've been here more than my little flat. This house is now more of a home to me than the other place ever was.

I throw open a window and let in some fresh January air. The figure in the bed stirs, turns over and faces the other way, away from both me and the weak winter sunshine, which now falls in a neat strip across the foot of the bed.

She won't get away from me that easily. My son never wanted to be parted from his bed either. I pull back the covers now, just as I used to do with him. Waking my boy sometimes felt like dragging him from a grave.

She moans and pulls the other pillow across her head, burying herself deep within the fibres.

I turn my back to her and pull open the wardrobe doors. If I have to bathe and dress her myself, then so be it.

A plain jersey top in my favourite shade of yellow catches my eye along the rail of hanging clothes. I've never seen her wear it before, but this will do. Perhaps it's something from her life before motherhood? With her recent weight loss, she should have no problems fitting into it again.

I lay it on the mattress beside the prone figure and return to look for some accompanying bottoms. My eyes fall on the suitcase shoved carelessly in the bottom of the wardrobe.

The dark canvas bulges. Clearly, the case has been largely untouched since its return trip. Although, the zips have been parted roughly, as though some items were hastily pulled out at some point. I pull out the case, and the resulting vacuum causes belts, shoes and handbags to spill out and fill the void.

'That will keep us busy later.' A good clear-out will keep

us occupied nicely. Goodness knows my daughter-in-law's vanity has inspired too much hoarding. As if I had such a collection of nice things to adorn myself with when I was her age.

Unzipping the suitcase reveals there aren't any clothes in here. Just towels and toiletries. A bottle of colourful raspberry shower gel has leaked all over everything. It has long since dried, leaving red smears all over the neatly packed towels. I pull out a horribly stained bath sheet and find my breath forced from my body as though I have been punched.

At the bottom of the case lies a handful of unwrapped gifts. Birthday presents my grandson never had the chance to open. It would have been his birthday the day after he and my son perished.

My eyes sting painfully as they move on to the shiny blue paper I scoured the shops for months ago. Although it seems like much longer now.

Before I have the chance to think about it, my treacherous fingers peel the paper from the box; this action shouldn't have been mine to make.

The navy-blue box is printed with fine silver letters.

For you, Grandson.

I pull open the box, and I once again see the gift I put so much thought into. I chose something that he would be able to keep forever. Something so personal, it couldn't ever be given away or sold. I never imagined it would outlast my grandson by so much.

My fingers are once again unwelcome as I pull on the chain and pull the pristine silver compass from the box. He never even got to touch it. My vision becomes blurred as I read the words engraved inside the case.

Happy birthday to my dearest Jacob.
May you always follow your heart and find your way
home.

All my love, Granny xx

After months of fighting against it, a wail of misery finally escapes my mouth. I launch the compass against the wall, and I'm only vaguely aware as it falls back onto the dusty carpet. The glass face is cracked and broken.

My daughter-in-law has finally moved from her bed. I hear her voice, but I don't care now.

Nothing matters anymore.

44

'Ali? Are you OK?'

I spin around and have a shock when I see who is behind me. My mouth opens in surprise.

It takes me a moment to recognise the woman who comes into my view.

Rebecca.

This doesn't look like the mundane employee who turned up for work in my shop every day until recently. This Rebecca looks more like the one I saw at the exhibition evening. The one who laughed and joked and seemingly remained ignorant when someone defaced one of my works right under her nose.

Today, Rebecca wears her hair back in an immaculate ponytail. Her faded highlights have been coloured over. She is dressed in what must be her finest black trouser suit under a long navy coat, far removed from the T-shirt and puffa coat she turned up in when I hired her.

Now she looks over at my twisted pose with concern. 'Are you all right? You look flustered?'

'Fine.' I straighten my back and attempt a shrug. Part of

me is outraged she is talking to me as though nothing has happened, as though she hasn't disappeared from work without explanation. 'I just came to the city to do some Christmas shopping. You know how it is.'

She seems taken aback for some reason. 'Oh,' she says, looking at me in confusion. 'I thought you might be doing something work related?'

I stare back at her for a moment. 'No. I don't know why you would have that idea.'

'I don't know. I'm obviously mistaken.'

'Yes, you are.' My lip trembles despite myself. I don't want to break down in front of her again. I've made that mistake before. For all I know, she is the one who set up the fake meeting in the first place.

'Look, I feel like we should talk. Do you want to get a coffee?'

'No, thanks. I've already had one.'

She sighs. 'Please don't be like this. I mean, you have every right to be angry with me. But please don't be. I want to explain.'

'Maybe you can explain what you are doing here,' I say suddenly, realising how unlikely this meeting is. 'Why have we run into each other in a busy city neither of us live or work in?'

Rebecca looks down at the dirty pavement, looking miserable all of a sudden. 'I think I've blown things with you at the studio. You reposted the job ad, didn't you? I was at a recruitment agency looking for a new job. It's not far from here.'

'So you haven't followed me here?'

She looks at me in alarm and shakes her head earnestly. 'No. I honestly was at a recruitment agency just around the corner. Then I saw you as I was leaving. It was a coincidence. I care about you, Ali. And the business too.'

'If you cared about the business, you wouldn't have

stopped turning up for work without even an attempt at an explanation. Where have you been?'

Rebecca hesitates and bites her lip. I consider the fact that she may be about to lie to me. She doesn't know what to tell me, in any case.

'Well, forget it,' I say, deciding not to give her a chance to reel me into whatever she is planning. 'I've got to go.'

'Wait!' she says as I turn to leave. There is something like desperation in her eyes now. 'I didn't mean for any of this to happen. I just ... things just got on top of me. You must understand how it is.'

'What could you possibly have to deal with? You don't have a partner or any children to worry about. Or maybe you have. Everything you've told me has been a lie.'

She looks genuinely hurt. If there is one thing to be said for Rebecca, it's that she is a good actress. 'No, it hasn't. I've tried to be honest with you, Alison.'

'Really? Because I went to the address you told me you lived at, and the people who live there had never heard of you.'

Even Rebecca can't hide the flash of alarm that crosses her eyes. 'Oh.'

'Yes, that's what I thought. Honestly, I don't know what to think anymore. Nothing about you has been real. You've pretended to be my friend whilst doing goodness knows what. You were there at the exhibition when one of my photographs was destroyed. Then you pretended to have no idea who had done it–'

'I wasn't pretending. I had nothing to do with that.'

'Then the electric board at the shop had water poured into it. You knew exactly where it was and how it could have been sabotaged. I must have looked like a right idiot when I was sitting there wondering how it had happened. Then Adam got food poisoning after I'd left him with you. And there was the note stuffed into his bag that night. Of course, there was the fire that was started at his birthday party too. It could have burned the house down.'

She shakes her head, a flush appearing in the bit of neck showing above her neat white collar. 'I told you the fire was an accident. I must not have extinguished the match properly like I thought I had. I was mortified, I told you. You can't seriously think any of the rest was me? Is that what you've been thinking?'

'Oh no, of course not. All of it just happened to occur when you were around or nearby. You had access to everything that went wrong. Then you just disappear without a trace. When I try to find you, it turns out you gave me a fake address and telephone number.'

She shakes her head. 'It wasn't fake. It was just old. That number was from when I *did* live at that address.'

'Nice try, but the couple who live in that house said they've lived there for years.'

'Couple?' Rebecca's eyes look watery all of a sudden. 'What did the woman look like?'

I shrug. 'I don't know. She didn't have a specific look. She had a sort of wide face and a chunky gold chain around her neck. Mainly she had a blank expression on her face when I asked about you. Does it matter?'

She smiles sadly. 'I didn't realise he was living with her now.'

'Who?'

'My ex-boyfriend, Alex. His parents left him that house. If you went there, then that was who you saw if he said he's lived there for years. It used to be my home too. Until he kicked me out when I found out he was cheating with that ... well, with her.'

'You expect me to believe that?'

'You should do. It's the truth.'

'Then why didn't you change the address on your CV?'

She shrugs. 'It was a nice neighbourhood for applying for work. I loved living there until it all turned sour. But I found it got a better response when I applied for jobs than using an ex-council flat address.'

I stare at her for a moment. 'That wouldn't have bothered me.'

'Wouldn't it? You said yourself what a nice house I lived in. You were impressed, admit it.'

I shrug sheepishly. 'You should have told me the truth. It wouldn't have mattered to me. I thought we were friends.'

'We are.'

I avoid her eyes and stare instead at a piece of greying chewing gum attached to the smooth pavement. 'Then how do you explain all the other things that have happened when you've been around? Like when I caught you touching the baby's things. And then I find some of it is missing.'

'I don't know.' She looks at me imploringly with her sparkling blue eyes. 'But I promise you it wasn't me.'

'What about that night at the adult learning centre? I caught you there when I shouldn't have. Then you disappeared. Why go off when you were telling the truth?'

She closes her eyes and takes a deep breath. 'Because I wasn't telling the truth about why I was there. I swear I haven't done anything bad to you behind your back. But I made up the reason for being there that night. I hadn't come out of a pottery class.'

'Why did you lie about it, then?'

'I didn't know how to tell you the truth.'

'Which is?'

'I was at a group therapy session.'

I think of the classroom I saw at the Lakeside centre with the circle of chairs. 'What's wrong with that?'

'Nothing, but I knew it would lead to further questions

that I didn't want to answer. You're the best friend I've had for ages. I just didn't know if I was ready to talk about it still.'

'Talk about what?'

She glances around at the bustling pedestrians before answering, but they act as though we are invisible. 'A few years ago – I was attacked. One night when I was coming home late from the off-licence I used to work at. Some guy jumped me as I was on my way to the bus stop. He must have been watching me for a while because it happened so quickly, as soon as I stepped into a quiet street. And well, what happened next wasn't very nice. This is the first time I've spoken about it to anyone.'

'What about your sister?'

'She doesn't know. Alex knew, but he blamed me. He acted as though I were cheating on him. He didn't understand. I don't think it was long after that he found someone else and started cheating on me. I know I'm better off without him in the long run. Without him, I've had more spare time. That led me to start taking martial arts classes, which has been good for me. They have taught me how strong I can be – physically, at least. But what happened with Alex still hurts, especially now I know he stuck with her, from what you said.'

'That's terrible.'

'Anyway, that's what I couldn't tell you before. I didn't know how to find the words. I'm so sorry, Ali. I've let you down. I don't blame you for firing me. I just thought I was going to have to explain everything like I had with Alex. He reacted so badly when I hadn't expected him to. I didn't know what you would think of me. I just dreaded having to explain myself. It's brought it all back, the memories. I've just been hiding in the flat the whole time. Until today. I'm running out of money, and you'd already announced that you were looking for someone else.'

'Rebecca, I'm sorry. I never would have done that if I'd

known … I would have understood. I just wish you'd come to me. You can talk to me about anything, you know. I'm your friend.'

She nods. 'Thank you. It means so much that you know.' She dabs at her eyes gingerly with the back of her hand to keep her mascara intact. 'Look, I don't know why all those other things have happened to you. But if you thought it was me, then maybe you need to be careful – because it wasn't – I promise. I would never do you any harm. But it sounds like someone else might.'

45

I t feels so good to be busy in the kitchen. I'm relied upon now in this house when once I was barely allowed over the threshold. I know if I weren't here to cook lunch, my daughter-in-law wouldn't eat properly at all.

The pan comes to a boil just as I drop in some bow-tie pasta, but I skip the salt. I'm all too aware of how harmful it is for toddlers to consume too much sodium.

A knife slides easily into the butternut squash I remove from the oven. It gets chopped up and dropped into the blender with the cheese sauce.

But when I turn the dial to blitz the mixture, nothing happens. The time is absent from the microwave too when I glance around. We must have had a power cut. How annoying in the middle of cooking.

A rumble on the stairs announces the arrival of my daughter-in-law. She appears in the doorway, her hair sodden. Beads of moisture run down her bare shoulders and legs. *I'll have to get the mop out,* I think to myself.

She looks around, agitated, and flips the light switch to no avail. 'What's happened?'

She looks at me, confused. 'Everything just went off when I was in the shower.'

'Power cut,' I tell her.

She stares absent-mindedly at the drips she is causing on my white kitchen tiles. I can almost see the long-dormant cogs whirring to life once again in her head. She moves a hand to her forehead and closes her eyes.

'My bank account,' she says. 'The money must have run out by now. All the bills are via direct debit in my account. I should have kept on top of it ...' Her eyes open again, and she looks around the room as though seeing it for the first time. 'It's so strange that the power company didn't send a reminder though.'

'Oh, I think they might have sent something like that,' I say.

Her gaze snaps in my direction. 'What? When?'

'Oh, they've been bombarding us for months with their nonsense. With not a thought as to what we might be going through!'

I look over her wet form covered only by a hastily wrapped towel. 'Are you going to put some clothes on? I never would have allowed your husband to turn up to lunch naked, I'll ask the same of you if you don't mind? You'll like what I've made today. I found a way to add some hidden veggies into the pasta.'

She stares at me with her mouth open as if I have sworn at her. I've always hated her attitude towards me. It's disappointing to see it re-emerge now. We've been getting along so well for a while.

'What are you talking about?' she says.

'You're always complaining what a fussy eater Jacob is. But he likes pasta. This dish seemed like the perfect thing for him.' I gesture to the various pots and pans dotted around the kitchen when she continues to look blank.

She is quiet for a few moments before she speaks again, watching me closely. 'You threw the bills away. What did you think was going to happen if they were ignored?'

I sigh, returning to the food. 'Don't be ridiculous. All your post is in the drawer there.' I gesture, jabbing a knife in the general direction.

I pour the contents of the blender cup into a bowl and find a fork to start mashing. This will take some elbow grease. Jacob hates lumps in his food. It needs to be silky smooth.

My daughter-in-law pulls open the drawer beside me. Envelopes spill out onto the tiles below her feet as she does so. She swears.

'I won't tolerate that kind of language under my roof, I say. Now go upstairs and put on some clothes.'

I look around to find her staring at me again. 'What is it now?' I ask her.

She pulls the towel around her more tightly, watching me intently. 'I noticed a lot of my things are missing upstairs. I can't find a lot of my clothes. Where are they?'

'These are family cottages,' I say, picking up the knife again and chopping some cucumber sticks. 'There isn't the space for clinging onto unnecessary things.'

'Unnecessary?'

'You had those clothes you used to wear to work. You won't need those anymore since you lost your job.'

Her eyes return to the faint pattern of the tiles.

'And then there were all those heavy bottles of perfume and bags of cosmetics,' I go on. 'You haven't used those for a while. And how many pairs of high heels do you think you need? I didn't own a single pair when I was raising my boy. There just wasn't space for it all. You know that. It's much better in here with the extra space.'

'How dare you. You've got no right to go through my things and throw them away!'

I turn away from the chopping board to her. She eyes the knife in my hand warily.

I sigh impatiently. 'I didn't throw them away. I took them to the charity shop for you. Took me two or three trips, it did. And you were there. We had a clear-out together, remember?'

'No, I don't remember that.'

'Well, that's because you wouldn't leave that lazy bed of yours. I had to do the work myself.'

'Get out,' she says abruptly.

'What?'

'Please leave.' She moves to the hallway and pulls open the front door, standing behind it to shield her wet form against the cool spring air.

She turns to me when I don't move. 'Leave this house and do not come back.'

46

'That sounds creepy,' Rebecca says, staring out at the road ahead of us. 'Isn't there any chance this Richard guy didn't just get the time or day wrong?'

'No. I checked the emails he sent loads of times. He was pretty clear. He doesn't sound like the kind of person to get mixed up. I mean, he is in charge of an entire school, a good one too. Now that I've had the chance to think about it, I've realised the whole thing was set up.'

Rebecca is quiet for a moment, and when I glance from the motorway ahead of us back to her, I realise she is staring at me. 'I know you don't believe me. You think I'm being paranoid. Thanks for not saying it though.'

She smiles weakly. 'No, I believe you. I don't think you imagined any of these things happening. I just can't figure out who it might be. You're so nice. Why would someone go to all this trouble to get at you? I mean, what are they gaining by it?'

I smile back at her. It's hard to tell whether she is simply trying to humour me, as she is only very recently back in my good books. Or could she be right about someone wanting to harm me?

'I don't know. I've tried to figure it all out this whole time. It just makes me tired.'

She throws me a sharp look. 'You do look tired. Have you been sleeping any better?'

Her words throw me back to the threatening message I received on Facebook. But I believe it wasn't Rebecca who sent those messages now. How could I ever have suspected her? 'No. Dan wants me to wind the business down.'

'But you've worked so hard.'

'I know. The business is going better than I ever expected.'

'But Dan wants you to let it all go? It sounds like what you said was written on your website.'

Dread bubbles in my stomach. 'I've been thinking the same thing. But he wouldn't do it. He just wouldn't.'

'Are you sure? He might not think he is doing anything bad. Maybe it's just his way of getting you to work less, just like he said?'

'No. It's not his style. I know him. We've been together for years.'

'So you think he couldn't be keeping things from you? Alex kept things from me. It was ages before I found out what he was doing behind my back.'

I think about the devastating things I've been hiding from my husband and hope that he has treated me with far more respect.

'I heard you two had a row,' Rebecca says.

I glance at her sharply. 'How did you hear that?' I think of Julie. I've never thought of her as a gossip, but she does have a prominent position in the local council. Could she have spread my and Dan's private business through her workplace? Perhaps she was more shocked than I thought to find her son on her doorstep after our falling-out?

'My sister,' Rebecca says simply. 'One of her neighbour's children goes to Rishworth Primary, same as Adam. She heard at the school gates that you kicked your husband out one night after an argument.'

My mouth drops open in shock. 'How could someone know that?'

Rebecca shifts in her seat. 'I think that Helen woman was spreading it around. She was gleeful about it, apparently. She sounds like a real nightmare. Someone needs to teach her not to shout her mouth off.'

'But I don't understand. How did Helen find out that Dan spent the night at his mother's house?'

Rebecca looks at me, puzzled. 'Oh. I thought Dan spent that night at Helen's house. That's what my sister heard, anyway.'

My white fingers grip the steering wheel hard. A horrible sinking feeling creeps over my shoulders. Dan didn't say where he spent the night. He didn't say a word about that night at all. I simply assumed he went to Julie's house. And he didn't correct me. How stupid have I been?

'He didn't tell me,' I say, struggling with the connotations of this new piece of information.

Rebecca puts a firm hand on my arm and squeezes. Her grip is strong, almost painfully so. But I know she is just being supportive, and I'd rather not be without it right now.

'I'm so glad you are here,' I say to her.

'Me too. Everything will be all right now I'm back.'

47

Rebecca steps out of the Christmas set after sprinkling another packet of iridescent confetti over the scene. 'I'm so glad you're giving me a second chance, Ali. I've missed being here so much. I wanted to come back but didn't know how. I don't know what I would have done without you.'

'That's OK.' I smile. 'What do you mean anyway?'

'It didn't exactly go well at the recruitment agency. I have experience, but I'm not qualified to do anything other than shop work. And most places already have their Christmas staff sorted. In the second place I tried, the woman took one look at my address, and that was it. It turns out she used to live in Rishworth herself and knew the area. She was a right snooty cow. Talk about bad luck that I had to run into her. I thought Manchester was far enough away from here not to bump into anyone.'

'I know the feeling.' I smile.

She laughs. 'Yes, small world, isn't it?'

'Seriously though, the place I used to work at wasn't far

from where we saw each other the other day. You might have even passed it yourself.'

'Maybe. You don't mean that swanky glass skyscraper full of offices, do you? The one near the river?'

'Yes, that's the one.'

'Wow. I can't imagine leaving a job like that if I could get one. You're so brave.'

'Not exactly. I guess I haven't been entirely honest with you either about the past. I told you I left that job to work for myself. The truth is, I got pressured into leaving by the other people who worked there.'

'Oh no. I hate people who do that. What happened?'

I fiddle with the pen on my desk nervously. I've never talked about this with anyone other than Dan. 'I had a sort of breakdown. It was after Adam was born. I guess I had some kind of postpartum depression or something. It spiralled out of control. One of my colleagues set me off one day, and it got ugly. I didn't stay long after that.'

'That's horrible. Didn't you get any help for it?'

I shake my head. 'No. I got a little worse after I lost my job. It meant everything to me. So I started trying out different ways to earn money instead. It wasn't easy, as the job had paid well. We struggled when it was only Dan's income. That's why this place was so important to me. And that's why I can't give it up.'

'Even though Dan thinks you're working too hard?'

'He worries too much. I can understand what I was like before when I wasn't thinking straight. I would know if it was happening again. I know what to look out for.'

'You really are brave, you know.'

I laugh, embarrassed. 'Stop saying that.'

A wild thought strikes me now that I have confided one of my secrets. How about I share another one? I teeter on the edge of the decision for a moment before I come to my senses. I stand up abruptly and bustle about making coffee for us. I'm grateful to have Rebecca back; I can't push it. Nor can I ever tell anyone what I have done.

Ever.

Rebecca's familiar fragrance wafts around me as she approaches. She opens up a packet of custard creams and puts some onto a plate for us. 'So, can I ask what happened with Dan? Did you ask him about the night he spent with Helen?'

'No. I tried to bring it up a few times over the last few days, but I just can't do it. We have argued before. But we're in a good place now. I trust him.'

'Oh.'

'I know you think I shouldn't, but I just can't bring myself to start another argument. I have Adam to think of. If he weren't around, then I would have confronted Dan right away. It's different when you have children, you know. I can't explain it if you're not a mother.'

Rebecca's voice drops so quickly it scares me a little, and I look at her. 'I almost was,' she says quietly. 'I was pregnant when I was with Alex. Then, when I was attacked that night … I lost the baby.'

'I'm so sorry.'

'I'm better now. At the time I was a mess. Alex didn't go to the hospital with me. He had been out drinking with his friends. He was out of it.'

It's unusual to see Rebecca unhappy.

I put my arm around her slumped shoulders. 'Is that why you were upset when we did that school shoot?'

She nods. 'The baby was something else that was stolen from me that night. I got some of my confidence back when I started my group therapy sessions and even more so when I started taking martial arts classes. But nothing I ever do will bring my baby back. I was going to have a little girl too.'

ANOTHER PROMISING ENQUIRY comes in just before lunch.
Rebecca takes charge of the call, and I decide to let her. She
has turned out to be right about every other decision. I know
I need to relax and trust her more. And besides, she insists on
handling it, so I make the lunch run for us both. I brave the
November chill as I venture up towards the high street
bakery.

I select a new sandwich flavour I know she will like, and I
order her favourite chocolate fudge cookie for both of us.

I'm talked into a meal deal and have to wait for the atten-
dant to produce two hot chocolates. I stand to the side to let
the other member of staff process the rest of the queue that
has built up behind me.

As I do, I realise two women near the end of the line are
both staring straight at me. One mutters something under
her breath and looks away, but the other remains with her
gormless gaze fixed on me, unmoving.

I try to focus on watching the drinks being poured as the
member of staff opens up the machine to refill the cocoa
mixture. But when I glance back again, the woman is still
staring at me as though I am a television.

Anger bubbles at my insides. *What's her problem?*

'Excuse me?'

I glance over my shoulder and realise the young man
serving me is waiting impatiently with the card reader
outstretched.

'Oh, sorry,' I say as I tap my card on the machine. 'I must
have been miles away.'

I collect the food and drinks awkwardly and move to the
back of the shop. I'm almost at the threshold, but I'm
painfully aware of both women watching me as I leave.

I know I shouldn't say anything. I know I should leave,

but I can't help but turn back to them and meet their stares. 'Is there a problem?' I ask abruptly.

The woman who had looked away before does so again, moving forward in the queue, apparently trying to decide on a sandwich from the display refrigerator.

The other one's face, however, is pulled into a horrible sort of smirk that infuriates me. She obviously finds something amusing.

'What's so funny?' I ask her as the heat rises in my neck and cheeks.

She does nothing but stare back as though my growing fury is entertainment to her. Her friend nudges her on the shoulder, and she finally faces the counter too. I'm about to say something else, but I catch the elderly man behind the women eyeing me nervously, and I think better of it.

Once I leave the shop, I realise the women may not be strangers after all. Now that I think about it, I've seen their faces vaguely before – outside the school gates.

It doesn't take much imagination to figure out what they'd been talking about before I caught them staring. This is all Dan and Helen's doing.

I'm suddenly aware that my fingers feel greasy. I look down and notice that, in my anger, the bag with the cookies inside has been crushed.

After dropping the bag in the bin, I stand out in the cold at the end of Mill Street and breathe deeply. It is a good few minutes before I feel calm enough to return to the shop.

48

I used to have nightmares. Just like everyone else, I suppose. Now when I wake up, I can't say it was all just a dream.

My consciousness has been dragged from the same place as always. The sun was glorious and bright, but the horror was real. Now that I'm awake, there is no way what happened could ever be blown away by a blissfully warm wind drifting up along the Algarve.

I glance at the clock. It's still only 4 am. What could have woken me at this hour? It can't have been long since I finally drifted off after worrying about the situation with Dan. I hate to be the one to rock the boat, but Rebecca tells me I'm being too lenient by not confronting him. Not that she knows the full truth.

I roll over gently and stare at the back of his head. His sleeping form is so peaceful. It's hard to imagine that he has been so duplicitous. Why wouldn't he have told me where he spent the night? Did he conceal the truth because he was staying with an old friend and there was nothing to tell? Or is it because something happened that he can't confess?

The worst thing is that Helen will have gone out of her way to tell everyone she can about the incident. Even if there was nothing to tell, she will have made something out of it and left the imagination of others to run riot. She has always been the same.

I remember some of the rumours she started about a new girl in secondary school, and my stomach runs cold. I'm sure none of it was true, but by the end of the term, Helen had spread so many lies about the girl that she broke down one horrible afternoon in an English presentation.

She ran out crying to the chorus of laughter. After that, I never saw the girl again. I heard she transferred to a school in Manchester. But then again, it was Helen who told me that. In reality, the girl could have gone anywhere or done anything. I just like to think that she didn't hold me partly responsible, as I was Helen's friend.

I pick up my phone and, in the usual dance of my fingertips, check my emails and Facebook account.

There are no new messages. I suppose that's a good thing. It just proves that whoever set up that meeting in Manchester wasn't Richard Neal. I have no idea who it was though, which disconcerts me more. Was Helen behind everything? Maybe I haven't given her enough credit, but she was never that clever. She must have changed. Have the years as a lonely single mother transformed her enough to be so devious?

My throat is dry, so I carefully creep from the bed with thoughts of a drink. My feet now automatically follow the quietest route from the room, avoiding the most worn floorboards that might disturb Dan's sleep. Downstairs, I shut the kitchen door, flip on the light and run a glass of water. My eyes sting as the cold liquid runs down my throat.

I peer through the kitchen blinds; the low temperature has coated our dark car in frost. Inside, the kitchen tiles are threatening to make my feet numb.

The red digits on the microwave burn in the darkness. It's almost five now. I'm wide awake. My nerves tingle. I keep looking around me nervously, as though something is off in the periphery of my vision.

Then something happens that makes me freeze, my numb feet firmly planted on the tiles. A faint sound reaches my ears.

I listen, straining hard. My head moves this way and that, trying to detect the source of the sound.

It stops. Then a few moments later, it starts again.

At the bottom of the stairs, I realise the intermittent noise isn't coming from the ground floor.

My heart hammers in my throat as I head upstairs and come to a stop outside Adam's bedroom door. The sound is coming from inside his room.

I push the door open and look towards the bed. Adam is sleeping peacefully. His breathing is slow; the sound definitely came from here though. I crouch beside him and check, just as I did when he was a tiny baby. It's a good thing he is such a heavy sleeper. I just wish I were more like him.

I stand up. All is still and silent again now I'm in here.

As I turn to leave, an eruption of noise causes me to stop with my fingers on the door handle. The sound is eerie and ethereal, and it takes me a few moments to realise where it is coming from.

Adam's nightstand. The walkie-talkie I haven't got around to confiscating is making bizarre noises.

I snatch it up. My cold fingers fumble blindly in the dark with the buttons, trying to shut the thing up. I haven't found the off switch, but something I've pressed brings the sound of the handset to an abrupt halt.

The silence lasts for a few moments; then I think I hear something else. Movement of some unknown person coming through the handset. Then through the static, I hear it. Whispering.

'*Jacob.*'

49

A horn blares behind me as I pull into my usual spot on the bungalow-lined street near the school.

A man in a sharp suit glares at me angrily through the window as he pulls past my Fiesta in his Range Rover. I'm bewildered for a second and wonder why he is staring at me. Then I realise I didn't indicate before slowing down in front of him.

I move to raise my hand in an apologetic gesture, but the glossy caramel tint of his vehicle has already disappeared around the corner.

I'm so exhausted, I feel as though I am moving around in a daze. As though the barrier between dreaming and consciousness has finally dissolved completely.

Crossing the road with Adam, I scan every face we pass. It's not my imagination now. I see many look back at me for more than just a brief moment.

And there is whispering now that their attention has been turned in my direction thanks to Helen and Dan. Any one of the staring faces could be the voice I heard in the night. It was so distorted, it would be tough to place. In the same way, I could easily have misheard what was said. My mind was playing tricks and filling in the gaps in the low-quality sound. Anyone with a handset on the default channel could have been on the other end of the walkie-talkie.

My hand remains firmly on Adam's shoulder as we get to the gates. The only other place where Adam is safe.

He sees me coming in for a kiss and a cuddle before we part, and manages to dodge me. He steps quickly over the threshold to the playground and leaves my empty arms wanting.

I hear a stifled laugh behind me and turn to see one of the mothers I encountered in the bakery in town, the one who stared relentlessly. Her little girl releases herself more casually from her mother's arms as she slips inside the safety of the gates too.

She looks up and catches my eye. 'Always desperate to get away, yours, isn't he?'

'No.' It sounds abrupt, but I wasn't expecting someone to talk to me directly. Especially not her. 'He's just a boy. That's what they do, I suppose.'

'I wouldn't know. I can't imagine having boys.' Her murky round eyes are fixed on me as she talks.

'I only have the one,' I say firmly.

'Yeah?' She shrugs. 'I didn't ask.'

'No, but you were staring. I think you should mind your own business.'

Her face takes on the ugly look she had worn a few days ago. Somewhere between a smirk and disgust. 'I think you should watch what you're saying, if you ask me.'

'I'm not the one going around staring at people when I should be minding my own business. How dare you.'

She is quick to retort, raising her deep voice so that other parents and their children turn around. 'How dare *you*, you mean! Don't talk to me like that. I can look at who I want, thanks!'

'Mum, what's happening?'

I glance through the diamond fence and see that Adam has come back over to investigate the sound of raised voices. The woman's daughter appears behind him, looking between us adults, wide-eyed and tentative.

Both children are moved along and away from the fence by Mrs Turner, the teaching assistant from Adam's class. Adam throws inquisitive glances at me over his shoulder as he shuffles away.

Mrs Turner snaps her head in our direction. 'Is there a problem here?'

The other woman shrugs, puts her hands inside her pockets and slinks away.

Mrs Turner's sharp features scrutinise me from behind her glasses. 'I don't take kindly to squabbling in the school playground. I would expect parents to know better, Mrs Burnham.'

'It wasn't me. I was just ...' The other mother has disappeared, I realise as I look around. Now only a handful of parents remain as the bell rings and the children start to filter into the school building. Their eyes keep flicking in my direction.

I sigh. 'There isn't a problem. It won't happen again.'

She nods sharply. 'That's right it won't. How can you expect children to behave themselves when the parents set such an example?'

My mouth opens in surprise. 'You're not talking about Adam? He's so well-behaved.'

'He is a model pupil. I couldn't ask better of him. I'm just worried that things aren't ideal at home. He tells me it upsets him when his parents have arguments.'

'What? When did he say that? We don't argue.'

She raises her thin eyebrows at me.

'Well, we do sometimes disagree about things,' I admit. The heat rises in my cheeks and I realise what it feels like to be one of the children under her care. 'Everyone does.'

'Be that as it may, I don't appreciate it when domestic issues spill over into the school environment.'

I realise she is talking about the situation with Helen and Dan. Now it's affecting Adam, which is the last thing I wanted. Even Mrs Turner has heard the rumours; it's safe to assume Mrs Evans also knows. Perhaps they discuss these matters over coffee at break time?

Anger bubbles inside me. Is there anyone in this town who doesn't know my business?

50

I'm due at the shop to open up, but I send Rebecca a text and ask her to do it whilst I run an errand. She has her own set of keys now, and she texts back promptly to let me know she is happy to open up. At least there is one person I can rely on.

The lack of sleep is exhausting me. The day is dull and dark, which doesn't help. My reactions are slow as I drive.

The clips of a supermarket delivery lorry fly about beside me ominously in the wind as I pass. It makes me wonder what would happen if the gale that is whipping up tipped the whole thing over onto my little car.

The restaurant car park is busy as I pull into it. Inside the detached building, I'm pounced upon by the head of house. He asks me if I'll be joined by anyone else.

'I'm sorry,' I say. 'I don't want a table. My husband is a chef here. I need to speak to him.'

The man's stubbled face sinks, and he drops his overly polite air at once. 'It's Dan you're looking for, is it?'

'Yes, that's right.'

'He's not on the breakfast shift today. He won't be here until lunchtime.'

'Yes, he is. He told me. He's been on the morning shift this week.'

'No, it's Will on breakfast today. Has been all week.'

'That can't be right,' I say quietly as I scan my memories to check it's not me who is at fault. But I distinctly remember Dan leaving in his uniform this morning. The image is clear in my mind.

I read the name tag of the head of house: Nigel. This is whom Dan complains about, or rather, it was. I realise he hasn't spoken to me about work for a while, or about anything in fact.

Nigel sighs impatiently as he gathers menus together and drops them on the front desk beside us. 'Look, why don't you just call his mobile and find out where he is?'

'He should be here.'

He turns his palms upwards and looks at me, exasperated. 'I can't help you. I promise I'm not hiding him under a table. I think I can be trusted to know the staff rota in my own place.'

He looks past me to a young family walking in with screaming children. Nigel's face takes on the same fixed smile he initially greeted me with, and I have no choice but to leave again.

A hailstorm beats down upon me as I dash back to the car. The wind drives it painfully against my cheek and forehead, and I sit shivering in my Fiesta for a few minutes whilst I try to get my thoughts organised.

Dan specifically mentioned being on the breakfast shift. He is a bad liar, always was. Only it used to be about his whereabouts just before my birthday or our anniversary and he wanted to conceal the surprises he'd been planning. I know that isn't the case this time around, however.

If I weren't so preoccupied myself, I would have noticed.

Dan has taken advantage of the fact. Why has he been lying to me?

The image of Helen's broad, smug face swims before my eyes. The way she laughed at Dan's jokes at the birthday party can't be dispelled from my mind. Nor can the way she walked gleefully down the street beside Dan when they went out afterwards.

My hands shake with fury and shock as I call his phone. There is no answer on the first try. He can't be driving, as I've got our car. There is no excuse at all for him not to pick up.

Rage boils inside me as I try again. And again.

On the third attempt, he answers, just when I'm about to conclude he will keep ignoring me.

'Hello?' His voice is tentative.

'We need to talk.' I try to keep my own voice neutral but fail. 'Where are you?'

'I'm at work right now. Can't it wait until later?'

I stare straight ahead as my eyes fill with tears. I knew Dan and I were over long ago. But I wasn't prepared for everything to come to an end in one definitive moment. Especially with everything else going on. Not when I need my husband the most.

'You're not at work, Dan,' I say. 'I've just been in there. I'm sitting in the car park after Nigel has told me you're not on this morning. Nor have you been there all week.'

He sighs. 'You shouldn't have done that.'

'No?' I hear the waver in my words now. 'Why is that? You seem to have somewhere better to be if you lied about being at work.'

'Look, I didn't want you to find out like this.'

'Find out what?' Tears flow freely down my cold cheeks. Rebecca was right – I should have been suspicious of Helen after all. The thought brings me no satisfaction. I was a fool to ever think better of the man I've spent most of my adult life with. This is surreal. Dan and I are actually having this conversation.

'You're right,' he says. 'We do need to talk. Are you still at the restaurant? Wait for me there. I'm coming over.'

'Why can't you just tell me what you have been up to all this time now? I can't believe this. I've been running myself ragged trying to provide for our family whilst you've been doing goodness knows what!'

'It's not like that. Let's talk about this.'

'Don't bother trying to lie to me. I know the truth. Everyone does – even Adam's teachers! I know you spent the night with Helen after our argument. Will you deny it?'

'It wasn't like that!'

'Sure it wasn't! I've had to deal with everyone staring and talking about me all over town because of you. I've had enough, Dan. This was a long time coming and you know it!'

'Alison – I need you to listen to me for a minute.' There is clear desperation in his voice now. And something else in the background – a woman's voice. I immediately think of Helen.

'Don't bother.' I end the call and immediately bring the engine to life. I want to get out of here before Dan arrives. He won't be allowed to talk me around. I know what he has done now.

The headlights gleam brightly upon the sodden bricks of the restaurant.

I've been hiding so much from him for so many years. Did I think he wouldn't do the same to me eventually? I can't help but wonder what else Dan could have done behind my back.

Hailstones crunch and slip under my tyres as I pull away from the car park and back onto the road.

51

How did I ever think being forced from my daughter-in-law's care was a bad thing? Being ejected unceremoniously from the home of my son and grandson was hurtful, I must admit. It had been an unexpected jolt. Shocks like that make me remember what really happened, and I don't like that. The only way anyone can make it through life is fooling themselves into thinking that everything will be OK; I'm not any different. If Little Miss Perfect thinks keeping me out of the family home will stop me from being with them, then she has another think coming.

I told her so via several texts. She still hasn't responded to any of my latest messages. In my last one, I merely suggested taking over some of the household chores so she could spend some quality time with Jacob at home.

I hate it when his parents leave him at the local daycare facility. Is the care of strangers better for her child than his own flesh and blood? I said this to her in my messages, but still, she won't answer me now.

Her indifference makes my blood boil. I feel it throbbing in my head now as I pick up the phone. I hardly hear the dial tone above the sound of my own heart in my ears.

She has the audacity not to pick up. How dare she? After everything I've done for her. She would have perished too if it weren't for me taking care of her in every spare moment I had.

I've done nothing for myself all this time. I never have. The only joy I've ever had is when I've held my son and grandson in my arms. My only real use was to care for my little ones. It always has been.

What am I supposed to do now?

The only contact I've had recently is from my boss. She tells me she will have to let me go if she doesn't hear from me by the end of the week.

You used to be so reliable, she said in her message yesterday. She doesn't understand how much I have to do here at home in my flat.

The phone is still in my hand. I start dialling the number for my boss. I suppose it's about time we spoke. It must be weeks now since I turned up for work.

Then I hear something. Pipes. It must be coming from the bathroom. A toilet flush, I think. Then I remember. It's my son. Perhaps he is in there with little Jacob before dinner.

Dinner. I look through the open door to the kitchen. Nothing is cooking. In fact, it's getting dark, and all the lights are off. The curtains haven't even been shut yet. It doesn't look at all homely.

What will little Jacob think? He gets so afraid of the dark.

I put the phone back down and move around quickly, illuminating the dim rooms. I wonder what I can make for us to eat that our fussy little eater wouldn't reject.

An evening with my family should brighten things up in

here. Perhaps they will even stay over for the night? Yes, I will insist upon it.

The three of us will stay in my flat and keep the darkness out together. It will be cosy.

Facing the evening without them would be unbearable.

52

Mutters and stares face me as I turn up at the school gates in the afternoon. But I ignore them. With Rebecca by my side, I find I can focus on the sound of her voice instead of the scandalous whispers that have followed me recently. I force myself to see only the details of her face and not the ones that turn in my direction as we wait. It's now that I notice her freckles are brought out even by the weak winter sunshine that illuminates the day.

'If you ask me,' she says as she picks up the thread of our conversation earlier at the shop. 'The teaching assistant was bang out of order for saying anything. If I'd been there this morning, I would have had more to say to her. It's not right that they gossip about the kids and their families.'

I smile, grateful she is here with me. This is the support I should have had from Dan. He has always been so quick to take the other person's side, especially when I questioned the judgement of the teachers. It's so nice to hear someone tell me I'm not imagining things. It's not nice to think that an unidentified person is out to get me, but for my own sanity I need to know the truth.

I glance beyond the scattering of faces now and then. Dan will likely turn up and try to talk me round. That's the main reason Rebecca is here – to provide moral support in case of a moment of weakness.

But as the bell rings and the children slowly start spilling across the playground, I realise he isn't going to turn up. I've been nervously anticipating his arrival, but the lack of his presence is like a stab in the heart. The fact he didn't come is further proof of his guilt and deception. He must be too ashamed to face me after all.

Adam appears suddenly from behind a dense group of Year 6 boys. He doesn't bother with mere greetings.

'Where's Dad?' he asks as soon as he is near enough.

'Hello to you too,' Rebecca says to him.

'Your dad isn't supposed to be here,' I say. 'I've been picking you up all week.'

Adam eyes me suspiciously. 'Are you and Dad breaking up?'

I open my mouth, unsure what to say. Then I catch Helen nearby, watching me. My stomach twists before I return my gaze to Adam. 'No, of course not. Let's go home.'

We stop off at the supermarket on the way, and I find the assistant takes one too many glances at me as she scans our shopping through. Has she heard the rumours too? My face burns as I ignore her. Instead, I try to smile along with Adam as Rebecca play-acts an animated struggle to stay away from the convenience sweets and chocolates positioned at the checkout.

A note of disappointment bites at me when I open the door to our cottage and find it empty. Dan isn't waiting for me here either. It must be over.

Rebecca uses the toilet when we get inside. Then I hear the boiler ignite and the pipes screeching to life upstairs.

'We usually use the downstairs sink if you want warm

water to wash your hands in,' I say to her as she returns. 'The system is so old. The water takes forever to heat up otherwise.'

She shakes her head. 'No, it's for you. I'm running you a bath. I put loads of bubbles in it with that muscle-relax stuff on the side.'

'Oh, that's Dan's. His mother bought it for his birthday.'

She shrugs. 'I think you're the one who needs it. Best make the most of it before he takes it with him.'

I sigh. It's been such a long day, and I can't think of the day when Dan will load up a vehicle with the remains of his half of our life together.

'No, I can't,' I say as I look towards the washing machine. 'I have to look after Adam. I need to empty his school bag and check for homework. Then I need to wash and dry some uniform for tomorrow.'

'Don't worry about it. Anyway, it might do the two of you good to have the day off from the gossiping teachers and toxic mothers at the gates. He can have a Friday off now and then. We can have a three-day weekend. We could go somewhere maybe, have a day out.'

Adam's bright face turns in our direction as he kicks off his shoes. 'Can we, Mum? That would be *amazing*.'

I frown. 'Adam can't just skip off school. I don't think that's a good lesson to teach him.'

She shrugs. 'I bunked off loads, and it never did me any harm. This is just one day we are talking about. I can handle all the rest of it whilst you have a nice soak.'

'I'll think about it. Just let me get the uniform in the washer. Adam's got mud up his last good jumper. He needs it for tomorrow if he goes in.'

She takes hold of my shoulders and steers me through the hall and towards the bottom of the stairs.

'I'll do it. You deserve a rest. You do too much. Let

someone help you for a change. I'm here now. I'll get everything sorted out, no problem. Dinner will be ready by the time you come back down.'

I look in on Adam in the living room. He is absorbed in his cartoons.

Rebecca begins to move about in the kitchen. I guess she is getting started on her famous chilli she has bigged up all day. She certainly seems to know her way around the kitchen.

Upstairs, it feels opulent to walk in and find a bath running for me. Already, a full cloud of fluffy bubbles blooms on the surface of the water.

I move to turn off the taps, worried about the cost. I'll be responsible for the bills alone from now on, and I'll have to be mindful of what is spent in the house. As if I weren't already.

As I undress, I look uncertainly at the bathroom lock. Usually, I wouldn't bother with it, just in case Adam should need me. But now I look twice at it before sliding the small bar across.

My foot slips on excess bubble bath as I lower myself down. For a moment I panic, thinking I will slip beneath the surface before I regain my balance.

The water is far too hot and deep, and I struggle to keep my chin out of the foam as I recline. It's been a long time since I had a bubble bath, but I don't remember having one less relaxing. I feel guilty, as Rebecca meant well.

My mind keeps replaying all the unpleasant things that have happened lately whenever I shut my eyes, just like it does in the darkness at night. It strays downstairs to where Adam is left without my supervision. I hope Rebecca is looking in on him now and then. Did he have a drink when he came in? I haven't managed to judge his liquid consumption today from what he left in his lunch box bottle.

Despite all these troubling thoughts, I find myself

becoming drowsy after a few minutes. My eyes drift closed against my will. I'm more exhausted than I thought. The warmth of the water wraps itself around me and lulls me further into its bliss.

The doorbell rings. It's frantic and repeated.

I shift position and realise water has made its way into my mouth. A cough erupts from my throat as I sit up.

The doorbell rings again, multiple times in quick succession.

Who could that be? Thoughts of Julie coming over to collect Dan's things trouble me as I reach for a towel and drip my way downstairs in a hurry.

At the bottom of the stairs, I see Rebecca has beaten me there. Through the crack she has opened in the front door, I see Dan's stressed face. He looks grey, and the lines around his face are tauter than ever.

'Alison,' he says, spotting me, 'what's going on? I can't get in. The door was bolted from the inside. Why is the chain on?'

'I – I didn't realise it was.'

Rebecca mutters to me, 'Sorry, Ali. I thought you didn't want to see him.'

'That's fine.' I turn back to Dan. 'What do you want?'

'To start with, I'd like to be allowed into my own house! Can one of you please unlock the front door? Or do I have to scale my own gate and go in the back?'

'Don't bother,' Rebecca retorts quickly. 'I bolted that one too.'

Dan swears. 'Ali, please let me in. This is nuts. I want to talk. I tried to find you at the shop today, but it was shut. And you had already picked Adam up from school by the time I got there this afternoon.'

Rebecca gives me a warning look and shakes her head subtly. On our on-location shoot today, I already told her that

I would probably back down if Dan turned up apologetic. The last thing I want to do is create an unstable home for Adam. He is my priority.

'You've had your chance,' I say to him. 'You should have thought about that before you spent the night at *her* house. You've been lying to me.'

'I've already told you. I can explain everything.'

'If there was such an innocent explanation, then I would already know it. Face it, Dan. It's over.'

I move forward and push the door closed, sliding the bolt firmly across.

53

Rebecca puts her arm around my shoulders and squeezes tightly. The idea of her taking martial arts classes now reconciles with my image of her. She has a lot of hidden core strength that must have come from many hours of practice. I suppose that should make her extra useful to have around if someone out there wants to do me any kind of harm. It's so lucky that we ran into each other in Manchester. I don't know what I would do right now without her.

'I'm so proud of you,' she says. 'You held up.'

'Thanks. I wasn't sure I would.'

'This is the right thing to do. It might not always feel like it. But you can't stand for cheating. He'll only do it again. Trust me, I know.'

A sudden noise startles me in the otherwise still hallway. It's Dan. He opens the letter box and attempts to peer through the many dark bristles. 'Alison? Please open the door. I know you are there. You can't hide.'

Rebecca drops her voice to a mutter and leads me quietly into the narrow kitchen. *That's what he thinks.*

Back in the kitchen with the hall door shut, she rescues a pan of rice from boiling over. 'He'll give up eventually.'

The doorbell rings again. 'You just have to let him get this out of his system first.'

Adam appears in the doorway. 'Who is that at the door?'

'No one,' I say, looking at Rebecca for support.

'Why are they hanging around for ages?'

'It's just a salesperson,' I say. 'Ignore it. Maybe you should wash your hands for dinner.'

He pulls a face. 'Why would a salesperson keep ringing and ringing?'

Rebecca points her wooden spoon at him. 'Because it's a persistent one. Now, are you going to wash your hands, or what?'

Thankfully the doorbell has quietened by the time we all sit down to eat. The food is spicier than I expected. It gets me in the throat on the first mouthful.

Adam takes another gulp of water.

'Don't drink too much,' I tell him. 'You'll give yourself a stomach ache. Are you sure you don't want me to make you a sandwich instead?'

'I'm fine,' he insists, picking up his fork again and shovelling up more chilli.

'Sorry,' Rebecca says. 'I didn't think it would come out so hot. I tried to tone it down, but that's not my usual brand of chilli powder.' She turns to Adam and pats him on the back. 'You don't have to eat it just to be polite, you know.'

'I'm not. It's really nice. Mum's food is always boring. She never cooks spicy stuff.'

I shrug. 'I thought he was still too young for that sort of thing.'

Rebecca laughs as Adam takes another gulp of water. 'Bless, he's just like me. He's suffering, but he loves it!'

I smile politely as I stack the dishes and cutlery afterwards. Rebecca puts her arm around Adam's shoulders and congratulates him on managing to clear his plate.

In the kitchen, I realise my phone is alight with another missed call from Dan. There is a voicemail too. I put my face in my hands after placing the dishes in the sink.

This is all too much to deal with right now. I wonder where he is. Has he taken refuge with Helen again? Or will he be spilling our secrets to his mother instead?

Suddenly, there is an eruption of banging in the dining room. I rush back through to find Adam and Rebecca staring at the window.

I gasp when I see a face outside in the dark and the rain.

It's Dan. He looks soaked through, even with the hood of his coat up.

'Dad?' Adam moves to the back door to unlock it, but Rebecca catches him by the shoulder and pulls him back.

Dan nods and points to the back door, shouting through the glass, 'Unlock the door, Adam!'

Adam turns to me, a look of shock upon his face. 'Why have you two locked him out? Is this because of Eric's mum?'

So Adam has heard something too. Anger stabs at me when I consider how young Adam and Eric are. They shouldn't be bogged down with the troubles of us adults.

Rebecca closes the curtains, but Dan bangs on the glass again. It's a deep, booming sound that can be heard through the whole of the ground floor of the small cottage.

'Upstairs,' Rebecca says. 'Adam, why don't we go up to your room and play with those walkie-talkies I got you?'

'I can't find the other one.'

'Well, let's go and do something else, then.'

She follows Adam upstairs, and I move to the living room to shut the curtains in there too.

I expect Dan to follow and try to communicate through the glass, but he doesn't. With all the curtains and blinds shut now, I can't see out. He could be anywhere out there. I brace myself, wondering if the next sound I hear will be him breaking through the glass with something heavy.

But it's all gone quiet. I find it unnerving.

Upstairs, I walk into Adam's room to find Rebecca laying out a deck of cards across the carpet. There isn't a great deal of floor space, and she resorts to short, narrow rows in the space between Adam's bed and the door. The rest of the room is still dedicated to Dorothy's things. With the three of us, it looks overcrowded.

It's been a while since I have come in here when Adam is playing and not settling down to bed. His desk was moved up into the loft to make way for the baby furniture, and he has since done his homework at the dining table instead. Mrs Evans told him off for getting gravy on his English workbook.

The completed Lego sets and toys that once adorned the shelves have also been moved into a box and shoved beneath Adam's bed.

A shrine. That's what my little boy's room has become. Why should he have to live like this?

I watch Adam's bright blue eyes as they scrutinise the cards as though he might be able to see through them with enough concentration. He has been so good throughout all this. He has been patient. Not once has he complained. He's such an angel.

As he counts his stack of cards at the end of the game, I say quietly to Rebecca, 'I think it's about time I tackled this room. There's no sense in keeping everything. Would you help me?'

She looks up and smiles in surprise. 'Of course, if you are sure you are ready?'

I watch Adam's face break into a broad grin as he realises he has won by a long shot. 'I am. It's time to move forward.'

'Good. The three of us can get started first thing in the

morning. Adam will be delighted to see his room come back together. We need a big strong guy to help us with the changing table.'

She reaches over and gives his upper bicep a playful squeeze.

Adam smirks back at her. 'Yes! That would be great. But I thought you said we were going on a day out somewhere? Eric went to that escape room place last weekend. Can't we go to that?'

I shake my head quickly. 'No, you are still going to school tomorrow. I meant Rebecca and I will have a sort-out in here whilst you are away.'

Adam groans loudly. 'Boring.'

54

I awake abruptly. It's completely dark. I have the vague sense that something isn't right. I fell asleep with a deep sense of unease. It takes me a few moments to remember what has happened.

Then it hits me in a rush of pain and anguish when I remember what Dan did and why he is gone.

But then, why can I feel his body now pressed against mine?

I look over my shoulder abruptly, and I have a fright in the darkness when I don't recognise the figure beside me.

In a few blinks, Rebecca's sharp cheekbones come into focus in the dim room. Her hand is draped across my hip. Now that I am conscious, I feel her gentle breath on the back of my neck.

Perhaps that's what woke me up? I hope it's not Dan trying again downstairs.

It's past 3 am, however, so I think it unlikely. But my husband has surprised me recently. Who knows what he is capable of?

I know from experience that I will be awake for a long

time just lying here. My heart still pounds fearfully for an unknown reason. All the reasons I have to be stressed flood my brain once again.

With difficulty, I extract myself from beneath Rebecca's sleeping hand without waking her.

Downstairs, I routinely check all the locks. I peer out the windows, afraid of what I will see, but there is nothing out of the ordinary. Dan must be long gone. I try not to picture where he is spending the night.

In the kitchen, a light flashes on the washer-dryer to signal the end of the cycle. I had forgotten about the load with the events of dinner. I close the kitchen door and flick on the light.

The laundry will need to be dry before the morning. I'm determined Adam will continue at school as normal, no matter what his parents are going through. He will need the normality, for sure.

I freeze, however, as I grab the still-damp fabrics from the machine. It takes me a moment to recognise Adam's usually white polo shirts. They come out of the machine now dark pink. A few even have dark grey streaks on them. I'm baffled until I find that his PE jogging bottoms are in here too. The dark dye has run all over his school jumpers too, leaving them irretrievably stained.

I swear. This can't be happening. Adam needs to go to school later this morning. I've got so much to sort out. I don't want to ask Dan for a favour at this point. He needs to know he has no chance of proving me a poor mother in any custody case he might throw my way.

It looks like Rebecca will get her way after all. Adam will be delighted.

A buzz from the dining room makes me realise Rebecca's phone is still in the pocket of her coat draped over a dining chair. I slip my hand inside and place it on the table with the thought that she will see it when she wakes up.

Then I see the sender's name: Dan.

I blink and think I must have misread it. Why would Rebecca even have my husband's number?

But I press the power button to see the screen again. There is no mistake. Dan has sent Rebecca a text in the middle of the night.

My mind swims with possibilities. Just hours ago Rebecca was keeping up the pretence of barely knowing Dan. She was hardly even civil to him. At least, that was how she acted for my benefit.

It was she who locked him out. But she also had the idea of Adam not going to school today. Now his uniform is ruined. She has got her way.

She suggested that Helen was after my husband. But did Dan look guilty when he told me they were just friends? Did she run into me by accident in the city?

I run my tense fingers through my hair and realise that the reality is far worse than I have imagined at any point.

There is no one I can trust at all.

Everyone has lied to me at some point. But I won't let any of them win. Now I need to keep my baby safe.

I don't care that it is barely past four in the morning. Action needs to be taken. Now.

I pull on my coat and grab my car keys.

55

My boss sent me an unpleasant letter a few months after Charlotte kicked me out. I'd never been sacked from a job before. My tears of anger and humiliation didn't last long, however. I couldn't blame her for firing me. What choice did she have? It must have been a while since I turned up for work. I've lost track of time for so long. But it doesn't matter.

At first, I thought it would be something for the better. I was able to spend more time with my son and Jacob. Though, eventually, the power went off in my flat too. Not only was I chilled to the bone and in darkness day and night, but the dwindling supplies in my kitchen cupboards weren't the same eaten cold from the tins without a way to heat them.

It was early when I got dressed in my dingy flat that morning. Usually, I would have flipped on the light switch and checked my appearance before I left the house, but I couldn't that day. I don't know what sort of impression I made when I arrived at Rishworth Primary on my first day as a teaching assistant.

The headmistress smiled and shook my hand warmly

when I arrived. It was almost like she had no idea that morning was the first time in months I had spoken to other people. I'd only left the house a handful of times for food and supplies before then. When I dressed for work that morning, it showed on my figure that I had neglected to eat properly.

But I found myself automatically slipping into the role I've fitted for years in my professional life. I used the right phrases as I spoke about my many years of teaching experience, and it seemed to please the headmistress. If even the shell of a person I was then could be disguised by a veil of normality, it made me wonder what kind of half-life I'd been living all these years. Part of me was alarmed at how easily the headmistress was fooled. The other part was grateful to have money again. Food and warmth. Somewhere to be. People who relied on me.

The children were the same as in my old school. A sea of little faces that watched me with interest. I saw their eyes move over the sharp collarbone visible beneath my collar. The lines of my face must have become more pronounced, as were my cheekbones.

I wonder if I have gained any weight since then. Have my years now of Rishworth Primary staff meals made me any less gaunt and haunted by the horrors of my past? It's always a relief at lunchtimes to sit down to a staff school dinner. If it weren't for that, I probably would have starved by now. The simple food provides me with the energy I wouldn't bother to prepare for myself.

I'm grateful for the nourishment, even if it is tasteless and bland. But perhaps it is me. Maybe I've lost the ability to feel and enjoy over the years since it happened.

September signals the beginning of a new school year. It brings in a new batch of children. To me, they all look the same. The same set of characters walk in through the door: the no-hoper who can aspire to be nothing more than the class clown, the bully, the pretty girl with hand-tied ribbons in her hair, the bookworm and all those faceless forgettable children in between.

After lunch, it's time for me to listen to the children read. Up close, their cheeks are so young and round like my son when he was small. Especially one boy in particular.

He has a full head of dark hair, just like my son's. Same brow bones too.

And those eyes. The same tint and shape that is etched into my memory forever. I wonder if I'm imagining the familiar bright blue hue that glows with the sunlight streaming in through the window.

Then again. I'm sure that I am not.

It's exactly the same.

56

It's cold in the shop when we arrive. It's dark too.

Adam is still groggy after being pulled quietly from his bed and bundled into the car. 'Why don't you switch on the lights, Mum?'

'Not right now.'

'But why not?'

'It will be daylight soon. You need to get some more sleep before then though.'

I use the blankets from the Christmas set and the display in the window and make Adam a sort of makeshift bed in the kitchen area of the shop.

'I'm too hot,' he complains, tugging at the thick jumper I dressed him in on our way out of the house.

'You'll cool down once you lie still. It's draughty down here on the floor.'

He is safely out of sight. As am I. No one can see us from the outside. If we turned on the lights, it would give us away instantly. Besides, it's best if Adam doesn't see how much I am shaking as I settle him down.

'What's going on?' Adam asks me as I pull the velvet

blanket up to his chin. 'Why can't we go home?'

'We will. Just not at the moment. Or maybe we will make a new home somewhere else, just the two of us.'

The part of Adam's face that is illuminated by the street light outside looks puzzled. He watches me closely. 'So you and Dad are splitting up. Like Eric said?'

I stroke his smooth plump cheek gently. 'It's for the best, I promise. Everything will be all right.'

'But why? What did Dad do that was so bad?'

'He ...' I struggle to find the words to explain to a child. 'It's hard to explain.'

'Why are we hiding?'

'This is just until I figure out what to do next. It's safer if people don't know we are here.'

'What would happen if they did?'

I shrug and try to keep my voice steady. 'They might come and take you away from me.'

'Why?'

'Try to get some sleep now.' I settle myself down beside him, spreading my thick coat over us for extra warmth.

The occasional car drifts down the street now, headlights sweeping quickly across the ceiling.

Adam's eyes drift shut as I stroke his head. His voice becomes slower. 'What about Rebecca? I thought she was our friend.'

'Yes,' I whisper. 'So did I.'

Despite my elevated level of tension, I find myself able to lie still beside Adam as his breathing becomes low and steady. I envy his ability to drift off into oblivion.

All is still and quiet for a long time as we lie peacefully beside each other. I wish we could stay this way forever. One way or another, there will come a time where he isn't by my side, whether merely by choice or some other force.

As I'm replaying the last few interactions with Dan in my

mind and trying to piece them together, the silence is shattered by a sudden noise coming from the front door.

My heart hammers, and I sit bolt upright.

I am on my feet as a bundle of letters drop onto the mat.

Quiet descends once again, and I breathe heavily as I stare at the post in the entranceway. I glance around and see Adam remains undisturbed. If only I could exist that way.

It takes a while for my breathing to return to normal. I pace back and forth a few times before I pick up the mail. The menu of the local pizza outlet does nothing to distract me from my woes, nor does an invitation to join the local church.

A formal-looking letter catches my attention, and I tear into it. As I read the message inside, I feel as though I've downed a whole glass of cold water at once. It's a sternly worded letter from the local council.

Someone has reported me for noise disturbance. The date printed is of the exhibition. That wasn't very recent. Who would have remembered all this time later? Only someone close to me. Someone who wants to see my business destroyed. That narrows it down to three people. Helen, Dan and Rebecca.

I pull out my phone and switch it on for the first time since yesterday. Dan was trying to get through so many times, and I wasn't ready to talk to him yet.

But now I am fuming. I want answers. Wasn't he the one who disagreed with me starting this business in the first place? He was the one telling me to take it easy all along. He was the one who wanted me to wind the business down and reject inquiries. Then I get a fake client in the form of Richard Neal supposedly offering me an amazing contract.

Now it seems obvious that it was Dan. What if he set up the meeting as a trick? He wanted to test me, and I failed.

He answers immediately when I call him. 'Alison? Are

you all right?'

'No, I'm not. I want to know what the hell you think you are doing?'

'What do you mean? Please calm down. I want to explain.'

'Why don't you explain why I've got a letter from the council. Someone complained about me. It was you, wasn't it?'

He sighs. 'I don't know what you are talking about.'

'Of course you don't! Don't play stupid with me. How dare you interfere with my business? You know how important it is to me. Why try to ruin it?'

'I'm not trying to destroy anything. I don't know what you are talking about. All I want is for you to be well. You've been running yourself ragged. This business is exhausting you. You've been acting like you were before. After you had Adam, you were down for ages.'

'And whose fault is that?!' I spit at him suddenly, erupting into tears. 'If you hadn't constantly accused me of cheating, then we could have been happy.'

'I know I was out of order back then, but I don't see how it would have been any different now. Look, you aren't thinking clearly. You weren't sleeping properly then either. It's all happening again, Ali. When you get better, you'll see. I just want to help you.'

I shake my head. 'What else have you done?'

'I haven't done anything to harm you, I swear.'

'Why don't I believe you? I suppose I'll be in touch soon to make arrangements. We'll need to get everything sorted out.'

'Please don't do this.'

'I have to. There is no way I'm letting you get away with cheating on me. The whole town is talking about me behind my back because of you and Helen.'

'I already told you nothing happened. I had nowhere else

to go. Mum was away in Bournemouth that night. There weren't any vacancies in any of the local hotels, only the five-star one up on the hill. But it was so expensive you would have gone ballistic if I'd paid for a night there. Helen had texted me earlier to arrange a play date with Adam anyway. I didn't see any harm in it, I promise.'

I go quiet as I consider his version of the story. 'You're making this up.'

'I'm not. It's the truth.'

'Then why didn't you tell me this at the time?'

'You didn't give me the chance. I was banging on the door most of yesterday when you locked me out. You wouldn't answer the phone. What was I supposed to do, Ali? I tried phoning Rebecca too, but she kept rejecting my calls.'

'I noticed you texted her in the middle of the night. Why do you even have her number?'

'I gave it to her at the exhibition. Just in case I couldn't get through to you at any point.'

'You didn't mention it. Anyway, it's a flimsy excuse. Perhaps you liked having an attractive woman's number hidden from your wife?'

'What? Alison, this isn't you talking. I want to tell you the truth about everything – like work. Nigel cut my hours down. I didn't want to tell you in case you thought you needed to work harder at the shop and put more pressure on yourself. I've been trying to find another job.'

'You're making all this up. It's too convenient.'

'No, please try to listen to what I'm saying.'

'Don't patronise me.'

'Look, I'm coming over to the house. Will you let me in this time? We can talk properly.'

'I'm sure you have invented a neat little excuse for every-thing, haven't you? Well, I'm not at the house, so don't bother turning up.'

'You're not at the shop this early? This is what I meant by working too hard, Ali. You're depressed. Your priorities are messed up.'

'I'm not there either,' I say quickly, thinking fast and realising I can test him at the same time. 'I'm in Manchester. I've got a meeting with a big potential client.'

Dan sighs. I can't tell if he knows I'm lying. It's hard to gauge from his reaction whether he invented the false meeting with Richard or not.

'When will you be back?' he asks now, sounding tired. 'I just want you to be well again. I want us to be like we were before. It's been a long time, but we can work on our marriage.'

I bite my lip. I've longed for Dan to be the man I married for so long. Now I don't know what I want.

I've been tricked too many times lately. I've forgiven and trusted only to be proven wrong time and time again. I haven't imagined all the bad things that have happened to me, no matter what anyone else says. No more will I let it happen.

I end the call and look over to Adam. He is still sleeping peacefully, although he shifts slightly now.

I look back at the calls section of my phone. Then something strikes me from the uniformity of Dan's name in the missed calls list. He isn't the only one to have phoned me recently.

There is another name I never expected to see in my call history.

Charlotte, my class tutor. Her name is listed more than once.

My stomach clenches so violently that I think I might be sick. Why would she be calling me? There is only one reason I can think of.

She knows my secret.

57

I've never been so keen to go to work in my life. Now it's what drives me to get out of bed in the morning. Just the thought of seeing the precious boy is enough to make everything else melt away.

I know now. The truth is more beautiful than I ever could have imagined. Everything makes sense. This has all happened for a reason. It's not all behind me as I had thought.

True, my son is gone, but now I am being blissfully haunted by the memory of him.

The warmth of the sun through the window envelops us in class as I sit and listen to him read. Even certain elements of his voice strike a chord in my memories.

I feel as though I'm caught in the trappings of a strange spell. It's like the years have melted away, and I am young again with my son beside me. Only this time, I treasure him even more.

I make sure there is a copy of my boy's favourite story in the school library for him one day. He takes to it like a dream. They could be twins.

I'm so excited to tell my daughter-in-law the news. She sends a condescending reply back. I'm not the one who needs help if she refuses to accept the miracle I've discovered.

I'm excited when we set off to the zoo with the rest of the class. Our first real day out together. But I'm distracted by a petty squabble between two girls at lunchtime as we all sit in the picnic area. When I look for my favourite pupil, I realise he isn't here.

He has wandered off. Mrs Evans sends me to find him, and I become more and more panicked when I scour each section of the place and find he isn't there. How could he have disappeared so quickly?

I pass the deep moat surrounding the chimpanzee enclosure, and fear hammers in my heart. Don't the idiots that run this place realise how dangerous water is for children?

But the surface is still and black. People wander about and chatter happily. Nothing has happened here.

It's the gift shop where I find him. As soon as I spot his full dark head next to a display of stuffed animals, I grab him by the arm and pull him to me. I shout at him for scaring me. He bursts into tears, and people stare at us.

I release the grip on him; it was tighter than I thought. My heart breaks to see him upset. I hold him to me and rub his back soothingly. At the counter, I pay for the toy gorilla he was holding.

Outside the shop, I put it carefully inside his bag. I don't want Mrs Evans to see I've bought a student something so expensive.

'It will be our little secret,' I tell him.

58

I spend the rest of the morning frantic, not knowing what to do. Within the confines of the shop, I can only pace back and forth to the kitchen area and into the back room. It's a loop I'm stuck in, like a bird that flies repeatedly around a cage. I've run out of places to fly to.

My fingers confirm the sanctity of the lock on the back door again. It feels too flimsy. It would be too easy for someone to break in.

This place isn't safe either. We need to move. As soon as Adam is awake, we will get in the car. Maybe we can go and visit Mum? Even as I think it, I realise it is too obvious. It surely would be the first place people would check.

Adam and I will have to move. We can start a new life elsewhere. But the only business I've proven myself good at is photography. And then that requires an online presence. I could be tracked down with just a few clicks.

Dark shapes start to move past the window now as the day gets going. I scrutinise each one as they pass, convinced I will see a face I recognise.

It never occurred to me that Charlotte could be the one

behind everything. Perhaps it was her whom I've seen here and there where she shouldn't have been? When I signed myself up for her evening class, I thought she had no idea who I was. I had been so certain I was safe turning up there week after week.

But was I naive? Or did it occur to her who I was after a while? She already admitted to knowing more than she should about my personal life. Did she know who I was when she handed me her card with her number on it? It seems so plausible now.

She could have been the one playing games with me all this time. Why didn't it occur to me sooner? It would have been more than easy for her to have hacked my website. She is the first person who would have been able to guess the password.

My stomach burns. I'm running on empty after the spicy meal I struggled to get down yesterday. I dread to think what state Adam will be in when he wakes up. In the kitchen, I quietly open up the biscuit tin. It's empty.

I move to the window and peer out at the street. It's daylight now, and people are milling about. It never gets busy enough in Mill Street to ever hope to slip amongst a crowd and sneak out unnoticed.

I check again that the bolts are securely across on the front door. It's locked as securely as possible.

I creep past the sleeping form of Adam on the floor and open the door to the backyard.

Locking the door firmly behind me, I make sure I'm not being watched before heading off in the direction of the nearest convenience store.

I intend to make a hurried purchase of sandwiches and Adam's favourite flavoured milk before I return. But there is a queue. Now that I am in a rush too, the general store seems further away than I remembered.

Almost half an hour has passed when I'm scurrying back to my shop. I just hope Adam isn't awake yet and wandered off looking for me.

I slide the carrier bag of food onto my wrist and put my keys into the lock. As soon as I step inside the shop, however, I realise something is wrong. The air isn't still like I left it. It has been disturbed.

And I can hear voices.

59

As I rush forward into the kitchen, I spot Rebecca standing over Adam's stirring form.

'Get away from him!' I scream, dropping the bag of food.

Rebecca jumps in alarm and moves back instinctively. She raises her hands in defence as though I have advanced on her with a weapon.

If I had more warning, maybe I would have picked up a loose brick from the yard, but I haven't. I feel completely unprepared.

Then I remember Rebecca knows martial arts. I thought she would help to protect me. Now I realise she could injure or kill me with ease alone here in the shop.

'How did you get in?' I demand.

'You gave me a key, remember? So I could open up if you are running late.' She reaches into her pocket and pulls out her set of keys. She holds them up, and an attached fluffy pom-pom charm swings about. 'I didn't know where you went. I didn't realise you would have come here so early.'

She glances down at the makeshift bed on the floor where

Adam now sits up, watching us as though we are one of his cartoons.

Rebecca looks back at me again. 'Did you two sleep here? What happened? Did Dan get in? I don't understand. You were there last night when we went to sleep.'

Adrenaline still courses in my blood. Rebecca is acting every bit the friend I desperately need right now, as she always does. 'I saw the text on your phone from Dan. You didn't once mention that you had his number stored.'

She shakes her head, bewildered. 'I don't know. I didn't think anything of it. He just handed it over in case I ever needed it. I just saved it, that was all. I've never called it. He was pestering me with calls yesterday, but did you see me pick any up?'

'No, but–'

'That's because I didn't. You know me. I'm your friend. I would never do anything behind your back. It's you who is hiding something, let's be honest.'

Blood surges to my head, and I feel faint all of a sudden. 'I don't know what you are talking about.'

She lowers her voice and moves towards me as Adam watches my face curiously. 'I think you do. I was hiding something a few weeks ago too. But I told you the truth, and I'm sure you will tell me your secret in the future if you want to. If it's never, then that's fine. I'm here for you. I'm so glad we found each other.'

I shake my head. 'It's all very convenient though and always works in your favour. Like when we ran into each other in Manchester. I've been thinking – that can't have been an accident.'

Rebecca sighs, and her imploring look drops for a second. I'm sure I have her now, she has to admit.

'No,' she says. 'You're right. It wasn't a coincidence. I saw your Facebook post. You posted it from the cafe saying you were meeting an important new client. I know how nervous you get about pushing for sales. I thought if I turned up, I could help you clinch the deal. I wanted to make up for disappearing on you.'

I shake my head. I fear I'm being talked around again. 'But what about Adam's uniform? You didn't want him to go to school, and then suddenly the load of washing was ruined on purpose. You can't deny it. You must have known what would happen if you put all those colours and whites in the machine at once at such a high setting. You did it to get your own way.'

She shakes her head. A look of confusion comes upon her face. 'No, I separated the colours. Adam was there. Whilst you were in the bath, I gave him a lesson on how to do laundry. I put the whites in first on their own, I swear. I don't know how they could have got mixed up. Tell your mum, Adam.'

She looks down at the boy behind her for some support, but he avoids her gaze. He looks at his hands instead.

Adam reddens in the cheeks, and his eyes look watery all of a sudden. 'I'm sorry,' he mumbles. 'I wanted to go somewhere fun instead. Rebecca said we could have a day out somewhere.'

'You little bugger ...' Rebecca mutters to herself, folding her arms. She sighs and turns back to me. 'I'm sorry. I didn't catch him doing that. He must have bunged it all in when I was cooking.'

'No, I'm sorry,' I say. 'I was too quick to suspect you of everything.'

'Well, you have had a lot of other things going on,' she says softly, reaching for my hand and giving it a squeeze. 'No one can blame you for getting a little paranoid when weird stuff is going on inside your own house. I guess you just don't know who to blame.'

I sigh. 'That's the thing. I think I do now.'

60

BEFORE

I have to be careful at school. I had thought I'd felt Mrs Evans watching me a few times as I spoke to Adam. But then I look around to find she isn't. It's my fear making me paranoid.

In the mornings before work, I find myself impatiently sitting on the sofa in the flat, thinking about the time we will spend together in the day.

He tells me all sorts of things about his life at home. He tells me about how *Mum* starts all sorts of businesses in the pursuit of financial stability, how she is currently starting a photography studio. He tells me about the baby girl she has recently lost. How tragic. When the truth comes out, this woman will realise that she has no surviving children. Hopefully, she is not the dramatic type.

I listen intently. I want to know everything about him. Every step of his journey up to this point must be etched onto my memory. I need to discover how this could have happened.

Despite my daughter-in-law's ignorance, I know this is the

right thing to do. Charlotte has always been awkward when it comes to me.

She doesn't see that we need to do this.

One day after school, I have nothing but the thought of an empty flat to return to. So instead, I drive over to Charlotte's cottage.

She won't be back home from work for a couple of hours, but I don't mind waiting. These days she teaches courses at the local adult education centre. I've familiarised myself with her routine. Today, I know she is due home sooner after an earlier class.

Although lately, she has become a tad unpredictable, gallivanting here and there at all sorts of hours. Goodness knows what extracurricular activities she has been up to. I do hope she isn't dating again, the traitorous bitch. If she is cheating on my son, then I don't want to know about it.

Sometimes, I like to park on this street lined with cottages and sit and remember. I even used to close my eyes and imagine that when I open them, I will exit the car, and my son will greet me at the front door.

But I don't dare leave my vehicle when I know Charlotte isn't far away. Only when she is safely gone for an extended period do I deem it safe to use the key I've kept hidden all these years; it's a good thing Little Miss Perfect didn't think to confiscate it from me in her haste to kick me out. The cottage is largely the same as it was inside; I find that comforting.

I park a little way up the street so she doesn't notice me. She doesn't need to be given the opportunity to avoid me like she does when we see each other around town or in the supermarket.

The time I wait is used to consider my wording carefully. I've been thinking about confronting Charlotte properly for weeks with the truth. She has ignored my text messages, and in hindsight, perhaps it wasn't the most sensitive way to spill the news of what I have stumbled upon.

Any good mother would be delighted at such news. I know I would be if someone told me there was a chance my son was still alive somewhere. But I live in the real world; I know that will never happen. There is only hope for Adam now.

A flutter of nerves fills me as her car pulls into the road. She doesn't spot me, and I give her time to settle inside the cottage before I ring the bell.

Just as I am getting ready to step out of my little car, another vehicle cruises down the street. My hand reaches for the door handle, but something causes me to freeze.

I recognise the driver as a parent from my school. But not just any parent. It's Alison Burnham, the woman who thinks she is Adam's mother. She doesn't live in these cottages, but ones very similar on the other side of town.

What is she doing here?

I worry for a moment that she will see me sitting inside my car. But she doesn't. She simply drives slowly down the road, her attention noticeably elsewhere. At the end, she turns and disappears.

This is a quiet residential street, not a through road to anywhere. There is no reason for anyone to drive down here, especially not a local who should know better.

And besides, I didn't imagine the way her eyes lingered on Charlotte's cottage, did I? I might have imagined things in the past, but not this. The vision of her actions haunts me.

She was driving too slow, as though to get a deliberate view.

61

Rebecca's confused face looks at me sideways as we trundle along the outskirts of Accrington. 'I don't understand. Why would your tutor have done all that to you?'

I shake my head. 'I can't explain it. But I know it's her now.'

Deep down I think I knew all along. Who else would have poured such malice into the things against me? The time and effort put into everything that has happened to me recently would surely have ruled out Helen if I had thought about it logically. Even if she had wanted my husband, when has she proven to have ever put so much energy into anything? I was wrong to ever suspect her.

There is only one person with the motivation to strike out at me repeatedly. Charlotte. She has been playing games with me all this time. She must have found it hilarious when I was the one who approached her through her class. Why did I have to do something so stupid?

Anyone else in my position would have stayed well away. It was only my compassion that drove me to fear for her well-being. Most other mothers would have thought only of their child and themselves.

Now I'm facing this impossible situation. She knows. Why hasn't she done anything about it? Was punishing me so important that she held off reporting the situation to the authorities?

Rebecca folds her arms again. 'It wasn't that long ago that you suspected me of being behind everything. Don't you think you are jumping to conclusions?'

'No, I don't. I've thought about it. Everything fits. The phone calls, the flowers, the fake meeting and the voice at the other end of the walkie-talkies. She told me she knew about the exhibition we held – it must have been her who took that bit of photo. She must have been there when I wasn't.'

I reel off the list of events as I drive, more to make sense of it all myself. 'The way the messages were worded fits too; my website getting hacked – Charlotte would have known the password to get in and mess with it ...' I trail off, thinking. It's all so obvious now.

'I don't think she would know your password,' Rebecca says with an almost soothing voice, as though she is trying to make me see reason. But I've already seen it.

'Ali,' she goes on, 'I've come to know you pretty well, and I don't think I would be able to guess your password. The only way your tutor would know it is if you told her, or typed in the same one in front of her.'

'No. The password is Adam's birthday.' I glance across at her, expecting realisation to dawn across her face, but it doesn't.

She merely looks puzzled again. 'So?'

'It's hard to explain.' I look up into the rear-view mirror and see Adam's bright blue eyes trained on mine. He's been watching us closely as we drive, listening. He looks increasingly unsettled on the back seat.

'It's OK,' I tell him soothingly. 'Mummy is just going to have a little chat with someone.'

Rebecca rests her elbow on the passenger armrest and buries her forehead in her hand. 'I don't know about this. Why don't you just try calling her again? You've got both her numbers in your phone. Try her landline again.'

'She isn't answering. You watched me call her loads already. This must just be one of her games.'

I make the familiar turn into the car park of the Lakeside centre. My heart sinks when I realise Charlotte's car isn't here.

'This isn't right,' I say. 'We have a class scheduled for this evening. I know she teaches classes throughout the day on a Friday. She said so.'

'Unless she was lying,' Rebecca says. 'Maybe that was part of the conspiracy too.' She attempts a smirk, but her face looks too strained to pull it off.

'I'm not denying she is clever and sneaky. She somehow found a way to take Dorothy's baby clothes from the house, for starters.'

Rebecca sighs, and there is quiet for a moment inside the car, which is punctuated by Adam. 'Mum, that was me.'

I spin around in my seat. 'What do you mean? What was you?'

'The baby clothes. The super girly ones – I stuffed them down the back of the changing table. And that fluffy pink rabbit.'

'What? No, you can't have.'

His round cheeks redden, and he looks miserably at the car floor. 'I just didn't want Eric thinking I had a girly room when he came over on my birthday. I didn't want him telling everyone at school that I had pink stuff in there. I'm so sorry – I didn't mean to.'

Rebecca turns back to me with a look almost like *I told you so.*

'Adam isn't behind everything,' I say to her imploringly. 'He can't be. It's not like he set up a fake Facebook account to send me messages or set up false meetings. And he was asleep when someone spoke to me through the walkie-talkies in the middle of the night.'

'You didn't tell me about that one.'

'Well, it was just a few days ago.'

'Maybe it was a contractor or something nearby?'

'No, it was the middle of the night. And it was a woman's voice.'

'What did she say?'

I think of the name that had been uttered. The one that sent the hairs on my arms standing on end. 'Something only Charlotte would know.'

'Well, maybe that was Adam too. For all we know he was talking to a friend when he should have been sleeping.' Rebecca looks desperately towards the back seat again. 'Were you talking to someone? Eric maybe?'

Adam's heart visibly pounds in the collar of his T-shirt, but he shakes his head as tears spill down his full cheeks.

'Look, I have to do this,' I say as I unclip my seat belt and get out of the car. 'I can't go on like this anymore. This whole thing has been driving me mad. It ends today. I'm going to ask at the front desk, see what's going on. They might know where Charlotte is.'

Rebecca unfastens her seat belt too. 'I'll come with you.'

I turn back to face her through the open window. 'No. Stay here with Adam. Do the windows up and don't leave him. I'll be back in a minute.'

Rebecca looks pale beneath her freckles, but I'm pleased to see she does as she is told before I slip inside the automatic doors of the Lakeside centre.

62

It's not my imagination. This woman knows the truth. Yet she sits on it. To think I actually felt sorry for her. But she knows and hasn't told anyone. How long has Alison Burnham been hiding this monstrous secret?

Intuition tells me where Alison is heading alone after dark this evening, and I'm not being proven wrong. My thoughts are so much clearer than they have been for years. It's like waking from a long nightmare. Finally, there is a ray of light in my otherwise dismal existence.

This is no trick of the mind. I've been slipping in and out of waking dreams of my family for so long that sometimes it has been hard to tell where reality starts again. But now I know. This is real. I really do have a grandson who needs me. He is my priority now.

Up ahead on the road, Mrs Burnham makes another turn. So I do too. My heart pulsates strangely in my chest. The blood rushes loudly in my ears because I know where she will turn next. It's a wild sort of satisfaction that strikes me as I position my vehicle at the other end of the car park. I remain inside the car and watch as she enters the building of the education centre.

As I followed her, I had my suspicion of where she was going. The lights are on inside Charlotte's classroom. Occasionally, I've come here purely to see her. But not tonight. Now I see her class file inside the room. And Alison is amongst them. I was right. This can't be a coincidence.

She holds a photography exhibition one night at her shop. Feeling bold, I make sure I'm there during the evening. It's easy to slip amongst the crowd, and I'm not disappointed. There is a *stunning* shot of Adam up on display. A lump forms in my throat when I see it; I took a snapshot of my boy, Steven, at the seaside once in a strikingly similar pose.

The idiots around me jostle about for the free booze and food; they are too busy talking and laughing about nonsense and don't notice me tear a strip from the print.

Alison doesn't seem to be in attendance either despite the fact she is supposed to be hosting the evening. She is sloppy and careless, nothing like Adam. That part of her could be written into her genes, something the boy in her care is thankfully immune from.

That certain day of the year rolls around again, as I knew it would. My grandson's birthday. Of course, I knew the date even before he told me. In school, he talks excitedly about what he wants to receive and how *Mummy* has hinted she will deliver on all his wishes this year. I want to get him something special, but I know I can't. Buying that gorilla at the zoo got Alison asking questions. I was forced to allay her fears over the phone afterwards when she feared a stranger had given it to Adam. The old feeling of exclusion rises in me again. Perhaps that is what pushes me to have the flowers and the words of sympathy sent to Alison at the birthday party. It would have felt strange not to have done something to mark the occasion.

When she starts a website for her latest venture, I set it as my browser homepage. The heading at the top reads:

Alison Burnham: Photographer & Post-Processing Artist.

In reality, it should read:

Wife, Mother, Liar & Cheat.

How dare she do this?

Doesn't she know what I've gone through? And my daughter-in-law too. Is that why Alison has worked her way into Charlotte's life? To assess the damage? Something tells me she isn't working herself up to make an announcement any time soon.

Alison Burnham needs to be rattled. She thinks she can skip about freely with the child who should be in my and Charlotte's arms. Well, she will learn that nothing is free.

She will pay the price.

I want to physically shake her. But I know that if I do, I won't ever stop. Then I will lose the chance to ever be near Adam again. By now she knows my face from the school gates, so I must keep my distance. I was lucky she wasn't at the exhibition when I arrived.

I start a fake Facebook profile and send her carefully worded messages. It doesn't feel like much, but I know from what Adam tells me that Alison has trouble sleeping. It's not hard to see why now. I really do know what keeps her awake at night.

It's hard to hold back from asking her directly how she let go of her real baby and took home ours. The questions are burning at my insides, but I know that will be the end of tormenting her.

Eventually, the truth will have to come to light, but not

yet. I've waited years; what's a few more weeks? It's not enough to simply take Adam back. Alison needs to think about what she has done. So instead I tell her she should have kept a better hold of her baby.

She never replies, but I know the messages get through. As do the phone calls timed for when she gets into the shop. Over the weeks, I've seen the circles beneath her eyes darken. That careless streak causes it to show; eventually she starts turning up late for school.

One day, I decide to see what will happen when she thinks an important potential client requests to meet with her. It's my day off, and I walk past the little coffee shop a few times over the hour. She wouldn't recognise me in my hat and scarf even if she looked this way, but Alison isn't looking out the window. She has her laptop open, and I imagine she has seen what I've done to her website by now.

Each time I go by, I see her already nervous demeanour slump closer to her table as she realises no one is going to turn up. She is unsettled, but I know my feeling of satisfaction is only temporary. Whatever I do to Alison, whether sabotaging the electric supply to her precious business, following her or startling her through the walkie-talkies her friend bought Adam, it will never be enough. I can never do to her what she has done to my family.

I haven't yet decided when I'm going to bring this little game to an end. But today, when I go to visit Charlotte at work, I am surprised to find she isn't there. But I do spot Alison's car parked outside. I see her leave the car and rush inside the building, but movement persists inside the vehicle. It's Adam, even though it's a school day.

This must be the moment I've been waiting for. I don't feel prepared, but it must be time to put things into action.

Today is the day.

At the front desk, I'm kept waiting as the receptionist takes her time on the phone. She eyes the fingers that I drum anxiously on the front desk. I have the feeling she slows down on purpose.

Finally, she puts down the receiver and addresses me again. 'Charlotte Pritchard's IT class has been cancelled today.'

'Why?'

'She called in sick yesterday. She was supposed to have contacted her students to let them know. Didn't she tell you there wouldn't be a session today?'

I open my mouth to respond, but someone cuts across me.

Turning around, I see it is Rebecca. 'Yes, that must have been what that missed call was,' she says, nodding. 'Right, Alison?'

'I don't think that's why she was calling me,' I say. 'Why wouldn't she just leave a message?'

'I don't know. Maybe she didn't have time if she was calling all her students. Or she wanted to speak to you and make sure you definitely got the message and didn't turn up anyway.'

I turn back to the receptionist. 'Do you have another number she can be reached on?'

'I'm sorry,' she says. 'I can't give out your tutor's home number. I'm sure the class will be resumed next week. Perhaps you can talk to her then?'

I shake my head. 'I've already tried calling her landline and her mobile this morning. She's not answering. If she was ill, then she would be at home, wouldn't she? Do you know anywhere else she might have gone?'

The receptionist stares at me with her mouth slightly open. She looks from me to Rebecca before she shakes her head. 'I'm sorry. There's nothing I can do.'

Rebecca puts one of her firm hands on my shoulder and starts to steer me away. 'Thanks anyway,' she says over her shoulder as we walk away.

I still feel the eyes of the receptionist on the back of my head. I wonder if she is friends with Charlotte. It's not hard to imagine they might leave the building together at the end of the working day and go out somewhere together.

'Why did you do that?' I say to Rebecca once we are far enough away.

'Do what? She didn't know anything.'

'Didn't she? How do you know she wasn't covering for Charlotte? They work in the same building. They are probably all friends.'

'What? I don't think that's true. You still haven't told me why your tutor would start a vendetta against you.'

I shrug and avoid her intense eyes. Instead, I look through the glass frontage to the bare trees beside the lake. 'I don't know. I asked you to wait with Adam in the car.'

'I was wondering where you got to. Adam is too. Come on.

Let's go home. Maybe we can plan a day out somewhere after all?'

We exit the building and step out into the cool air. The sun has painted everything gold in the car park, and the day is unseasonably warm. But after leaving the overheated building behind us, I start to shiver even beneath my coat.

I rotate my shoulders a few times, trying to ease the tension that is causing my muscles to cramp. Something isn't right. I just can't place what it is.

As we approach the car, I realise immediately what is wrong.

Adam isn't in the back seat.

I rush over and pull open the door, but I can already tell it is empty. Adam has gone from the car.

Once I'm satisfied that Alison is inside the Lakeside centre, I make my move. My heart bursts into an erratic stream of beats as I get closer and the front passenger side door flies open. Another woman emerges and jogs briskly up to the building too. She disappears inside the glass doors, and I realise that this will be my only opportunity.

I tap on the glass at first so as not to alarm him, and when recognition crosses his face, I pull open the back door. The poor thing already looks shaken, red-faced and watery-eyed as though he has been crying. How dare Alison treat my grandson this way?

Adam tells me his mother is scaring him. She is acting strangely and won't let them go home. As I unclip his belt, he tells me *Mum* made him sleep on the floor of her shop.

'It's OK,' I say. 'Your father asked me to take you away from her. He wants me to bring you home. He is excited to see you. He sent me to pick you up.'

Like any good pupil, he follows his teacher's instructions without question. He climbs into the back seat of my car, and

I tell him to put his seat belt on as we pull out of the car park and onto the dual carriageway.

Charlotte may be ignorant, even when a miracle presents itself at her feet. But she can't ignore one when it is staring her in the face. She can't brush me off like a piece of dirt and dismiss me now. Not when I present the evidence to her in the flesh.

65

Rebecca raises her palms to me in a placating gesture I could do without. 'He could have wandered off somewhere nearby.'

We are still in the car park, and I pace back and forth, unsure of what to do or where to go. The only thing I know is Adam is gone.

'Maybe he wanted to see the lake?' Rebecca suggests, staring over in the direction of the choppy water.

'The lake?' I look over too. I hadn't even thought of that. But Charlotte wouldn't harm her own child. It has been me on the receiving end of her punishments. I think back to when Adam came home with the stuffed gorilla from the zoo. He had said it was a female stranger who bought it for him. It should have been obvious then.

Now she has taken my little boy somewhere.

I shake my head as I stare vacantly through the bare branches and trunks. Adam's bright red coat would stand out against all the muddy brown. 'No.'

'Well, maybe he needed the toilet?'

'This is the only building for miles, and the only way

inside is through the front doors. It was only us in that foyer – you know that – we would have seen him.'

Rebecca looks towards the band of trees towards the lake. 'Maybe we should check over there. He could have wandered ...'

I groan in frustration. 'He's not the wandering type! I know him. He wouldn't do that. She's taken him!'

'Who?'

'Charlotte!'

'But she isn't here! This is one place we've established she definitely isn't, remember?'

I run my fingers into my hair. 'No ... she must have ... I don't know. Maybe someone has been helping her. But I know it's her. She's come to take him back.'

Rebecca stares at me, bewildered. 'Back? What are you talking about?'

I look back at her. The delicate hue of her eyes is illuminated by the weak winter sun.

Everything I've done has been to keep Adam in my arms. Now he has been snatched from them.

It's over. I've failed as a mother. Charlotte could have taken Adam anywhere. I can't find him on my own. I want to race to him but have no idea which direction to start.

My voice comes out in a choked whisper. 'Adam isn't really my son.'

'What?'

'He's Charlotte's. Somehow they got mixed up shortly after they were born. The hospital was overcrowded when I gave birth, and I ended up going home with Adam instead of my own baby. Charlotte took mine. But Charlotte is Adam's real mother. Now she knows.'

'How would she have found out?'

'I don't know. It must have been my fault. I signed up for her evening class to get to know her. I was worried about what her life was like after losing her husband and what she thought was her baby in an accident. I felt so guilty for keeping hold of Adam and not saying anything. If you realised your baby wasn't dead after thinking he was for years, wouldn't you do something to get him back?'

Rebecca is stunned into unnatural quiet. She swears and puts her palm to her forehead as she processes the information.

'We need to call the police,' she says after a moment.

'No.' I shake my head. 'I'll lose him forever if we do that. If we can find where she has taken Adam, we can still get him back.'

'And then what, Alison?' Rebecca stares at me incredulously. 'If what you've said is true, she isn't just going to roll over and let you keep him, is she?'

I put my face in my hands. 'I can't think about that right now. He's hardly ever been away from me since I brought him home from the hospital. I just need to get him back. I want to tell him that I love him and that I'll always be his mother.' My voice breaks, and I look up and see tears in Rebecca's eyes now too.

'He doesn't know Charlotte,' I say. 'She could have told him all sorts of lies. He'll be so confused. I need to get to him ...'

She sighs. 'But we have no idea where she would have taken him. The most likely place is her house. Maybe that is why she wasn't answering the phone – because she has taken Adam there. Or got someone else to. That's why we need the police. They'll have access to her address.'

'You think she would take Adam to her house?'

'Why not? Even if she was planning on doing a runner with him, she would need to pack some things first. This can only have been a spur-of-the-moment thing, surely. No one knew we were coming here. We just need to find out where she lives.'

I come to a decision as I look from Rebecca's strained expression to my car behind her. 'You could be right. I already know where she lives. Maybe you could go over there and look for Adam?'

'Aren't you coming with me?'

'No. I just thought of somewhere else she might be.' I dash over to my car and pull out some paper and a pen.

'This is her home address,' I say, handing over a scrap of paper that I've hastily scribbled on.

She takes it from me and stares at it.

'I know where her partner lives too – I'm going to check it out. She might think it's less obvious if she hides Adam there. He could have been the one helping her. You can call for a taxi from here.'

I jump into the driving seat and fire up the engine. Rolling down the window, I say to her, 'But no police if they aren't there. Promise me, Rebecca.'

She looks at me blankly as I reverse and pull away towards the car park exit. But I can't stop. I feel certain Rebecca was right in her hunch that Charlotte took Adam to her home.

As I make the turn out of the car park, I still see Rebecca watching me before she disappears out of sight.

The journey over to Charlotte's house is a nightmare. There aren't any real hold-ups, just a series of nuisance drivers who seem to have been placed in my way on purpose. I sound my horn when the motorist up ahead dithers about and chooses to let yet another pedestrian cross.

I don't have time for this, I think as another vehicle waits obediently for the traffic lights to turn from flashing amber to certain green.

Finally, I manage to find a point to overtake an elderly driver who cruises along for a parking space near the golf course.

The play park is bustling with figures of children and adults as I drive past. I focus on the road to blot it out. I don't want to consider how Charlotte would have held my baby's tiny hands as he toddled over to the slide or the swings. I don't want to picture Steven as he walked him home afterwards, maybe stopping at the newsagents around the corner for sweets.

I push my foot down on the accelerator, ignoring the faces of the parents at the park as they turn around in disapproval.

The blood pounds in my head as I turn onto the road with Charlotte's row of cottages. Her usual red car isn't on the driveway when I park outside. Instead, a smaller green one takes its place. She must have switched vehicles.

So that's how she got past me at the Lakeside centre. She was there after all.

A sudden change in vehicle is cause for suspicion in itself. Especially this one. It's a noticeable downgrade from her usual glossy Skoda. This little green one has a scrape all down the side.

I freeze on the driveway when I realise I've seen this car before. Adam and I have passed it at least a handful of times on the way to school recently.

My chest becomes tight. Charlotte has been closer than I thought all this time.

This is all my fault. I should have noticed sooner. Why have I buried my head in the sand when the obvious was staring me in the face?

When I'm presented with the front door, I realise it would be ridiculous to knock. I try the handle, but find it locked. So I move around to the side of the house and follow the narrow path to the backyard with thoughts of the back door.

These old cottages in Rishworth are all virtually identical externally. But Charlotte's has a larger grassy garden with a small conservatory encasing the back door.

I swear under my breath. But when I try the handle, I'm surprised to find it gives in my hand.

My breathing sounds desperate and almost ragged as I step inside the quiet house.

It is silent as my feet trespass upon Charlotte's immaculate dining room floor. But someone must be home. The car I'd seen near the school is parked on the driveway.

There is no immediate whisper of Adam as I tread further. I have the strangest feeling he isn't here at all. The dining table is lacking its chairs, almost as if to show that no one could be hiding beneath.

The difference in layout inside the cottage throws me. All this time, I pictured my little boy being raised in a house that was the same as ours. But I was wrong.

My breath is suddenly taken away when I draw level with the refrigerator in the kitchen.

A photo of Adam is stuck with a chrome magnet to the centre of the gleaming white door. It is the scrap that was taken from the exhibition, but the edges have been cut straight. Still, it looks oddly out of place in the otherwise neat and pristine kitchen.

In the living room, I clap my hand to my mouth when I see something that makes me gasp out loud.

Adam's bright red coat. It has been thrown across the sofa. I snatch it up and hold it to me. The lack of heat emanating from the fibres tells me it hasn't been very recently discarded.

My shoes hardly make a sound as they tread hurriedly up the thick carpet of the stairs. A dark stain runs from the doormat in a stream all the way up the luxurious pile to the top step. It is obviously out of place in such an otherwise well-presented home.

My palms sweat as I grip the bannister for support. But it is equally silent and deserted up here. I quickly race from room to room. The modern bathroom borders on clinically clean, but it is small like ours at home and certainly doesn't conceal my little boy.

Nor do either of the two bedrooms. They remain still and quiet. If it weren't for Adam's red coat clutched in my hands, I would think that I've made a mistake in being here now.

I'm just turning to go back downstairs when I see it.

On the bedside cabinet, there is a photo frame. My

stomach twists as I reach out and raise it closer. Steven's round face smiles and points at the camera. His eyes are so much like Adam's. The boy in his arms looks inquisitively at the person behind the lens. The image blurs as I reach out to stroke the infant's precious cheeks.

Then a noise from downstairs makes me drop the photo. The frame clatters noisily onto the bedroom carpet as the jangle of keys stops on the ground floor.

I hear footsteps upon the expensive tiles downstairs come to an abrupt stop too.

I freeze, hardly daring to breathe.

The new arrival knows I'm here.

Alison's car has appeared on the street whilst I've been out. I guessed where she was speeding off to when I saw her race past the park. The conservatory door is open when I get back to the cottage too. I distinctly remember shutting it behind me.

Our guest has let herself in. I don't remember officially inviting her.

Her footsteps are loud and clumsy as she descends the stairs. I'm so glad she hasn't taught Adam to be like her. He is so much more gracious.

She stops dead in the living room doorway when she sees me.

'Mrs Turner,' she says, shaking her head, 'what are you doing here? I'm looking for Adam. Do you know where he is?'

She is easily confused. Adam is much more intelligent, thank goodness. He gets that from his father.

'He isn't here,' I say.

She takes a step towards me. 'But where is he? This is Charlotte Pritchard's house. How do you know her? She has taken my son – I need to find him.'

'He isn't your son, so you can stop the pretence, for a start. Charlotte is plainly his mother. She would have every right to take him if she wanted.'

I've found a certain vocal tone and the way I draw myself up sometimes when I'm giving pupils a telling-off is effective when addressing certain adults. I'd had Alison down as one of them, and I'm not disappointed. She shrinks before me now as if she were a nine-year-old.

She recovers herself enough to speak. 'So you're saying she hasn't got him?' She raises the coat in her hands. 'But I found this on the sofa. It's Adam's – it has his name in it. He must be here. You have to help me find him.'

'I won't be doing that,' I tell her flatly. 'The last thing I will allow is for Adam to be returned to your hands. You can forget about ever getting him back. Do I make myself clear?'

Her mouth opens as she stares at me stupidly. 'I don't understand. You're one of his teachers. Why would you say that?'

'I say it because it is the truth – something you have done your best to bury. Isn't that right?'

She shifts her weight from one foot to another awkwardly. 'I don't know what you are talking about. Look, there has been a mistake here. My child is missing.'

I laugh in shock at her audacity. 'Do you still think you can get away with it? I know you got my messages. You see, I do know *what keeps you awake at night*. Did you think I was lying?'

Her eyes widen. 'You sent those messages? Not Charlotte?'

I open my mouth to answer, but a noise causes me to stop and turn my head. The sound of a key negotiating the lock of the front door makes me smile. 'Why don't you ask her yourself?'

68

My heart pounds in my throat as Charlotte lets herself into her house. For a moment she is oblivious as she removes her coat. But she gasps and stops dead when she catches sight of me standing in the hallway.

Her wide eyes move quickly from me to Mrs Turner behind me in the living room. 'What the hell?' she says faintly.

Mrs Turner strides forward, pushing past me to greet the new arrival in the hallway. 'Charlotte,' she says. She nods her head towards me. 'Look who is here.'

Charlotte's look of confusion grows as her eyes flick between me and Mrs Turner. She is smartly dressed today in a trouser suit like Rebecca's when I saw her in Manchester. Her hair is as neat and sleek as always as it frames her face.

She shakes her immaculate head. 'What are you doing in my house?' she demands of the older woman. 'I thought you didn't have a key anymore?'

Mrs Turner ignores this and drops her voice a little. 'This

is her,' she mutters to Charlotte. 'This is the woman I told you about.'

Charlotte presses her hand to her mouth and looks mortified all of a sudden. 'Oh my goodness. Evelyn, please. I told you to get help.'

'I'm not the one who needs help. You can't deny reality any longer, Charlotte. I've got proof now. You can't deny a fact when it is staring you in the face. I've got the boy I told you about!'

'Where is he?' I say suddenly. 'What have you done with my son? I want to see him, please.'

Charlotte's eyes widen in horror now. 'What did you do, Evelyn? Have you really taken her child?'

'Out of the three of us, I'm the only person doing the right thing!' Evelyn Turner says, her voice rising. The tiny birdlike eyes behind her glasses gleam. 'I'm keeping Adam safe.'

I step forward and look at her imploringly. 'But where? He'll be scared and confused – I just want to see him.'

'I'm not going to tell you.'

'That's it.' Charlotte pulls out her phone. 'I think we've heard enough. I'm calling the police now, Evelyn. I would have done it sooner if I'd known you were going to pull a stunt like this.'

'No, don't!' I move forward and raise my palms to her pleadingly.

She stops with her finger above the call button on her screen. 'Why not? Hasn't she kidnapped your son?'

'Look, I don't want any trouble–'

Evelyn huffs and nods sternly. 'I bet you don't! And, no, you haven't heard anywhere near enough yet, Charlotte. Alison is going to tell you the truth. That's why I brought her here today. Go on, Alison.'

They both look at me expectantly.

Charlotte still has her phone in hand, ready to dial. 'What

is she talking about? Look, I think this has got way out of hand. I'm calling the police now.'

Evelyn makes a sudden movement and snatches the phone from Charlotte. 'Not yet,' she says simply, as though we are merely pupils in her class who need to be verbally restrained. 'You have to hear what Alison has to say to you.'

Charlotte stares at the other woman, open-mouthed.

But Evelyn hasn't noticed. She looks at me and nods as if it's the prompt I need. But I shake my head.

'Tell her, Alison. Charlotte needs to hear the truth. Explain how you came to have her baby in your home. Tell her how you've lied and kept the truth hidden all these years.'

Evelyn steps forward and points a bony finger at me. 'Look Charlotte in the eye and tell her Adam isn't her son.'

69

Horrible silence rings in Charlotte's living room. I don't dare look up at either of the other two women, and I find myself staring at the plush carpet instead.

Evelyn turns back to Charlotte and gives a frustrated sigh. 'She's been raising your boy like he is her own. His name is Adam. Alison is the reason you don't have a child anymore. Jacob was her baby all along, Charlotte. Listen now. And look at me when I am talking to you! What is the matter with you?!'

Charlotte looks sombre as she runs her fingers through her immaculate blonde hair. 'Not this again, Evelyn. We discussed this. Jacob *was* ours, and he died. He drowned.' Her voice breaks, and I feel my own heart wrench too as I bite back tears myself.

'You just haven't taken it well, Evelyn,' she goes on after a moment of silence. 'That's why you need to get some help to put it behind you. It's what I did, and now I've moved on.'

Charlotte looks at me with tears in her beautiful eyes.

'You shouldn't have stopped me calling the police. Pass me your phone.'

She reaches out her hand, but I shake my head. 'No police. I just want my little boy back. You have to make your mother tell me where she has taken him.'

'Mother-in-law,' she corrects flatly.

'That's certainly right!' Evelyn adds. 'Adam is my Steven's son. There's no denying it. Put them side by side at the same age and they could be twins! I would know my son's face anywhere! I raised him – all by myself, I might add. He never got shipped off to daycare. Nor did I have parents or in-laws to help me, as you did, Charlotte. It was just me and him, always. Do you think I wouldn't recognise the boy I spent the best years of my life with? It is his face I see whenever I shut my eyes. His features are permanently etched into my memory. Then I saw Adam in school one day, and I knew instantly. No mistake or coincidence could make him look exactly the same.'

'No.' Charlotte sighs and dabs at the corner of her eyes with her hand. Her perfectly applied eyeshadow has been distorted. 'It's just a coincidence. They both have dark hair and a similar eye colour. That's all.'

'But you didn't know Steven as a boy!'

'I've seen photographs.'

'That's not the same thing. A few blurry snapshots here and there was all I had of his childhood, apart from my memories. You can't compare.'

'Yes, I can. I've seen the photos you sent me from Alison's portfolio, Evelyn. There is some resemblance. But all boys of the same age with similar colouration are going to look at least a little bit similar.'

'You ignorant bitch!' Evelyn stares from Charlotte to me and back again with wild eyes that gleam now with tears. 'Look at you, the pair of you! I don't know which of you is worse! Alison for stealing the baby and lying. Or you, Charlotte, for letting it happen! Then you choose to deny it when I bring it to your attention! How dare you? I've arranged everything for you, Charlotte, so you could have him back. And this is how you act? Well, you both will be sorry you didn't believe me!'

'What are you going to do?'

'I'm going to make sure he is safe from your clutches – both of you! After today, no one will be able to hurt Adam ever. Neither one of you will ever be able to get to him again!'

Charlotte looks fearfully at her mother-in-law now. 'What are you thinking, Evelyn. Don't do anything else you can't take back. Give Alison her son back, now. Did you bring him here?'

When I see the terror and uncertainty in Charlotte's eyes, I realise she has no idea what her mother-in-law is capable of either. She has underestimated her already.

Adam's coat is still clutched in my hands, and I realise he should need it. Why would Evelyn have taken it from him? Has she done something unforgivable already?

The answer makes my stomach jolt, and I feel like I might be sick. I put my hand to my mouth. This is such a nightmare. I just want Adam back. I can't stand another second not knowing where he is. My baby needs to be back in my arms, even if he will be taken from them straight away again.

'Tell me where he is,' I say.

Evelyn is quick to snap back. 'Not until you admit what you have done!'

My hands shake as I grip Adam's coat. 'All right, I will.'

I turn to look at Charlotte, fighting down the nausea that threatens to overcome me. 'She was telling the truth. Adam wasn't ever my baby. He was yours.'

70

Charlotte looks at me as though I've gone mad too. 'I don't understand. Why would you say that?'

'Because it's the truth!' Evelyn moves from one foot to another. She is clearly delighted. 'Haven't I been telling you all along, Charlotte? You thought I was mad. But even you can't deny the truth when it is coming from someone else's lips.'

'No.' Charlotte shakes her head. 'This can't be right. You must be mistaken.'

'I'm so sorry,' I say, ignoring the look of excitement on Evelyn's face. 'I didn't mean to lie. I've wanted to say something for so long, but I couldn't. When I first found out Adam wasn't mine, I had no idea what had gone wrong when I had the results of a DNA test in my hands. I was so confused. I was more shocked than anyone to find out neither myself nor my husband shared any genes with the baby we had been raising as our own. Eventually, I realised the mistake must have happened shortly after the birth. My baby was taken very quickly by the midwives, almost as soon as he was born. He wasn't breathing properly, and he was rushed to the baby care unit. He never even had a tag put on before he was taken away. There just wasn't time.'

'That sounds so much like Jacob's birth ... he had a heart problem ... and he was taken from me.'

'I guessed that's how it happened. Steven told me Jacob had been in the baby unit.'

Charlotte looks at me, surprised. 'You knew my husband?'

'Not very well. I met him once or twice at the local daycare centre. The one on Church Road. I took Adam there for a little while when I went back to work. Steven and I got talking when we were waiting outside for the place to open. We found out Adam and Jacob shared a birthday. I just knew then. Steven had such similar eyes to Adam ... He confirmed Jacob was born in the same hospital too. Steven told me Adam was lovely. A credit to me, he said.'

Charlotte presses her neat fingertips to her smooth cheeks and shakes her head. 'This is all too much. It can't be right.'

'I'm sorry. It all seemed so obvious to me what had happened when fate threw us together as it did. I know I should have said something. But I just couldn't. I'd been raising Adam for over a year when I met Steven and Jacob. Adam was my child in so many ways. I couldn't imagine letting him go. But then I wanted the baby in Steven's arms too – I was so confused – I didn't know what to do. I couldn't talk to anyone about it. So I did nothing. I told myself I would do the right thing eventually, I just needed time to process everything. And then ... it was too late. Jacob was gone forever. And I didn't want to be left with nothing. So I didn't say a word.'

Charlotte stares at me, her eyes wide as she processes what I've said. Her pale pink cheeks are unusually flushed with colour. 'So you kept hold of my baby even when you knew I was grieving for yours?'

I nod, tears spilling silently down my cheeks.

Evelyn breaks the silence. 'That's not all she did though. Was it, Alison?'

I shake my head. 'I don't know what you mean. Look, I've done what you wanted. Let me see Adam now. Take me to him.'

'Not yet. You still have something else to confess to us.'

'I don't. That's it. I need to see Adam – now.'

'You know, Alison can't necessarily be blamed purely for her inaction. I distinctly remember Steven told me about a certain someone at daycare – a *friendly* other parent. He mentioned meeting a mother who had talked him out of investigating some developmental problems Jacob was having. I wonder if you remember, Charlotte.'

Her daughter-in-law shakes her head. 'It was so long ago.'

Evelyn sighs. 'But you must remember how the daycare centre was worried about Jacob when he was enrolled. They noticed he was behind in certain areas. There were things the other children did without blinking an eye when Jacob struggled. The staff found it was tough to get his attention. And they pointed out he should have more words in his vocabulary. And then there was the way he refused so many foods. Jacob was your and Steven's only child, Charlotte. You didn't know any better. But the daycare centre told Steven.'

Evelyn turns to me, and each word is laced with venom now. 'My Steven would surely have listened to people with experience if it hadn't been for that *helpful* mother he had spoken to about the matter.'

I squeeze my eyes shut, remembering the interactions Steven and I had all those years ago. I talked him out of getting Jacob assessed for learning difficulties. My own ability to lie surprised even me. I told Steven that even if Jacob was fine, the diagnosis process would strain them all.

Steven believed me when I said that I had a friend who

faced the same situation, and the child developed normally as they grew older. Some children just needed more time than others, I told him. Now I wish more than anything that I hadn't been so convincing.

'I was scared. And confused.' When I open my eyes, I see them both staring at me. The shock and disgust on Charlotte's face is too much to bear, and I look back at the carpet. 'I wasn't ready for my life to be turned upside down. You can't blame me for that.'

Evelyn jabs a bony finger towards me. 'Yes, we can!' She shakes her head. 'It always stuck with me how Steven chose to listen to a peer over a professional. Isn't the power of peer advice fascinating? You must have been pretty convincing. It wasn't until recently that I thought about it again, and the pieces clicked into place. It was you, Alison.

'You stopped Steven from starting the process that could have saved his life and that of your baby. But you made sure that Jacob stayed away from any authorities who could have raised awkward questions. The whole thing might have unravelled back then with just one blood test.'

'I didn't know what would happen,' I say flatly. 'I wasn't ready to give up the baby I'd been caring for all that time. In my mind, he was already my child.'

'Meanwhile, Steven and Charlotte struggled here with yours. Jacob was still alive when you started lying. Everything would have been different, and we all could have gone down a different path. Your baby would have lived if you hadn't procrastinated. It's all your fault, Alison. No wonder you can't sleep at night! You must think about your baby in the water. How his lungs filled up as he drowned. I know my Steven did his best to save him, but the sea doesn't forgive. None of that needed to happen. That will surely haunt you for the rest of your life!'

It's Charlotte's eruption of grief that breaks the silence

now. She covers her mouth with a hand. My despair has gone beyond the tears that I've shed over the years; it lives silent and dark somewhere inside me. That's where Jacob exists. I can only remember him in the first few moments of his life as I held him to me, warm and still sticky from the birth. He will never leave me.

'I'm so sorry, Charlotte. If there was a way to turn back the clock and make everything right, I would.' I reach out and move to touch her shoulder, but she pulls away.

'No,' she says. 'This is all too much right now. I wasn't prepared for this today. I need a few moments alone.'

Her eyes are full of despair as she looks from me to Evelyn.

Lost for words, she sweeps from the room. The heeled boots she hadn't had the chance to take off are heard on the stairs. The floorboards give and creak upstairs in what I know to be the master bedroom.

I wipe my cheeks and my eyes with my sleeve in an effort to compose myself. I take a deep breath. 'I've done everything you asked for. Please let me see Adam. Where is he?'

Evelyn considers me from behind her glasses for a moment before she speaks. 'You know, even when Jacob was alive, I barely saw him. Steven managed to talk Charlotte into letting me babysit here and there. But it wasn't enough. I had imagined being a grandmother would be like becoming a mother once again. Being with Adam even just at school has made me realise what that would be like. I'm not just going to roll over and let you two pass him back and forth between you. I know I won't get a look in.'

'That's probably just as well after everything you have done to me in the last few months. I think Charlotte is right. You do need to get some help.'

'That's disappointing to hear. But it doesn't surprise me.

You and Charlotte are oddly alike. But I have no intention of sharing Adam via less than a three-way split.'

She rummages in her coat pocket for something. She pulls out a box of matches.

'You don't have a choice,' I tell her as I watch in confusion as she pulls out a match and lights it.

'Yes, I thought one of you would say that. Actually, yes, I do.'

She pulls open the front door, then turns to look down at the floor. I follow her gaze to the dark stain I saw earlier. The one that runs from the doormat all the way up the stairs. I realise too late what is about to happen.

She drops the match and disappears, shutting the front door behind her.

71

F lames erupt in front of the door, blocking the way out. They spread with alarming speed up the stairs and eat at the canvas artwork on the walls. I back away in horror, staring at the flames that catch upon a fluffy scarf on the coat stand now. It tips over and spills fire moving hurriedly in my direction.

Out of instinct, I spring into action and away from the heat. I find myself in the conservatory and grab for the door handle, expecting it to give as it did earlier to allow me entry.

But the thick white handle is secured firmly in place. Evelyn must have locked it when she arrived to find me here. Forcing my weight against the door does nothing.

I need something to break the glass.

The dining table behind me is missing its chairs. I'd thought it strange earlier. Now I realise Evelyn has thought this through carefully. She planned for me to be here. She had laid some kind of accelerant on the carpet of the stairs before I arrived and waited for me to turn up. She must have been lurking somewhere nearby.

As I pull open cupboards frantically, looking for something heavy, I remember the faces at the park around the corner. I raced by so fast and avoided looking in their direction.

Adam always nags me to take him to play parks. I bet that's where he is. But it's too late now. I'm trapped in the house.

The shrill screeching of the smoke alarm erupts upstairs. Then something else. Above the roar of the flames and the high-pitched sounding of the alarm, I hear another sound.

Screaming.

It's Charlotte. In my panic at seeing the fire, I forgot she went upstairs.

She is trapped inside this house too.

Those ungrateful bitches deserve everything that is coming to them. If they hadn't been so difficult in accepting the truth, then I might have considered some sort of compromise.

But I know Charlotte too well. I shouldn't give the past a chance to repeat itself. Without my Steven around, my daughter-in-law will make sure that I'm the odd one out again. I won't risk being like Alison, left with nothing.

My stomach flutters now. It's time to act fast. Adam and I will have to get far from here. Somewhere where no one will find us. I'll raise him by myself. He doesn't need to turn out like either of his mothers.

It will be like having my son back again. Only this time, I'll make sure he finds himself a better wife. She will have to be strictly vetted before I allow him to commit himself.

It takes less than two minutes to walk around the corner to the park where I left Adam. Although it is unseasonably mild today, I hope he hasn't become too cold. He insisted on taking his coat off when we got to the house. He is always the same at school. Always one of those whom I have to nag to dress appropriately for break time. He has inherited that difficult streak from Alison or maybe even Charlotte. Steven was never at all disobedient. It's handy this park was here. I didn't want Adam to witness what happened at the house just now.

As I let myself in through the gate, I scan the faces at the swings and the roundabout. Panic bubbles in my stomach. He isn't here.

Adam is gone.

A roaring wall of flame greets me as I move back through the ground floor. I can't see Charlotte, but I can hear her upstairs somewhere. Her terrified screams somehow chill me more than the blaze itself.

I want to call out to her, but the smoke burns my lungs and stings my throat. Uncontrolled coughing erupts in my throat, and I gag. But it's the heat that repels me the most.

I'm forced to turn back in the living room. The fire has crept into here too, biting at the curtains and licking at the cushions of the leather sofa.

The smoke has reached the kitchen now. It stings my eyes as I frantically search for something to break the glass with. Tins and packets spill out across the worktop in my panic. A jar of dark sauce smashes onto the tiles, and I almost slip in it as I take a can and smash it furiously against the glass sheet of the locked door I came in through.

Despite throwing all my force into it, nothing happens. The room is starting to look foggy now, and my eyes stream as I spot a tall cupboard almost concealed behind the conservatory curtain.

I rush over and pull open the door only to be greeted with an array of cleaning products – an apron and spray chemicals, bottles of bleach and sponges. All things that would fuel the blaze. Then I spot an iron.

It's heavy as I grab it. I try not to look at the orange glow that now moves across the living room rug as I return to the door.

The pointed end of the iron shatters the first pane of glass with the first blow. I put all my weight into it and aim again, targeting the second sheet. Panic rises in me when it takes several desperate impacts to crack and splinter like the first.

The work is exhausting, but I think of Adam's small soft hand in Evelyn's bony one. The thought gives me the strength to deliver the last few strikes. There is now a hole large enough for me to climb through.

There is heat touching my back now. So I don't waste time as I gingerly squeeze through the hole in the door. Jagged shards remain stuck in the frame, however, and one tears at my shoulder. Another at my arm. Sharp pain sears the skin of my leg too, but cool air greets my face as I finally make it out into the garden.

I collapse onto the grass in the back lawn, coughing and spluttering. Tears run down my face.

It's relatively quiet out here. Until I hear screaming. Charlotte's voice is louder out here.

I look back up at the house and see her leaning out through an open upstairs window above the conservatory.

She looks down and sees me. Our eyes meet. It suddenly occurs to me that if Charlotte didn't make it out, then I would retain full custody of Adam. Evelyn wouldn't stand a chance after what she has done. That's if anyone could find her.

The flames must have crossed the landing into the bedroom now or, at least, be lapping at the door. Charlotte knows it too. I can see the terror in her eyes.

'How far away are they?!' she screams down at me.

'W-What,' I stammer, but I realise she probably can't hear me.

'How long until the fire service gets here?! Didn't they tell you?!' She coughs and glances behind her. I swear I see a warm orange glow reflected in her pale hair now.

I shake my head. 'I haven't called them.'

'What!?' she screams. 'I can't hear you!'

'I'm sorry!' I close my eyes, and it's suddenly Adam's face that I see. I imagine if I got to see him again, having to explain to him what happened here today. I can't tell him that his real father is dead, and his real mother died when I was right there with her, mere feet away.

If I left Charlotte now, I would never be able to live with myself. I already carry the loss of Steven and Jacob with me every day. Dorothy too. I have the opportunity to do the right thing, and I won't let anyone down this time.

My legs are weak as I scramble to my feet. I flatten my palms against my cheeks as I stare at the situation in front of me.

'What about the fire brigade, Alison?!' Charlotte screams in between intermittent coughs. Smoke starts to stream out of her open window now too. 'Will they get here soon?!'

'There's no time for that, Charlotte! You're going to have to jump – *now!*'

She shakes her head, wide-eyed. 'No! I can't do that.'

'Yes, you can! Just get onto the conservatory roof and you're halfway there!'

'No. I'll wait.' She coughs again and glances behind her.

'You know there isn't time! Just climb out the window!'

'I can't do it! I can't climb. It's too high up!'

'Yes, you can. Steven was strong. The newspaper said he fought against the current for so long. He stayed alive to try to save Jacob. Now you have to stay alive – for Adam!'

She squeezes her eyes shut and shakes her head.

'Charlotte, please! Do it now! I can't get up there. You have to help yourself.' When she doesn't move, I scream at her again louder than I've ever screamed before. '*Please!*'

Before I realise it, Charlotte has her hands on either side of the window frame. Then I see the heel of her boot. Then the other as she squeezes her way out. She looks down in terror at the sloped and pointed roof of the conservatory and drops down onto it.

There is a moment when her fearful eyes widen further. Her arms flail in mid-air, and she loses her footing as she slips off the roof.

After a frantic rush around the park, it's obvious Adam is gone.

No! I left him too long. I hadn't expected to be caught up at the house as long as I was. Time got away from me. And so has he.

Where could he have gone? In desperation, I get down on my hands and knees and peer into the tunnel at the centre of the play structure. I do the same with the pretend shop area, but it's just small children inside.

My tights are laddered as I get back up again. I look around and catch a man on the nearby bench watching me. He is alone and watches me unblinkingly. We have to watch out for loners hanging around the school. This person seems too well-dressed to fit the profile of the people we have to report though. A small girl emerges from the tunnel and runs to the man as I stare back at him.

'Daddy,' she says, 'did you see me go through?'

I turn away. I'm grasping at straws here, but I'm becoming panicked. It won't be long before someone notices what I've done to Charlotte's house. Fear strikes my heart when I consider Adam going back to the burning building.

He was left with strict instructions not to leave the park until I came to pick him up. At school, he has been told time and time again in assemblies not to go off with strangers.

Out of the corner of my eye, I spot the father of the little girl now talking with a mother of a toddler. They both stare unabashedly in my direction as they mutter something to each other. I suppose I must look strange, being the only childless adult.

I exit through the gate and think of hurriedly retracing my steps to the house in search of my little boy. But just as I make the turn at the end of the road, I see a sight that makes my insides turn cold.

Adam *is* with a stranger. He holds the hand of someone I don't recognise as he is led further into the distance.

My legs are weak with panic as I set out after them. What will I do if I can't get him back? I have nothing if I don't have him. Adam is the light of my life, and I can't exist without him.

They turn another corner before I make it to the end of this street. My breath comes in ragged bursts. It's been years since I've run like this. I've been physically tried today already. Moving Charlotte's dining chairs into the shed earlier wore me out.

I'm weak and trembling by the time I catch up with the pair. I'm shocked to see it's a woman who has taken Adam. *How dare she? Who does she think she is?*

My limbs tremble from the exertion and the adrenaline. The only thing I have on my side is the element of surprise. I'm prepared to use it as the woman says something to Adam and turns back to the pavement ahead.

Adam is depending on me. I'm all he has left, even if he doesn't even know it yet.

This is my moment. I summon my remaining energy and force myself forward.

75

It's like I watch Charlotte's fall in slow motion. My life has been a waking nightmare for such a long time, and it continues now. It's as though I'm observing another horrifying night-time vision as Charlotte's twisted form slips head-first down the pointed white roof of her conservatory.

Before I know what's happening, I'm anticipating her landing, and I rush forwards.

But I can see I will be too late.

In a panic, I reach out for her blindly. The force of her motion causes me to lose my footing too, and we both fall hard to the concrete patio.

My back collides painfully with the hard ground, and Charlotte writhes beside me. She whimpers in pain, fresh tears streaming from her eyes. Lines of black mascara run down her cheeks. Her hands clutch instinctively for her ankle as she bends her knee up towards herself.

'It's broken,' she mutters, more to herself than me.

'It's OK,' I tell her as I wince in pain myself. 'I'm going to call for help. Evelyn can't have got far. I'm calling the emergency services now.'

I groan as I ease my arm from beneath Charlotte and force myself to sit up. As my shaking hand rummages for my phone, I see that it is red and bloody. Long gashes have torn into the back of my hand, and I realise there are shards of glass lodged into my fingers. It's only when I see them that I feel the sting of the wounds.

'It's all right,' I say as tears run down my face again now. Like Charlotte, I'm mainly talking to myself.

Sirens form a high-pitched note above the wind. Someone else must have called for help already.

The sound of glass shattering somewhere above our heads causes me to flinch and throw myself over Charlotte's nearby form.

'Everything of Jacob's was in there,' she says flatly, her weary voice close to my ear. 'His clothes, his toys.'

I pull a wincing Charlotte to her feet. 'We need to get away from the building.'

'All the photographs too,' she sobs as I drape her arm over my shoulders and urge her along the narrow passageway beside the cottage. I'm sure I hear the sound of crashing from inside before we emerge on the other side.

'Not all of them,' I tell her quietly. 'I kept a cutting from the newspaper article somewhere safe. I would imagine you remember the picture they used.'

Neighbours from the other cottages are spilling out into the street now. They stare up at the burning building, which is now flickering orange at the windows. Smoke billows up in a tall cascade into the otherwise blue sky above.

A police car rounds onto the street. The sirens halt as it stops near the house. The doors are thrown open, and the occupants spill out. A young officer is quick to approach me. He glances at the burning house. 'Is there anyone still left inside?'

I shake my head. 'No. It's just us.'

'There is an ambulance and a fire engine on the way. Keep back from the building.'

As the officer retreats to the car, I see someone else emerge from the back seat. It's Rebecca.

My mouth opens in surprise. 'What are you doing here?'

Before she has the chance to say anything, I realise there is a smaller figure appearing from behind her. Adam.

His lip trembles as he looks uncertainly at my face. I worry that it is slightly sooty like Charlotte's, whose weight I'm still supporting. I can see at a glance that my clothes are torn, dirty and bloodied in some places.

Adam eyes Charlotte cautiously too.

'It's OK,' I say to him as I reach out my free arm. He throws himself against me, and I give him the biggest one-armed hug ever, as though it's my last.

I feel Charlotte's silent sobs rack through her body beside me as if they were my own.

Rebecca takes Charlotte from me and helps her to a low wall nearby.

I stroke Adam's hair gently. 'I'm fine,' I tell him. 'Are you OK? Did Mrs Turner hurt you?'

He shakes his head as he rests it against me. 'Why did she do this, Mum?'

I don't know what to tell him. Charlotte catches my eye as I hold him to me, and I hope this isn't the last time I get to do this.

I look at Rebecca, who is peeling up Charlotte's trouser bottom to look at her injured ankle. 'How did you find Adam?' I ask her.

'Well, I almost didn't because someone sent me to the wrong address on purpose. I could tell you were lying, Ali. There was no way you would let me check out her house by myself when you wanted to go so much.'

I sigh. 'I'm sorry. I thought you would try to stop me from

coming here. I was in a hurry. I knew Adam had been kidnapped.'

'Yes, you were right. I'm sorry I doubted you. That Mrs Turner is a right psycho.' She presses a hand to the side of her head, and it's now that I realise she is bleeding too.

Charlotte looks at the red stain in Rebecca's mousy hair. 'What did she do?'

'She just attacked me in the street. Jumped out at me without any warning, she did. I'd found Adam at the park on his own, and I was trying to find Charlotte's house. Then that Turner woman grabbed hold of me and pulled me to the ground. She is a skinny thing, but I wasn't expecting it. I got knocked down, and I hit my head on the kerb as I fell. I'm going to have a right headache tomorrow. I wasn't going to give Adam up though. Turner gave him a right fright. Luckily, I'd called the police before I set off, and a pair of cars were driving past when she pulled that little stunt. They took her off in one car. We came over here in the other.'

'But how did you know Adam was at the park?' I ask.

'The receptionist at Lakeside gave in and handed the address over when I explained the situation. I got a taxi over here. The driver was having trouble finding this place too. All these cottages look just the same. Well, they did.' She looks behind us. 'All the smoke gives this one away now. Look at the state of it. Anyway, I saw Adam when we were driving past, and I got out there.'

'Thank you,' Charlotte says as Rebecca tends to her ankle. I can tell as much as my friend can that she isn't just talking about the help with her injury. The gratitude I feel towards Rebecca goes far beyond words. I'll never be able to give her the thanks she truly deserves for what she has done today.

I once again catch Charlotte's eye. It's now that it hits me that everything is about to change.

I t's been a few months since Charlotte fell from her roof and broke her ankle. Today, you wouldn't notice anything was ever wrong with it as she steps out of her car and walks through the gate of the cemetery.

All of our various superficial injuries have healed. It's only deeper down that our scars remain. No one will ever forget what Evelyn did. Nor is there any hiding from the truth we must all face.

When the judge announced the official custody verdict, it felt like a knife through my heart. A fair split, she decided.

And just like that, Charlotte gained access to her son. If she is struggling to cope with the news still, she is hiding it well. There's only one person who has been more hit by the news, and that's Dan. The truth hit him like a heavy weight.

Perhaps it's the sudden change in the dynamics of our home that changed how we see our marriage. It had become stagnant, routine. I think we had both come to question our decision to be together in the first place. But now we have a fresh perspective on things. Now we are rediscovering each other and remembering why we fell in love in the first place.

It will be a long time before he will forgive me for keeping such a devastating secret from him. Likewise, it will be a long time before I forgive him for accepting help from someone I haven't thought of as a friend in the longest time. I know we have a long way to go, but at least we have started our journey back to being us again. We were assigned a therapist after what happened with Evelyn Turner. He has been so helpful. He has taught me how to trust my husband again.

Charlotte smiles warmly as she approaches us and wraps Adam in a hug. She looks radiant in the sunshine with her long purple coat that sets off her hair. In return, her son gives her an awkward sort of, 'Hi.'

Adam glances at me, as he always does when his real mother arrives. He doesn't seem sure how to address her. It's too soon for him to consider calling Charlotte *Mum*, but I'm not sure he ever will. This is a lot for him to take in.

I'm happy for Charlotte that Adam warmed to her. He always seems to have a great time when he is away at her new house.

The court's ruling that we keep Adam for weekdays and Charlotte gets him at the weekends is provisional. I know that will change in the future, especially as Adam grows closer to his mother all the time.

Charlotte straightens up again and greets me and Dan. It seems obvious all of a sudden that she wants to talk about something she can't in front of Adam.

'Adam,' Dan says, 'why don't you take Charlotte's flowers, and we can go on ahead, eh?'

As the pair lead the way through the graveyard, Charlotte moves in closer to me.

'Did you hear?' she asks in a low voice. 'About Evelyn?'

'Yes, I did. I got a phone call this morning. They said she killed herself last night.'

'Yes.' Charlotte is quiet as we walk for a few moments.

She squints through the spring sunshine at Dan and Adam, who are busy in conversation themselves.

'I hadn't seen it coming, to be honest. I thought she might try to hang on until she got out. You would think she might have wanted to see Adam again. I've been having nightmares about it, actually.'

Charlotte puts a hand on my arm. 'Yes, me too. Maybe she just decided she couldn't wait that long. The thought of her has stopped me from sleeping soundly for a long time. I just didn't think when I woke up, my dreams would become real. There was always something off about her. I used to say so to Steven, but he always said I was being silly.'

'What I don't get is how she did it either. I mean, aren't there systems in place for that in mental health care hospitals? You would think the staff would recognise if she presented a danger to herself.'

'They obviously didn't think she did. I didn't. I underestimated her too.' She fiddles with the fine gold chain beneath her collar, which I know now holds her and Steven's wedding rings. 'I'm sorry I didn't report her behaviour sooner. She was always a little strange, in my opinion, but she was Steven's mother, so I put up with it. After we lost Jacob and Steven, her mind kept slipping back and forth as though she couldn't bear to remember what had really happened. At that point, I was a mess myself. When she mentioned her suspicions about Adam and you to me a little while ago, I thought she was deluded. I wanted to tell you, give you some kind of warning. I gave you my card with my numbers on it in case she showed up. But I never dreamed she would take things so far.'

'Or that she was right.'

Charlotte smiles weakly. 'Yes. She had behaved so strangely for so long that it never occurred to me she was telling the truth.'

'I know what you mean. She was the teaching assistant in Adam's class. She was with him virtually every day. I met her, spoke to her even. She seemed harmless enough, even if she was a little strict. I guess you never know what is going on with someone inside their head. What secrets they hide.'

'Very true.' She glances sideways at me. 'So how are things with you? I noticed you have a new website up.'

I smile. 'Nothing gets past you, does it? Yes, the business is doing great. But I'm making sure I have more time for Adam and Dan.'

'Did you sort out the issue with the council? Rebecca mentioned you had some kind of complaint.'

'Oh, that. Yes, they just gave me a warning. It seemed so much worse at the time, when I got a letter arrive out of the blue, and I didn't know what the consequences would be. I didn't know who had triggered it at the time either.'

'Did you find out who it was?'

'Yes. It was someone I used to be friends with.' I pause for a moment and consider how up in the air everything must have been for me to consider Dan had made the complaint. Rebecca learned from one of the mothers on the school run that it had been Helen who had contacted the council and wasted no time in gleefully sharing the information with her clique. 'But that's all sorted now. How about you? How is your new job?'

'Great. Everyone is so nice. It's much steadier than teaching classes here and there.'

'That's good.'

We fall quiet as we reach the pair of headstones I have visited for so many years on my own. This isn't our first visit together. The therapist said we should all come here a few times for Adam's sake. He said it would help him to process the information. In the spirit of what he said and with Rebecca's help, I've finally taken the last of Dorothy's things from

Adam's room. I'll always keep the tiny set of sleepsuits though to remember her.

Adam lays Charlotte's daffodils at Jacob's headstone and looks thoughtful for a moment. It's not hard to see why Evelyn became so enamoured by him.

My and Dan's mums are enjoying their regular visits now too. Now that the truth is out in the open, there is no reason to keep them away. I want to make the most of my time with Mum. She is delighted to see more of me, Dan and Adam. Knowing the truth doesn't seem to have dampened her affections; as far as she is concerned, Adam will always be her grandson as much as he will always be my little boy. We are scheduled to have Sunday lunch tomorrow with her and Julie.

Dan will be cooking. He's got a new job as head chef at a four-star restaurant in Blackburn. We've been enjoying some of the new dishes he has to prepare at home as he has honed his techniques. The money is a great improvement. We are about to exchange contracts on a three-bedroomed place on the outskirts of Rishworth. Dan will be closer to work, and we can start afresh, away from all the memories the cottage has held. I can't wait.

I hand Adam the colourful bunch of flowers that Dan and I chose with him this morning. He turns and lays those down too. I see fresh roses on Steven's headstone and realise Charlotte must have been down here alone to pay her respects to her husband. It makes me feel for her that she lost Steven as well as Jacob.

I want to convey this to her on the walk back to our respective cars, but I don't know how to put it into words. The sun is shining, and the sky is a beautiful shade of blue. It seems like a day to look ahead, not back for once.

Charlotte glances at me as Dan takes Adam to the car and makes sure he is strapped in. 'So how are you doing?'

'Well, as I said, the business is going great. Dan has been promoted. We are going to be moving to a bigger house soon.'

'No. I meant you, personally. You haven't mentioned your feelings. Although, if your therapist is as thorough as mine, you might have spoken about them already. Mine said we should make sure we talk to each other about how we feel.'

'I don't know. I have to adapt, I suppose. Like you have. This hasn't been easy for anyone.'

'You are right. I think you're doing really well.'

Dan straightens up and looks over at me. I put my hand up to give Charlotte and me a minute, and he sits in the driver's seat.

Charlotte stares into the distance at the tree on the cemetery hill for a moment and looks thoughtful.

'What is it?' I ask her.

'You know I was just thinking about something Evelyn said once that stuck with me. It wasn't long after Steven and I got engaged, and I wasn't sure how to take it. She said it in casual conversation, but it was sort of like a veiled threat.'

'Oh? What was it?'

'She said that when you have a little boy, you are destined to lose him eventually. That he would get married and leave you behind. He would forget, she said.'

'Yes. I can see what she meant.'

Deep down, I always knew I would have to one day share Adam with someone else. One way or another.

ABOUT THE AUTHOR

Did you enjoy *Just One Lie*? Please consider leaving a review on Amazon to help other readers discover the book.

Ruth Harrow was born and raised in England and graduated from university before embarking on an unfulfilling career in an office job. She eventually put pen to paper and her debut psychological thriller, *In Her Footsteps*, was published in 2018. It quickly became a bestseller. Following the success of her first novel, her second and third books followed shortly afterwards. She lives in the UK with her husband, two children and chocolate Labrador, Rolo.

Want to connect with Ruth? Visit her at her website.

https://ruthharrow.com/

ALSO BY RUTH HARROW

Printed in Great Britain
by Amazon

12188552R00236